CITY

OF

SPIES

Mara Timon is a native New Yorker and self-proclaimed citizen of the world who began a love affair with London about 20 years ago. She started writing short stories as a teenager, and when a programme on the BBC caught her interest, she followed the "what ifs" until a novel began to appear. Mara lives in London and is working on her next book. She loves reading, writing, running, Pilates, red wine, and spending time with friends and family – not necessarily in that order.

MARA TIMON

CITY

OF

SPIES

ZAFFRE

First published in Great Britain in 2020 by
ZAFFRE
An imprint of Bonnier Books UK
80–81 Wimpole Street, London, W1G 9RE
Owned by Bonnier Books
Sveavägen 56, Stockholm, Sweden

A CIP catalogue record for this book is
available from the British Library.

ISBN: 978-1-83877-070-9

Also available as an ebook

3 5 7 9 10 8 6 4 2

Typeset by IDSUK (Data Connection) Ltd
Printed and bound in Great Britain by Clays Ltd, Elcograf S.p.A.

Zaffre is an imprint of Bonnier Books UK
www.bonnierbooks.co.uk

For my parents, without whose love and support I would not be where I am now. I could not have asked for better, and miss them every day.

Character List

* = real name, verified via print or online resources
~ = fictional characters in other novels

France

Pierre Alaunt: A Resistance fighter

Jean-Roger Demarque: A Parisian neighbour of Elisabeth's

Antoine Gamay: A French fisherman

Köhler: ("the grey-haired man") A German secret service operative

Franc and Christiane Laronde: Relatives of Madame Renard with links to the Resistance near Rouen

Elisabeth de Mornay: (codename Cécile, aliases include Nathalie Lafontaine, Solange Verin, and Veronica Sinclair) An agent within Special Operations Executive

~Edith Renard: A friend of Elisabeth's, with links to the Resistance in Paris

Alexander "Alex" Sinclair: A Mosquito pilot from the 105 Squadron

Michel, Armand, and Mireille: Resistance fighters

Portugal

Rupert Allen-Smythe: A diplomat within the British Embassy

* John Grosvenor Beevor: Former SOE station head in Lisbon

* Hans Bendixen: Kapitän, head of the Abwehr's Naval Intelligence in Lisbon

Alois Bergmann: A German assassin

Martin and Rosalie Billiot: French nationals living in Estoril, Portugal

* António de Oliveira Salazar: Prime Minister of Portugal from 1932 to 1968

Adriano de Rios Vilar: A lieutenant within the *Polícia de Vigilância e de Defesa do Estado* (PVDE), Portugal's Surveillance and State Defense Police.

Claudine and Christophe Deschamps: French nationals living in Estoril, Portugal

Sabela Figueiredo: Elisabeth's housekeeper

Eduard Graf: Formerly of the 7 Panzer division, now a Major in the Abwehr (the German military intelligence service)

Matthew Harrington: A diplomat within the British Embassy and godfather to Elisabeth

Count Javier: A Spanish count living in Estoril, Portugal with his wife Laura

Hubert "Bertie" Jones: (Code name "Ulysse", aliases include Pete Aldridge) A Special Operations Executive agent shipwrecked in Portugal

Betty Jury and **Nicola Langston:** Secretaries at the British Embassy

* Agostinho Lourenço: ("The Director") Captain of the *Polícia de Vigilância e de Defesa do Estado* (PVDE), Portugal's Surveillance and State Defense Police

Andreas Neumann: Leutnant, formerly of the 7 Panzer division, now a lieutenant in the Abwehr (the German military intelligence service), and adjutant to Eduard Graf

Pires: A Portuguese man selling information to the Germans

Julian Reilly: An Irish novelist living near Estoril, Portugal

Gabrielle Ribaud: A French national living in Estoril, Portugal

* Amália Rodrigues: A Portuguese fado singer

Major Haydn Schüller: An SS officer based in Lisbon

* Baron Oswald von Hoyningen-Huene: German Ambassador to Portugal from 1934–1944

Mrs Willoughby: Bertie Jones' housekeeper

Great Britain

* Vera Atkins: Assistant to section head Colonel Maurice Buckmaster, and his de facto second in command, responsible for the recruitment and deployment of British agents in occupied France

* **Colonel Maurice Buckmaster:** ("Buck") Leader of the French section of Special Operations Executive

~**Kathryn "Kat" Christie:** A friend of Elisabeth de Morney

~**Big André,** ~**Jérôme,** ~**Dominique,** and ~**Robert:** Code names for Special Operations Executive agents that Elisabeth trained with

Other Persons of note:

* **Pietro Badoglio:** Marshal, an Italian general who became Prime Minister after the Italian Council voted to depose Benito Mussolini

* **Ronald Campbell:** The British Ambassador in Lisbon

* **Wilhelm Franz Canaris:** German admiral and chief of the Abwehr, the German military intelligence service from 1935 to 1944

* **Leslie Howard:** An English film actor/movie star. He was actively anti-German and rumoured to be involved in British Intelligence. Returning from a trip to Lisbon, his plane was shot down by the Luftwaffe over the Bay of Biscay

* **Benito Mussolini:** ("Il Duce") Prime Minister of Italy from 1922 to 1943

* **Henri Philippe Pétain, Maréchal:** A hero from WW1 who served as the Chief of State of Vichy France from 1940 to 1944

* **Harold Adrian Russell ('Kim') Philby:** An MI6 operative in charge of the subsection dealing with Spain and Portugal. Philby was later discovered to be one of the 'Cambridge Five' – double-agents working for the USSR

* **Erwin Rommel:** ("the Desert Fox") A German general who served as field marshal in the Wehrmacht (Defence Force)

***Otto Skorzeny:** A lieutenant-colonel in the Waffen-SS, he led the successful rescue of Benito Mussolini from where he was imprisoned in the Appenine Mountains

* **John Vereker, 6th Viscount Gort:** Commander-in-Chief of the British Expeditionary Force (BEF) in France

Part 1
Paris, Early June 1943

Chapter One

The café's door chimed, allowing in the evening breeze, the hum of street noise, and a man. He shuffled past, head down, shoulders stooped. His right hand, deep into his pocket, signalled to us that he'd been compromised. Sorrow ripped through me; Pierre Alaunt was a good man, and a friend to the Resistance.

'He's being followed,' Michel muttered. 'Two goons. Ten paces behind him.'

Which meant they weren't here for Pierre; they were here for whoever approached him.

I rotated my glass of Pernod and stretched my fingers. It was less than two months since I'd narrowly escaped a Nazi ambush, and no one had yet identified me. I was in no hurry to put myself back in the Nazis' cross hairs, not with a set of forged papers hidden in my handbag. Michel nodded; five minutes and we would leave. It was just long enough not to look suspicious.

'When will you speak with your Uncle Maurice?' Michel lit a cigarette, and slipped the case into his breast pocket.

'Uncle Maurice' was my commanding officer, Maurice Buckmaster. As the head of Special Operations Executive's French Section in London, he would need to know that Pierre was no longer reliable, and get word to whoever else Pierre worked with. I took a deep breath, inhaling Michel's nicotine, and wishing the Nazis hadn't taken such a dim view of women smoking.

'Tomorrow.'

A glass shattered on the floor. The woman who had dropped her drink was unfamiliar, and if she worked with the Resistance, it wasn't through our cell, but that didn't stop Pierre's shadows from mobilising. One of them moved towards the woman who had dropped her drink while the other blocked the door. A low rumble of voices rose and then subsided at a sharp glance from the first man.

'*Merde*,' Michel muttered, the only visible sign of his nerves.

I finished my Pernod as the goon finished searching the woman's satchel and signalled for her to move to the door. His colleague would search her person for anything suspicious, like the set of forged documents hidden in the lining of my handbag. My fingers explored the underside of the table for a nook, a nail, anything to hide the documents on, but found nothing.

The goon searched two other tables before coming to us. Michel's shoulders arched in a Gallic shrug. He retrieved his documents from his breast pocket and handed them across with a neutral expression. I hoped I looked as blasé as I placed my own papers on the table. The goon's nose flared as his thumb stroked my photograph. His head tilted to one side, watching my reaction as his fingernail worried the edge. His eyes were black, almost opaque, beneath a single dark brow. A corner of his mouth rose. From across the river, Notre Dame rang half past ten. I met his gaze.

'Curfew's approaching.'

4

He tossed my papers onto the floor, watching them scatter. Michel shook his head, warning me to hold my tongue. Teeth clenched, I dropped to my knees to collect them. The goon stepped closer so that his crotch was level with my eyes. Options ran through my mind. I could easily disable him. Even kill him. But for what purpose? A fleeting satisfaction followed by incarceration? Holding that thought in my mind, I waited. Ten seconds. Twenty.

He stood back and pointed to the man at the door. I'd passed the first hurdle; the second would be worse.

The second thug emptied my handbag on the table, watching as the detritus of my daily life scattered across it. I caught the compact before it fell to the floor. Buck had given it to me the night I parachuted in to France last December. I ran my fingers over the words etched onto it. *Bonne Chance*. I hadn't thought I'd need luck back then, but I wouldn't mind a healthy dose of it now.

He stared at my silver cigarette case, and I held my breath. The Nazis had decreed that smoking was unladylike. I refrained in public only because I had to. Would he use that as an excuse to arrest me?

'It's mine,' Michel said, picking it up. 'The lighter as well.'

Snatching the case from his hand, the thug opened it up, inspecting it. It wouldn't be the first time I'd used it to carry notes, but this time it was empty. He slid out a cigarette and lit it. Blew the smoke in Michel's face.

'Is it?'

'Her bag is big enough to carry it.'

'So it is.'

The goon peered inside, and then ran his fingers around the interior, feeling for any anomaly. He must have touched the papers, felt the ridges in the lining. The tingling in my spine intensified.

My bag was thrown aside as he moved to inspect my coat. I tried not to sigh. The coat was clean; the danger passed. Michel was shovelling my belongings back into the bag when the goon rotated his finger. I followed his instructions, turning while he patted down my back. I focused on the wall, trying not to react, but when he reached around me and fondled my breasts, my temper erupted.

'*Cochon!*' I whirled around and barely stopped myself from driving my knee between his legs.

He gave me a slow, smarmy grin. It was a challenge; he wanted a reason to arrest me. A reason that his fat fingers hadn't found. I was seething, but not stupid. A trip to the Gestapo's headquarters wasn't on my agenda. I raised my head, looking down my nose at him. He laughed, and waved us through, as if it were all a game.

'Opportunistic sod,' I growled once we were on the other side of the door.

'Fucking pig,' Michel agreed. He put one hand at my back and guided me into the crowd. 'Do not forget – they are closing in,' he murmured. 'You must be careful, Cécile.'

'Always.'

We walked together as far as the Pont Neuf. As he leant in to kiss my cheek, Michel reminded me: 'No unnecessary risks, *ma chérie.*'

Pierre Alaunt was proof that sometimes being careful wasn't enough. I mentally formed the message to Buck as I passed the darkened lamp posts that lined the bridge. The City of Lights, temporarily extinguished. And yet, there was something oddly comforting about it. In daylight, it was easy to get distracted. The dark allowed the senses to come alive. Only in the moonlight would I have noticed the man on the far side, scuttling along the Quai des Grands-Augustins, hunched into a dark coat despite the warm night.

A sensible woman would continue home, but he held my attention. Memory put a name to the face: Jean-Roger Demarque, a collaborator who lived in my district. If he was up to something, I wanted to know what it was. Ignoring Michel's warning, I followed him.

Demarque eased down a side street, pausing outside a bistro where a group of German soldiers tried to persuade a pair of women to stay for one last drink. He looked around and, satisfied that he'd attracted no undue attention, stepped inside.

The blackout curtains were drawn, hiding him from sight. In truth, I'd already risked too much. With the incriminating second set of papers in my bag, and curfew fast approaching, I needed to get home. Whoever the little weasel was after would have to fend for themselves.

Instead of moving, I counted the seconds with each heartbeat, with each couple rushing past.

Five minutes later Jean-Roger emerged, flanked by a German officer and two soldiers. I followed at a discreet distance as he led them into the labyrinth of Saint-Germain, weaving through the little streets to an unassuming building. Wrought-iron balconies hung like dark lace from the second and third floor windows, and the flowers in the window boxes were lovingly maintained.

By my landlady.

That bastard had led the Germans to my home.

The officer banged on the door with the butt of his gun.

My landlady was a good woman, but she wouldn't risk her life for me. How long before my image was nailed to buildings and signposts?

I shoved my hair out of my eyes and forced my breathing to slow. My backup flat was on the other side of Paris, and the house where I stored my set and transmitted from was in the suburbs. Too far to go without getting caught for breaking curfew. Assuming that the Gestapo weren't already waiting at those locations.

That left only one option.

Madame Renard had proven her loyalty to the Resistance and to me – standing fast in the aftermath of a Gestapo ambush, in which I'd been shot twice. Despite being under suspicion herself, she hid me, wounded and feverish, in her cellar. It wasn't fair to put her in danger again, but there was no other choice. If Demarque knew where I lived, he knew the name I was using. A quick flare from my lighter took care of that problem. Pulling the loose thread in the lining of my bag, I retrieved the spare set.

Voices echoed in the night as a gendarme questioned someone. I eased around the corner to see him shaking his head at a young couple. Shivers racked my body, and sweat trickled down my spine. Madame Renard's home was less than a quarter of a mile away but seemed farther away than London.

I doubled back to make sure I wasn't followed. Spent the better part of an hour ducking in and out of the winding streets until I was convinced it was safe to turn into the small alleyway leading to Madame Renard's house. Torn between regret for involving her and my own need to survive, I paused before raising my hand to rap once on her door, almost too soft for an old woman to hear. The bolt scraped open and one gnarled hand pulled me into the house. She closed the door firmly behind her and leant back against it.

'What happened?'

'I need a place to hide for the night. My cover was blown.' Her face paled and I added, 'No one followed me here.'

'Of course they didn't.'

She folded her arms over her bony chest, the Luger a lethal black mass, incongruous against her yellow dressing gown.

How on earth had she acquired a German pistol? And a Luger at that? Then again, if anyone could, it would be Madame Renard. She had enough food stashed in her cellar to single-handedly stock the black market, so why not a Luger? She set the gun down on a side table, and led the way into the kitchen.

'I'm sorry to ask this of you, madame.'

'Faugh!' She waved her hand dismissively and uncorked a bottle of wine. 'What happened?'

'Someone sold me out.'

'A friend?'

'A neighbour. Jean-Roger bloody Demarque. I'm not sure why, but I don't suppose it matters, damn him.'

As I removed the last cigarette from the silver case, the memory of an awkward dinner invitation, followed by a polite but firm refusal surfaced. At the time, he seemed to take the rejection well, but that was months ago. Had he been planning his revenge all this time, or had he found some shred of evidence? It took three tries with the lighter before the blasted cigarette ignited. I sucked in the smoke, savouring the familiar rush before exhaling a cloud of smoke and nerves. 'I don't suppose it matters,' I repeated.

'I don't suppose it does.' Madame Renard placed two glasses on the table and shooed her cat off a chair. 'Where will you go?'

'Out of Paris, obviously.'

'That's not much of an answer, Cécile.' She pushed a glass across to me. 'Is there somewhere you can go?'

'The couriers escort downed airmen to the Normandy coast. They use trawlers to take them back across the Channel.'

'You're going home?' Her voice was flat, making her opinion clear.

'Don't be absurd.' I toyed with the glass, wishing my hands would stop shaking. 'I'm sure they'll need another wireless operator up north. Maybe someone to co-ordinate the pickups.'

The old lady stood up and rummaged in the pantry. She put the battered tin of biscuits in the centre of the table and sat down. On the lid, one of Alphonse Mucha's redheads pouted, a heavy-handed reminder of happier times. I pushed it away.

'Thank you, but I'm not hungry.'

Madame Renard treated me to another condescending look and opened the tin to reveal a stack of photographs. Arthritic fingers flicked through them, pausing now and again, until they lingered on an image. She put it on the table and turned it around so I could see.

Two men flanked a young woman in a floral dress, standing in front of a stone cottage. A breeze had caught her hair, and

10

her hand was raised, holding her locks in place. The man on the right was a bit older, perhaps thirty, and bore a family resemblance to the woman. The man on the left was shorter, but had a strong bone structure and a determined chin.

'A good-looking set,' I said.

She harrumphed and jabbed a finger at the man on the left.

'My nephew, Franc Laronde, outside his house with his wife Christiane and her brother.'

I forced back a bad feeling and waited for her to continue. She took her time, picking up her glass and taking a delicate sip.

'They live near Rouen.'

'Madame, with all due respect, this isn't the best time to matchmake.'

She wheezed, spraying the burgundy over her hand. Then the laughter erupted.

'Cécile, you fool, Franc is part of the Resistance. If you can get to him he'll help you, or at least introduce you to someone who can.'

I opened and closed my mouth a few times before my voice caught up.

'Madame, I don't know what to say!'

'A simple thank you will do. Now, fetch me the Michelin map from the parlour, and I'll show you how to get there.'

As the birds fly, it didn't look far. If the trains were running, I would be able to get there within a few hours. Only the railway stations would be the first place they'd look for me.

'Perhaps a boat up the Seine,' I mused out loud.

'Still too obvious. Try a bicycle.'

'I don't have one.'

'Take your friend Juliette's. She left it here, and I don't think she'll be back in Paris anytime soon to protest.'

'No, I don't suppose she will.'

Juliette, or rather my fellow agent Dominique, had boarded with Madame Renard. In the aftermath of the ambush, Dom had been arrested and taken to the Gestapo's HQ on Avenue Foch. She'd escaped, and as far as I knew, had successfully disappeared.

Madame Renard's eyes narrowed. 'You do know how to ride a bicycle, don't you?'

I'd ridden on the handlebars a few times. What was there to it? You sat, you pedalled, and you got where you needed to go. Anyone could do it.

'Of course I can.'

Madame Renard's lips pursed. I met her gaze with all the innocence I could muster until she sighed.

'Sleep for a couple of hours. You'll go just before it gets light.'

The alleyway was deserted, but it was foolish to think no one watched from behind the shutters and blackout curtains. Madame herself watched from the doorway as I wheeled the bicycle on to the street and straddled it.

'Perhaps you're waiting for the Second Coming?' she asked, her voice low.

'Ha, bloody ha.'

I tossed the strap of my handbag over my head and straddled the frame. She held up a finger for me to wait and disappeared into her house for a moment before returning with the Luger, a book with a postcard tucked a third of the way in, and a box of chocolates.

12

'Never go to anyone empty-handed,' she advised.

Did she realise that where I was going, the Luger was a more effective asset than the sweets?

'Cécile, for once, try and be subtle. Use the chocolates first.' She tucked the chocolates and the pistol into my handbag, but held back on the paperback. Curious, I reached for it.

'*The Count of Monte Cristo*?' I blustered. 'Have some faith, Madame!'

Wearing a familiar expression of pained patience, she waited until I removed the postcard. On the front was the striped cathedral at Marseilles. On the back was a brief note, pleasantly bland as all postcards were these days. The message wasn't on the card – it *was* the card. Two friends I had long thought captured or dead had written that card. For me.

'They're alive?'

My voice was thick and I fought to hold back tears. I couldn't cry. Not in public, not even in front of Madame Renard.

'So it would seem,' she said. 'And if they can beat the Boche, so can you. Keep the card if you want, but also keep the book. A woman alone looks suspicious, but one with a book, oddly less so.'

The smile didn't reach her eyes, and she looked down as her gnarled fingers buckled my bag closed. Madame was a tough old girl, and although she tried to hide it, she cared. So did I.

'I'll be fine.'

'I know,' she said. 'Don't worry. I'll make sure the right people know about you. And your neighbour. Now, get out of here.'

Swallowing the lump in my throat, I grasped the handlebars. If it were anyone other than Madame Renard, I might have paused

13

for a hug, a last kiss on the cheek, a murmur of thanks. But even if I knew how to extend the sentiment, Madame was too crusty to accept it. I took a deep breath, steadying myself. Looked up to clear my own eyes. The last rays of the moon provided just enough light. As long as no one stopped me, I'd be in Rouen tomorrow or, worst case, the day after. I glared at the red metal frame, willing it into submission. Refusing to comply, it wobbled a few times and pitched me into the gutter. I cringed at the noise and looked around, but there was nothing, not even the twitch of a curtain.

Madame Renard muffled a snort. 'Shall I fetch someone to hold the saddle for you?'

'You shall not.' I dusted off my stinging palms and rose to my feet. 'I'll be fine.'

'Yes. You said. Would you like a plaster for your knee?'

I glared at the thin red trail snaking its way down my leg.

'I've had worse.'

'I remember.'

She flicked her fingers at me, urging me back on the bicycle.

It took three more tries before I was able to leave the street. My hands ached from the death grip they had on the handlebars, and sweat made my dress stick to my back. At this rate, it wouldn't be a day or two before I got to Rouen. It would be a week or two.

And I'd arrive in an ambulance.

It was barely dawn but vehicles were already queuing up to have their papers and vehicles inspected at the checkpoint leaving the city. So far I'd been lucky. No one stopped me as I weaved my way through the streets. There were plenty of posters fluttering in the breeze, but none with my face on them. How long my luck would last was a different question.

'You!' The German-accented voice boomed out.

The young soldier held his assault rifle in the crook of his arm as he pointed in my direction. I looked over my shoulder, but there was no one behind me. I pointed at my own chest.

'Me, sir?'

'*Ja*. Come here.'

I raised my chin and cycled around a horse-drawn cart and the two Germans peering underneath it. The man holding the reins looked away as I passed.

'Your papers?'

The soldier cradled a rifle in one arm. He thrust the other out for my identity card. I handed it over with a weak smile.

'Madame Laforge?' Pale eyes darted between my face and the photograph.

'Lafontaine.'

'Yes. Of course. And where are you going so early this morning?'

He stood so that I was half-blinded by the sun. I shielded my eyes with my hand and allowed the all-too-real wobble to enter my voice.

'My aunt is ill and has been asking for her son. She's sent me to collect him.'

'From where?'

'Halfway to Caen.'

'You couldn't use a telephone? Send a telegraph?'

'Not if I expect him to answer. Or to come and see her.'

A reluctant smile teased his lips. 'Like that, is it?'

'I'm afraid so.'

'And you're going to get there on the bicycle?'

I held up my raw palms. 'If it weren't important, do you really think I'd voluntarily travel on this godforsaken thing? My cousin has a permit for a car. He can drive us back.'

The corners of his mouth twitched as he returned my papers. 'Have you never heard of a train?'

'Of course I have.' I shrugged and lied. By the time he checked, I'd be long gone. 'I've also heard the British bombed the line.'

His smile froze. 'Again? Damned Tommies,' he muttered and waved me through.

Chapter Two

My death grip on the handlebars eased as the miles passed, but I was wary of stopping. Partially because I was eager to get to Rouen, but more out of the fear that if I stopped too long, the muscles in my shoulders and legs, already burning, might cease working.

I stopped late that night at a half-burnt barn, slept for a few hours and left before daybreak against the protests of my sore body. Fuelled by desperation, I cycled through the pain and the sun had already set by the time I rode past the stone cottage from Madame's photograph. It was a mile or so outside the nearest village, and set far enough back from the road to be almost hidden from view.

Circling the cottage would bring unnecessary attention. I did what I could to make sure there was no tail before coasting to a stop in front of Laronde's house. My knees buckled as I slid from the bicycle and dug my fists into the aching muscles to coax them into action. Slipped Madame Renard's Luger into the waistband of my skirt, and adjusted my cardigan over it. Combed my hair and applied lipstick to make myself look respectable. My gloves hid the blisters, but there wasn't much to be done about the scraped knees, other than hope no one would notice.

The couriers claimed nine out of ten homes would open the door to a resistance member, but that one in a hundred would summon the police. Laronde might open the door, but would he betray me?

I leant the bicycle against a tree and took out Madame's chocolates, just in case I had been seen. With the reassuring weight of the Luger at my back, I knocked on Laronde's door. Instead of the silence I'd expected, the door opened and I was pulled inside. A bright light shone into my eyes, almost blinding me. I stepped backwards until I pressed against the door.

'Who are you?' a voice demanded in French, the accent low and guttural. German. His dark hair was slicked back from a wide forehead, accenting small porcine eyes set too close to each other. He wore a well-tailored suit rather than uniform.

Hello, Gestapo!

Sod the subtle approach; I would have to brazen it out.

'Just what's this all about?' I demanded, throwing off his arm and stepping to the side. A second man, taller and slimmer with a scar that bisected his cheek, pointed a Walther PPK at me. I jabbed my finger at him. 'And you put that away. You're liable to hurt someone with that!'

'Where is he?' Pig-eyes asked.

'Who?'

'Who do you think?' he snapped.

'Franc Laronde? If I thought he wasn't in, do you really think I'd be here?' Sweat trailed down my back, but my voice remained even.

'Why are you here?'

'Madame Laronde kept an eye on my mother while I was away.' I held up the box of chocolates. 'I brought her a thank-you gift.'

18

'At this time of night?'

'It's still before curfew. Besides, I've only just returned!'

'Where were you?'

'Your papers!' the other man barked.

'Yes, of course.'

I put the chocolates down on a side table and, keeping my back to the wall to avoid them seeing my hidden gun, rummaged in my bag. I should have left the Luger in there; with both men watching my every move, it would have been easier to grab.

'Black market chocolates?' Scar sneered.

'No. Just old. And probably stale. You can have them.'

Maybe Madame Renard had poisoned them.

'Papers, Madame!'

'Yes. They're at the bottom of my bag. As usual,' I grumbled.

He grabbed it from me and began to root around for them.

Despite my compliance, Pig-eyes raised his left hand to strike me. Instinct, months of training, and a deep-seated anger at the situation dictated what happened next. I deflected his blow and drove my right fist into his nose. He rocked back and before he could recover, I gripped his shoulder and slammed my knee into his groin. He doubled over, resting his pistol on his thigh and gasping for breath. Blood poured from his nose, pooling on the rug.

Despite its small size, Scar's PPK sounded like a cannon in the small parlour. Dust settled from the ceiling and I locked my eyes with Scar's.

'Who are you?' He pointed the pistol at me.

'Who are you to bloody attack me?' I growled, calculating and recalculating my options.

19

He stepped closer. 'I will ask you again: who are you and why are you here?'

I'd rehearsed this, was trained for this with sergeants correcting me until I could do it without even thinking. A cold confidence settled over me and I pulled Pig-eyes erect, his back to my breast. Wrapped my hand around his and shot Scar between the eyes. As he crumbled, I buried the pistol's nose in the fleshy folds of Pig-eyes' chin and fired again.

His body hit the floor with a low thud. A trickle of blood traced its way from the third eye in Scar's head, disappearing into his dark oiled hair. They were dead, and I'd killed them. I fired another round into each of them. Just to make sure. Because either they were dead, or I was.

I stuffed the chocolates back into my bag and bolted, in case anyone had heard the shots and called for reinforcements. Grabbed the bicycle and pedalled hard, throwing myself behind a low rock wall only when I heard a vehicle pass. Cringed when I realised it was a transport, heading towards Laronde's house.

Forcing my heartbeat to slow, I considered my options. Fleeing on the bicycle wasn't possible. Too many people could have seen me and quite frankly, there was no way I'd be able to out-pedal the Gestapo. Franc Laronde was gone, maybe dead. He wouldn't be able to help me, and without him, how in the blazes would I find the Resistance? What else was there? Hot-wiring a car? Without the right papers, I'd be caught at the first checkpoint.

I closed my eyes and remembered Madame Renard's map. The lines criss-crossing the countryside. She was quite right: passenger trains were too risky.

But there was one other option, and it wasn't far.

Chapter Three

Dim starlight revealed the men in dark coveralls, milling around outside a medium-sized station house on the far side of the tracks. Casks were lined up on the platform, ready for transfer. I breathed a small sigh of relief. I wouldn't have long to wait for the train, and guessed that if it stopped here, then there would be other local stations like this, transporting wine east to Germany, or south towards Vichy. And frequent stops would give me plenty of opportunities to slip off once it was safe. Once far enough from Rouen, I'd be able to formulate a plan to get in touch with the local Resistance cells.

I crouched in the bushes and waited. Heard the engine before I saw it, clacking along the tracks, followed closely by flat carriages carrying tarpaulin-covered tanks. The train slowed as the container carriages came into sight and I crossed the strap of my bag over my head, leaving my hands free.

Getting on board proved surprisingly easy. Using the train itself to block me from view, I hauled myself onto the junction between the carriages and eased over until I could grip the lever. The sounds farther down the train hid the creak as I eased the door open and slid through, grateful that there were no locks. And if there wasn't much room between the casks to manoeuvre, at least I was reasonably certain this carriage wouldn't be opened until the train reached its ultimate destination. I eased to the floor and allowed myself to smile.

With a jolt, the train began to move. Braced against the casks, I held the Luger in my hand. Just in case.

The rhythm of the rails and the swish of wine had a lulling effect, and I only realised I'd slept when my head bumped against the wooden barrel. Pins and needles tortured my legs and I shifted as much as I could. How much time had passed? Was I far enough from Rouen yet?

Clickety-clack.

It was less than two days since I'd fled Paris and the journey was worse than I'd imagined. How did the couriers do it? Did they get used to the constant fear? The confinement? The overwhelming stench of burgundy that seeped from a broken cask?

Clickety-clack . . . *THROMMMM* . . .

The rhythm changed. It didn't undulate. It was loud, insistent. And frightfully familiar.

A sick feeling radiated from the pit of my belly as I realised that trains were bombed all the time, and this train pulled more than just local vintages.

Oh, hell!

I tucked the Luger in the back of my skirt and scrambled to my feet.

An explosion rocked the train. Bracing myself, I leant hard on the latch. It moved easily enough, but the door refused to open. The blasted thing was either broken or disabled, and the RAF were trying to make sure the whole damn train was as well.

Another bomb exploded but the train continued forward. How the bomber could have missed a large object, following a predictable trail, was something I could only be grateful for, and if I had any chance of survival, I had to get out.

22

A whistling sound ended in a loud BOOM! The train shuddered and rocked from side to side.

Please, God, don't let me die this way!

The carriage leant too far to the left. Wood protested, cracking. A couple of casks slipped their restraints and crashed into the little space by the door. I dropped to the ground and shielded myself as best I could as the train derailed and rolled. My stomach rolled with it, and I gagged.

Would Baker Street learn what had happened to me? Drowned in a cocktail of wine and vomit. What then? Would the very proper Miss Vera Atkins, Buckmaster's second-in-command, write to my mother?

Dear Lady Anne.

I regret to inform you that your daughter, while on assignment, drowned in a sea of burgundy. You'll be proud to know she did her best . . .

To what? Drink her way out? A high-pitched giggle escaped, ruthlessly cut off by a sob.

Think of the scandal! my mother would wail. If she could be bothered to read the letter.

Pull yourself together! Miss Atkins's cool voice cut through my panic. *You know what to do!*

I forced a breath into my lungs, and another. I'd get out all right. Sod the scandal, I wasn't ready to die. I pushed myself free of the casks and fought my way to the door. Any sound I made was inaudible over the roar of the engines and screaming voices.

23

Another bomb threw the carriage as if it were a child's toy. I made myself as small as I could, held on until the motion stopped. I'd been battered by the casks, but nothing was broken.

Smoke stung my eyes and filled my lungs. I doubled over, choking, and this time I allowed the bile to escape. Wiped my mouth clean with the back of my hand . The carriage wasn't yet ablaze, but I was surrounded by wine casks. Wooden casks, in a wooden carriage. On a train that also carried munitions. I had to get out.

'Shit, shit, shit!'

Splinters clawed my legs as I sloshed through the spilt wine. The carriage lay on its side, with the sliding doors above and below, and the smoke thickening.

Desperation reinforced determination. I began to climb towards the door. Grasped a piece of metal that must have once circled a barrel. Ignored its heat and wedged it between the doors, working it until they slid open with a screech of protest.

Damn it, I will get out!

I dried my hands on my skirt and reached up. Gripped the door jamb harder, pulling myself up and through the door. I crouched on top of the carriage to minimise my silhouette and took stock. The engine and first three carriages of the train disappeared into the distance. The bombers too were fading into the night. The train had become a conflagration. And four soldiers, guards I guessed, stood about one hundred feet away, cradling rifles.

Crouching low, I moved to the far side and slipped over the edge, my feet finding purchase on the undercarriage. The metal was hot, and my hands were already blistered. I didn't feel either,

24

yet. The next carriage exploded, the blast flinging me from the carriage. I moved with it, rolling as I hit the ground.

The countryside was flat and open; there was nowhere to hide. Making myself as low as I could, I ran from the blaze and the soldiers guarding it. I'd be damned if I allowed them to catch me now. I ran, Luger in hand, until I found a small copse of trees. A quick glance behind confirmed that I hadn't been followed and I allowed myself to drop to my knees and gasp for air.

I stayed that way for several moments. Until I felt cold metal press against the back of my head.

Chapter Four

I slowly raised my hands.

'Drop the gun,' the voice growled.

I lowered the gun to the ground, realising that the voice, a raspy baritone, spoke English – with a slight Scottish burr – although without seeing him I could make no assumptions. It could be a trick to get me to compromise myself, although covered in blood, sweat and smoke, it wouldn't take much. Leaving the Luger on the ground, I raised my hands, turning to look at him.

He wore the simple cotton shirt and trousers that RAF men often wore under the flight suits. His sandy-blond hair was plastered to his head, but his face was clean-shaven. He was probably shot down within the last few hours, and ditched the helmet and flight suit along with the plane. Sensible, although the cut of his clothing, not to mention the Webley pointed at my forehead, marked him as foreign.

'What's yer name?'

'Nathalie.'

'Good. Ye speak English. Where are we?'

'France.'

The pilot winced. A bruise was forming high on his forehead. The skin hadn't broken, but it was probably enough to give him a monstrous headache.

'I kind o' figured that much. Where in France?'

It was a good question, and as I had no answer, I shrugged.

'Alexander Sinclair,' he said. 'RAF. I need you to take me to the Resistance.'

I looked down at myself before meeting his gaze.

'Don't really know where to find them.'

He looked as if he wanted to challenge that until his shoulders drooped. He stared up at the moon.

'Damn.'

'Put the Webley away. I don't know where they are, but I didn't say I wouldn't help you. Just not while you're pointing the gun at me.'

'Why?'

I shrugged, not entirely sure of the answer.

'We'll look less suspicious travelling together.'

'And ye're already running from something,' he guessed. 'What?'

'Nothing that concerns you.' I got to my feet and dusted off my hands on my bottom. 'Unless you're planning to shoot me, put that damned English gun away.'

'You have a plan?'

I didn't, but that didn't stop me from improvising.

'For now, we walk.' I pointed in the direction away from the burning train. 'I need clean clothing and you need something that looks less English.'

'British,' he corrected, in a way that seemed more automatic than condescending.

Refraining from pointing out that while the French might note the difference, neither they nor the Germans would care, I started walking. He tucked the gun away and caught up easily.

27

After a mile or two of silence, I murmured, 'That bruise is fresh. When did you get shot down?'

'Couple of hours ago. We hadn't dropped everything on the bombing run, and the squadron leader thought it was a good idea to drop them on the train. Didn't see the 109s until it was too late.' His wry smile faded when he took in my singed clothes. 'Stupid idea.'

'That was you, wasn't it? The squadron leader?'

His shrug was as good as an answer.

'Got into the RAF, despite the accent, because I could fly. Moved through the ranks because I was better at staying alive than a lot of good men. One stupid decision and here I am.'

'Well, you're not dead yet, so that's a bonus. Let's keep moving.'

We took turns standing on guard, back turned, while the other washed in a stream. Sinclair again turned away when I filched a blouse and skirt from an unattended clothes line. The skirt was too short, and the blouse a bit loose. Neither of us would stand up to scrutiny, but from a distance, we were passable enough.

We stayed off the main roads, opting for the less-travelled ones, as much in the hopes of finding Sinclair more appropriate attire as it was to avoid unnecessary attention.

In England road signs were removed or altered in case of a German invasion. Assuming French road signs were reliable, we just skirted another town near Vouvray when we heard the roar of a motorcycle. I pulled Sinclair back into the shrubbery and lay flat beside him. His breath caught in his throat as the motorcycle slowed.

'Through your mouth,' I whispered.

'What?'

'Breathe through your mouth. It's quieter.'

He nodded, his hand clenching his sidearm. The motorcycle stopped and the driver helped the man in the sidecar out. The latter stretched, and pushed his driving goggles onto his forehead. Hand on the flies of his black uniform, he ambled towards us.

'SS,' I mouthed at Sinclair.

The man's trousers were now undone and he was braced to relieve himself. He was close enough that if he looked to the side, he'd see Sinclair.

The man must have heard something and his head turned towards us. There was no thought, and no other option. My hand tensed, fingers pressed together. Thumb up, palm down in a familiar gesture. In two long strides, I was out of the brush and striking the back of his neck next to his spine.

No one could have been more surprised than me when he crumbled to the ground. The move was well-practised, but had never been used outside the practice grounds. There was no gunfire, but the second man fell, a small blade quivering from his eye.

'Gunfire echoes. I didna think we'd want to attract attention.'

He was right, and from what I could see, capable of handling himself. Maybe there were worse travelling partners.

He pulled the knife free from the dead man and was about to clean it on the black tunic when I stopped him.

'He's about your size, isn't he?' I said.

And with a similar fair colouring to Sinclair; an idea began to gel. We made quick work of plundering the bodies and hid them in the woods. They would be found, but hopefully not until we were long gone.

I fiddled with the strap for the goggles, watching Sinclair from under my eyelashes. Dressed as an *SS-Untersturmführer*, he looked frighteningly authentic. His Webley was out of sight and the German's Luger was holstered at his side. I swallowed hard, and tamped down the visceral fear that the uniform brought as he straddled the BMW.

'Most officers are driven.'

'No' when they have a girl wi' them. Stop arguin' and get in the sidecar.'

I shook my head at this demonstration of male ego, and slipped the goggles over my eyes. Sinclair fired up the engine and revved it a few times.

'Where to?'

'They'll expect us to head to Vouvray or Tours. Maybe north, towards the coast. We'll go south, I think. At least for now, then we can head west. We'll need to keep to the small roads.'

'I don't know these roads.'

'South,' I repeated, pointing. 'And don't forget to drive on the right-hand side.'

We skirted Vouvray and picked up the road leading south. The first checkpoint was at Montbazon, a simple barrier manned by two soldiers with a third sitting in front of a little hut. I held my breath as we approached. Had my description made it this far? Were alarms raised about the missing SS soldiers and their vehicle? Or the dead Gestapo thugs in Rouen? What if we were stopped and the Scot questioned? He had no French, and probably not a lot of German, if any. If we were caught, we'd both be shot as spies.

The same thoughts must have been running through Sinclair's mind, but his expression, or what showed beneath his goggles, was stony. Maybe even arrogant. He didn't stop for the checkpoint, just slowed the bike enough to allow the guards to see the SS flashes at his neck.

His gamble paid off. The two guards snapped to attention and saluted us, the third moving quickly to remove the barrier. I counted to twenty before releasing the air from my lungs. Sinclair glanced over. One corner of his mouth twitched and he winked.

We drove for another hour before stopping in a small village. Sinclair stretched before helping me from the sidecar. He patted down his pockets and thrust a wad of French francs into my hand.

'Food and beer,' he directed, before stalking off behind a tree to relieve himself.

For someone who had baled from a plane, cracked his head, held me at gunpoint and killed an SS officer in less than twenty-four hours, the Scot was doing rather well. But there was one other thing to do first, even more important than food. I spat on a handkerchief and cleaned the grime from my face. Applied a coat of lipstick and sauntered through the town until I found several broadsheets nailed on a board in front of the post office, captioned with names, aliases, and alleged crimes. Even with a healthy dose of imagination, none of the likenesses bore any resemblance to me, or anyone I knew. With a forced smile, I walked into the shop, surprised to find it well-provisioned. A young woman, neatly attired, put down her duster.

'May I help you?'

I hummed a response and wandered through the aisles. Most of the goods were local, which explained a fair amount. A small area stocked beer and wine, in the blue bottles that had become common since the start of the war.

'It's a beautiful day for a picnic.' The woman's voice, high and strident, jerked me out of my thoughts.

'Yes, I suppose so.'

Unfamiliar with the labels, I directed her towards a bottle of red table wine and a locally brewed beer for the Scot.

'I haven't seen you here before.' Her brown eyes narrowed as she studied me.

'No. Just travelling through.'

The woman's eyes narrowed again. Her voice was chilly as she quoted me an inflated price for my purchases. I gritted my teeth and handed her a note. Turned away without waiting for my change.

'Have a good day, madame.' Her voice dropped when she added, 'Hope you get bombed, collaborating bitch.'

With one hand on the door frame, I turned and stared at her. Animosity blossomed, palpable between us. It was nothing short of foolish. If I were the collaborator she accused me of being, I could make life difficult for her, and still she showed defiance. I didn't know if it made me proud, or sick.

We stopped at an open field far enough from the town to risk speaking in English. A handful of trees clustered into a corner, under which Sinclair set up the little picnic.

He took a swig from the beer bottle. 'Not bad.'

'I'm sure the shop girl would be glad to hear it.' I sat beside him and looked at the meagre feast. 'Damn, I forgot to buy glasses. And a knife . . .'

I looked meaningfully at his ankle where he sheathed the small blade.

'You're no' using my sgian dubh to serve lunch.'

He ripped off a piece of bread and stuffed it into his mouth.

'No? Well, fair enough. Your little dagger has other uses.'

'That it does,' he said through a full mouth.

He moved to one knee, and pulled the knife from his sock.

'Can you teach me how to throw it?' I asked. 'Like you did this morning?'

He eased back and looked at me with calculating eyes. So far, he hadn't commented on the bloodstained clothes he found me in, or the ease with which I'd killed the SS man earlier. It wouldn't last.

'First I want to hear how an English girl comes to be in Occupied France.'

'Wrong turn at Brighton?'

'Ye're wanting me to guess?'

'Go ahead. This could be fun.'

I leant back, enjoying the sun on my face, and a rare moment of peace. When I opened my eyes, Sinclair was giving me an odd look.

'What?' I asked.

He shook his head. 'Ye're one cool customer, Nathalie. Do you kill men often?'

'Only when they're trying to kill me.'

I looked away. How could I explain that the moment I thought of them as men – as sons and husband, fathers and lovers – I was done for? It was easier to pretend they were the dummies we used in training – mannequins moving on unpredictable tracks.

His warm hand closed over mine. 'You did well.'

'I'm still alive,' I murmured.

He squeezed my hand and, reaching, produced a multi-tool pocketknife from a pocket.

'Let's hope you stay that way.'

He unfolded a small metal curl and worked the cork from the wine bottle.

'Convenient,' I murmured.

'Ye can thank the uniform's previous owner.'

He handed me the bottle, laughing as I raised it to my mouth. Harsh tannins assaulted my tongue, and I struggled to swallow. I looked at the label. It wasn't the wine I had selected; the shop girl must have switched it. Damn her.

'No' a good vintage?' Sinclair drawled.

'Better than what you can find in Scotland.'

I took another mouthful, more carefully this time.

He squinted into the sun. 'That doesna take much. Ye'll be fluent in French then?'

'*Oui.*'

'Why is it so hard to get you to talk?'

'Usually it's hard getting me to shut up,' I admitted.

His full mouth twitched and I was surprised at how much I was enjoying his company. He took another swig of beer and sighed.

'At least one of us can speak the native lingo. I can't speak a word, short of finding . . . ah. Yes. No French.' A red flush crept up his cheeks.

'Finding a whore?' I guessed. His eyes raised in shock. Did he think I'd never heard the word? 'You can say that in French but you can't order a glass of wine or a loaf of bread?'

'One phrase isn't that hard to remember,' he said. 'Dinnae get me wrong – the nuns tried to teach me French in school. The "Auld Alliance" and all that. It just didn't take.'

Catholic, then. And well educated, for all he dismissed it. Coupled with the comment about his accent when we first met, a picture of Alex Sinclair was beginning to form: of a man who achieved whatever he set his mind to, despite the odd 'stupid decision'. A useful ally to have.

'How's your German? The Boche can get away with not speaking French, but you may have a problem if you don't understand German either. Did the nuns manage to drum that into you?'

'Never thought I'd be needin' it.'

I frowned. 'Your head injury will buy us a bit of time, but not a lot. My German is passable, Squadron Leader. I'll teach you enough to get us through.'

'Alex.'

'What?'

'"Squadron Leader" is a mouthful. Ye may as well use my name. Alex.'

'No. Your name is . . .' Bracing one hand on his chest, I reached into his breast pocket for his papers, opening them with a flourish. 'Heinrich Weber.'

He grabbed them back and repeated the name.

35

'No. The Germans pronounce W's like V's, and ch's, well, rather a bit softer than you would.' I demonstrated, exaggerating the sounds. 'Try again.'

'Hein-rik Vayber.'

'You know, he probably goes by Heini.'

I struggled to keep a solemn expression. He stared for a few seconds before bursting out in laughter.

'Fine, then.' He got to one knee. 'Ye teach me what you can, and I'll teach ye how to throw the sgian dubh.'

That afternoon we made a game of it, although it was anything but funny. Chances were that I'd never need to throw his knife, but how well he grasped the language could make all the difference to our survival. He'd never be able to speak well enough to fool the Boche, but as long as he could fool the French, we'd be fine.

'We should keep moving.'

I reluctantly gathered our things and allowed Sinclair to help me up. He had a nice smile and a sharp dagger. There were worse travel companions.

The countryside passed in a blur of farms and vineyards, interspersed with small towns and villages, all but indistinguishable from one another until the motorcycle stuttered. Sinclair guided it to the side of the road and cut the engine.

'What's wrong?'

'Out of petrol,' he said.

'And your German isn't good enough to get more. Even if we had petrol coupons.'

He gave me a dark look. 'We passed a town a couple o' miles back. We can turn around or keep walking until we find the next town. What do you think?'

'There's still plenty of daylight. Let's keep going.'

When those SS soldiers were reported missing, someone would start looking for the vehicle. I'd trained as a wireless operator, not a courier. All I had to go on were my instincts, and they told me to keep moving.

Alex pushed the bike off the road and removed the goggles and leather helmet, flinching as it brushed over the bruise on his forehead. Fresh blood seeped through the bandage.

'Are you all right?'

He shrugged and echoed my own words: 'I'm alive.' He removed the motorcycle's identity plate and buried it some feet away, stamping hard on the earth. 'Let's keep it that way, eh?'

Sinclair took off his jacket and slung it over his shoulder. Without the stripes and lightning bolts, he was Alex once again, no longer SS officer Heini Weber. It was a dangerous look, but the sun was hot, and a man, even an SS officer, might relax when walking alone with his girl.

'Do you have a plan?' he asked.

I didn't, but wasn't about to admit that.

'Our best bet is to link up with the local Resistance. Then we get you on a boat back to Blighty.'

'What about you?'

'If they'll have me, I'll stay here. Continue working with the Resistance.'

His tone was a cross between curiosity and suspicion.

'Why wouldn't they have you?'

That surprised me; I'd expected him to ask why they would want me.

'I . . . ah, I've had a run of bad luck lately.'

He burst out laughing. 'You think?'

'Don't be difficult. If there aren't any posters warning people about me yet, there may be soon enough.'

Now he was serious. 'What have you done?'

I met his eyes, offering no apology.

'I've survived.'

Necessity proved a better teacher than the nuns, and we continued the German lessons as we walked, peppering them with a light banter that allowed both of us to pretend that the danger had receded. As his confidence grew, Alex spoke of his home, his family, his love of flying.

'Ye're a very good listener, Nathalie,' he said. 'But ye don't offer much, do ye?'

I wanted to talk to him, to tell him what had happened, how I got here. Already a strange sort of bond was forming between us. The couriers hadn't really mentioned this phenomenon, and I hadn't thought to ask whether it was usual or not. Whether they were able to keep themselves remote from the men they escorted, because I knew I was slipping.

Despite that, something held me back. Maybe it was my training, maybe the experience working with the Resistance, but I knew what a careless slip could do. I could offer Alex my friendship, but not my trust. Not yet.

'It's easier that way.'

He could have said something sarcastic; I knew my reply stung, but instead he nodded.

'Fine. But please, whatever ye do choose to tell me, let it be th' truth.'

Very aware that I hadn't even given him my real name, I tried to smile.

'Moving forward,' he added.

'Thank you.' I nodded. 'Are you upset?'

He seemed to think about that for a few steps.

'No. Your secrets are yer own to tell.' His smile was shy. 'Maybe ye'll tell me when ye're ready.'

'Maybe.'

He looked at the sky, clear and starry. The moon was nearing full and was bright enough for a pilot to see by, a drop to be made. We could have continued walking, but my legs hurt, in fact, my entire body ached.

'Let's bed down here,' he suggested before I could. 'It's a mild night, and maybe safer out here in the middle of a field, than in a town.'

'Sensible.'

I dropped my handbag and sank to the ground, ignoring his laugh. Under normal circumstances, I'd have suggested that we took turns sleeping, but if either of us was awake in five minutes it would be nothing short of a miracle. I stretched out, using the bag as a pillow, the pistol at my side.

'The wildlife will let us know if anyone comes close.'

Alex was slower to lie down. 'Nathalie?'

I opened one eye. 'Yes?'

He rested his head on his neatly folded tunic. Stared at the sky and said, 'I'm glad ye're here.'

His hand reached across and squeezed mine.

Unsure whether he saw my smile, I closed my eye and answered, 'I'm glad you're here too, Alex. Goodnight.'

What woke me was Alex's nightmare. Arms like steel pulled me close against his chest, the buttons of his shirt digging into my cheek. His teeth ground together, making a horrible sound, and his face contorted as if he were in pain.

'Alex?' I squirmed to free myself – to breathe.

He mumbled something and released me, rolling to his side in a foetal position. Awake now, I studied his face. It was difficult to believe I'd only just met him. Impossible to comprehend how much had elapsed in that time – in the last week, for that matter. I reached out, lightly holding his shoulder until the nightmare released him. His features softened to childlike innocence. Brushing a lock of sandy hair from his face, I impulsively dropped a kiss on his forehead.

Strong arms pulled me back, this time protectively. Chaste as it was, it was the first time I'd slept in the arms of a man other than my husband. He would be horrified if he could see me now. A filthy ragamuffin, in the arms of a strange man. A spy on the run.

I bit my lip and turned away from Alex. Philip wasn't here to judge me; he'd left to go to war, and became one of its casualties. I'd get Alex Sinclair back to England and then would find myself another Resistance cell to work with.

There was still work to be done.

Chapter Five

A pleasant monotony of wheat sheaves waved in the breeze, one field indistinguishable from the next, until something marred the uniformity. A slim line slashed through the field, about a third of the way in. Swearing reverently, I moved towards it, the pain in my body dissolving with budding excitement.

'What do you see?' Alex asked, following me.

Two faint, parallel ruts bisected the field. I squatted beside one depression and allowed my fingers to trail along it.

'A plane landed here.'

He looked around, gauging the distance.

'Pretty impressive flying if they did.'

'They're a pretty impressive lot.'

I knew this from experience; a flak storm had buffeted my plane as we crossed the Channel. The old bomber that had carried us was badly damaged; smoke billowed from one of the engines, visible through the window. A shard had pierced the wall, narrowly missing the dispatcher's head. If the rent in the hull allowed the stench of petrol and kerosene to escape, it did little to salve our fear.

My fingers curled into talons, digging into the bench. Across the aisle, one man genuflected in a continuous motion, pausing only to check his harness. The other, who didn't have much of a neck to start with, retracted what little was left into the folds of his jump suit, like a large drab turtle.

The dispatcher yanked open the hatch.

'Get out! NOW!'

As the only woman on board, I was first through the joe hole. Any drop was risky – the Germans were known to infiltrate and ambush the Resistance – but a blind drop bordered on suicide. We could have landed in an empty field, or the middle of a German platoon. Or on top of their offices. And still the option to drop was better than staying on the Lancaster.

Those were the longest fifteen seconds of my life.

It was December, and cold. The snowdrift I'd landed on was a scant cushion but at least it wasn't a pond or a river. A small dark animal – maybe a fox or a cat, with yellow eyes that reflected the moon – stared at me for a few moments until it silently disappeared into the night. In the sky, three other 'chutes trailed from the plane, and with our weight gone, the bomber began to climb. I never found out if the pilot made it home.

Alex hunkered down next to me, touching the ruts.

'The tracks look recent. Maybe a few days old. The Resistance?'

'The Resistance don't have their own planes.'

'So the RAF then. D'ye think the Resistance are active here?'

'So it would seem.'

The only question was how to find them.

The next village was small, with a single main street meandering through it. A post office and village shop sat on one end, on the other, a hotel and a restaurant. Some buildings had advertisements painted on them while others allowed vines to creep up the sides. On the whole, the town looked well maintained, if not prosperous. Possibly explained by the swastikas, flying from most buildings.

'Why would the Resistance operate so close to a town like this?' Alex asked. 'What wi' the town clearly supporting the Nazis?'

I had no ready answer. It was dangerous, maybe even foolhardy, but looks could be deceiving.

'Perhaps they believe that by supporting the Nazis – at least on the surface – they'll reduce the risk of any retaliation? Or maybe the Resistance has enough eyes and ears in town, maybe even with the police, to warn them of any action ahead of time?' It wasn't likely we'd ever find out, and I shrugged. 'It wouldn't be my first choice, but we haven't eaten since finishing off the bread and cheese for breakfast.' I gestured to the restaurant's entrance, under a neat green and white awning. 'Fancy a bite to eat?'

'Is that wise?' Alex asked. 'I cannae speak French *or* German.'

'Hiding in plain sight. They wouldn't expect anyone like us to stop here, so there might not be so many questions.'

It was a calculated risk, but given the more than fair chance that we had already been seen entering the town, it would seem only right that we stop to eat. It might reduce the question as to why an SS officer was walking *anywhere*.

'If we stop for a newspaper,' I thought out loud, 'then you could hide behind it and leave the ordering – and the conversation – to me. All you need to do is grunt in the pauses and we'll be fine.'

'Ye're married, aren't you?' he joked, but looked unconvinced. He ran his hand through his hair, his blunt fingers gingerly exploring the scab on his forehead. His stomach rumbled, sealing the deal. 'Any paper in particular?'

'There won't be a lot of options. Point to something that looks like it's written in German and hold out a note. You'll be fine.'

Uncertainty flashed in his eyes before he nodded, the corners of his eyes tightening in grim determination. A faint smudge ran down the side of his face. I sighed. Reaching up to caress his cheek, I dusted it off.

'I'll wait for you over there,' I said, indicating a low stone wall shielded by a cluster of trees.

His back was as straight as any officer's, the swagger as authentic as it could be, as he made his way into the shop. I watched until the door closed behind him, and reached into my bag. Under the guise of brushing my hair, I studied the town. It had a strange feel to it, retaining its vigilance even after its neighbours had lapsed into a wary tranquillity. People bustled past in groups of two or three, under the watchful eye of the German soldiers.

Alex reappeared with the newspaper and a remote expression. I met him halfway across the street. Tucking my hand in the crook of his arm, I allowed him to escort me down the street and into the restaurant.

The restaurant was quaint. Murals decorated the walls, giving it the atmosphere of an establishment that was trying hard to be more than it was. Not unlike the short man in the pristine suit who swanned up to us.

With a smarmy grin and a not-so-discreet glance at my cleavage, he asked: 'May I help you?'

'A table for two.' I took hold of Alex's hand.

'Do you have reservations?'

One chubby finger consulted a well-worn book with very few entries.

'Thank you, the table there will do just fine.'

Twenty-five years of watching Lady Anne's tactics hadn't gone to waste. Without waiting for his answer, I swept past him to a table in the corner with a good view of the door. The maître d' scurried out of our way, any protest silenced by Sinclair's black uniform.

Alex took the corner seat and snapped open the newspaper. I sat on his left, with a clear view out of the window.

The waitress brought wine that was slightly better than what I'd bought the previous day. Her nose flared as she took my order; she would tolerate the Germans – she had no choice – but collaborators might find their food seasoned with spit *du chef.*

The door banged open as a group of men entered. Like us, they brushed past the maître d' and claimed two nearby tables, pushing them together. Unlike Alex, they wore no uniforms, but I didn't need to hear their accents to know they were German. And plain-clothed Germans in France meant one thing: Gestapo.

I swallowed the dust at the back of my throat at the thought that they might notice that his trousers didn't match the tunic. Or what they'd do about that.

'Wine!' one demanded, and he pinched the waitress's bottom.

In a saner world, if one of them had pinched mine, I'd have smacked him into next week, but this world was no longer sane, and the waitress was too wise to show any indignation. She moved out of reach, a fixed smile in place. If she ordered the chef to spit in my food, these men were likely to get something worse.

Alex's hands, holding the paper in front of his face, tensed, the veins standing out. I brushed one with the back of my hand, and tried not to look apprehensive.

'So, my dear,' I prattled in rapid-fire French, hoping that these soldiers would see only what they expected to: a silly woman boring her man. 'I forgot to tell you I saw dear Annette yesterday,' I said in a stage whisper and began to bore even myself with some fiction about a woman who'd had an affair and found herself pregnant.

Alex's newspaper crackled but otherwise he showed no interest. The story wasn't that uncommon, but I hoped dull enough to deflect any attention from us.

The waitress set the plates down and retreated, neatly avoiding the Germans, who were now banging on the table like naughty children. The bottle of wine on their table couldn't be their first.

There was a slight tremor in Alex's hands as he folded the paper and placed it on the table. He centred his plate and looked at me expectantly.

'*Bon appétit*, Heini,' I said.

'*Bon appétit.*'

Nerves made his voice harsh, but improved the accent. Alex's full lips had tightened and his naturally fair skin had gone white.

Most of the Germans seemed preoccupied, but one of them – an older man with a rugged face and grey hair – inclined his head, acknowledging Alex. Alex responded with a curt nod and just the right amount of disdain for an officer to show a comrade from a rival organisation. Despite the salute, the grey-haired man watched us, his expression giving nothing away. Had I missed an incriminating image? Did he know of me? Recognise me from Paris? Was it Alex who had captured his interest? He looked the part, but had his accent given us away?

Hoping for the best, I reached out to caress Alex's jaw. Allowed my fingers to drop to the collar of the black uniform. Alex played along. He took hold of my hand and raised it to his lips. He glanced over and met the grey-haired man's eyes. Raised an eyebrow, challenging the other man before putting my hand on the table and turning his attention to his meal. The grey-haired man took a deep pull from his beer glass and raised it to me in a mocking salute. I breathed out, grateful Alex hadn't seen it, or at least pretended he hadn't. Pushing my fork through my food to test any unwanted ingredients, I too pretended not to notice.

Alex shovelled another forkful of lentils into his mouth. The grey-haired man still watched us, his expression crafty. A dark shiver slid down my spine. The others murmured to themselves, their heads held close. Every moment or two they cast the odd glance our way.

Alex's muscles were tense; he wouldn't last much longer.

'I'm boring you, aren't I, darling?' I reached across and stroked his hand.

He stood so suddenly that his chair slammed back against the floor. Silence blanketed the room and all eyes focused on us as Sinclair pulled me to my feet and clamped his mouth on mine. Someone wolf-whistled and he flung a few notes on the table. Grabbed me around the waist and slung me over his shoulder, pausing only to let me grab my bag, before striding out the door.

As we left, my last look back was of the German soldiers, on their feet, laughing and applauding. All except the grey-haired man who, still seated, again raised his glass at me.

'I'm sorry,' Alex murmured. 'I couldn't think of another way to get out of there.'

Still slung over his shoulder, I hissed: 'You think this isn't drawing attention to us? Put me down, you oaf!'

My toes touched the ground only briefly before he cradled me in his arms.

'Put your arms around my neck,' he ordered. 'The auld bastard is still watching – we need a hotel for the night.'

I obeyed as he made his way through the door of the nearest hotel.

'One room, please,' I said to the startled clerk, trying to preserve what dignity I had left.

'I . . . I think we may be full.'

The man's Adam's apple bobbed nervously as he licked the tip of one finger and ran it down a page in the ledger.

'Put me down, darling,' I told Alex.

The Scot might not have understood my French but understood the tone. He set me down on my feet and, with one hand on my waist, took an aggressive step forward. His glare was more eloquent than any words would be and the clerk shrunk back.

'Ah yes,' the clerk squeaked, running his hand through thinning hair. 'Yes, we do have a room. Last one left. Room five. Down the hall, on your left.' His hand fluttered in the general direction. He pressed a key into Alex's hand and looked, wide-eyed, at both of us. 'It's one of our best rooms.'

'Thank you.' I took hold of Alex's hand. 'Come, darling.'

Alex glowered at the clerk for a final moment before stomping towards the room. He locked the door behind us and leant back against it. Slowly, his body slid to the ground, his forehead resting against his knees. I didn't know whether to go to him or remain quiet. After a few moments, he spoke – his words so soft I had to struggle to hear.

'I had to get out of there.' He raised his head but looked through me. His blunt fingers pressed against his temples, disrupting the beads of sweat forming at his hairline. 'I had to get out of there. They were taking too much notice of us.'

It was easy to forget that Alex wasn't trained for a spy's shadowland. For him, enemies were marked with crosses and friends with stars and circles. It wasn't less dangerous, but it was straightforward. This couldn't be easy for him. Hell, with all my training, it wasn't easy for me.

I sank to the floor and rested a hand on his shoulder. There were no words that could make this situation right, but perhaps it would be enough to remind him that he wasn't in this alone. He shook off my sympathy and lurched to his feet.

'I'm fine. Just tired.'

Feeling strangely rejected, I moved out of his way, watching as he stumbled to the bed and fell across it, face down. He was still fully clothed, his legs hanging off the edge, when his breathing evened out.

I couldn't promise him that things would be better in the morning. Couldn't promise that we'd even see the new day, but whatever was coming, he needed to be ready. I unlaced his boots, gently pulling them off and putting them neatly beside the bed. Removed the socks, lightly touching a blister that had formed and broken some time during the day. He'd never complained. About anything.

I tried to be gentle when I pulled his legs onto the mattress, but didn't dare remove any more clothing for fear of waking him. The lines began to fade and his colour returned. I closed the curtains and began to work on his papers, altering them as best I could. It didn't need to be perfect, just good enough to withstand the cursory inspection of one Nazi to another.

Sinclair cried out, shuddered, and jerked upright, eyes wide and staring. He blinked a few times, orienting himself.

'Are you always plagued by nightmares?'

'What?'

'You were tossing and turning. Once or twice you called out, but I couldn't understand what you're saying.' Then I added: 'Thank God.'

He sighed and rubbed the stubble bristling his face.

'I was back in my Mozzie, getting shot down. Fielding was screaming. But this time, I couldn't get out. Tim Fielding, my navigator, was a good man. Got himself hitched three months ago to a lass from Stirling. I stood up for him.' He stared into the distance. 'Christ, I have to tell Caroline.'

'I'm sorry.' The words were inadequate, but what else could I say? 'At least you survived, Alex. They didn't get you both.'

'No,' he said. 'They didn't. What time is it?'

The stubble gave him a dangerous look, but with the pride of Deutschland clean-shaven, he'd stand out in a heartbeat. We'd need to stop at a chemist for supplies, and not just for him. Auburn roots gleamed at my hairline, and if not many SS officers were bearded, not many Frenchwomen were redheads.

'It's just gone eleven.'

Rhythmic thumping from the next room indicated that at least someone was having a good time.'

A faint smile curled his lips. 'What time is curfew?'

'About five minutes ago.'

'You're not sleeping?'

'No.'

'Of course not.' He stood up and stretched, vest pulled tight against a lean abdomen. I turned away as he reached for the shirt. 'Ye want to check out those tracks?'

'There's no guarantee they'll be there tonight, but linking up with the Resistance is our best chance. Take whatever you have – we won't be coming back.'

Nodding, he inspected the papers before slipping them into his breast pocket and moving towards the door.

'Not that way,' I whispered, pulling the heavy drapes from the window.

'Wait here.'

He stepped out of the window and disappeared into the night. He may have good instincts but one passing soldier, one question that couldn't be answered, and there would be one less Scot.

Minutes dragged, plagued by doubts and fears before a twig snapped outside. It was likely Alex, but there were no guarantees. I fumbled for my gun and pointed it at the window.

Someone tapped on the glass and I held my breath. Another tap, and then, softly, he murmured my name.

51

'Jesus!'

I slid the gun into my waistband and scrambled out of the window, grateful that the room was on the ground floor, and even more grateful that he hadn't been picked up.

It took less time to reach the field than I anticipated. It was cloudier and the moon's dim light was barely enough for us to find our way. An owl hooted and a fox screamed – the sound uncannily human. A flock of birds took flight from the other side of the field, winging their way north.

'Someone's there,' he murmured. 'Birds don't move like that unless they're startled.'

We reached for our guns, knowing we could be walking into a trap.

A twig broke somewhere ahead and Alex pushed me gently behind him. We crept forward in single file, unsure what we were creeping towards. It could just as easily be a group of Germans as the Resistance.

Any sensible person would get out of there. What's wrong with you?

It wasn't uncommon for the Germans to find a field, or some other place the Resistance used. They would put it under surveillance, until they could spring their trap. That's what had happened last spring. We made it out of there alive, but at a high cost: I'd been shot twice, and Dom had been arrested. Recovering from my wounds, I hadn't been able to help with her escape, but the news she'd survived, relayed on the back of Madame Renard's postcard, gave me hope.

The snick of a gun's safety preceded a voice demanding we raise our hands above our heads.

'French,' I breathed. 'They're speaking French!'

It was my own hope that spoke; not all Frenchmen were on our side, but my instincts told me that this was the Resistance, and that we hadn't found them so much as they'd found us. Smiling broadly, we raised our arms.

Against the pale wheat, dark shapes began to materialise. Men, women too, moving surrounding us.

'An SS dog and his bitch,' someone sneered.

'If he's dumb enough to come out by himself, then he's dumb enough to die here.' The voice rang with authority and hatred.

'Repercussions?' Another voice. No less strong, but pragmatic.

'We're not Germans,' I protested, my optimism turning to bile.

'Sod the repercussions,' the first man said. 'Take them into the woods and shoot them.'

Chapter Six

The Resistance fighters formed a loose circle around us. There were six of them: two women and four men. Their faces maintained the same expression, resolute bordering on hatred. Their guns, a mix of handguns and rifles, American, British, and even German, gleamed dully in the moonlight.

'He's not a German,' I told them. My hands, still raised, turned outwards in protest. 'I'm not either. He's an RAF pilot. We're English!'

Sinclair stiffened, but he didn't correct me.

'Is that so?' The man who'd just sentenced us to death stood forward. 'Then why's he wearing an SS uniform?'

The words were out before I could stop them: 'Well, I couldn't get him to the bloody coast in his RAF kit now, could I?'

'I like this one – she has spirit,' one of the other men said.

'Collaborating bitch,' someone else disagreed.

'Take the blasted gun!' I pushed my pistol into a pair of waiting hands and jabbed Alex in the side. 'Give them the Luger, will you?'

He handed over his gun, but he was looking at me with a strange expression in his eyes – like I was a creature he'd never seen before.

'What?' I asked.

Alex continued to stare at me with an expression midway between horror and fascination. Was he surprised that a woman would snap back? Or did he resent being told what to do by one? When our future was being discussed around us, and in a language he didn't understand, he'd have to deal with that hurt on his own. We had bigger problems.

'Who are you?' the Frenchman asked, echoing Sinclair's unspoken question.

'You can call me Cécile. Most of my friends do, anyway.'

Actually, none of the people I called close friends these days knew my real name. And those who knew the name I was born with would be horrified to see me now.

Alex's shoulders stiffened and he looked away.

'And who *are* you, Cécile?'

The man stepped closer, and despite whatever he felt for me, the Scot moved in front of me, shielding me with his own body. His chivalry was misplaced. I put a hand on his shoulder and stepped around him.

'I'm an agent for Special Operations Executive,' I said. 'Check with Baker Street. Or better still, give me a wireless and I'll contact them myself.'

The leader gestured for his men to circle us and herded us westwards in silence. We weren't restrained but we were no less their prisoners. We would be treated as the enemy until proven otherwise. My feet hurt and I was exhausted, but no one would tell us how much farther we had to travel.

'Your new friends seem better at asking questions than answering them,' Sinclair noticed. 'How did you know they were on the right side?'

'If they were Germans, they wouldn't have called you an SS dog.'

His full lips twitched. 'And if they were tryin' to trap a few Resistance fighters?'

'Then we'd have been stuffed the moment you opened your mouth.'

He grunted and we passed the next few minutes in uneasy silence. Every so often he would flash me a wary glance, as if he was trying to gauge how much he should worry based on how worried I was.

The man in charge paused at the side of the path and waited for us to catch up.

'Tell me, Cécile. What do you do for Baker Street?'

'That depends on what's required. And who's asking.'

'I'm the one with the gun. Good enough?'

'No,' I bristled. 'You're not the first man to wave a gun in my face, and if you were inclined to shoot me, you'd already have done so.'

He might not understand the words, but my tone was clear enough.

'Steady,' Sinclair cautioned. It was too late for that.

'You're asking me a lot of questions, but I don't know who *you* are or what *you're* doing here. We passed a town that has more swastikas than Berlin. We're heading away from that place so I'm guessing you're not going to bring us to the Boche, but I'm not going another step until we have some answers.'

He returned my gaze. 'You're not in a position to negotiate.'

He was right, but that didn't stop me from folding my arms across my chest and giving him a mutinous look.

'Oh hell,' Sinclair groaned.

The Frenchman's dark eyes narrowed as he considered me. Finally he nodded.

'You can call me Michel.'

'And the second question?' I prompted.

'Let's just say I've nothing against the Germans, so long as they're on the other side of the Maginot Line.' His mouth twisted in a wry smile. 'I'd like to think I'm helping them go home.'

Despite myself, I laughed. Alex, unable to follow the conversation, looked taken aback. Without taking my eyes off the Frenchman's, I laid one hand on Alex's arm to stop any reaction.

'Fair enough, Michel. As I said, I'm a pianist. Been working in France since December.'

He understood the slang. 'How does a wireless operator get lumped with chaperoning pilots?'

'Abject masochism.'

Alex, catching the gist of the conversation, looked offended. Michel met his gaze, and with a slight nod, switched to English.

'Wasn't manning a wireless exciting enough? They say Jerry can pinpoint you in half an hour these days with their radio detection finders.'

'Less than that.'

'You must be good.'

He looked at me appraisingly, and I stared back. Michel was about forty, but he wore his age well. While his dark hair shone with silver glints, his face was strong and spoke of his confidence and character. It would be good to work for someone like him.

'I can hold my own,' I said.

'And him?'

'Ask him,' Alex said. 'Him might no' speak French, but does fine wi' English.'

'Or Scottish.' I tried to lighten his mood, but from his dark glare I was, apparently, unsuccessful.

'And how did you come to be here?' Michel asked.

'Shot down by a swarm of 109s.'

'Bomber or a fighter?'

'Six o' one.' Sinclair straightened his shoulders and raised his head proudly. 'I piloted a Mosquito.'

'Beautiful plane.' Michel clapped Alex on the shoulder and moved on to a trio of men farther ahead.

'She was,' Sinclair whispered, mourning the de Havilland as if she were a lover. Then he sighed. 'I'm guessing that Cécile isn't your real name either?'

'Not any more than Nathalie is.'

'Complicated woman,' he murmured.

When we neared a farm, Michel dispersed most of his people and fell into step with Sinclair. The remaining woman walked in silence beside me. She was pretty, with long curly hair and an air of naïve sweetness. I didn't think she was the one who'd called me a collaborating bitch, but looks could be deceiving. Or at least some of them.

'He's not bad looking, your Englishman.' The woman's voice was carefully modulated, but the coquettish tilt of her head and the way she played with her long curls when she looked at him, gave more away than she, perhaps, intended.

'Don't call him English if you want to get anywhere with him,' I advised. 'He's Scottish.'

She nodded, her lower lip pouting as she processed this information. For a few moments, she studied me. 'Is he your lover?'

Heavens, she was blunt.

'He's in my charge. At least until I can get him to safety.'

'I hope you can do so.' She didn't take her eyes off me for a long few moments, before commenting, 'But you have not answered my question.'

Michel had brought us to a farmhouse surrounded by a couple of outbuildings. He unlatched the barn door, holding it open as the men entered. Aching feet and exhaustion made my voice curt. 'No. He's not my lover, and for what it's worth, I'm not a German spy. I don't know how long we'll be here, but by all means, try your luck with him.'

Moving past her, I tried not to laugh at her expression, and joined the men in the barn. Once we were all inside, the door was secured and the windows shaded. Several lamps were lit and crates rearranged to form a circle. Michel pulled the young woman aside. He spoke too softly for me to hear, but whatever it was, it didn't please her. With one last backwards glance at the Scot, she grabbed a case held out by another man and all but stomped outside.

'Going to check on my story, I imagine,' I murmured to Sinclair.

'I don't like this,' he said.

'We're the new dogs in the village,' I explained. 'The pack is sniffing us out, trying to determine whether to accept us or run us off.'

'Or kill us.'

'Also an option, but I don't think so.'

'Because you're Special Operations? What does that mean anyway?'

'I'm a spy.'

It wasn't entirely false, but it was a very small part of what an SOE agent was trained to do: explosives, firearms, unarmed combat, sabotage. In short, our job was to prop up the Resistance and make life as difficult as we could for the Nazis.

'I'm the link between the Resistance and London. Usually,' I added wryly. I turned to Michel. 'Now that we're here, and safe for the moment, would you be able to tell us what you're planning?'

Michel uncorked a bottle and poured four glasses.

'You stay in the loft tonight while Mireille, as you guessed, verifies your story. If you are who you claim to be, we will help you get you to the coast. If not?' He shrugged, his eyes dark and inscrutable. 'Then perhaps someone else will find you.'

Your body, he meant. I took a small sip of wine and nodded. We were outnumbered, and I wasn't inclined to fight if I didn't have to.

He glanced at his wristwatch. 'When you finish your wine, go upstairs and sleep while you can. Whatever happens, it will not be before dawn.'

I moved behind a bale and quickly changed into a cotton shirt and trousers one of the men had thoughtfully provided. When I returned, Alex had rolled up a spare blanket and positioned it lengthwise in the centre of the old mattress. He lay on his side, facing away from me to preserve my modesty. His uniform was neatly folded on the floor beside him.

'I dinnae like this,' he said. 'He's planning something.'

'Of course he is. And right now we're a complication. I don't think he likes having us here any more than we do.' I sat on the mattress and plaited my hair. 'Once the girl validates my story, we'll be on our way. You'll be back with your squadron in no time.'

It sounded like a naïve platitude, even to my own ears, but Sinclair didn't question it. Instead he blew out the candle and allowed darkness to descend. He lay quietly until his breathing evened out.

Sleep was far more elusive for me. I was less worried about Michel's men than I was the rest of the journey. Each handover came with risks. Would I find someone to escort Alex the rest of the way, or would I have to take him back myself? And if we made it back to England, what then? He'd rejoin his squadron, of course, and I'd be debriefed; there was a school in Wandsworth we used for that. And then what? How long before Buck redeployed me? And then where? Paris wasn't safe. Nor was a large swathe of northern France. Perhaps Alsace? Or maybe Free France?

Sinclair's arm crashed down on my chest, interrupting my musings. He moaned again, clearly in the midst of another nightmare.

'Alex?' I threw his arm off and shook his shoulder.

His eyes snapped open – wide and staring. He looked straight at me but didn't see me. He breathed in fast pants, as if he'd been running.

'Alex?'

I touched his jaw with my free hand, feeling the rasp of his stubble under my fingertips. His hand grabbed mine as his gaze locked on to me. His hazel eyes sharpened and then went dark, reading something in my face that I wasn't aware of. Before then.

His fingers moved to my cheek and then the back of my head, gently pulling me forward. My heart pounded as Alex guided my lips to his. He tasted of red wine and desperation. The planes of his chest were hard, and I braced myself against him until his arms came around me, pulling me over the blanket that separated us. He held me tight, his body pressing mine into the old mattress. When his hands found my breast, my breath caught in my throat.

'Nathalie,' he murmured, pulling the cotton shirt from my shoulders.

In the two years since Philip's ship sank, I had never been tempted to take a lover. Alex was a stranger; I knew little about his background, his aspirations, or his desires. He hadn't mentioned a wife but that didn't mean there wasn't one waiting for him at home. But he was a good man, I was sure of that, and equally sure that in that moment, I wanted him as much as he wanted me. In that loft, with half of the local Resistance resting downstairs, it was me he turned to and, when the time came, my name he called out, the sound muffled against my neck.

Once his breathing eased, he rolled on to his back, pulling me with him. Brushed a lock from my forehead and pressed my head to his shoulder.

'I should apologise for that, but I canna bring myself to.'

'Nothing to apologise for,' I murmured.

My contentment was more than physical until the realisation hit me that, not only had I fallen into bed with him after only knowing him for two days, I had unwittingly turned myself into the wireless girl, Mireille's rival. And in this situation, where neighbour informed on neighbour for less, she now had the advantage.

Chapter Seven

I slept well, for the first time for weeks feeling almost safe. By the time I woke, Alex was gone, likely into the hub of activity in the room below. I took my time getting ready before joining them. Michel sat at the table, a steaming mug of ersatz coffee untouched at his elbow. His freshly shaven face was half-hidden behind a copy of *Le Figaro*, while Alex leant against a wall as the animated little wireless operator smiled up at him. His response was polite but it wasn't until his eyes met mine that a slow smile spread across his face.

'Good morning,' he said, already moving towards me.

'Good morning. There's been news?'

Michel set aside his newspaper. 'London has confirmed your story. It would seem your exploits are rather infamous in certain circles, madame.' His voice was calm, but his eyes were amused. 'I am almost disappointed to see you leave. However, Armand spent the night forging travel documents, and I would not wish to disappoint him.'

'Certainly not,' I murmured, under no illusions.

He might have wanted another wireless operator in his cell; he might have even wanted another SOE agent. What he didn't want, however, was someone who would draw too much attention to his activities.

'You, *Monsieur*, will remain Heinrich Weber. He's fixed the work *Madame* did to those papers. The photograph of Herr

Weber will have to do. Your colouring is the same, and your features similar enough that differences can be explained away with weight loss, age, and experience. I'm sorry. There just isn't time to have a new photograph taken.'

'Thank you,' Alex murmured, pocketing his papers.

Michel gestured to the wireless girl, who had so far been following our conversation from a safe distance, her eyes never leaving Alex.

'Mireille and Claude will go on ahead to arrange your passage, or at least the first leg of it.'

'You're sending a pianist? That seems a strange choice.'

'She has other duties here, and knows the contact. Claude knows the roads better than she does, he can protect her.'

His voice, while directed at us, left no room for debate. Mireille, shoulders dropped, followed a wiry man out of the barn.

'They won't be back until nightfall. Stay close to the barn today. You'll leave at first light tomorrow.'

We nodded, and stepped outside into the sunlight. Meandered along the perimeter of the barn, and then took a seat on a low stone wall under an apple tree, and far enough away from the others to give an illusion of privacy.

'Why first light? Why no' during the night?' Alex asked.

'That eager to get away from me?' I teased. 'I'm sure Mireille wouldn't be too upset if you decided to stay.'

He pretended to consider that for a moment.

'Aye. She's sweet, and bonny.' Unable to maintain a straight face, he grinned. 'But I'm no' daft enough to throw over a woman who can handle herself like you do, for a wee thing like her.'

'If that's what you want –'

Still smiling, he kissed the top of my head.

'I don't. I am, however, keen to hear more about these "exploits" of yours.'

'Michel, and probably your bonny wee lass, made more of it than there is.'

'I dinnae believe you.'

I shrugged. 'The Official Secrets Act trumps your curiosity.'

He seemed to consider that, and then, unbelievably, the Scot had the unmitigated gall to tickle me.

Secrets intact, even if my virtue wasn't, we climbed down the ladder an hour before dawn, for Michel's briefing in the barn's large room.

'As you may know, the Germans have closed most of the fishing channels heading north. If you head towards England, you'll be caught in their net. So you will head for Spain. A fishing boat will take you as far as Bilbao. From there you take a train to Madrid. Your embassy will arrange your trip home.'

'Spain?' Alex's face broadcast his dismay.

How long would it take us to get back? At least by checking my credentials with Baker Street, Mireille had let Buck and Vera know that I was here, and still alive.

'Be careful. The border police arrest people sneaking into the country,' he added.

How many people like Alex, like me, had he helped? He wouldn't answer even if I asked.

Instead I simply said: 'Thank you, Michel.'

He rubbed his eyes. 'The boat is called *Le Rêve*. She's not big and certainly not pretty, but she's fast and hasn't got caught yet.'

'The Dream,' I translated. How appropriate.

'It's white, edged in blue. The man who'll take you is called Antoine Gamay. You'll be able to spot him –'

'He has eyebrows like caterpillars,' Armand said, demonstrating by waving his fingers from his brow.

Michel wasn't amused. 'Not now, clown.'

Armand shrugged, good-naturedly, and handed Alex a thin envelope with Spanish notes.

'You'll need this when you cross the border,' he said. 'It's the best we can do, but don't let anyone find it on this side of the border. I'll drive you to the outskirts of the village. I can't go any farther without being recognised. You'll want to buy provisions there. Make it look like an impromptu picnic.'

'But instead of heading out on a yacht, we find a fishing boat?' I asked. 'Wouldn't it be better to leave tomorrow morning dressed as fisherfolk?'

Michel shook his head. 'Too risky. Every day you remain brings you closer to being captured.' He rubbed his eyes. 'Even if you looked the sort, and you don't, fishermen don't usually take their women on the boat with them. Bad luck, you see. So you get on the boat, and you all get below – out of sight. Fast. Got it?'

He waited for both of us to nod before holding out his hand, first to Alex and then to me.

'God be with you.'

Despite Michel's faith in Mireille, I wasn't convinced. Trusting anyone else was dangerous, and Alex had chosen me over her. She didn't strike me as vindictive, or foolish enough to risk someone she was interested in to destroy a rival; then again, I hadn't expected Jean-Roger Demarque's betrayal in Paris. My fingers stretched and clenched in turn, wishing for the comforting grip of the PPK, knowing that it wasn't possible without attracting undue attention.

The village wasn't large, but was comfortable in its anonymity. Fish-sellers and restaurants touted the local catches, and the small harbour at the edge of town was mostly empty, the fleet of ketches and trawlers having already gone to sea. If it wasn't picturesque, at least it did possess a wall devoid of broadsheets with Alex or my likeness on them, a boat that would take us away from France, and a village shop.

Wearing the SS uniform and a grim look, Alex stomped beside me, deep in thought. He waited until we were far enough from the nearest person to risk sharing those thoughts with me.

'I know we dinnae have much time left, Nathalie. But I wanted to thank you.'

I raised an eyebrow and tried not to smile when he blushed.

'No' for that. Well, yes, for that too. What I meant is that ye're doing your best to get us out and I ken I'm no' helping.' He rotated his shoulders as if trying to shift an uncomfortable weight. 'And that hurts. I dinnae like not being able to hold my own.'

'For someone who wasn't trained for this, you're holding up amazingly well. Sure you don't want to trade a Mozzie for French lessons and a wireless? I think I know someone who'd be willing to teach you.'

He snorted, but his expression softened.

'No' cut out for it.' He linked his fingers with mine. 'You told me what you were yesterday, but ye ken what I am as well. I cannae make you any promises, Nathalie, but . . .' He took a deep breath and his words came out in a rush. 'When we get back, will ye allow me to call on you?'

I stared at him. Suddenly he looked young and awkward.

'Alex, just how old are you?'

'Twenty-three.' A wry smile. 'One of the oldest in the RAF, I think.'

It was experience, I supposed. Losing his friends, his wing-men, must have made him mature quickly. I had guessed about twenty-five. A three-year difference between us wasn't so bad, but five?

'Christ, Nathalie, stop laughing. I ken ye're older, and I dinnae care. Will ye step out wi' me, or no?'

I leant over and kissed his cheek.

'Count on it. Now, go and look for the ship while I buy food for our "picnic".'

Still smiling, I walked into the village shop and watched as the woman lined my purchases on the counter. As she tallied the cost, I glanced out of the window.

A pall fell over the square as a dozen drunk soldiers formed a rough circle. It wasn't large enough to kick around a football, but whatever was in the centre held their full attention. Just outside the circle, standing apart but intent on the proceedings, was the grey-haired man we had seen in the restaurant, hands clasped behind his back. He wasn't participating in their game but he wasn't stopping it either. Whatever reason he had for being here boded ill for our escape; he struck me as too observant not to notice us or to wonder what had brought us here.

One of the soldiers, a big brute of a man, kicked forward. An unearthly shriek carried on the wind and I came close to knocking over the parcels. Someone was in that circle – a woman. What could she have done to deserve that?

The old woman at the counter met my eyes, and then glanced away. Her face was harsh with years of sun and toil, but her eyes were kind.

'Jesus have mercy on her soul,' she muttered. 'Resistance. Foolish enough to get caught. Brave enough not to speak.'

She stared at her hands, before systematically putting my purchases into a wicker basket.

The woman's shrieks subsided to whimpers, almost drowned out by the cheering soldiers.

'Why didn't they just arrest her?'

I was unable to take my eyes from the tableau.

'And pass on the fun?'

Bitter, angry tears trembled in her eyes. They widened as she realised her mistake: her sympathy for the woman and her cause was too clear, and for all she knew, I was one of them. I wanted to reassure her – wanted to help the woman on the street – but anything I did would jeopardise our escape. And I had no desire to join her in the centre of that circle.

The whimpering ceased. A soldier reached into his tunic and took a long gulp from a silver flask. Passed it to the next man. Their game seemed to be breaking up. One man spat and clapped another on the back before they moved off, falling in behind the grey-haired soldier as they crossed the square, leaving the woman crumpled like a broken doll. Her long dark hair curled protectively around her – shielding her in death as it couldn't in life.

We had to leave before the grey-haired man saw us. I threw a couple of notes onto the counter, grabbed the basket and scanned the village for Alex's tall form. He stood nearby, his body stiff and vibrating with anger. Where my instincts directed me to take the distraction as a divine gift and use it to escape, Alex's directed him to act. I grasped his arm, holding him back.

'You don't know who's watching,' I hissed, hoping no one would hear the English.

'They killed her, Nathalie.' His voice was filled with the horror we both felt.

'There's nothing we can do.'

He shook off my grip and straightened his tunic.

'I didn't sign up to turn a blind eye to that.'

Held together by horror and determination, he strode to the fallen woman. For a second, I imagined green eyes under that long hair – the friend who had fought beside me.

It was lunacy. I knew this woman wasn't Dominique. Even if it was, Dom wouldn't want me to jeopardise myself for her. But I was no more able to stop myself than I was able to stop Alex.

Ignoring the drunk soldiers, he turned the woman over. Her face was beyond bruised – it was broken, her cheekbones shattered, teeth missing. Blood flowed from her nose and a dozen or more cuts. Under the gore, brown eyes stared sightlessly at the sun. Whoever she was, even her mother wouldn't be able to recognise her. But it wasn't Dom. Of course she wasn't; little Dominique would have fought back.

My relief was short-lived.

'Mirielle,' Alex murmured, seeing past the disfigurement to identify the pretty girl who'd gone to arrange things with the fisherman. I'd known I'd see her again, but not like this. Had they been watching her? Had they caught her before or after she spoke to the fisherman with the caterpillar eyebrows? The old woman said Mireille hadn't talked, but how could she know?

'We need to go, Alex. Now.'

'No,' he whispered, throwing off my hand. Then louder: 'No!'

He pulled his gun from its holster and pointed it at the soldiers, his Viking features twisted in hatred.

'No, Alex,' I whispered, horrified. 'Don't . . .'

The Luger coughed; a soldier fell. The grey-haired man unholstered his sidearm as the others stared, confused by Alex's SS uniform. He stood statue-still, squeezing off shot after shot, bullets arcing as the Luger's knee joint expelled and chambered cartridges. And yet, the enemy advanced.

Until Alex's gun clicked on an empty chamber and the knee joint stayed up. He stared at it, then at the oncoming horde.

'Shite,' he breathed.

'SHIT!' I dropped the basket and pulled him away as the Germans returned fire. 'Dolt!' I accused. 'Idiot!'

There was no word strong enough to describe the sheer lunacy of his actions.

'They kicked her to death, what was I supposed to do?' he panted, running alongside me. We turned towards the harbour, and I hoped the fisherman was still waiting for us. 'An' where the devil was Claude? He was supposed to protect her!'

He pointed at a small white skiff moored at the end of the pier, bobbing on the tide. An old man in a dark cap sat in the waning light, polishing the metal bracings. I yanked my pistol from my bag as we thundered over the planks.

'Go!'

The old man threw the rag aside and stood, mutely watching. A shot rang out, the bullet almost hitting him. He dropped to a crouch, with his hands locked over his head, and crawled to the ropes mooring the boat.

I hunched forward and leapt across the gap between the pier and the boat, my gun remaining pointed at the fisherman. My left hand hit the deck first, the wood scraping the scabs from my palm and the skin from my knees. My elbow gave way but neither my pistol nor my will wavered.

'Cast off!' I ordered, the sound of gunfire and Alex's footfalls ringing in my ears. 'Now!'

The old man released the lines as Alex landed on top of me, slamming me into the wood and shielding me from the Germans' bullets. The skiff bucked once or twice before it turned and caught the tide.

Sea spray kissed my face, and Alex's body was a comforting weight. My eyes were still trained on the old man. He was short and squat, with a face lined by years in the sea and sun. Armand was right; he sported the longest eyebrows I'd ever seen. They were like a thing alive, an anemone or some other such creature.

On the pier, the grey-haired man stood at the edge, still firing even as we moved out of their range. He pointed to the harbour master's hut and one of his men ran to it.

One man and one woman: fugitives. Assassins. They saw me pull the gun on the old man; they would think I'd shanghaied the boat and give chase.

'Alex,' I said, 'get off me – I can't see.'

He remained silent and heavy on my back.

'Damn it, Alex!'

I pushed back with my good shoulder, and he obligingly rolled on to his back. The man who stood outside the hut argued with the harbour master as we shot forward – one small fishing boat amongst many.

Victory surged through me.

'We made it, Alex,' I breathed. 'You'll be back in Blighty for the weekend.'

He remained silent. One arm was lightly draped across his chest, and his hazel eyes were closed, his face relaxed. I hoped he hadn't hit his head again. It seemed like ages, but it had only been a few days since his plane was shot down. I shook him.

'Wake up, you oaf. Alex, we *made* it!'

My hand froze on his chest; it was damp, far more so than our last sprint would warrant. I raised it, horrified to find it covered in blood. With the coppery stench came a rising panic.

'Alex?'

He didn't reply. He didn't move.

'Alex?' *Oh God, no. Oh God, Ohgodohgodohgodohgod.* 'Alex! Open your eyes, you Scottish bastard! Don't you dare leave me!'

I fumbled for the buttons on his tunic, ripping them from the cloth. The pings of metal on wood was lost in the rush of the sea; the denial roaring in my mind.

His shirt was stained crimson but his face was serene in the evening's light. The boat bucked against a wave and I looked up at the old man. Saw the pity in his eyes.

I stretched out alongside Alex, resting my head for the last time on his chest.

'My name . . .' The words were soft, forced through the lump in my throat. Important, even though he couldn't hear them any more. 'My name is Elisabeth.'

My tears mingled with Alex Sinclair's blood as the skiff shot out of the harbour and headed south.

To Spain. Where we would be free.

Chapter Eight

The fisherman sewed Alex into an old sail, his eyebrows as protesting as my soul as the second man I loved, or could have loved, slipped beneath the surface.

He's not Philip.

I knew that, of course. My husband's ship had been torpedoed years ago, but the memories, the emotions were as fresh as if they were yesterday. We must have landed near Bilbao at night, or at midday. It didn't matter; I remembered little of the journey. Blocked out the walk to the city and the train to Madrid. Clad in the fisherman's clean shirt, I looked like a street tramp, but at least I wasn't detained.

The walk from the station to the embassy was measured by the pain of blistered feet, and an aching soul.

Of my interview with the Consul-General at the embassy, I remembered a bit more. He sat across a sea of mahogany from me, a tall man, powerful – with the aura of a doer rather than a pencil-pusher.

'My name is Elisabeth de Mornay, code name Cécile. Special Operations Executive in London.'

'What can I do for you, Miss de Mornay?'

His fingers twirled a gold pen in circles on his desk. Mine couldn't have been the first interview of this type he'd had to endure.

I didn't bother to correct him. 'I need to get back to London.'

'Why?'

'My cover was blown,' I explained. 'I need to debrief with my CO.'

'And who might that be?'

He had to know who Buck was, but I played along.

'Major Maurice Buckmaster. Chief of F Section.'

The C-G considered his response as an ormolu clock on the mantle tracked the time.

'Why should I believe you?'

He stood up and poured himself a brandy. It was rude of him not to offer me one, but now was not the time to lecture him on manners.

'You shouldn't.'

He raised his eyebrows, sipped his drink and waited for me to continue.

'Contact Baker Street. Buck will vouch for me.'

Outside the window, palm trees swayed in the hazy light as people bustled along the streets, preoccupied with their normal day-to-day lives. Did they know what was happening? Did they care?

I was sick of war, sick of death. Would anyone blame me for walking out of the door and disappearing into the throng? There were worse things than sitting out the rest of the war in obscurity, and I'd done my part. Transmitted twice a week to London for six months before leaving Paris. I was exhausted, mentally and physically.

The war could go hang.

The C-G poured two fingers of Carlos Primero into another glass and handed it to me.

'I'd be a fool not to.'

The correct response was: 'And you're no fool, sir' but I was too tired to play the game.

'May I ask what you were doing in France?'

'You can ask.'

'But you won't tell?'

'No.'

He smiled wryly, and sipped his brandy. 'You got out alone?'

Hazel eyes and Viking cheeks; Alex's shade stood at my side.

'No, not exactly.'

'Where are they now? Exactly?'

'At the bottom of the Atlantic.' There was no pleasure in watching him cringe. 'Not by my hand,' I added, although he didn't ask.

'I'll need names, of course.'

'Yes, of course.' Alex had family, and they deserved to know that he had died a hero. 'Squadron Leader Alexander Charles Sinclair, of 105 Squadron, was shot down near Vouvray with his navigator Tim Fielding. Fielding died in the crash and I was escorting Sinclair out of France. We'd almost made it.'

The C-G pushed my glass closer to me.

'I have a feeling there's a story there.'

'There's always a story. Just not always a happy ending. He tried to save a woman who was beaten to death by the Nazis. He was shot and I wasn't. Because he shielded my body with his own.'

The C-G's mouth twitched. 'You loved him?'

The truth was bitter, and this time it demanded a voice. He deserved at least that much.

'I only knew him for a few days. With more time? Maybe. I liked him, and I respected him, and that's a good start. But he was my responsibility, at least while he was with me, and I let him down.'

'How so?'

'I couldn't save him.'

'I rather think he made his own decision, Miss de Mornay. There wasn't much you could do the moment he confronted the Nazis.' He looked away and drained his glass. 'Where are you staying?'

'I've taken a hotel room in the city,' I lied.

'Where?'

'Close enough that I can be here by 10 a.m. That should give you enough time to contact Baker Street and decide what to do with me.'

'You know I can't let you go.'

I moved back to the window.

'You'll stay here, a guest of Dona Araceli Ortega.'

'Guest?'

'She has a town house nearby and will see to you until your Major Buckmaster tells us what to do with you.'

The C-G opened the door and talked in soft tones to a porter. The man was stout and swarthy, bowing to me before ushering me out. He called for a car and driver. Closed the door for me and stood back as I was driven away.

'The Hotel Orfila, please.'

It was the hotel I'd stayed at five years and a lifetime ago. On my honeymoon. I wasn't sure why I said it; the C-G wouldn't risk letting me disappear.

The driver smiled in the rear-view mirror, showing kind eyes and yellow teeth. He ignored my directions, driving to a private house, four storeys high, in a fashionable part of town.

'Safe,' he said, as if such a place still existed on Earth, and opened the door for me.

I stayed in Dona Araceli's house for two days. Elegant women and smartly dressed men bustled in and out, asking questions, offering sympathy and Spanish brandy. They spoke to me in kind tones, and of me in hushed whispers.

Finally, a man came to the house with thin hair slicked back over his head and the smell of someone who ate too much garlic. He presented a small valise to me with a flourish.

'What is it?' I asked, without any real interest in the answer.

'Clothing. Beautiful things.' He flashed his teeth in what could almost pass for a smile.

'Why?'

'For you,' he said, confusion clouding his expression. 'What pretty woman does not like such things?'

After waiting around in Dona Araceli's cast-offs while the ruddy C-G decided what to do with me, I was in no mood to contemplate what this meant. I retraced my steps into the parlour. He followed me, and pushed the case into my hands.

'Please, señora. It is a gift.'

'Gifts rarely come without a price.'

In the end, I acquiesced. He waited outside my bedroom door as I changed into a new dress. I glanced out of the window. Would

80

they give chase if I climbed down the trellis and slipped from their grasp? Pity I couldn't be bothered. But wherever they were taking me, I wasn't about to go unarmed. My guns had been taken into 'safekeeping', but I still had Alex's little dagger. Whether they believed my story that I wanted to personally return it to Alex's family, or whether they thought it was harmless enough, leaving the sgian dubh in my custody was considered a safe compromise.

I secured it to my thigh using a silk scarf, clipping the ends to minimise any bulk and leaving them where they fell. Let the C-G and bloody Dona Araceli wonder about that. I closed the door behind me and brushed past the man in the hallway.

'How beautiful you are, señora,' he said.

His eyes lingered on me as he reached for the case and escorted me to a limousine with diplomatic tags and darkened windows. He stored the valise in the boot and slid into the passenger seat beside the chauffeur.

Instead of driving east to the city and the consulate, we drove west. There was a plan afoot, but for the life of me, I couldn't muster the energy to care.

The heat increased my lethargy. Hazy sunshine burned off by midday, turning the sky a shade of blue that hurt my eyes. I prayed for rain and an end to the cloud that had insulated me since Alex's death.

The men had stopped trying to make conversation, leaving me to stare out the windows of the limousine at the passing countryside, arid and red.

On the fourth day we reached a checkpoint. It was bigger than the ones we'd passed, and I roused from my stupor as we stopped at the barricade. The C-G's man, still sitting beside the chauffeur, handed over three sets of papers.

One of the men riffled through our documents, holding each up to the light and comparing our faces to the photographs. He leant around the chauffeur to have a closer look at me. I stared back, uninterested.

Finally, he grunted and returned the papers.

'Welcome to Portugal,' he said.

As if that should mean something special.

Part 2

Lisbon, June 1943

Chapter Nine

We passed through three towns connected by long stretches of barren before pulling to the side of the road. A dusty motor car with a Portuguese licence disc was already parked there. Heat emanated from it, surrounding it in a wavering halo, and a short round man with slicked back hair leant against the bonnet, smoking and fanning himself with a newspaper. He tossed the paper into the passenger seat.

'Good trip?' he said, exhaling a cloud of bitter smoke.

The C-G's man shook his hand while the other transferred my case to the other vehicle. He opened the door for me.

'End of the line, beautiful.'

It should have sounded ominous and I should have been terrified. Being driven across a border and handed over to a man who looked like a tuskless boar wasn't an everyday occurrence, but if they wanted to kill me, they would have done that back in Spain. Whatever the plan was, they wanted me alive for it so I allowed the man to help me to my feet.

'Do you have another one?' I asked the boar.

He looked at me stupidly.

'May I have a cigarette?' I clarified.

His grin revealed yellow teeth and the remnants of his lunch, but he reached into his jacket and handed me a battered pack. I allowed the nicotine a few moments to reach my head before I sighed.

'Now what?'

The short man inclined his head as the second of my two erstwhile chaperons closed the door and disappeared down the road.

'Now my turn to drive you.'

He wouldn't say where or why; just grinned. I sighed and leant back. It didn't really matter.

The taxi stank of garlic and unwashed male. An icon of Jesus and a photograph of António de Oliviera Salazar, the prime minister, looked beatifically down from the sun visor. The driver produced a flask and unscrewed it.

'You want?'

'No, thank you.'

The driver hummed tunelessly to himself as small towns and villages flitted by. Brown grass was punctuated with dark green trees and houses painted in pale shades of cream and yellow, pink and peach, with red tiled roofs. After the greys of London and Paris, the colours were blinding. I tried to watch where we were going, in case I needed to find my way back, but we moved fast, frequently changing direction, vehicles and drivers. Whoever had summoned me, wanted me there without tail or trail. And they appeared not to care if I was armed: my Luger and PPK had been returned, hidden in the false bottom of my valise. The latter was now stashed in my bag. Just in case.

The sun was setting as we skirted the capital city and entered a town called Estoril. I caught glimpses of the ocean with its faint salty tang, like the tears shed for a gruff Scotsman.

The driver stopped halfway down the hill in front of a high stone wall.

'Your home,' he explained.

'Oh.' I brushed aside a tear under the pretext of a yawn. 'What do I owe you?'

It was a silly thing to say; this wasn't a black cab, and I hadn't sanctioned this trip.

'Is taken care of,' he said, although he made the motions as if I'd just passed him a note. Instead of change, he pressed a pair of keys into my palm. 'For the doors,' he explained.

'Fine. And who do I need to thank?'

He seemed to think this amusing.

'You thank me for driving.'

He cleared his throat and hurried around the car to open the door for me. He took my case to the gate, watching while I unlocked it and admired the cottage. As much as I appreciated the high wall, I was delighted by what lay behind it. Two jacaranda trees guarded the front door and purple bougainvillea crept up cream-hued walls. A large blue and white tile of a mermaid basked next to the door.

The driver set down the case and tipped his hat. His voice was low as he warned, 'Be careful. *Bufos* watching.'

The term was unfamiliar. I was fluent in French and German and passable with Spanish and Italian. Portuguese, on the other hand, was a mystery.

'Buffoons?'

His eyes were sad as he shook his head.

'Watchers. Informers. Everyone is *bufo* in Lisboa.'

He pronounced it *Lishboa*, making even the name of the city seem evil. He tipped his hat again and drove off.

I closed the gate and, hidden between the stone wall and the jacaranda, slipped my hand around the PPK. Just because the house was dark didn't mean it was empty. I toed off my shoes to prevent them from making noise on the tiled floor and eased the door closed.

The dining room lay to the right of the foyer, with a long mahogany table, eight chairs on either side and a silver candelabra stationed in the middle, the candles unlit. The room smelled of beeswax and fresh flowers. Behind it, the kitchen was just visible, with a small wood table and clean countertops. There were no unwanted guests in the pantry, just a plethora of consumables. More than I had seen in years.

I returned to the hallway, isolating each sense and allowing it to expand until I was able to detect a faint hint of cigar smoke and expensive cologne. Whoever it was was foolish. Gun firmly in hand, I followed the trail down the hallway to a parlour.

The curtains had been drawn against the evening air and the eyes of the *bufos*, but the red glow of the cigar gave away the man's position – a dark silhouette sitting in an armchair. My hand was steady as I aimed the gun at the centre of his chest. I counted out half a dozen heartbeats before speaking.

'Who are you and what do you want?'

'Do put that away.' He consulted his watch, although the room was too dark to read the time. 'You're late.'

English, and with an accent that spoke of privilege. That could have been faked, but there was something about it that

88

scratched at the back of my memory. I tightened my grip on the pistol and opted to play along.

'For what?'

He ignored the question.

'You were supposed to be here an hour ago,' he drawled.

If I had problems seeing his face, he was equally disadvantaged.

'Blame the driver.'

He stood up and took a step towards me.

'Oh, for heaven's sake, Lisbet, put that away. If you couldn't shoot me five years ago, you're not going to do it now.'

Memories crashed over me. The young friend of my father's who had pushed me on a swing. Always encouraging me to learn more, do more, laugh more. Until the day he relayed my mother's ultimatum. He still wore the same cologne. I should have remembered that.

'Why don't you turn on the lights, Lisbet?'

'Turn them on yourself.'

Seconds ticked by before Matthew Harrington flicked the switch on the wall. Not much had changed; his dark hair was Brylcreemed back from a tanned, aristocratic face, although the widow's peak had receded a bit and, like his moustache, was now peppered with silver. The nose was still aquiline and imperious, and his black eyes watched beneath thick eyebrows. Clad in Savile Row's best, he looked like an elegant bird of prey.

'When did you lose your manners, old girl?'

'About the time I realised you didn't deserve them.'

He moved to the sideboard, chuckling.

'What do you want, Matthew?' I demanded. 'Assuming, of course, it was you who sent for me.'

He looked at me over his shoulder, one brow raised.

'What makes you think that was my doing?'

'Wasn't it?'

Ice clinked into the crystal glass and he didn't bother hiding a smug smile.

'Of course it was. Do sit down, old girl. Surely you can't fault me for watching out for my family?'

I shook my head. 'You can't have it both ways. You told me that the moment I married Philip, I was divorcing my family. Well, I married him. Stick to your side of the bargain.'

He held up one finger. 'Your mother's words, my dear. Not mine. I did make that clear at the time.'

'And because you were her lackey, you're now blameless?'

'Is that really the question you want to ask me?'

'No,' I snapped. 'I've already asked it – you just haven't answered. Why am I here?'

Matthew shrugged. 'You dropped out of sight a few years ago.'

'Not my decision,' I growled, allowing him to relieve me of my pistol and put it on top of the piano. He was right; I wouldn't shoot him. Yet. And I didn't need a gun to disable him.

'So he forced you?' He raised his eyebrows in mock disbelief. 'And here I thought it was mutual. So where is the loving husband now?'

'At the bottom of the Atlantic.'

'Sorry about that, old girl. You should have said.' His voice was sympathetic, but Matthew was well connected and would have known about Philip's demise, maybe even before I did. 'You didn't have to cut us all off, you know.'

'What did you expect?'

Matthew waved his hand, the long fingers dismissing my ire.

'Better judgement, since you ask. First there was that incident with the Christie girl's boat. And if that wasn't mad enough, you had to start running with the Baker Street Irregulars. Yahoos,' he sniffed. 'What they don't blow up, they shoot. You could have at least chosen Six or the Foreign Office if you wanted to be a spook. I could have arranged something.'

As if I would have asked him for anything.

He stepped closer, holding up a long strand of my hair.

'Whatever possessed you to colour it?'

I pulled away. 'Not many redheads in France.'

'Not enough redheads anywhere.' He smiled, flashing strong, if slightly long, white teeth. 'You do realise if you'd gone blonde, you'd be a dead ringer for Veronica Lake?'

It was a familiar jibe, and one that didn't deserve an answer.

'It's brown until I find the first hairdresser with a bottle of dye.'

He hummed a reply. 'I wouldn't do that just yet, if I were you.'

My eyes narrowed as my head began to throb at the base of my skull. 'Why not?'

He flashed a polite smile. 'Be a dear, get a bottle of wine and share a glass with your old godfather.'

'Do you really need to remind *me* of family obligations? Remember, *old boy*, that I don't have them any more.'

I left the room, giving myself the space to think. My father often referred to his protégé as 'the Spider', noting that Matthew wasn't just drawn to intrigue – he orchestrated it. And now he

91

expected me to become a willing pawn in his schemes? Not bloody likely.

'Lisbet?' His low voice called from the other room. 'I do hope you haven't shimmied out of a window.'

'Stinking Spider.'

I rummaged through the kitchen for a bottle and corkscrew. As my hand closed around the little metal device, I saw Alex open a bottle with the dead German's jackknife. I had few options on that day, no connection to the Resistance, no way to get us to safety. Just instincts, and his death was a reminder of how that had worked out.

My options weren't much better now. Alex was dead. Philip was dead. The only 'friend' I had in this country was my godfather – a man my father had trusted, and whom I had trusted, until he relayed Lady Anne's ultimatum. But he needed something, and as long as I was useful, he would protect me. Contrary to his claim, I wasn't family – I was an asset.

Grabbing two crystal wine glasses from a cabinet, I returned to the parlour, determined to show no weakness. Put the bottle and glasses down on a coffee table, and looked around for the first time. The room was small but well appointed. A brocade sofa the colour of double cream was flanked by two matching armchairs. Across the room, under an oil painting of a grandee, was the piano. It had seen better days but despite the humidity, it was still in tune.

'You always played well.'

'Yes? Well, I've played a different sort of piano for the past year.'

'Ah, yes. The wireless.'

His bland tone confirmed that he knew what I did for SOE, and the cloak-and-dagger nature of my arrival – and his – gave an indication of what he wanted. I played along.

'Who lives here?' I asked.

'You do.' Matthew handed me a glass and raised his own in a silent toast. 'Tell me about France.'

'Why?'

He was silent, his black eyes locked on my face as he waited for me to continue.

'It's all classified. I'm sure you're aware that I signed the Official Secrets Act.'

'I'm quite sure my clearance is sufficient.'

'I'm quite sure it is.' My polite smile matched his. 'Have some-one look it up.' I sipped the wine, watching him over the rim of the glass. 'What do you want me to tell you? What it feels like to be shot? To shoot someone? It's different from a distance as opposed to close up, you know.'

'I know.' His quiet voice took the wind from my sails.

'There was death in France, Matthew. Too much death. Some was under my watch, some by my hand.' My shrug was any-thing but an apology. 'As you said, they're a bunch of yahoos I run with.'

His face remained impassive. 'No one ever said you took the easy path, old girl. Not your nature, maybe too much of your father in you.' I looked away, but Matthew continued. 'Nine lives your father had. Like a cat. You're the same, Lisbet.'

'Sure. I'm a cat, all right. A black one.'

He chuckled, and pressed my glass into my hand.

'Even better, dear one. They know how to hide in plain sight.'

Matthew Harrington, aristocrat, bureaucrat and a plethora of other 'rats, clinked his glass against mine.

'*À votre santé, ma chatte noir.*'

Chapter Ten

'How much do you know about Portugal – about Lisbon?' Matthew held the empty wine bottle up to the light, frowning. Muttered something about evaporation and poured two glasses of Carlos Primero from a bottle on the sideboard.

'Not a lot, I'm afraid,' I answered, accepting a cut crystal brandy balloon. 'I know they're neutral, or at least, technically so.'

'Right you are. Dr Salazar, like Franco in Spain, favours the Germans. Or rather, the Italians – there used to be a portrait of Il Duce hanging in his office. Might still be, for all I know. The rest of the country, however, favours the Allies. It's a delicate balance.'

'He's sitting on the fence because he doesn't want to be deposed?'

Matthew's long fingers traced the grooves in the crystal.

'The only problem is, he's not sitting on the fence. No, my dear, be under no misconceptions – Salazar's early reforms gave the country a modicum of stability, but his policies are conservative, Catholic, and as I said, Fascist. We gave him lists of suspected German and Italian spies. Would you care to guess what happened to them?' He paused, one eyebrow raised. 'No?'

His nostrils flared and his voice became condescending.

'Allow me to give you two examples. Mind you, in each case, we provided them with solid evidence of the gentleman's activities. The result of this "Portuguese justice"? In the first case, Richard Schubert left Portugal for Spain. That, at least, was an act of expulsion although the Portuguese refused to do more. Why? Because according to their penal code, spying in Portugal against another country is *questionable* and expulsion is the only option.'

'Questionable?'

'And I quote: "It is unclear whether espionage is a punishable offence under Portuguese law if it's not against Portugal." Under duress, Salazar just changed the law, but it doesn't apply retroactively.'

'And the second example?'

I could have pointed out that the Boche were most likely equally irritated that people like Matthew were still walking around. Or me, for that matter.

'Ernst Schmidt – and I'm not sure if they're their real names, mind – was arrested and then released. He now boasts that the Portuguese police dare not hold him.'

'So one is free to wreak havoc in Spain until, I imagine, he finds a way back in, and the other has set a bad precedent. Forgive me if I'm wrong, but don't we have a treaty with the Portuguese? I remember reading about a speech Salazar gave reaffirming it just after the start of the war. All the newspapers covered it.'

'Very good, and yes, we do. Salazar not only confirmed it remained intact, but also stated that Portugal wouldn't take advantage of its neutrality to make money from the war. The only one who seems to believe that tosh is Campbell. Thinks that Salazar will come to the rescue if things get bad enough.' He made a rude sound. 'And I'm damned if I know what it'll take for things to get "bad enough".'

I raised a brow. 'Ronald Campbell? Isn't he the ambassador here?'

'Yes, and you might not want to get too close – he knew your father. Might recognise you and blow your cover. Inadvertently, of course.'

'Noted.'

'Good. As to the situation, if he had more sense, he'd press for all of Bendixen's lackeys to be arrested.'

'Bendixen?'

'Hans Bendixen, Head of German Naval Espionage in Portugal. And for every one we find, there are countless more at large. Furthermore, Salazar –' his voice dropped to an icy timbre, sarcasm oozing from each syllable – '*swears* that we are barking up the wrong tree. Agents we list as minor fry are key men and vice versa. He protects them while claiming to support us as well. Lisbet, this is serious business. Lisbon is the only neutral capital on the sea. People sneak in and out every day. The Hotel Avenida even has a "secret passageway" to the train station, for Christ's sake.'

'Not so secret, then,' I murmured, impressed despite myself. And for the first time in weeks, intrigued.

'Informants are on every street corner, with three others peering from behind the curtains, ready to run to whoever offers the highest price.'

'Not much different from France.'

97

I put down my glass, trying not to remember how Jean-Roger Demarque's treachery could have landed me in the Gestapo HQ on Avenue Foch.

'They're everywhere.' He rubbed the bridge of his nose. 'When you meet someone, Lisbet, always assume they're a spy. Perhaps even a double agent.'

'And you want someone here you can trust.'

'No, my dear.' The light in his eyes dimmed and he looked tired. 'I *need* someone I can trust. Each week it's something else. Assassinations. Kidnappings. That bloody fiasco with the *Ibis*.'

I felt silly asking the question, but to be fair, I hadn't had the leisure of reading a newspaper for weeks.

'What fiasco?'

'Last week the German Junkers shot down a commercial plane over the Bay of Biscay. A scheduled flight from Lisbon to Whitchurch that didn't go over the war zone.'

I hadn't realised there was an exclusion zone anywhere near England or France, but surely if a bomber could be modified to drop agents, why couldn't a commercial plane be refitted to carry something rather more dangerous?

'Ah.'

'No, in this case there was no Trojan horse involved. There were innocents – or at least non-combatants – on that plane. Seventeen dead, including the crew. This was the third plane they attacked and the first one they managed to shoot down. With Leslie Howard on board.'

'Who?'

'The actor. You know the one – he played in *Of Human Bondage* and *Gone with the Wind*.'

I had a vague memory of a man with a long face and soft voice.

'Oh, yes. He played Ashley Wilkes. He's dead?'

'You *would* remember that role. Not his best work, of course, but that's what he'll be remembered for.'

'What else should he be remembered for?'

'The chap was rabidly anti-Nazi. Did what he could for us. Came over with his agent for a series of talks about film, but spent time trying to shore up support with the local propagandists.' He shook his head, frowning. 'A very brave – and clever – man.'

'That's why he was shot down?'

'So some say. Others say Jerry thought Winnie was on the flight.'

'Churchill? Was he really over here?'

'Doubt we'll ever know. If he was here, I didn't see him.'

Still holding his glass, he moved to the window and twitched aside the curtains.

'What do you want me to do?'

'Just mingle. Preferably with the Germans. Be friendly with everyone but friends with no one. Keep your eyes open. They'll be wary of you, do what you can to be accepted.' He shifted his shoulders, as if his jacket had suddenly become too tight. 'I want to know if the things you hear are consistent with what they want us to know.'

'They?'

'The Portuguese. The Germans. The Italians. Hell, even the Yanks. You choose.' He drained his glass. 'I won't come here again, Lisbet. We'll arrange dead letter boxes and go-betweens. When we meet in public, pretend you don't know me.'

'Easy enough. Is there anyone here that might know me? From *before*?'

'Before?'

'Before I married Philip. Before I dropped out of society. Before the war.' I shrugged. 'Before.'

'Lisbet, it's been five years. With the dark hair, I barely recognised you. I doubt your own mother would.' He had the grace to look chagrined.

'And if she did, the old dragon would look away and keep walking.' With a bitter smile, I forced the rage back into its cage and changed the subject. 'What's your link to Special Operations?'

'I have no direct link to your little club.' He held up a single finger, stopping my next question. 'No indirect link either. SOE doesn't hold much sway here.'

'That doesn't sound right. Buckmaster never missed a chance to get more people into France. I can't believe his counterpart here would be so lax.'

'Have you ever met John Beevor?' Matthew delicately crossed one leg over the other.

'No, I don't think so.'

'Headed up SOE here for a couple of years. A foolish man playing a double game.'

I sat up straight, alarm coursing through me.

'Double agent?'

He held his hands up. 'No, no. Double game. He established a network with the left-wingers. The Communists opposed to Salazar –'

'So what? We did that in France as well.'

'Yes, my dear. But Beevor also danced with the Legião Portuguesa. Heard of them? No? Bunch of chaps who formed an armed militia specifically to fight the Red Wave.'

'Ah,' I said.

'Ah, indeed. And then there are the disputes between the Legião and the state police, the PVDE. Bloody amateur. His boys show up for a "little chat" with someone—'

'A kidnapping?'

He inclined his head in silent acknowledgement. 'Only to be met by the PVDE. Too many holes in the organisation. Too unreliable.'

'And this is who you want me to work for?'

Underneath the horror was a vague certainty that there was more to the story than Matthew was telling me, and not just about John Beevor. I hadn't met the man, but I had heard of him. 'Foolish' wasn't a word often used to describe him.

'Don't be absurd. He's moved on, but the damage is done. No, my dear. Best that no one even knows you're in the country. You're not going to work for Special Operations here. You're going to work for me.' He shrugged. 'Call it a secondment if it makes you feel better.'

It didn't. But I had run out of options.

Once Matthew left, I prowled through my new lair. The public rooms were on the ground floor: two parlours, a formal dining room, a WC and the kitchen. On the first floor, three bedrooms and a large bathroom. The enormous copper bath was tempting and I set the water running. Threw in a handful of bath salts from a jar on a shelf before undressing.

The looking glass wasn't flattering. The woman in it had gone from slim to gaunt. Long brown hair escaped its chignon, and auburn roots showed at the hairline. Dark circles ringed tired eyes, but for the first time for weeks, they held a hint of their old sparkle.

Matthew's offer was intriguing. Unlike the work I had done in France, where survival meant blending into the background, here I was setting myself up as live bait, and with the ability to bring the fight to the Germans. It was a welcome change.

I slipped into the cool, fragrant water. Closed my eyes and began to relax. The bath smelt of flowers and spices, the evening air of jasmine and the sea, carrying with its scent the sorrowful sounds of a distant guitar.

Matthew's offer wasn't philanthropic. He wasn't looking out for me; he was looking out for himself and his country. And as long as I remembered that, and worked for the same things he stood for, he'd look out for me as well, as much as he was capable of. His attention came at a price. It always had.

When my fingertips were sufficiently wrinkled, I towelled myself dry, wrapped myself in a piece of flannel, and padded down the hall to the master bedroom. It was lovely, hung in shades of cream and beige. A large vase of flowers stood on the dressing table opposite an enormous bed.

My case and bag lay just inside the door. Across the room, the cupboard cracked open, and I cursed myself for not doing a better job securing my home. I reached into my bag for my pistol, feeling its familiar weight. On silent feet I moved to the wardrobe. I took a deep breath before allowing the gun's muzzle to widen the gap.

What greeted me took that breath away. Instead of a person lying in wait, there hung a glorious array of colours. One side contained stylish yet sensible clothing for everyday – but the other made me want to weep. Tentative fingers brushed across silks and satins, the like of which I hadn't worn since before the war. I held an emerald green Balenciaga gown to my chest and I felt my knees go weak.

I'd play his game. And I'd play it on my own terms.

Operation Black Cat. I liked the sound of that.

Chapter Eleven

Matthew had set up my new identity, supported by all the required documentation. Solange Verin was a widowed Frenchwoman of independent means and vague political allegiance. She had a housekeeper – appropriately vetted by Matthew's people – a required accessory for someone of Madame Verin's stature, but I drew the line at a chauffeur. From what the taxi driver said, there were enough *bufos* around to track a person's whereabouts. I didn't need to make it too easy for them.

With a growing understanding of how the city worked, I began to establish Madame Verin, finding an odd exhilaration in allowing rumour to work in my own favour as for the first time for years, I became the hunter instead of the hunted.

At the chemist in Estoril, two fashionable Italian women gossiped about an event at the Hotel Aviz. I made a mental note to have a drink there later.

My manicurist, gesturing to a frumpy blonde, whispered that the Abwehr were better known for their sexual exploits than for any intelligence, either gathered or innate. Barring one or two, she added.

That wasn't comforting – it only took one man, one person to find out my secrets.

The milliner revealed the Portuguese obsession with French designs, even as they were frowned upon by the state. This supported Matthew's political assessment, although Estoril, inhabited by a strange mix of exiled royalty, aristocrats and officers, refugees and spies from at least a dozen different countries, seemed to play by a different set of rules. The capital was farther up the river, but based on the bored look of the bank teller when I exchanged rather a large amount of French francs into Portuguese escudos, in this suburb lay the real power.

By mid-afternoon, I'd dropped my parcels at the villa and applied another dose of brown dye to my hair. Finally groomed to a state that even Lady Anne wouldn't be able to find fault with, I followed the hordes down the hill towards the beach. It was enough for the first day. I would secure a safe house in another part of town and a few disguises later in the week.

Graceful hotels lined the street, and at the base, a small castle stood behind arches that reminded me of the ruins I'd seen on Rome's Palatine. Beyond that, a large garden led up to a casino. I meandered along the beach before stopping for lunch at a yellow building with a steeple reminiscent of a dunce's cap. The Tamariz.

Smiling, I followed the maître d' past a group of Germans at the bar and a table of Englishmen, their suits still crisp despite the heat. I sat under a large umbrella on the terrace, acclimatising to the warmth and the seemingly comfortable way the nationalities interacted with each other here. I ordered lunch in French, allowing my voice to carry.

'One of ours,' a women at the next table murmured, approving.

'But supporting who?' another asked.

There were three of them: middle-aged *Parisiennes* with an impressive range of diamonds and double chins. Over the low din of clicking crystal and silverware on porcelain, the wheels of Estoril's rumour mill began to churn.

The black lace mantilla swept across my shoulders, secured by a large marcasite cat at the cleavage of the Balenciaga gown. If it concealed the dress's neckline, it also hid the puckered bullet hole the Germans had left on my shoulder last winter. Walking into the casino by myself would be bad enough, but that was the sort of gossip I wasn't prepared to deal with yet.

The doorman held open the doors and for a moment, I was back in London. *Before.* The air was scented with a familiar mix of French perfume, cigarette smoke and sweat. The colours of the gowns and uniforms were as blinding as the light refracting off the heavy chandeliers. Walking through the doors, I entered a warped version of the world I'd deserted five years before.

With a small clutch bag in one hand and a glass of champagne in the other, I exchanged a handful of notes for chips, trying not to smirk as a man, hair combed back from an Eastern European face, swanned past, a woman clinging to each arm. There was something horribly clichéd about him, giving me more than an inkling about the games being played here.

Perspiration beaded more than one brow, as much from the heat as from the games. A man with silvering hair and a long Gallic nose sat at one of the tables, surrounded by a group of unsmiling men. He rubbed his pencil moustache and threw in a few chips. It wasn't difficult to gather that he was out of his depth. I turned away, taking no comfort from his situation.

The atmosphere was almost surreal, with warring factions politely moving past one another. That being said, they did appear to keep to tables with other like-minded individuals.

At the roulette table, a slim, pale man in a white dinner jacket stood with a group of uniformed Germans. While his posture wasn't ramrod straight, nor was it the deliberate slouch of a British aristocrat. The ironic twist of his lips made it clear he wasn't above having a laugh at Jerry's expense.

I moved past to the next table and placed a small stack of chips on Black 22. The silver ball whirled as I took a small sip of the first champagne I had drunk for years. If people thought conventional forms of gambling were exciting, they should try jumping out of a plane into occupied territory. I grinned widely when the croupier pushed a stack of chips towards me. Held back part of the winnings and pushed the remainder to Red 12. The silver ball again danced along, dipping into the red pocket.

'*Mein Gott*,' a man with sun-bleached hair murmured. His face was tanned, but fleshy, with the soft look of a diplomat rather than a front-line soldier. 'Lucky *and* good-looking.'

'Try your luck,' an older, elegant man laughed. Unlike his younger companion, this man, perhaps in his late fifties, exuded both confidence and charisma.

He tipped his head at me as the younger man approached.

'Good evening, Fräulein . . .'

'Frau,' I corrected, focusing my attention on the spinning ball.

'You speak German!' he exclaimed. 'Splendid! Can I buy you a drink?'

'I already have one.'

'Then finish it and I'll buy you the next one. Perhaps you can share your luck with a simple soldier.'

I raised an eyebrow to let him know I was unimpressed.

'You make your own luck, sir.'

'Please. My name is Jurgen Kuhne. And you are?'

'Too old for you.' I moved my winnings to another square.

'You're French, aren't you?'

The puppy placed his chips next to mine, his hand grazing my wrist. The shudder was hard to stifle. And in Portugal, maybe I didn't have to. I gave him a pointed glare.

'And?'

'And I have not seen you here before. You're new to Estoril?'

I looked over his shoulder to glare at the other man. He'd moved, and was now speaking with two other men: a German major, and a taller man, perhaps half a head above the others. He wore a dark dinner jacket, but everything about him screamed *Military* – his straight posture, the dark hair cropped close. His eyes crinkled at something the suave older man said.

Clinically speaking, the major was more attractive, with a square jaw and bright blue eyes that slanted like a cat's. But where all three men emanated confidence, Cat-eyes bordered on arrogance.

As if sensing my attention, the tall man looked straight at me. His face was arresting, with high Teutonic cheekbones, a nose that was a touch long, and dark, deep-set eyes that seemed to miss little. His half-smile faded as he studied me. I held myself still, unable to move. Unable to fathom my reaction to a complete stranger, and a German one at that.

When a striking brunette in a diaphanous yellow gown linked her arm in his, a surprising disappointment hit me.

'Beautiful, lucky, and, apparently, quite rich,' a French voice drawled from behind me.

'Who?' I asked absently.

The Frenchman in the white dinner jacket chuckled. 'Why, you, my dear. Haven't you noticed?'

He cleared his throat and indicated a rather large stack of chips that had replaced the handful I'd thrown there some minutes before. The Frenchman was right. In less than an hour, I had done very well.

'Have you had enough of the child's attention already?' The Frenchman was perhaps thirty or thirty-five, with fair hair that waved back from a high forehead. His voice held the slightest of slurs, but his eyes were clear, regarding me with lazy curiosity. 'Dreadful bore that he is.'

'That isn't a very nice thing to say.'

'Never claimed to be nice. Don't worry, he doesn't speak a word of French, the ignorant bastard. Not many of their lot do. Julian Reilly is my name. At your service.'

He grabbed my hand and bowed over it, while the young Herr Kuhne looked unhappy. While Reilly's French was flawless, his name was Irish.

'Citizen of the world,' he corrected, although I hadn't spoken aloud. 'But if you tell me your name, madame, I shall rescue you from the attentions of the barbarians.'

'That seems a fair deal.' Despite myself, I was amused at his outrageousness. 'I am Solange Verin.'

'Then come with me, Madame Verin, and I'll introduce you to all the wrong people.'

He held his arm out to me.

'And won't that ruin my reputation?'

'You have a reputation? How delightful!'

His devil-may-care grin exposed crooked teeth and dimples. He opened his mouth to speak when the hubbub in the room suddenly muted. Nervous glances swept to the door and the young lieutenant who entered. He paused, scanning the room, and made his way slowly towards the tall man. It was a painful procession; he didn't limp so much as force one leg in front of the other. His gaze was fixed straight ahead, refusing to acknowledge the hostile stares that followed his progress.

'Who is that?' I asked.

'Ah. That poor sod is the Herr Leutnant Andreas Neumann.'

'What happened? Why does everyone dislike him?'

'Dislike? Nothing of the sort.' Julian looked uncomfortable. 'We don't dislike *him*. What is hard to bear is that he reminds us of our own mortality.'

As the lieutenant passed, the woman in yellow joined a pair of women, watching the young man exchange words with the major and the tall man. I edged closer, curious. How he could remind them of their own mortality? So he limped. A lot of soldiers did.

'I don't understand how Eduard can bear to talk to that man. Much less look at him.'

The Canary didn't bother to lower her voice and her Spanish-accented syllables were clear in the almost-still room. I blinked. The young lieutenant may have moved awkwardly, but he was

110

beyond beautiful, with a face as finely drawn as a Botticelli angel. The lieutenant stiffened, but otherwise showed no emotion, waiting for a reaction from the major and his colleague. When I met the Spanish woman's eyes, she sneered.

'Well, look at him, will you?'

'I have.'

The lieutenant's expression was stony when he turned towards us. If the right side of his face was hauntingly beautiful, the left side was something out of a horror movie. Scar tissue radiated up from his collar, drawing down his eye fractionally, giving the impression that half his face was melting off. All signs of life faded from that hideous mask, except for a tiny spark in his piercing eyes, that otherwise would have been chilling. He didn't respond to their jeers, holding himself with an unapologetic honour that made me respect him, in spite of the side he fought for.

'I have looked.' This time my voice carried. It was foolish to draw attention to myself, but for my own honour, I couldn't allow the Canary's bad manners to go unchecked. 'And I hope that if you ever must endure whatever that man went through, that you will be shown the compassion that you deny him.'

The lieutenant didn't respond, maintaining his rigid posture, the beautiful side of his face showing no emotion. He saluted the tall man and limped to the door. Just before he exited, he looked at me. I met his eyes without flinching and smiled.

'Well, if you didn't have a reputation before, you do now.' Julian's droll voice sounded impressed. He pressed a glass of champagne into my hand. 'You find all the wrong people all on your own.'

'You don't know how true that is,' I murmured.

'Don't listen to Julian, my dear.' A woman appeared, linking her arm in Julian's. She leant her head against his shoulder and watched me with savvy eyes. She was a few years older than I, but pretty, with chestnut curls set off by a deep violet silk frock. 'What you did was very brave.'

'Why brave? He wasn't going to attack me.'

'No, my dear. Brave to antagonise our Spanish friend. Laura can be a right bitch.'

'Claudine!'

'She can, and you know it, Julian. Why her husband puts up with her, or her philandering, is anyone's guess. It's not as if she's even subtle about it. He –' she indicated the tall man – 'is only the latest in a very long line.'

Claudine ignored Julian's rude suggestion and tilted her head to the side, long earrings catching in the heavy jewelled torque at her neck. One hand idly released it as she stared at me.

'I know you.'

'I really don't think so.'

Mild panic had me push away the thought of the tall man with the Canary, mentally flicking through the catalogue of my contacts. And coming up blank.

She tapped one fingernail against her teeth, dark eyes narrowing.

'Yes, I believe it's you. You moved in to the cottage across the way from me yesterday. I've seen the deliveries to your door all week. I meant to stop by earlier to introduce myself but completely forgot.' She reached out a hand for mine, her ankle wobbling as she moved from Reilly's arm. 'I am Claudine Deschamps.'

'Pleased to meet you, Madame Deschamps.'

'No, you're not,' Reilly interrupted. The words were rude, but his tone affectionate. 'She's one of the people you really don't want to know. Go away, Claudine.'

She made a little moue with her mouth. 'Don't be nasty, Julian. Christophe is losing at the tables again, and I will have an unhappy enough time when I get home.'

'I fail to understand how that's my problem.'

'I can make it your problem, if you wish.' She linked her arm back in Julian's. 'So how are you finding our city? Other than the obnoxious Spanish countesses, irritating Irish novelists and little German lapdogs, that is.'

'That's quite a list, Madame Deschamps,' I smiled. 'And despite that, Lisbon seems quite lovely.'

'It can be catty as hell. Get used to it.' Using her champagne flute, she gestured around the room. 'Anyone who's anyone is here. From all sides of the conflict, and some people representing more than what you'd first think. But good – I like you, Madame Verin.' She shook my hand. 'I'm about to collect my husband from the tables. It'll be quite a messy scene for which I'll apologise in advance, but if you'd like us to drop you off at home, do let me know.'

'Thank you. I appreciate it.'

She blew a kiss at Julian and sashayed across the room with a deliberate grace, attracting enough attention that people might not notice how drunk she was. She paused once or twice along the way, kissing a cheek or shaking a hand before stopping at the blackjack table in front of the man with the pencil moustache and losing streak. Voices were raised as the man and woman stood nose to nose, animosity pulsing between them.

'Foolish man,' Reilly murmured, watching them over the top of his drink. 'She's a good girl, loves him desperately. He, on the other hand, loves the cards.'

Reilly reached into a pocket for a gold case and a monogrammed Zippo. He lit two cigarettes and handed one to me. The voices on the other side of the room rose, and Claudine's hand flashed out to slap her husband's face. She reached into her handbag and threw down a combination of chips and notes. Stormed away, brushing tears from her face. Her husband sat down. Piled the stack neatly in front of him, and slipped the notes into his breast pocket. Gestured to the dealer for another card. Julian jammed the cigarette into his mouth. He exhaled a great cloud of smoke and downed the rest of his whiskey.

'Well, Madame Verin. There goes the rest of the night as I find myself once again your neighbour's chaperon,' he said. 'You might just have lost your ride home, unless you're willing to share a seat with Claudine?'

Matthew had suggested that I move in the German circles, but accessing them via the German-sympathising French would be more convincing. I tucked my clutch bag under my arm and smiled.

'Why not?'

Julian's car was a two-seater with an engine that roared like a Lancaster. The Portuguese valet dropped the set of keys into the

Irishman's hands and stood back. His gaze ping-ponged between Claudine and me, and I hoped he was more curious about the logistics of the drive home than what he thought would come later. Claudine had one hand on the dashboard and the other on the gearstick as she shimmied into the car. Huddled close to Julian to make way for me as the valet closed the door.

'Hold on tight, madame,' Claudine murmured as Julian revved the engine.

He slid the car into gear and rocketed from the car park. I gritted my teeth as we made a sharp left turn away from the casino. Behind us, moonlight danced on black water, beauty over deep currents that could suck a soul under.

'Tell me where!' Julian screamed over the engine as we climbed the hill.

I pried one hand from its death grip on the door to point at my villa. Julian waited for me to pass through the gate before driving off, one arm across the back of Claudine's seat.

Chapter Twelve

An insistent knocking catapulted me from sleep into panic. Only the Gestapo came calling at night; only they made that sort of racket. Damn it, I was *careful*! I grabbed a dress from the wardrobe at random, and slid my feet into a pair of shoes. I was halfway out of the balcony door, with my gun in hand, when I realised that it was mid-morning and here in Portugal, the Gestapo held no more sway than any other gang of street thugs.

Peering over the gate I caught a glimpse of the red highlights gleaming in my neighbour's chestnut hair.

'Inconsiderate cow.'

I returned to my bedroom and ran a comb through my hair. The sgian dubh on my thigh was more out of habit than caution, but there was no need for the PPK. I slipped it into my handbag and went to meet Claudine.

'Good morning,' I tried not to snarl.

'*Bonjour, madame.*' Her smile was too bright for the early hour. 'Have I woken you up?'

'Yes.'

'Ah, well, now that you're awake, I have decided to introduce you to Estoril.'

My compliance assumed, Claudine ducked under my arm and led the way into my house, chattering as she walked. Taken individually, her features were unspectacular, but the energy she emitted was engaging.

'Frankly speaking, my dear, you have stirred up an awful lot of gossip this morning,' she said.

'Me?'

'Oh, everyone's used to seeing Christophe being difficult. But you're new.' She laughed in a very self-satisfied way. 'Please don't take this the wrong way, but I'm delighted the old dears have found someone else to gossip about.'

'Dare I ask what they're saying?'

'Fiction.' She waved her hand airily. 'Like everything else here. My favourite story is that you're an actress, on the run after being caught *in flagrante* with Pétain!'

'You cannot be serious!' I laughed. 'The Maréchal is old enough to be my grandfather!'

'Does that matter?' She rummaged through my cabinets, finally putting two cups on the table. 'Where do you keep your coffee?'

The small bag of beans hid in the back of the second cabinet. I poured a handful into the grinder and cranked the handle. It didn't look like very much and added a few more. There was something calming about this process of making coffee.

'I'm nowhere near as interesting as that.'

'Perhaps. Perhaps not. But you are kind to small animals and mutilated Germans.' She rested her elbows on my table and dropped her chin on to her crossed hands. 'I'm assuming the bit about small animals.'

'Of course.'

It was hard to keep up with her. The smell of coffee began to infuse the room and I felt a little more alert.

'So what is your story?' she asked.

'Story?' I paused halfway to the cupboard for the sugar bowl. Claudine was a gossip, which could be as dangerous as it could – occasionally – be convenient. I fixed a bland smile on to my face. 'What do you mean?'

'Oh, you know. Where do you come from? How did you get here? Why on earth did you choose this place? And what made you want to defend Quasimodo?'

'Is he that bad?'

She looked confused. 'No, I don't suppose so.'

'And does *he* kick small dogs?'

'If he does, I've not heard of it.' She relaxed, seeing where the conversation was leading. 'But I suppose you're right. I sound like Laura, don't I? I confess, I've never spoken to him, but it was a tragedy, what happened.'

'How he got the scars?'

I poured the coffee and gestured for her to continue.

'The tank he was driving took a shell. This was fairly early on, of course. The major dragged his unconscious body from the wreck.'

'The major?'

The man with the blue cat's eyes and smarmy grin didn't seem the sort to save anyone other than himself. Did that over-whelming arrogance hide a selfless bravery?

'He received the *Ritterkreuz* that day. The major, that is. The attack was at his command and rather a victory.' Her voice had gone flat and I guessed that victory was against the French. 'Despite the injuries they sustained.'

'Really?'

I was impressed: the Knight's Cross was the Third Reich's medal of honour. I hadn't seen it at the major's throat last night, and blinked. He didn't seem the sort to tone down his merits. If someone earned that cross, they probably wore it pinned to their pyjamas at night.

She sipped the coffee and cringed. Fumbled for the sugar bowl and stirred in a spoonful. Tasted it and then added a second.

'Real sugar? I'm impressed. In any case, someone said that Rommel himself pinned it on the major, but you know how gossip is.' Disdain pulled her mouth into a small moue and I struggled not to laugh at the irony.

'So what's *your* story, Madame Deschamps?'

'Claudine,' she corrected with a stern look. 'I'll have been here two years in December. I never thought it would be this long. Didn't think the war would go on this long.'

She hadn't answered my question, from which I could only guess that she also had a past she preferred to keep quiet.

'Who did?'

'Oh, there are people enough who want it to continue. Who make sure it continues.' For a moment, her face darkened. Then she pushed the porcelain cup to the centre of the table and abruptly stood. 'Come, Solange. Your coffee is not fit for pigs. Let me show you this place you've chosen to call home.'

'The King of Spain lives over there.' Claudine pointed to a little castle near the beach. 'He's in exile, of course. As are half the people who live here.'

'And the other half?'

She laughed. 'Merchants, adventurers, and of course spies.'

Of course.

'Fancy an ice cream? Best one in the city is just ahead. Come on, you'll love it.'

Gino's Ice Cream Parlour was a thriving business. Not a single table under the green-and-white umbrellas was free, and a roiling file of children and adults led to a counter outside where a young man was busy scooping their *gelato*. Through the window, an enormous portrait of Mussolini proclaimed Gino's politics. I held back a sigh. Whether by intent or not, Claudine was ensuring that I was seen in the right watering holes.

'It's always like this,' Claudine said, grabbing my arm and moving fast to slide into a seat almost before it was fully vacated.

A middle-aged woman came to take our orders. Tendrils of hair escaped the chignon at the back of her head, falling in damp waves along her shoulders.

'*Buon giorno*, Signora Deschamps.'

She piled the empty glasses onto a tray and sponged down the table.

Claudine waited for her to finish before responding. 'Good afternoon, Carla. I'll have a strawberry gelato, please. And for my friend . . .'

I ordered a hazelnut gelato and watched three small children at the next table over attack their ice cream as Claudine prattled on.

'Bless her, she really could do with a bit more help here. It was better when her daughter was here, but Gino won't allow her to bring in anyone else. "A family concern" he calls this. Or something like that.'

'Where's the daughter?'

'She ran off with a sailor last year.' Her nostrils flared, showing her opinion on the matter.

'It's a common enough story.' I couldn't help myself. 'There's something about the uniforms.'

'You didn't!'

'No, I was already married when my husband joined the navy.' That part, at least, was true.

'And Monsieur Verin?'

'Is dead.'

The simple words didn't lend themselves to further conversation, and after murmuring her condolences, Claudine looked away. I stared over her shoulder at two women farther down the beach. They lounged in deckchairs, their faces half hidden behind large sunglasses with tortoiseshell frames, with a bottle of Johnson & Johnson's Baby Oil perched on a table between them.

'Americans,' Claudine said, following my gaze. 'I almost envy them.'

'Whatever for?'

'Ever met one?' a blonde woman with olive skin said, kissing Claudine's cheek and sliding into the seat beside her. She waved at the waitress as she spoke. 'Everything about them is larger than life. They play at war, having no idea what it's all about. What it's like to be bombed,' she said bitterly. 'So here they are, with their dollars and their white smiles and their naïveté. They think they're helping but everything they do makes this damned war last forever. But enough of politics.' A dainty hand waved away the subject. 'Welcome to Estoril, Madame Verin. I'm having a dinner party tomorrow. Do say you'll come, we're all quite curious about you.'

Claudine was right; the gossipmongers were already at work. I hadn't introduced myself yet, but she already knew who I was. I'd hoped to get my bearings before entering the fray, but wasn't about to miss the opportunity.

'I'd be delighted, Madame . . . ?'

'Ribaud. Gabrielle Ribaud.' She pulled a cream-coloured calling card from her handbag. 'The address is on the card, although Madame Deschamps knows where I live. By the way, darling, whoever is your husband talking to?'

Claudine went very still as she located her husband. She pushed her white-framed sunglasses farther up her nose and leant forward. Farther down the beach, he stood facing a man with fair hair and hands in his pockets. Christophe's shoulders were hunched in what should have been a casual pose. It was impossible to see his face from this angle, but from her expression, Claudine knew who his companion was, and wasn't pleased.

'Claudine?' I asked, curious.

'I don't know,' she lied. For some time, her eyes didn't leave her husband, until she threw down the spoon and stood up. 'Please forgive me, Solange.' She collected her things, fingers trembling. 'I'm so sorry to do this to you, but the sun's getting to me. I need to lie down.'

'Let me walk you back.'

'No, no. You stay and finish your ice cream. Gabrielle will keep you company. I'll be fine.'

Christophe's conversation had become animated, his hands gesticulating wildly. His companion had an unremarkable face, with both hair and chin retreating away from a prominent

122

nose and an even more prominent Adam's apple. It was the sort that you forget moments after meeting. Almost. The cut of his pale seersucker suit looked faintly English. From his company he kept at the casino, I'd assumed Christophe favoured the Germans, but this was the City of Spies, and I was beginning to realise, the moniker was well-earned.

Chapter Thirteen

For all that the Irishman, Julian Reilly, claimed Claudine loved her husband, both times I had seen them, they'd seemed at odds. And yet, they remained together. Expediency? Shared secrets? Or something deeper? I was curious, but the Deschamps weren't my priority.

My first three days in Estoril were busy. Under the guise of exploring the coastal towns of Cascais, Oeiras and Carcavelos, I secured a safe house and a number of disguises. I didn't have the documentation yet for a second identity, but that was something Matthew should be able to sort out.

By the time I returned home, I was exhausted. A note fell to the ground when I opened my gate, and I took a deep breath before opening it. Claudine, noting that I didn't have a car, was offering to pick me up at eight o'clock for the soirée at Gabrielle Ribaud's villa.

Two hours later, clad in a teal chiffon gown, I sat in the back of Christophe's Peugeot, listening to Claudine's monologue of the guests expected to attend the soirée, where they were from, and any little titbit of gossip associated with them. The quick glances she occasionally sent her husband weren't returned, and Christophe might as well have been a silent chauffeur.

Determined to summon a taxi for the return trip, I smiled back at her and counted the minutes until Christophe turned off the road onto a short drive. He stopped the Peugeot in front of a small but elegant villa and helped his wife, and then me, from the vehicle. It was the closest I had been to him. From a distance, he had seemed remote; up close, there was something repellent about him. His eyes. They were flat, emotionless.

I forced a smile and followed them into a villa that seemed only slightly more boisterous than Christophe. A servant opened the door for us, pointing the way through the house to a garden at the rear, scented with roses and jasmine. Gabrielle Ribaud rose to meet us; her dress was magnificent, but her face taut.

'I found out only a couple of hours ago. Horrible news. Martin Billiot was murdered.' Her voice was low and, unless I misread her, shocked.

'Murdered.' Claudine raised a hand to her mouth. 'How? Why?'

'Car crash.'

'Surely that could have been an accident?'

Could this city be so paranoid that even an accident was considered nefarious?

Gabrielle shook her head. 'They say he was driving.'

Her words were met with a hushed silence I didn't understand.

Finally, Claudine asked: 'Who told Rosalie?'

'One of the Director's men.'

'Who?'

Christophe's mouth pursed under his pencil moustache. 'Agostinho Lourenço, captain of the PVDE. They call him "the Director". He returned his attention to Gabrielle. 'Do you know who informed his wife?'

After a furtive glance, Gabrielle whispered: 'Adriano de Rios Vilar.'

It didn't feel right to capitalise on someone else's misery, but if I was going to make Solange Verin believable, I had to start now.

'Forgive me for interrupting, but who are the PVDE?'

Claudine glanced at her husband. 'The political police.'

'Why would they get involved for a simple traffic accident?'

'Because, Madame Verin, it wasn't a simple traffic accident. Martin Billiot had a driver. He never drove himself . . .'

Gabrielle glanced at me, her trailing voice indicating her unwillingness to postulate in my company.

I sighed, murmuring just loud enough for them to hear: 'And I left France because with the bombings it was no longer safe.'

'You don't strike me as being that naïve, Madame Verin.' It was the most I'd heard Christophe speak so far, his voice soft but derisive. 'Nowhere is safe. Especially not Lisbon.'

Martin Billiot's death rated a small column, almost hidden in the next day's paper – a not-so-gentle warning not to get too comfortable in Lisbon.

Needing time to myself, I ventured farther afield, taking a taxi along the Estrada Marginal. The coast road, the driver explained in broken French, was only completed a few years ago, as one of Salazar's great building projects. I tuned out his history lesson, fascinated by the flashes of blue water and rocky coastline. I planned to gorge myself on the sights I had missed on the way in: the tower of Belém, where the Portuguese World Exhibition was held three years ago, the palatial Mosteiro dos Jerónimos behind it, and the ruined castle on the hill in Lisbon.

Sandbags and barbed wire guarded the national treasures, but not like London or Paris. I knew Spain had tried to negotiate with Germany to extend her borders to the sea, and yet the Portuguese seemed more concerned about dissent from within than invasion from any outside nation. Newspapers barely acknowledged the food shortages, one thing that I had a hard time understanding, given how well Sabela Figueiredo, my housekeeper, provisioned my villa.

Despite my instruction, the driver let me out at the Rossio, a busy area which, from the looks of it, was the meeting point for refugees from across Europe. Figuring that being seen here would fit with my cover story, I took a seat between two families with a clear view out of the window. I ordered a cup of the thick black brew they called coffee and tried to block the stories being told around me: Jews who had been hiding for years before making their escape; Frenchmen who had fallen foul of neighbours, or the Gestapo. The trials they endured while waiting for a visa and the ship – or for the rich, the Pan Am Clipper – to take them to New York.

It was an interesting place, but not likely one a German sympathiser would frequent. I had already called for the bill when I saw the man stride past the window. For a second I considered letting him pass, but then my curiosity got the better of me. Throwing down a note, I followed my godfather into the warren of little streets – the Baixa.

It was a seedy part of town. Bridges arched overhead, giving the tourists a safe path above the grime, the scent of docks and of decay. Sailors weren't a particular lot, but worryingly, neither was my Matthew. He stopped in front of a short, round woman with a pockmarked face. She was young, with hard eyes and a straining décolletage.

I hid in the darkened doorway of a bar, horrified when Matthew followed the whore into a shabby building. In all my life, this was the one thing I never expected to see. I stumbled into a chair and, despite the early hour, ordered a brandy.

I wasn't naïve. With his wife in England, I didn't expect him to live like a monk, but to pay for company? I ignored the waiter's reproof and ordered a second drink.

'Hey, beautiful.' A sailor swaggered up to me, speaking Italian. 'You busy?'

Not sure whether to be amused or irritated by his intrusion, I chose the latter.

'Too busy for you.'

Too busy watching the brothel Matthew had disappeared into. Forty-six minutes later, he emerged, a smug smile on his face. My illusions began to crumble even as a little voice in my head protested that something was wrong.

He crossed the street and ducked into another alleyway. Matthew might not approve of Special Operations, but their trainers were effective. Blending into the crowd, I followed him to another bordello. The paint on the side was peeling, but the woman at the door smiled and kissed his cheeks. I sat down heavily on the kerb. This made no sense. He'd just left one whore; surely he couldn't still be feeling amorous?

Pushing away my shock, I ordered a cup of coffee from a reasonably clean café and, certain no one had followed me from the Chave d'Ouro, sifted through the facts.

Why is Matthew Harrington, renowned for his charm, visiting whores?

Stupid question. Why does any man visit a woman of questionable integrity?

Because a whore lacked the expectations a mistress might have?

Wait. Why 'integrity'? Why not 'morals'?

I sat up, accepting the chipped cup of coffee. Tapped my finger against it, cringing a little as it stuck to the handle. Why was one word was more important than another? What did my subconscious understand that I didn't?

Integrity. Honesty. Honour. Reliability.

What made them unreliable?

They sold their bodies to the highest bidder. A courtesan might have a choice, but these women were bought by the hour.

Or forty-six minutes.

A pair of sailors swaggered past with their distinctive rolling gait. The din of the crowds was nothing compared to the ringing in my head. Whores provided comfort – a safe port. And when a man feels safe, he won't be careful about what he says.

In London, there was a poster of a beautiful woman surrounded by men. Be careful, it warned. She's not as stupid as she seems. It cautioned viewers not to disregard women, although it should have suggested thinking twice about relaying any confidential information to *anyone.*

The penny dropped. Matthew wasn't rogering the whores – he was running them. An intellectual pimp. I wanted to find that distasteful, but this was the Spider. Tension ebbed from my shoulders and I leant back until I noticed that the waiter and two old men he'd served breakfast to were watching me. No wonder; I was a lone, well-dressed woman in a dodgy part of town.

Bufos, they are everywhere.

'My husband,' I said in Spanish, schooling my features to the hard, betrayed expression one would expect on a jealous wife. 'He likes whores.'

Their interest waned. I sipped the coffee, gagging on the bitter taste. If Claudine thought my coffee was undrinkable, she should try this swill. I pushed it aside and waited. Twenty minutes later, he slipped through the shadows, his fedora pulled low. He moved past the Bairro Alto, doubling occasionally. Passed Rato Square and headed towards Estrela, turning left on to the Rua de São Bernardo and skirting the gardens before halting at the gate of the British embassy.

Almost directly across the street stood another impressive building, with red swastikas flying from the windows. I chuckled to myself, wondering if each embassy stationed a man with binoculars on an upper storey.

I backed against a tree, dropped to one knee behind a bush, ostensibly to adjust the strap of my shoe, but careful to avoid watchers from either building noticing my face. Just beyond the gates, Matthew paused to speak to another man, and I was due my second shock of the morning: it was the same horsey man with an enormous Adam's apple that I'd seen with Christophe Deschamps.

Within moments, Adam's Apple adjusted the strap of the leather holdall on his shoulder and reached into his pocket for a pair of dark spectacles. He ran his fingers through his thinning hair, put on the glasses and walked out on to the street.

Spurred on by curiosity, I followed him. At least Matthew had taken *some* precautions against being followed; this man didn't, taking a taxi to the railway station. Three people stood between us in the queue; close enough that I heard him tell the man behind the counter that he wanted to see the sunsets over Cabo de São Vicente.

The tourist books mentioned the cape on the south-western point of Portugal, although I couldn't recall more than a photograph of a lighthouse and far too many birds. Closed my eyes and tried to envision the map. What was the nearest town, damn it?

Someone cleared their throat and I stepped forward, almost at the front of the queue. What was it?

Adam's Apple purchased a paper and a pack of Lucky Strikes, lit one and looked around. Lucky Strikes, and the same seersucker suit he'd worn the other day. He looked like a Brit trying to be an American. And failing miserably.

I dipped my head, hiding my face under the brim of my sun hat. The couple in front of me shuffled forward and bought tickets to Faro. It wasn't far from there. What was it? It started with an S. São, San.

A gentle nudge pushed me forward and the man at the counter raised an eyebrow at me.

'*Sim?*'

The word came out in a rush. 'Sagres, please. I'd like to purchase a ticket to Sagres.'

'*Sim*,' he repeated, sliding it across to me.

I reached the platform ahead of Adam's Apple. Bent down to adjust the strap on my shoe to allow him past. He took his seat in the front compartment of the third carriage. I entered the next compartment, sitting with a view of the corridor. If he was going to leave, I'd see him.

I opened my book and pretended to look engrossed, hoping it would deter anyone from sitting beside me, or even worse, distracting me with their conversation.

Cabo de São Vicente. I doubted that was his final destination, and I didn't believe his story about sunsets. Something was going on, and I was determined to find out what it was.

The heavy man across from me snored, his sonorous boom overshadowing the soothing clickety-clack of the train. He batted away a fly and jerked himself awake with a loud snort. He mumbled something and subsided back to sleep.

I sighed and returned my attention to the book, hastily bought at the station. Reread the page and realised I had no idea what it was about. Retraced to the beginning, dog-eared the corner of the page and stared out the window, wondering what the devil Adam's Apple was up to. I closed my eyes, just for a second.

And jerked awake as the conductor called out 'Sagres!'

Grabbed my book and handbag. A glance in the other compartment confirmed that Adam's Apple had already disembarked.

The platform was all but empty. A woman stood next to a man with a set of binoculars hanging from his neck, and a harried-looking mother herded three small children back to where her husband checked the times for the return journey. There was no sign of Adam's Apple.

With no pressing engagements waiting in Lisbon, I opted to remain on the chance that Adam's Apple was in Sagres. I rented a red bicycle that reminded me of the one I'd ridden from Paris, and asked directions to the lighthouse.

More irritated with myself than with Adam's Apple, I followed the coast road west. The sun began to dip as I tired. I'd gone as far west as I could without a swimming costume – which meant that this was Cabo de São Vicente. I might not have found Adam's Apple, but I'd see first-hand that sunset he had raved about.

I left the bicycle and wandered to the cliff's edge. I shouldn't have followed Matthew. Should have stayed in Lisbon. What the devil was I doing, chasing after a man I didn't know, on an impulse?

The low thrum of the waves caressed the rocks. The water was a deep blue, the beautiful colour too unreal to be on anything other than a gaudy painting. Farther out, a school of dolphins played and seagulls frolicked above the lighthouse farther along the coast. In a place like this, it was hard to believe there was a war on.

I stood up and dusted off my bottom. I'd check the lighthouse, and if Adam's Apple wasn't there, I'd return to Sagres. Worst case, I'd spend the night there and return to Lisbon in the morning.

In the distance, a trio of merchantmen steamed into sight. They were escorted by two frigates – British, by the look of them. If Philip were alive, would he be on one of those ships? I felt a pang in my heart, no longer the stabbing pain, but a longing for the man who'd been my husband for less than three years.

A seagull dipped into the water, shrieking its *joie de vivre*, and a different face superimposed itself over Philip's. A military man in a dinner jacket, whose dark eyes crinkled at the corners when he smiled.

'Where the hell did that come from?' I muttered, picking up a pebble and flinging it into the sea.

I'd never spoken to the man; what possessed me to even *think* of him? I gritted my teeth and concentrated on the rush of the waves.

Until they got louder.

And louder.

And the first plane screamed past. German Focke-Wulfs. I dropped to the ground, but there was nowhere to hide. There was just me, cowering on the blasted cliffs. But it wasn't me the Focke-Wulfs were hunting. A second plane thundered past, then a third, racing towards the convoy in the distance.

The fighters engaged, and the ships' enormous guns, rotating, retaliated. A Focke-Wulf disengaged, hit, but not severe enough to splinter. A German bomb hit a merchantman. Black smoke billowed from the ship as it listed to the side. Another Focke-Wulf was damaged, but dropped a bomb on a second merchantman before it peeled off. The bombers retreated, turning away as the British sailors jumped from the damaged ship.

The right wing of the damaged Focke-Wulf rose as it turned towards me. I cried out, pressing my hands closer over my head, as if by drowning out the sound, that awful roar, I could drown out my imminent death. My heard pounded, blood rushing though my veins. I was too young to die; I hadn't done what Matthew had brought me here to do. Hadn't completed my mission.

The Focke-Wulf screamed towards the lighthouse. If it exploded, I'd be caught in the conflagration. The plane passed, deafening as it screamed overhead. I braced myself for the stutter of machine guns but heard nothing over the roar of the plane, the waves, and my own blood.

The plane flashed past. It turned, this time over the ocean, and screamed out of sight.

'You bastard!' I howled, my hands still cradling my head.

Hating him for what he'd done; hating myself for my fear. I crawled forward, cursing and crying. The remaining two Focke-Wulfs were gone, and the convoy was slowing, picking up sailors from the water. The damaged hull of the merchantman was left behind, limping towards shore. I turned away; I could do nothing. Couldn't save those sailors any more than I could have saved my husband. Or myself, had the Focke-Wulf opened fire on me.

Streaks of lavender and pink replaced the oily smoke as sunset gathered. When the lights of the merchantman melted into the growing night, I picked up my bike and cycled into the dark.

Chapter Fourteen

The moonlit night reminded me of France. This time, I wasn't hauling my wireless, wasn't heading for a drop site, but every sense was still on edge.

The return to Sagres felt longer than the way out. Tired and cranky, I contemplated stopping to ask for directions, but the lorry that rumbled past moved at pace, and to avoid getting run down, I leapt onto the hard shoulder. Shielded by brush, all I could see was two men in the cab and a canvas cover concealing some cargo. It turned off the coast road, heading towards the ocean and a cluster of flickering lights.

I followed. The warehouse was two storeys tall, and well lit. Beyond it, a single speedboat was moored at the pier. Men milled around, looking bored, well-armed yet out of uniform. They were too far away for me to hear any words, but the guttural sounds sounded German. One man threw a half-smoked cigarette onto the dirt and ambled up to the lorry.

Whatever was going on wasn't above board. Hiding the bicycle in the underbrush, I freed Alex's sgian dubh from its sheath. It would provide little defence against a machine carbine, but with the Luger stashed in the chimney and my PPK under a floorboard in my bedroom, it was all I had.

Making a mental note never to leave home without a gun, even for sightseeing, I crept closer.

A guard stood at a barrier not unlike a level crossing. His attention was focused on the driver stepping from the lorry's cab and I skirted past unnoticed. The two men conferred for a few minutes before brushing aside the canvas awning to inspect the cargo.

What would require this level of security?

Prickly shrubs provided camouflage while I rubbed a handful of dirt on my arms and face, trying to blend into the night. Would Adam's Apple be here? Or had he travelled farther south to watch the convoy being attacked?

Someone barked a command and the other men began to unload the cargo. It looked like barrels, wrapped in sheepskins. Each barrel required two men to lift it, straining under its weight. The barrels were loaded onto a cart, and dragged into the warehouse.

Some ten feet away from me, the long grass stirred as a cat moved through it. It was missing half its right ear and several chunks of fur. The sgian dubh might not do much against a German assault rifle, but I'd be damned if I couldn't handle a cat.

The remaining ear twitched, and it turned, baring its teeth and hissing loud enough to warrant the officer's sharp command and disappeared into the brush.

'Goddamned animal,' one of the soldiers muttered, moving my way.

To be caught was one thing; to have the alarm raised by a feral beast was another.

The soldier strode closer, and sneezed. He wiped his mouth with the back of his left hand and muttered, 'Fucking cat.'

The knife felt slick in my hand and, muscles protesting, I crouched, ready to defend myself.

The man sneezed again.

'Waste of time,' he growled. Turned back to the warehouse.

The officer called out a question, to which the man shook his head and moved back into his position, passing less than five feet from me.

Once the lorry had been unloaded, the driver handed the officer a clipboard. Nodded as it was signed, then heaved himself into the truck and drove past the barrier.

'Well, how about that?' I murmured.

The quay was crawling with men, making it impossible to sneak closer. My legs ached from inactivity, but something kept me rooted to the spot, certain that whatever was going on hadn't yet finished. I stretched as best I could and allowed myself a faint regret that I hadn't brought a flask of coffee.

The moon was already dipping when a skiff tied up to the pier and the barrels were loaded onto the boat. They could have been the same ones, or different ones for all I knew.

The boat rode low in the water while the men on the pier fumbled for flasks and packs of cigarettes. What was in them anyway? Portuguese wine was pleasant, but not good enough to smuggle out. So what was it? Port? Spirits? What could be heavier?

Something at ground level caught my eye and I edged back as a creature tiptoed inches from my foot. About the size of my hand, at first glance it resembled a small lobster, but the narrow tail that curved over its back looked worse than the grasping claws. It swivelled to face me, its tail bobbing. I fell hard on my bottom, and grabbed the sgian dubh from my thigh.

Jesus Christ!

No wonder the cat had bolted. I had no idea if the little blade would even pierce the scorpion's armour, but I wasn't inclined to get close enough to even try. I dragged air in through my mouth, tamping down on the urge to scream. Edging back, I stepped on a dry branch and flinched.

I flicked my fingers at it, hissing, 'Go away!'

It didn't move.

If I threw a stone at it, would it run, or attack? Buck had always told us to expect the unexpected, but a *scorpion*?

With room to stand and swing a branch, I could launch the creature halfway to the sea. Only there was no room; standing would make me an easy target for the soldiers, and if I missed, the scorpion would get me. At least that would make for a less embarrassing letter to Lady Anne. Death by scorpion instead of drowned in wine.

I looked between the warehouse and the scorpion. Anger outweighed fear.

'Go,' I demanded in a harsh whisper, trying to keep the panic from my voice. 'Go!'

Its front legs bowed. Was that a warning?

'I tell you, there's something out there. You two. Go and check it out.'

Oh, hell.

'Fucking officers,' a soldier growled, stomping in my direction. 'Think they own the world. It's only a stinking cat.'

The scorpion retreated into the bushes and for a second, I wished I could follow it. Instead, I forced my heart to slow and crouched low to the ground. Trembling fingers gripped the knife. It wouldn't be much help, but at least it made me feel better.

'You think they don't?'

The other man used the muzzle of his rifle to check under the shrubs. The black barrel passed less than a yard in front of me. I could hear their grunts; smell the sweat on their bodies. With a little luck, they'd step on the scorpion.

'You'd think they'd do away with it, wouldn't you?'

'Christ, Sig, even the Reds have ranks. When did you turn into a commie?'

'Fuck off, Gast,' the first man growled. 'This is a waste of time. Let's go back.'

If they'd looked down, they would have seen me – they were that close. But they rejoined their companions in front of the warehouse, watching the motorboat slip its moorings and head south.

Stunned, I could only stare after them. Rank amateurs.

And thank God for that.

I edged backwards, careful not to make any noise until I could retrieve my bicycle. Dawn stretched lavender fingers across the sky as I followed the road until I saw signs for Sagres. The bicycle shop was closed but a nearby café was open. The coffee was hot, and if the roll was stale, it was edible.

Smuggling. Was Adam's Apple involved? Matthew? Christophe Deschamps? Both had spoken to Adam's Apple within the last week and I didn't believe in coincidence.

I trusted my instincts. Although I was as certain as I could be that I wasn't followed, I couldn't help feeling that I had missed something important.

Chapter Fifteen

My second cup of coffee sat cooling on the kitchen table when an insistent knock jerked me back from the table.

'Solange? Are you awake?'

I threw a rag over the spilt coffee and gave myself a few seconds to compose myself so that I wouldn't punch the woman. Took a few more deep breaths and made my way to the door.

'I'm bored,' Claudine said by way of greeting.

'You were born bored, Claudine.' I stepped back to let her in. 'Where's Christophe?'

Her Cupid's bow mouth tightened, white lines radiating out from her lips. Frustration as well as Nature was ageing Claudine.

'I don't know. Working, I suppose. He doesn't tell me where he goes.'

'I'm sorry to hear that.' I led the way into the parlour. 'What about Julian?'

'A new love,' she growled.

No wonder she was in such a foul mood. Her relationship with her husband might have been strained, but her affection for the novelist was clear.

'Oh, Claudine, I'm so sorry!'

She blinked. 'For what?'

'Well, Julian. You . . .'

She laughed with genuine amusement. 'Julian? You really thought that Julian and I . . . that we . . . Oh, Solange, you are priceless!'

'Well,' I said, offended, 'I don't really care if you are or aren't, but I am sorry . . .'

She put her hands on my shoulders and stared into my eyes.

'My dear, let me assure you, Julian is not my lover. It's not that I wouldn't, if I'm honest. But no. His tastes run to . . . Hm. Let's just say they're complicated.'

More complicated than an opinionated, alcoholic Frenchwoman with expensive tastes and dubious political leanings? Was that even possible? Still chuckling, she wandered around the room, picking up objects, only to put them down elsewhere. I moved behind her, replacing the clock on the mantelpiece.

'Can I get you something to drink?'

'Yes. A drink.' Her voice was soft, as if she was speaking to herself. 'I stopped by yesterday, but you weren't home.'

'No, I was out exploring. Is there something you need?'

'Not at all. I just wanted to see how you were settling in. It's been almost a week, already.'

Almost one week, hell. In the last twenty-four hours alone I'd discovered my godfather was running an intelligence network of whores out of the Baixa, almost got strafed by a trio of Focke-Wulf fighters, narrowly escaped a scorpion's bite . . . oh, and stumbled on some sort of smuggling operation. If Buck was impressed with my exploits before, what would he say now?

Forget Buck, my godfather would be incandescent. My job was to gather intelligence on the Germans, not to follow Adam's Apple or meddle with smugglers.

The clock was again moved to the side table.

'Claudine, what's wrong?'

She turned towards me, her dark eyes wide. 'Wrong? No. Nothing. Do let's go for a drink, but not here. Let's go down to the beach. You like the Albatroz, don't you? I'll drive.'

I grabbed my bag and hat and followed Claudine to a little black Peugeot with diplomatic tags. She slid behind the wheel and jammed the key in the ignition.

'I'm so glad to have met you, Solange. Did I say that?'

'No.' I stretched out my legs. 'But it's nice to hear.'

Claudine thrust the car into gear and pulled away from the kerb, narrowly missing a man on a bicycle. He held up his fist but his words were drowned out by the car's engine. She veered into the wrong lane while waving at a mother with two children. The woman yanked her children out of harm's way, almost throwing them against a fence. At the next turn, I was slammed against the door as we narrowly missed a man sweeping up fallen blossoms under a wall of purple bougainvillea.

'Are you trying to kill them or me?' I braced myself against the dashboard as Claudine manoeuvred around an elderly woman. 'Let's go to the Parque instead.'

My nails dug in to the leather as the hotel blurred past. There was no way the Peugeot could take the turn at the bottom at this speed. Claudine's nose wrinkled.

'Pah, too many Germans.'

'The Palácio?'

'Too many English. Relax, Solange. I never hit anything I'm not aiming at.'

'There's a first time for everything.'

143

Closing my eyes only made the ride worse. The shoreline was coming up fast as Claudine accelerated on to the coast road and headed towards Cascais. People and restaurants whipped past before she skidded into the car park.

'See? No new dents – no blood spilt,' she grinned and cut the engine.

The Peugeot spluttered before falling into affronted silence. It was a wonder Christophe allowed her to drive it. Or to drive at all. Singing came from a small church, no bigger than a garage, which stood in front of the restaurant.

'They're thanking God that you haven't killed me, yourself, and half the people on the coast. Just so you know, I'm walking home.'

She laughed. Linking her arm in mine, she led the way into the restaurant.

'A table for two,' she asked the maître d'. 'In the shade, please. My friend burns easily.'

'Of course, senhora.'

He signalled to a young man in a dark suit and a white shirt who led us to a table under an umbrella on the terrace. Claudine's eyes lingered on him as she slid into her seat.

'Perfect,' she sighed.

A short, round man weaved his way to our table. Beads of sweat stood out on his forehead as he placed menus in front of us. As I reached out for mine, she waved it away.

'Two Pernods. And have the other man bring them. The young one with the glossy hair.'

'Senhora,' he said and retreated.

Claudine turned to me with a little smile. I rolled my eyes, amused despite myself, and turned my face into the sun. She reached into her bag for a compact and a lipstick and preened when the young waiter set the sweating glasses on the table. Her long fingers were pale against the brown of his hand.

'*Obrigada*,' she purred.

'Would you like me to go for a walk?'

'Why on earth would you do that, Solange?'

The waiter seized the opportunity to retreat.

'What is wrong with you, Claudine?'

'Excuse me?'

'This mood you're in. I don't know what's happened, but something's wrong.'

She looked out to sea, then down at her hands, as if she wasn't sure if she should tell me anything, although she clearly wanted to. I lit a cigarette and waited for her to make up her mind.

'Christophe,' she sighed.

'What about him?'

'I don't know. Last night he left the casino to meet Hans and Haydn for a late drink.'

Hans? Hans Bendixen? Was that what Christophe was involved in?

Claudine twisted her wedding band around her finger.

'He came back at dawn.'

She stared out to sea. Then her expression changed; her eyes widened and her body went rigid. She took three fast steps to the terrace's railing. Her face was leeched of colour and she screamed.

'Bodies!'

The afternoon crowd surged to the railing to see the grisly tide. Some remained on the terrace sipping their cocktails, and for a moment, I was back in London. I was back in London and my friend Kat Christie was prying a flimsy piece of paper from my fist, reading aloud.

'Dear Mrs de Mornay, We are sorry to inform you that your husband's frigate came under heavy attack by German U-boats off the coast of Greenland . . .'

'Solange?' Claudine shook my arm, her brow furrowing. She repeated my name, but it was Kat's voice I heard.

'It badly damaged a German submarine, before taking a torpedo. I regret to tell you, Mrs de Mornay, that there were no survivors. Our condolences on your husband's death. He had an exemplary record and was a hero; much loved by his crew . . .'

I pushed on to the beach. In subarctic waters, Philip didn't have a chance, but these men . . . maybe they had a chance. The heels of my sandals caught on the stones, and I ripped them off, leaving them as they lay. Hot sand burnt my feet, and along with the bodies, the tide brought in shards of metal and wood, clothing and life jackets.

'English,' a low voice confirmed in a nasal American accent as he and two other men dragged a body out of the water. The sailor's uniform was tattered, his fair hair crusted with sand and seaweed. The tip of his nose was missing and wide eyes stared sightless at the sky.

Where the breakwater tamed the tide near a stone villa, an old man struggled to pull a second body from the sea. Determined to help, I threw myself into the surf, ignoring the tide dragging at my skirt and the rocks slicing my feet. I tried to grab an arm and missed. Where his arm should have been was nothing but algae and salt water.

'*Tubarão*,' the old man said. 'Shark.'

More a blast than a shark, I guessed, gripping the man's belt. Buffeted by the tide, we dragged the dead sailor on to the shore. He was also missing his left leg from the knee down. There was no need to check a pulse.

'*Morto*.'

Breathing hard, the old man fell to his knees, his gnarled fingers gentle as he closed the sailor's eyes. He crossed himself and said a prayer, the Latin strangely comforting. He bowed to me and stumbled down the beach.

Instead of the dead sailor's sandy hair, I saw Philip's dark curls. I brushed a lock of hair from his forehead and sat beside him. I would keep him company until someone came with a stretcher to take him away.

'I'm sorry,' I whispered, unsure if I was apologising to this nameless man or to Philip for that last argument, punctuated by slamming doors and shattered crystal. Had another woman sat by Philip's body and hoped he'd left home with a sweetheart's kiss on his lips?

'I think, senhora, that these are yours.'

I shielded my eyes against the blinding sun. A man held my sandals out to me; put them on the sand when I didn't move.

'It was very brave, what you did.'

His English was accented and I recognised the waiter from the Albatroz. Claudine still stood on the terrace, watching me. Had she sent him? Asked him to speak to me in English? Or was it his own initiative? I cocked my head as if I hadn't understood his words. When he repeated them in French, I shrugged.

'Anyone would have done the same.'

'No, senhora. Not everyone would go in the water after a dead English sailor.'

He had noticed the dead men's uniforms. There was no point in pretending I hadn't.

'He's still a man, regardless of what uniform he wears.'

For a moment his eyes mirrored my own exhaustion.

'You are a good woman, senhora.'

He left me alone with my memories, and a silent reminder not to trust anyone, no matter how innocent they seemed. I dug my feet into the wet sand, pushing against the mud, reality, and maybe my own nature, wondering what the devil I was doing here.

I expelled a deep sigh and glanced again at the terrace. There was no sign of Claudine, but in her place, watching me, was the man I'd seen sweeping away the dead blossoms near my villa.

148

Chapter Sixteen

Sadness turned to irrational anger at the human cost of war. Every time I closed my eyes, I saw the dead English sailor. I paced my villa, dosed myself with brandy, and only fell into a restless sleep shortly before sunrise.

The anger had festered overnight, and by mid-morning I stomped down to the cellar. A previous owner had decorated the walls with heavy walnut panelling, although why was anyone's guess, when there were serviceable rooms on the ground floor. Most of the walls now were hidden behind crates, boxes, and broken furniture. I pushed a trunk out of the way and chalked three concentric circles on the wall. My housekeeper, Sabela, was competent. She cleaned, she cooked, she provisioned the kitchen, and no doubt she informed on me. To Matthew, and whoever else bribed her. The holes in the wall were one of the things I made certain she knew nothing of.

I unsheathed Alex's sgian dubh. It had become second nature to strap it on in the mornings. I knew how to stab, to shoot, but I'd seen this blade fly, and that could be useful. Pacing to the far side of the room, I remembered what Alex said, and mimicked his stance from memory. Turned, and flung the knife at the wooden panelling. It landed with a soft thunk, quivering just inside the largest circle. I was nowhere near as proficient as he had been, but with practice, I was improving. Halfway through the session, the telephone rang. Leaving the knife in the wall, I raced up the stairs for the receiver.

'Yes?'

'Good afternoon, Solange. Did I interrupt you?'

Yes. 'No.'

'Oh. I wanted to see how you were. After yesterday . . .'

'I'm fine.' I wasn't, and even Claudine could hear it in my voice. Who would be after pulling a dead man from the sea? 'I'm not, of course, but I will be. It was just a shock.'

'Your husband was killed at sea, wasn't he? That was why you went into the water?'

'Yes.' I surprised myself with my own candour. 'It doesn't matter which uniform those men wore, they deserve a decent burial. I'd really rather not talk about that. I'll be fine.'

'Good. I'm glad to hear that.' She cleared her throat and forged on. 'I was wondering if you had plans for this evening.'

'Claudine, I'd rather not go back to the casino.'

'Oh, that's good. I wasn't about to suggest that. There's a small soirée tonight, a slightly different set from the people you met at the Ribauds'. I know it's rather last minute, but they really are nice people. One of Christophe's friends has found himself dateless, and I hoped –'

My mouth sagged open. 'You're trying to set me up?'

'Oh no. Nothing of the sort. Just something to take your mind off that. Come, Solange. Do this as a favour. For me. Can you really picture me at a boring German soirée, with pompous German officers and their frumpy German *Frauen*? You know how much they detest Frenchwomen! I won't have a single person to talk to!'

'I thought you liked the Germans.'

'I do. In small doses. Please say you'll come.'

Let them come to you, Matthew had advised. Well, thanks to Claudine the invitations were coming, along with the *bufos*. At the prospect of, perhaps, meeting Bendixen, a faint tingle crept up my spine.

'Very well, Claudine. I'll go.'

The doorbell rang at ten o'clock. I fastened the second sapphire earring and stood back to inspect myself. The matching necklace grazed the top of a low décolletage. My own jewellery was back in London, and over the last few weeks, I'd spent part of my casino winnings building a collection.

The Lanvin gown was stunning in its simplicity, cut as if it was made to order. Thick silk straps perched at the edge of my shoulders and crossed over my breasts. The waistline was fitted and the full skirt, captured at each hip, gave the impression of an A-line dress with a small train. Deep blue wasn't my favourite colour, but it turned my skin to alabaster and made my eyes enormous. Long kid gloves and silver ribbons in my hair completed the ensemble.

The bell rang again. I dabbed perfume at the base of my neck and applied a coat of red lipstick and opened the door, hoping the Deschamps' friend wasn't too awful.

Claudine kissed my cheeks and Christophe smiled, the emotion not reaching his eyes.

'Solange, may I present Major Schüller? Haydn, my lovely neighbour, Solange Verin.'

Ah, the Haydn he had drinks with the other night. I held out my hand to the major with the cat eyes.

'Haydn?' I asked. 'Like the composer?'

'Just so. A pleasure, Frau Verin.'

Claudine held up a bottle of Veuve Cliquot, sweating in the evening heat.

'A quick drink before we go?'

Christophe opened the bottle, pouring the champagne as the major wandered around my parlour, pausing at the gramophone.

'You look beautiful tonight,' I said.

Claudine's gown was a pale gold taffeta, sleeveless, with a high quilted neck and beading at the hem. Eye-catching, but not enough to camouflage the deepening lines on her face.

Her smile was wry. 'Do you really think so?'

The major clinked his glass against mine. '*Prost*. To new friends.'

His slow smile told me what sort of friend he was after, but I was determined to be polite.

'Where are you from, Herr Major?'

'Vienna. Have you ever visited it?'

'Once, when I was fourteen. It's a beautiful city. The opera house is exquisite.'

His eyes cut first to the piano and then to the gramophone, which now played a piano sonata composed by his namesake. At least he had a sense of humour.

'You like the opera?' he asked.

'No, Herr Major, I *love* the opera.'

He inclined his head. 'And who do you prefer? Bizet? Wagner?'

I was unable to prevent myself from needling him.

'Carmen was the only thing Bizet wrote worth remembering. And Wagner is too heavy for my tastes. I confess, I prefer the Italians – Verdi, Donizetti, Rossini. Not a bad note between them.'

'Italians,' Christophe muttered.

'Whatever you have to say about them, Christophe, you can't fault their music. Or their gelato.' Claudine flashed a fake smile and put her empty glass on the sideboard. 'Come, darling –' she linked her arm in her husband's – 'let's go.'

Christophe extricated himself, placing his flute beside Claudine's and making his way to the door. Her teeth bit into her lower lip as she trailed behind him. Schüller opened both doors on the right side of the Peugeot, settling Claudine in front and sliding into the back, pressing his knee against mine.

It was going to be a long night.

'He's handsome,' Claudine hissed once the men were out of earshot. 'Charming *and* well placed. Please be civil!'

'I am being civil.'

After all, I haven't stabbed the pompous bore yet, I silently added.

With a half-smile frozen on my face, I watched the room. Bronze silk curtains complemented the enormous oil paintings: nymphs and satyrs, lords and ladies, young men and old, with uniforms dating back to the Great War. It could have been one of Lady Anne's drawing rooms.

'For pity's sake, Solange! He's eligible! Make an effort, will you?' Her eyes widened. '*Please!*'

'Stop meddling.'

She gave me a filthy look and waggled her fingers, urging me in the Austrian's direction. He stood at a makeshift bar in the corner, flanked by Christophe and another man.

'Oh, very well.'

She was right – it wouldn't do to be a wallflower; there was always the chance I could learn something interesting. I accepted a glass of champagne from a waiter, and listened to snippets of conversation. Congratulations were being exchanged, but I had yet to learn what for. Perhaps the major knew.

'Fairly imminent, from what I'm hearing,' the man beside Christophe said. He was the man I'd seen the first night in the casino. The one who had pointed his young friend in my direction. I strained to catch the gist of the conversation before they noticed me. 'The only question is whether it will be Sicily or Sardinia.'

'Sardinia,' Schüller declared. 'Most certainly. And the Führer agrees. Troops have already been sent to reinforce the island.'

A laughing couple edged past me, causing me to miss his next sentence. All I caught were the words 'Marine' and 'Something something Major Martin'. Martin? That didn't sound like a German name. Perhaps a German spy? I sidled closer.

The older man sipped his drink. His eyes were unfocused, but his words were sly.

'Graf seems certain Sardinia is a bluff, that it'll be Sicily.'

'What does Graf know?' the Austrian laughed. 'Surely not more than the Führer!'

'No, I wouldn't think so.' The man paused, seeing me hovering. Schüller smiled. 'Ah, Frau Verin, I see you couldn't wait for a drink?'

I raised an eyebrow and held up my glass of champagne.

'Then it must be my company you're after,' he smirked, settling his free hand on my bottom.

I ignored their amused looks as I shifted out of the major's reach, intrigued enough by their conversation to ignore his bad manners.

'Please, don't let me interrupt you.'

'No, my dear,' the older man said. 'Don't let me interrupt you. A Viennese waltz is playing, and I am certain the Herr Major would like to show you off.'

'Thank you, Herr . . . ?'

'Von Hoyningen-Huene. Enjoy your dance.'

I forced a smile and held out my hand. 'Herr Major?'

'Haydn,' he corrected.

He nodded to von Hoyningen-Heune and, placing my hand on his arm, led me on to the dance floor.

'This soirée,' I began, my curiosity getting the better of me. 'Is it for any particular reason?'

'Why do you ask?'

He pulled me close as we twirled around a rotund couple, the woman glittering in diamonds, her gown straining at the seams. The man's upper body bulged over the top of what must be a corset.

'Because at every turn, people are congratulating each other. It's either that, or we're at a wedding reception and the happy couple are nowhere to be seen.'

Another officer danced past, paused and smiled at Schüller.

'Well done, Herr Major.'

Schüller inclined his head and I saw an opportunity for a *quid pro quo*.

'Is it my company he's congratulating you on?'

His blue cat's eyes danced. 'As well.'

Clearly he was enjoying being privy to something I was not. Either he'd tell me in his own time, or someone else would. Claudine, no doubt, would have all the relevant details by the end of the evening.

We danced in silence, pausing as one man after another met Schüller's eyes. He basked in their adulation. I stifled a yawn, hoping Claudine was as bored as I was.

'We concluded a successful venture yesterday,' Schüller finally offered.

'Venture?'

That was a strange choice of words. I'd expected 'battle' or 'campaign'. *Venture?*

'One that went according to plan. Again.' He slid his hand down my back.

Picking the gossip out of Claudine was a better option. I saw her crossing the dance floor, so I made my excuses and followed her to the lavatory.

'Are you having a good time, Solange? I saw you speaking with the ambassador earlier. Isn't he charming?'

'Who?'

She rolled her eyes. 'Baron von Hoyningen-Huene. Germany's ambassador to Portugal. Didn't you know?'

'No. I also don't know why everyone is stopping us every three feet to congratulate Major Schüller.'

'Didn't Christophe tell you?' Claudine asked, leaning close to the looking glass to inspect her face.

'Christophe didn't tell me anything. Your husband barely talks to me.'

She dusted her face, masking the signs of exhaustion.

'Christophe never talks to anyone. Don't take it personally.'

'I'm not. But your major is playing I-know-something-you-don't-know, and it's driving me mad.'

She grinned. 'So he is getting to you. I'm so pleased!'

I gritted my teeth. Schüller was getting to me, all right. If Christophe wanted to take an easy bet, he'd put his money on me slapping the Austrian before the evening was out.

'How can you not know!' a bejewelled matron exclaimed. 'And you with the Herr Major! A marvellous victory, our Luftwaffe sank two Allied ships the day before yesterday, and another one yesterday!' She leant in close. 'He received personal congratulations of the *Fliegerführer Atlantik*!'

Focke-Wulfs over the cliffs of Cabo de São Vicente. A burning convoy. Mangled bodies in the sea. Whatever else was happening with the smuggling, here was another threat: someone was informing the Luftwaffe of Allied ships leaving port, and I'd bet anything the trail led back to Haydn Schüller.

Chapter Seventeen

The Linha Ferroviária connected the coastal towns to Lisbon, for the people who didn't have a motor car or the funds to pay a driver, and by ten o'clock, the carriage at Estoril was still crowded. I took a seat and opened a newspaper a previous commuter had left behind. I couldn't understand the language, but it was useful enough to fan myself with, and occasionally swat away the hand of the overfamiliar man beside me.

The train terminated at the Cais do Sodré and I followed the other tourists past the Praça do Comércio with its statue of a very bored King José I, through the Arco da Vitória towards the Chiado, the shopping district. Side by side, the similarities of the window displays were hard to miss. Whether they supported Germany or the Allies, the same underlying themes were there. Like two companies plying completing products.

What was harder to miss was the *bufo*. Every time I turned around, he was there, and time was getting tight. I continued north to the Rossio, and the press of tourists, mingling and making minor changes to my costume until I felt certain that by the time I doubled back, slipping into the dingy bar at the edge of the Bairro Alto, the *bufo* not only was lost, but he wouldn't recognise me if he did see me. I sat down, ordered a drink, and waited.

*

'Be careful, my dear. You're dangerously close to acquiring the Portuguese melancholy,' the man lisped.

He slipped into the chair opposite and pushed across a glass with a couple of fingers of brandy. He was taller than most Portuguese, but had the same swarthy skin, the same round face crowned with black hair and moustache. What hadn't changed was the nose, aristocratic and aquiline.

'You need to learn to talk with those things,' I told my godfather.

'What things?'

'The pads fleshing out your cheeks. You're lisping like a little girl.' Paused for effect. 'Or a pansy.'

He graced me with a filthy look.

'Besides, it's not melancholy, Matthew. It's a hangover.'

'Good night at the casino?'

'Didn't go to the casino. German reception at some villa in Cascais.'

'You shouldn't drink so much – it's unladylike.'

'Since when have you concerned yourself with my manners?'

He tilted his head, conceding the point. 'Did you learn anything interesting?'

'Despite apparently meeting the German ambassador, all I have is speculation. Will the Allies run their way up the Boot from Sicily or cross over from Sardinia?'

'The consensus?'

'Sardinia. Their troops are already reinforcing the island, but who knows?' I looked at him closely. 'What do you know about a man called Martin?'

His face was carefully blank. 'Who?'

'Martin. A major in the Royal Marines, I take it.'

'It's a common enough name.' The tip of his nose twitched. For a diplomat whose life depended on deception, it would give him away in an instant, to anyone who knew to look for it. 'Why do you ask?'

My blasé tone matched his. 'I've never met the chap of course, but some of the Germans were discussing him.'

'How very interesting.' He scratched his nose and looked at me warily. 'What were they saying?'

'They stopped as soon as they saw me.' I leant back and smiled. 'Fancy telling me what's happening?'

He reached into his breast pocket for a silver case, extracted a small thin cigar and sniffed it.

'To be honest, old girl, I really don't know much. The chap was found dead in the water off the coast of Spain last month. Supposedly had documents of some sort on him, but as to what they were, I genuinely don't know.' He studied the cigar for a few seconds. 'Whoever he was, he was buried with military honours, poor sod.'

'Ours or theirs?'

His face was serene and the twitch had subsided. 'Theirs.'

'Ah,' I said. 'What did they find in those documents?'

Matthew shrugged. 'Your guess is as good as mine.'

'Well,' I raised my glass, 'to the major. Hope he really did die a hero.'

'Hear, hear,' Matthew murmured, raising his glass. 'And when we need all the heroes we can get.'

'So you *do* think invasion is imminent?'

'Which invasion, old girl?'

'Italy. What else is being planned?'

160

There had been rumours of an invasion of France, but the last one, Dieppe, had been a disaster. Was that it? Let the Germans think we were invading Italy and instead invade France?

'No idea, old girl.' He drew on the cigar, exhaling a small cloud of smoke. 'Yes, I do think an invasion of Italy is imminent. Sardinia seems as good a guess as any.'

I fumbled for my own cigarettes, allowing my godfather to light one for me.

'And what then? Do you think the Italians will depose Mussolini? Switch sides?'

'Italy won't switch sides.'

My hand froze, the glass halfway to my lips.

'What are you talking about? Of course they will.'

The speculation was rife – not only about Italy, but the impact her fall would have on the other Fascist states.

'They'll try, I'll grant you that, but it won't happen.' He sipped his brandy. 'They've spent the last few years as staunch allies to the Germans. Who'd trust them? No, my dear. Surrender is their only option. Unconditional. And then the ugliness begins.'

'You think the Germans will invade *Italy*?'

'They won't have a choice. Be surprised if plans weren't already in action. They can't afford to lose the Boot.'

'What aren't you telling me?'

'Nothing, actually. You know about as much as I do.'

I looked around. The bar was small and dank, catering more for locals than foreigners, but it had a feel, a vibrancy, which was rare in the European haunts. In the corner, a young man with a guitar sang *fado* in a rich tenor. On either side of him were men plucking on guitars – on the left a conventional one, on the right, a teardrop-shaped guitar with a lot more strings. The *fadisto*'s unintelligible words washed over me as I watched the man across from me. In a strange way, the disguise suited him. The heavy make-up gave him a swarthy look, and with the silver erased from his hair and moustache, he looked younger. Dangerous. Like a buccaneer in the films.

'Is this why you wanted to meet? To let me know the political lie of the land?'

He laughed – a deep rich sound. 'If you didn't know that by now, I'd be tremendously disappointed, old girl.'

'Why break your own rule and request a meeting? Awful lot of effort to lose a tail, for a social call.'

He sipped his brandy and replaced the glass carefully on the table. One fingertip rubbed the rim – delicate against the heavy tumbler, too delicate for the rough cotton shirt he wore.

'I saw you at the beach last week.'

'So?'

'The day the British sailors were washed ashore.' He watched me with hawklike eyes.

It was easier to talk about Mussolini's imminent fall, but I would never admit that to Matthew.

'So?'

He cleared his throat. 'So not everyone died.'

My pulse, which had been keeping beat with the guitar, accelerated.

'Well, that's good news.'

'It is, indeed.'

He was giving nothing away, and I was in no mood for games. 'All right, Spider. What do you need from me?'

162

He snorted. 'I was rather hoping you'd forgotten that nickname. What I need from you, my dear, is a favour.'

Another one?

'What sort of favour?'

'A survivor was washed up. Farther down the beach, near Carcavelos.'

'One of the men from the ships that sunk the other day?'

'You heard about that?' Matthew whispered. He looked around, but no one appeared to be interested in us.

The young *fadisto* accepted a glass and a searing look from the waitress. Patted his face with a towel and picked up his guitar.

'What do you think last night's reception was in honour of, Matthew?' He grimaced and I continued, 'Someone's keeping the Luftwaffe informed about the convoys. Someone with a wireless stashed nearby, I'd guess. Something needs to be done about that.'

'With four ships sunk in the last month, and a fifth damaged, we have some of our best men working on it.'

'If you'll allow a woman to speed things up, have one of your men look into Major Haydn Schüller. Not sure what his role is or where he's based, but I'm working on it.'

He nodded, rubbing his eyes. 'Appreciate that, my dear. Good job.'

'So – about this sailor. You want me to question him?'

'He's not a sailor. He's one of yours. Caught a ride home with our boys after he got into a spot of trouble.'

The *fadisto* launched into a new song. I didn't understand the words, but he sang with his heart and soul. It didn't distract me from one nagging worry: why would the Spider risk my cover when there were others better equipped to debrief the man?

'Ask one of the chaps here in an official capacity.'

'I can't.' His face darkened under the heavy make-up. 'I won't. I need you to do it.'

'Why me?'

'Because you were in France, and you got out. You know what it's really like.' He twirled the brandy in its glass and we both watched the amber liquid rise and fall in waves. 'I want to make sure he's genuine.'

'I thought you didn't want me compromised by showing up to one of your parties.'

'If anyone can disguise herself without – how did you say it? "Lisping like a little girl"? – it's you.'

His hand caught mine, and he brought it to his lips. He gave me directions and finished his drink.

'I'll expect you tomorrow. Shall we say three o'clock?' he said to me before leaving.

A middle-aged couple at the next table looked at me, the woman with curiosity, the man as if I emanated a bad smell. Women didn't sit by themselves in bars – at least not women with a decent upbringing. His lips pursed and he made a strange wheezing sound. The woman slapped him lightly on the arm.

With a bright smile, I made a show of lighting a cigarette and ordering another drink, enjoying the disgust that passed over the man's face.

I left the bar in the Bairro Alto and took my time wandering around the city, stopping in Chiado to buy a new hat, a scarf, and a pair of espadrilles. At each stop, making the slight changes that would return my looks to something the gardener-*bufo* would recognise.

He found me not long after I entered the Rossio, and this time I made eye contact with him. Walked to a café smaller, and less frenetic than the Chave d'Ouro, ordered two cups of coffee, and waited.

The man who joined me ten minutes later wasn't the gardener. This man was about my height, a couple of inches shy of six feet, slim, with olive skin, and large, beautiful black eyes – the sort that made people want to trust him, even if it was against every inclination. This man might be more of a spider than Matthew.

'Not so many years ago,' he said in softly accented French. 'these cafés were almost exclusively male.'

I looked around at the women and families surrounding me. 'Quite a lot has changed since then.'

'Yes, senhora. Even here.' He sat down across from me.

'I don't believe I invited you to join me, sir.'

He indicated the cup of coffee, cooling in front of him. 'Have you not, Senhora Verin?'

'Who are you? How do you know who I am?'

He nodded, expecting this reaction. 'My name is Adriano de Rios Vilar. You have heard my name?'

There was no point in feigning ignorance. Not yet.

'I believe you were the officer who informed Madame Billiot of her husband's demise?'

'Ah, yes. It was an unfortunate accident,' he said. 'And avoidable.'

'How does one avoid an accident?'

165

'He indicated that he was travelling in one direction, when in fact his intention was otherwise.' Little effort was made to veil the warning, and his forthright expression dared me to challenge him. 'Most regrettable.'

'Regrettable? For whom?'

The words were out of my mouth before I could stop them. What was I thinking of, toying with the PVDE?

A glimmer of amusement lit his eyes. 'For Senhora Billiot. And her husband, naturally.'

He raised the cup and took a small sip of the coffee, his gaze never leaving mine.

'Naturally,' I echoed. 'So, what is your interest in me?'

An elegant eyebrow rose as the cup was replaced in its saucer.

'Straight to the point, senhora? I admire that.' He threw a note on the table. 'Come. Walk with me.'

Despite his polite smile and cordial tone, his words weren't a request. My right hand dropped to my lap, brushing against the hilt of the sgian dubh, hidden beneath my skirt. It was scant reassurance, but all I had.

I forced a smile and followed him out of the café into the humid Portuguese twilight.

Chapter Eighteen

'Are you arresting me?' I asked as soon as we were far enough from the crowded café.

'Do I have a reason to?' he asked.

'In France, a reason wasn't required. People inform on friends and neighbours. Rivals. Do you want to know why I'm here? I know there are rumours, some of them quite colourful. The truth is, I'm here because a nasty little man couldn't take rejection. He pursued me from the start. And when he learnt of my husband's death, he was relentless. When he finally realised that his efforts were futile, he informed on me. So it was either be detained by the Gestapo, or flee. I chose to flee.'

It made for a good story, even more because every damned word of it was true. I hoped Madame Renaud and the rest of the Resistance had caught up with Jean-Roger Demarque.

'Were you? Part of the Resistance?'

'Don't be daft,' I snapped, then continued in a more amused tone. 'If I was part of the Resistance, do you really think I'd go to Portugal and spend my time with the Germans?' After another few steps, I turned to face him with my hands on my hips. 'And that's my rather dull, rather common story. I can't believe you shower this much attention on all émigrés.'

'I do not, no.'

For a moment, his expressive eyes betrayed his intelligence and determination. We walked for a minute or two in silence.

'Portugal is a small country. A neutral country, senhora. To maintain that neutrality, we must walk a delicate line . Before the war, we had few tourists, much less immigrants. And now you see, we are inundated with immigrants. Refugees. Some are desirable, they adapt to our climate, our culture. They add to our economy, and our society. Others, less so.'

Like Monsieur Billiot.

'And you think I'm . . . ?'

'That remains to be seen, senhora, and you have an uncanny ability to escape notice when, I think, it is convenient for you.' Before I could voice a protest, he gestured to a pair of shop-fronts. Side by side, they held similar propaganda, but each supporting different sides. Rios Vilar stopped in front of the German one. 'They say he is the last bastion, keeping the communists at bay.'

'So you . . .?'

'I do not care. Let me be clear – my interest is neither with the Germans, nor the British. It is Portugal. Only Portugal.' He held up a hand to still any comment. 'And, as with the other internationals here, as long as you keep your business to yourself and do not trip the delicate balance, I do not care what you do. But the moment that balance is tripped, Senhora Verin, you will have more than my interest to contend with.'

There was only one answer, accompanied by a polite smile.

'Then neither of us have anything to worry about, Senhor Rios Vilar.'

Rios Vilar consulted his wristwatch, and murmured a polite goodbye, leaving me in front of the shopfront with a photograph of the Führer staring out at me.

'Last bastion against communism, my foot,' I muttered, refraining from giving it the two-fingered salute.

Rios Vilar and his men had been watching me, but what had they seen? Had they come with me to Sagres, or had I lost them by then? And how much of the smuggling were they aware of – or worse, sanctioned?

He said he didn't care who I was and what I did, as long as it didn't tip the balance, but of course it would. That was what Matthew wanted, what I had been determined to do from the time I walked into Special Operations' office at Orchard Court and agreed to work for them. Did he know that? Did he know who and what I was?

And if so, was he friend or foe?

Chapter Nineteen

Wary of Rios Vilar's *bufos*, I took my time, ensuring they saw Solange in the crowds at the Rossio, before donning a blonde wig and a pair of dark sunglasses in a café's lavatory. It was a rudimentary disguise, but people often saw what they wanted.

I took two trams and walked along the Rua de São Bernardo, noting again how incongruous it was that the German embassy was virtually across the street from the British embassy. Continued down a handful of side streets to the address Matthew had given me. It was an office building, rather than a house per se. The sort favoured by small organisations that couldn't afford exclusive premises. The people coming in and out of the building were remarkably unremarkable. Much like the people who worked for Special Operations, who did a fair share of work at the flat in Orchard Court instead of Baker Street. It provided deniability, anonymity, and a venue away from the prying eyes of their neighbours.

At half past one, the lunch crowd returned to their respective buildings and I fell into step behind a pair of middle-aged men with the slightly glazed look that comes with one too many lunchtime martinis. I tucked a long blonde lock behind my ear, hoping no one noticed one more secretary returning to work. The man at the reception desk gave me a cursory glance as

I swapped the sunglasses for a pair with clear lenses and tortoiseshell frames. Sweat trickled down his forehead as he fanned himself with a large envelope.

A small statue of Christ stood on top of a stack of folders on a table of an unoccupied office on the first floor, proving itself an unusual and rather ineffective guard. I slid the top file out from under him and tucked it under my arm. Cruised the halls until I glimpsed my godfather sliding into an office at the end.

'May I help you?'

An older woman with the face of a bulldog blocked my way.

'I have a file for Sir Matthew.' I held it up for inspection.

'He's not in his office.'

She folded her arms over her ample bosom, daring me to pass.

'I think I just saw him, but if he's not in, may I leave it with you?' I asked. 'I haven't had time to eat yet and I'm absolutely famished.'

'You really shouldn't.' She eyed the folder hungrily.

For all I knew, it was someone's expenses, but drew it close to my chest.

'I suppose you're right.'

The bulldog's lips rose in a parody of a smile. 'Nonsense, I was only joshing. It's fine. We're on the same side, aren't we?'

I wasn't so sure, but I gave her a tentative smile. 'Of course. But, look, there he is.'

When she turned to look, I navigated around her, and slipped through the door Matthew had just entered. He was sitting at his desk with a set of files open in front of him. A few photographs were pushed aside as he rummaged through the papers.

'Thank you,' he said without looking up. 'Put it over there, will you?'

I raised my eyebrows and complied, but instead of leaving, I leant against the wall. The office was spacious, panelled in walnut, with a matching desk and green leather visitors' chairs. The third shelf of the bookcase held photographs, and I was drawn to it like a magnet. There had been no photographs in Special Operations' offices. There was some sense in that, although Matthew wasn't often one to take unnecessary risks.

'You may go,' he said, his voice sing-song.

'And I thought you'd invited me here,' I said, tossing my hat on top of the file.

His head snapped up, surprised. He blinked.

'Cat got your tongue?' I asked, pulling off my spectacles.

He laughed and stood up; closed the door on his way to me. He kissed my check before holding me back at arm's length.

'I was right. Blonde hair and you *are* a dead ringer for Veronica Lake.'

'Veronica Lake is just shy of five feet tall,' I reminded him.

'A taller version, then.' Smiling, he reached for the folder. 'No trouble getting in?'

'Disappointingly, no. It was harder to lose Adriano Rios Vilar's *bufos* than it was to get in.'

Sharp black eyes were suddenly interested. 'You've met him, have you?'

'Briefly. He gave me a polite warning not to disrupt the "delicate balance" of Portuguese neutrality.'

He paused, taking his time to slide the papers into their files, then stacking them on a corner of his desk. When he looked at me his eyes were serious.

'Do I need to tell you to do what you must to ensure you don't get caught?'

He didn't, and my expression must have been enough of an answer to him. This time, when he looked away it was to leaf through the file I carried in.

'Now then,' he said. 'What have we here?'

'Something I picked up along the way. Interesting, is it?'

'Not particularly,' he replied, leafing through it again.

I wasn't sure I believed him, and shaking off a faint regret that I hadn't read it, I wandered over to the photographs. Most were political: Matthew with Churchill; with HRH King George; standing at some formal function between two men I didn't know.

'John Vereker and Kim Philby,' he explained.

John Vereker, Lord Gort, was the commander of the British Expeditionary Force in France back in '39, and a friend of my father's. I looked closer, surprised at how he'd aged. I had no idea who Philby was, but had the impression from the way that Matthew said his name that, despite displaying the photograph, despite the man clearly being important, Matthew wasn't fond of him.

My eyes moved to a neat row of personal snapshots: Matthew's wife Eleanor, beautiful and remote; Edgar, his firstborn, proud in his captain's uniform, and rather more attractive than the spotty-faced nuisance I remembered. Matthew posed with my father in the next one, clad in white jumpers and floppy hats. Matthew held a bat like a walking stick whilst Dad held aloft the trophy. They looked ridiculously young.

In the last photograph, taken from a distance, a fair-haired young girl straddled the branch of a willow tree, her toes grazing the river beneath her. I picked it up, bemused. Looked at him for an explanation.

'You broke your arm jumping from that tree a week later,' he said. 'I suppose I should take it down now that you're here.'

I traced the lines of the image, feeling a certain sadness for the girl's loss of innocence.

'Well.' He cleared his throat. 'Let's get on with this, shall we?'

Replacing the photograph on the shelf, I sank into a visitor's chair.

'Yes. This man you want me to interview?'

'Hubert Michael Jones.'

'And what's Mr Jones's story?'

'Says he's from Shoreditch,' Matthew said blandly. 'The accent's about right. Picked out for special service thanks to a French mother. He trained with your lot and parachuted into France in July '42.'

'You seem to have the full story. Why do you need me?'

Matthew recited Mr Jones's curriculum vitae as if by rote. 'Our Bertie fell foul of Jerry and was incarcerated last November.'

'I landed in France just before Christmas, Matthew,' I pointed out. 'I wouldn't know him.'

'No matter.' Those elegant fingers waved away my argument. 'He spent the last six months at Adolf's pleasure in Fresnes.

Escaped and made contact with the local Resistance. He was smuggled into Free France before catching a ride with the Royal Navy, bound for the White Cliffs of Dover.'

'So if your Mr Jones wasn't on the *Volturno* or the *Shetland* –' I named the two ships most recently sunk by the Luftwaffe – 'where was he?'

'Sub. They had engine trouble before leaving French waters. Put in here for about twenty-four hours and were off again.'

'Until Jerry caught up,' I said.

'Until Jerry caught up,' Matthew confirmed. 'The little scrapper seems to have survived an awful lot.'

'You should congratulate him.'

'I will,' Matthew said, standing up. 'As soon as I'm convinced he's telling the truth.'

'What makes you think he isn't?'

'Bit too convenient, my dear. He gets out of Fresnes, out of France and is the only survivor from a *submarine*? A tad too convenient. But . . .' Matthew sighed, 'his company awaits.'

Grateful that the Consul-General in Madrid was more trusting, I followed my godfather up a flight of stairs. He stopped briefly in another office to pass on a file. It wasn't until the man turned that I noticed his Adam's apple. I stepped back and kept my head down, hoping he wouldn't notice me, or worse – connect the blonde in front of him to the brunette from the train.

A secretary carrying a silver tray with tea and biscuits met us on the top floor. Matthew held the door open, allowing her to enter first. The summer heat was oppressive and the interview room was stifling. Sweat gathered under my wig and I wondered how long I'd last before having to take the blasted thing off.

Jones sat at a low table. He was short and squat, with eyes too close together and a neck that must have been left in France. His nose had been flattened from repeated breaks and he sported a white scar above his left eyebrow. A newer wound oozed through the white bandage taped to what should have been his hairline. He might not have been a bad-looking man once, but wasn't likely to be again.

He was mopping his brow as we entered, his massive hand freezing on his forehead at the sight of me. Bright eyes raked me from head to toe.

'Hallo, Mr Harrington.' He greeted Matthew cordially and returned his gaze to me. 'Hallo, miss. And miss.'

He nodded to the secretary as she put down the tray, poured three cups, and retreated.

'Good afternoon, Mr Jones,' I replied, not bothering to introduce myself. 'I understand you have an interesting story to tell.'

'Ain't a story, miss.'

He put the white handkerchief down and I realised that his hands weren't that large per se. They'd been bandaged in several layers of white linen.

'Very well then. Why don't you tell me what happened?'

He shrugged. 'Where do you want me to start?'

'The beginning. I want you to tell me your full name and why you were sent into France.'

'Bert Jones, at yer service.' He pulled a non-existent forelock; what little hair Nature had left him with was shaved off.

'Please proceed, Mr Jones.'

'Started simple enough. I was about to be shipped out to France with my unit when I shot me mouth off an' got hauled in.

Someone looked at me sheet an' asked if I spoke French. Mum was from Tours, wasn't she?' He selected a wafer, crunching on it noisily.

'And you volunteered?'

He spoke through a full mouth. 'CO called me in for a chat. Asked if I wanted to volunteer for "Special Service". Me, I thought it'd be safer than having Jerry shoot at me.' He shook his head, disgusted. Brushed the crumbs off his chest. 'Safe, my rosy arse.'

'Where were you trained?'

'For what? Started off at Beaulieu, then went to a few other sites.'

He tried to lift the porcelain cup; cursed as it threatened to slip from his bandaged hands.

'Tell us about it,' Matthew suggested.

'What do you want to know? The shooting was easy enough. Weapons, then fighting without weapons. I was pretty good at both.' He smirked.

'I have no doubt of that,' I said. I also had no doubt that whatever skills His Majesty's academy at Beaulieu taught Mr Jones would be put to good use once he returned to the East End. Even if those hands didn't heal. 'What else?'

He ticked them off. 'Signalling, how to move about at night, how to blow up an old railway line. Enough to make me pretty clear about this "Special Service" bollocks.' He ducked his head. 'Sorry, miss.'

I waved away the apology. 'And afterwards?'

'Stomped about Scotland for a bit. Then learnt to jump outta planes and the like.'

He looked closely at me, as if trying to determine if he'd surprised me. It would take a lot more than that.

'And then off to France?'

'I was s'posed to be dropped into a field near Tours last February. I knew the area – Mum's people was still there. Supposed to recruit the lot of 'em, then train 'em up in weapons. Fancy that – me, the weapons instructor,' he snorted.

I'd have bet he had a criminal record back in England.

'They were waiting for us at the airfield. The lights looked right enough. Four of 'em, forming an L.' He raised the cup to his lips again; his hands had begun to shake. 'Could have been laid out with a square. "It doesn't get better than this!" the dispatcher said, and kicked us down the hole.

'Glad to have been out of the plane too, miss. You have no idea how it stinks in there. Kerosene and petrol. Vomit and fear. Terrible.' He rubbed a bandaged hand over his eyes.

'There was a woman on the plane, pretty little thing. Green as you like the entire flight, but she weren't the one to be sick. No, it were the lad from Liverpool.' He shook his head in disgust. 'So we dropped. Halfway down, searchlights caught us.

'The girl dropped first,' Jones said, his eyes faraway.

'Always,' I murmured.

The instructors did it to spur on the men. And if it was more dangerous, at least it taught us to be self-reliant.

Jones stared at me and, finding the answer he sought, nodded.

'She was almost to the ground before they started firing. The Scouse got it first, still in the air. Then the girl, caught up in her ropes. Me and the other lad, we got off a couple of shots but I'm guessing they didn't want us dead, or we would be.'

It was the same thing I'd witnessed last March. We had been warned of the ambush, but not in time to abort the drop. The agents were killed, and it was a small miracle that we survived.

'Who was the other man?'

'Claude? Stocky man, about forty or so.'

I met Matthew's questioning glance and shrugged.

'Do you know Claude's surname?' I asked.

Jones looked at me with narrowed eyes. 'You wouldn't understand, miss. We wasn't s'posed to talk about ourselves. Claude weren't his real Christian name.'

'And what was yours?' Matthew asked.

'What? Told you. Bert Jones.'

'Your codename?'

'Oh, that. Ulysse, if you'll believe it.' His lips twisted. 'Greek chap what went to war, then took twenty years to get home. A girl I sh— stepped out with liked her lit'ratcha.'

Jones' voice had tightened as if he wondered how long it would take him to get home, and who would still be waiting.

'Is Claude still alive?' I asked.

He shrugged. 'Last I knew he was still in Fresnes.'

'So he didn't escape with you?'

'No, it was just me an' Marc an' Robert.'

I'd trained with an operative called Robert. Would SOE use the same codename for different men?

'Can you describe them?'

'Which one?'

'Both, Bert,' Matthew answered.

'Let's see. Marc was tall and skinny, thick glasses. Bookish but a good laugh. His idea that we escape. He'd already worked

179

it out, but couldn't do it on his own, like. We talked, decided to keep it small. Just the three of us. The more what knows, the bigger chance Jerry'll find out. Right?'

Matthew nodded. 'How did you communicate?'

'Hard not to. We was all in the same cell.'

'And Robert? What did he look like?'

'Robert looked like he'd stepped out of a bleedin' Hollywood film. Dark hair, dark eyes. Like that *Gone with the Wind* bloke.'

I swallowed. Rhett Butler: we used to tease Robert that he looked like Rhett Butler. A cold certainty gripped me, knowing I was about to hear how another friend died.

'Right, Bertie. Back to your capture,' Matthew said. 'Where did they take you?'

'Avenue Foch. Fifth floor. Questioned me ten ways from Sunday, they did.'

'You said nothing?'

'Of course I bloody said nothing,' he snarled. 'What do you think I am?'

'Better than they are, Mr Jones, and that's all that matters,' I murmured. 'Please continue.'

Jones stared into his half-empty tea cup. 'You have anything stronger than this?'

Matthew called for an aide to bring a bottle of Scotch. Jones reached for the bottle of Laphroaig with an appreciative smile which quickly turned horrified as the bottle began to slip through his bandaged hands. He looked at me, ashamed of his weakness. Gently pulling the bottle from his failing grip, I poured a generous serving into his teacup.

'Thanks, miss,' he mumbled as those mittens cradled the porcelain, carefully raising it to his lips.

As he slurped the Scotch, his eyes closed and he made a curious little sound, almost a whimper. Matthew looked down at him with pity. Jones put down the cup and stared out of the window. The sun was high and shimmered off the street below, but I didn't think he saw that.

'It were never the same twice,' he said. 'Sometimes it was one of them, sometimes more. Sometimes in French, sometimes English. Sometimes with fists. Sometimes with batons.'

His voice was no much more than a whisper, as if speaking the words forced him to relive it.

My friend Dominique had been interred at Avenue Foch for weeks before Jérôme got her out. She was a woman, and tiny. She must have endured that, and worse. How had she survived it? I looked away, desperate to get that image out of my mind.

'Did you see anyone you knew while you were there?' Matthew asked.

'They threw Claude and me in a cell with another Englishman. But after the first few hours, we just ignored him.'

'Why?'

'Because he kept trying to get us to say things.'

'Things?'

'Like where we were from, where we trained, an' what we were supposed to do. Who else we knew. Same bollocks yer asking, matter o' fact. Claude played with him for a while, making up outrageous stories, but then he got bored.'

'Who was this man? Do you remember his name?'

'Called hisself Peter Fearson, but I think he made that up.'

'Why?'

'If you was a traitor, would you want people to know yer real name?'

Jones tried to rub his eyes, but the bandages got in the way. He stared at them as if wondering how they'd got there.

'No, I suppose I wouldn't.' Matthew wrote down the name; we'd run it past Baker Street later. 'When were you transferred?'

'Lemme check my diary,' Jones said.

He'd been through a lot and was clearly exhausted. His manners, on display for my benefit, were slipping.

'Roughly?'

'Spring, I reckon. The flowers were blooming. Little yellow ones.'

'Daffodils?' I asked. 'Tell me about Fresnes, Mr Jones.'

'Lovely parties. Champers . . .'

'Mr Jones, please don't waste my time.'

He shrugged. 'As I said, three of us in a cell. Me an' Marc an' Robert.'

'Where was Claude? Strange you wouldn't have included your mate.'

Jones shrugged again. 'Didn't see him much inside. In a different cell, mebbe a different section.'

'Did they question you again? In Fresnes?' I asked.

'Did they, hell!' he snorted. 'Same questions as Avenue Foch. Methods a bit worse.'

His shoulders hunched and his arms crossed his body. His actions seemed unconscious and when he caught my eyes on him, he looked away. He picked up the delicate china in those awful mitts and drained the rest of the cup.

It was the words he didn't say that made me believe him.

'Such as?' Matthew asked.

'Such as things not fit for a lady's ears.'

He didn't expect me to press him. In lieu of words, or sympathy, I refilled Jones's cup and tried to keep my mind from conjuring images of what my captured friends would also have had to endure.

'Fair enough,' Matthew said. 'We'll discuss that later. Tell me how you escaped.'

'Bloody brilliant. Marc was working in the laundry. The officers had him do their cleaning as well. He started to pilfer bits of their uniforms. Plan was for him to nick three – we put them on and walk out.'

'Did it work?' I was fascinated by the simplicity of it.

'Too bloody right it did. Sorry, miss. We didn't have papers, but reckoned we'd be able to meet up with the local Resistance an' they'd help out.'

'Did they?'

He shook his head. 'Didn't get far before we were stopped. I was in the bushes having a piss – sorry, miss – when a couple of Germans stopped to see if we needed a ride. Me, I stayed hid and watched. They saw that the uniforms were a bit mixed. Marc, he tried to brazen it out. Didn't speak a word of German, but there are French gaolers, y'see. He was a good bloke, Marc was. Robert, he panicked an' ran. Got shot in the back. The others, they dragged Marc back to Fresnes.'

Shot in the back. Not Robert, it couldn't be. He was always at the head of the pack, but watched out for the stragglers. He wouldn't have run; running would have confirmed his guilt.

183

He knew that. So why the devil would he do that? What would *make* him do that?

'So Robert is dead,' I asked, the effort to keep my voice steady.

'Yes, miss. Checked him myself after they left.'

'Then what?' Matthew asked.

'Didn't bloody wait for them to come back. Scampered out of there right fast, I did.'

'Thank you, Mr Jones.'

Feeling faint, I moved to the window. Several storeys below, the daily routine of a country not actively at war continued. Cars moved up and down the streets, men strode in and out of the gates, briefcases in hand. England seemed outside time – another reality. Or maybe Lisbon was the dream. How could Robert be dead? He deserved better than a bullet in the back.

'You met the Resistance then, Bertie?' Matthew asked.

Jones nodded. 'Had to lose the uniform so stole a shirt an' trousers off a line. Knocked on a door and asked for help. Took a chance an' got lucky. The lass what opened the door was connected. Passed me over to one bloke, then another. Then they put me on a boat. Thought the next time I touched ground it'd be Portsmouth.' His voice was grim.

I took a small sip of tea and topped the cup up with a splash of Scotch.

'And then?'

'It were night. Quarter moon. Enough light to see, but mebbe not enough to be seen. They gave me an inflatable. Told me to row towards the sub. Lads on the boat, they threw me a rope an' helped me inside. Always hated boats. Don't fancy the waves.'

He raised his cup, smelled the fumes, and put it back down.

'They gave me dry clothes. 'Splained that we'd dive to get away from shore then cruise on the surface. Faster, you see.' Jones bit his lip. 'Weren't long after that. Coupla hours, mebbe? I'm on the bridge and the radio operator sounds a warning. "Dive!" the captain says. No one talks but everyone moves. Orders are whispered. But intense, you know? The officers all pool together, talkin' too low for me to hear.

'"Another sub," one of them tells me. The radio officer is real pale, like. Pulls off his headphones and looks scared. Kid couldn't have been eighteen.'

His voice came in gasps, as if by increasing his speed he could outpace the torpedo.

'"Hang on!" someone yelled, and I did. Boat shook an' shuddered. Threw me against a table. The other blokes, they're hanging on. I don't know – mebbe it wasn't their first time. The captain yells down the 'phone. Someone hands me a Mae West an' I strap it on. Then a blast slams me against a wall. I smell smoke, fight my way up the steps. Some hands pull me back, some push forward. I touch something so hot it burns, but the water on the floors is rising. Fast.' His voice was desperate. 'Next thing, I'm in the water, holdin' on to a crate. I try to climb up on it but it won't let me. Keeps dropping me off. More hands pull at me, my legs. They want the crate too, but I kick them away. I have to, miss.' He looked at me, his eyes tortured by the ghosts of the other sailors. 'Or I'd be dead, too.'

He stared into the empty cup and repeated, his voice desolate: 'I had to – I don't know how to swim.' Tears coursed down his ruined face.

I looked at Matthew, unsure how to proceed. He looked equally lost. With no better idea, I refilled Jones's mug and poured another dram into my own.

'Hung on until my feet touched bottom,' he mumbled. 'Bloody cursed name. Bloody Buckmaster. Bloody war. Should have stayed in Shoreditch.'

Not unkindly I pointed out, 'Ulysses made it home, Mr Jones. It just took longer than anticipated.'

'Yeah, miss. Twenty fuckin' years.'

'I believe him.'

On the other side of his desk, Matthew scribbled notes in Jones's file. A large brandy sat untouched in front of me; his was already half empty. He paused, tapping the end of his pen against his teeth. His eyes narrowed at me before he spoke.

'Something struck you,' he said. 'When Jones spoke of his escape from Fresnes.'

'What makes you say that?'

'Lisbet, I remember when you were born.' He looked at me over the top of his glasses. 'I have seen you grow into a very clever young woman. Do you really think I don't know you?'

He was right. He knew my tells as well as I knew his. But if there was no point in lying to him, equally there was no point in telling him the full truth.

'The man shot during the escape. Robert. I trained with him.'

'Was he the sort to run?'

'I wouldn't have thought so, no. But everything is different when you're looking down the business end of a gun.'

He hummed a response and jotted more notes in Jones's file.

'What will you do with him?'

'Who? Bertie?' He looked up, surprised. 'I should pass him on to your lot, but I rather think he's been through enough. I'll arrange his chariot back to Baker Street. Let Buckmaster deal with him.'

'Fair enough,' I said, closing my eyes.

The first time I saw Robert was outside the red bricks of the manor house that Special Operations had taken over. His face was turned into the sun, too good looking for his own good, but without the arrogance that usually accompanied a pretty face. He was an athlete – a leader. At the front of the pack, maybe not always the first, but near enough. What had happened to that man? What made him turn his back and run? I knew I'd never know the answer, but that wouldn't stop me mourning my friend.

Matthew glanced at a clock and closed the file.

'Finish your drink, old girl. Looks like you could use it.'

'Expecting someone else?'

'Not at all.'

He flicked an imaginary dust mote from his sleeve, and glanced at a file on the corner of his desk, lying beside the one I'd brought in earlier.

I didn't want to go home; I didn't want to be by myself, with only my ghosts for company. I grasped at excuses.

'Anything interesting?'

A vertical line formed above his aquiline nose as he decided how much he could share with me. He moved to the window, clasping his hands behind him as he studied the German embassy across the road. The sun silhouetted him, granting him a halo that I knew he didn't deserve. His shoulders tensed when he turned back to me and asked:

'What do you know of wolfram?'

188

Chapter Twenty

Irritated at myself for not being as connected to the Portuguese scene as I'd thought, I hedged.

'I don't think I've met him yet.'

Matthew shook his head, not quite disappointed. 'Tungsten?'

My mental catalogue yielded the same results.

'Sorry.'

He sat back in the chair. 'It's not a who, old girl. A what.' He rubbed the bridge of his nose. 'It's a metal, non-ferrous, with a very high density and a ridiculously high melting point.'

Half of that sentence flew completely over my head, but I understood enough to hazard a guess:

'Weapons?'

'Put it in a shell head to harden it and it cuts through armour like butter. Our Teutonic adversaries have used it in anti-tank and anti-aircraft rounds for years.'

I tried to concentrate on what Matthew was saying, but chemistry and metallurgy, neither a strong suit of mine, were battling against my dead friend's Rhett Butler smile.

'Portugal produces most of Europe's wolfram. Spain has deposits as well, but produces maybe a tenth of what's done here. Despite our best efforts, Salazar sends a ready supply to Germany each month.'

'Can't we out-buy the Germans?'

'It's not like we're not trying. Hell, Lisbet, even the Yanks are trying. We're rationed. They appear not to be. Portugal shipped Jerry about six hundred tons last year. No reason to believe they're cutting that this year.'

'How much do we import?' He pursed his lips and I winced. 'Rather a lot less than six hundred tons? Can't we complain?'

Matthew tapped the folder. 'Copies of the letters sent to Salazar and his monkeys. Enough complaints to outmatch your mother. This one smacks of a naïveté that should be out-lawed. It asks –' his voice took on a mincing tone – '"whether the smuggling is done with the full knowledge and approval of the government". Bloody moron. Of course it is! Nothing happens here without Salazar's approval!'

One word snagged in my mind. 'Smuggling?'

Other images crashed through my mind: lorries unloaded at night; barrels transferred to a ship. Chemistry turned to mathematics: how many barrels passed through the quay that night? How many other quays conducted similar operations? How often?

'Oh yes. What the Portuguese don't officially export, they do so unofficially. Portugal is a small country with a big coastline. We have men monitoring the traffic in and out of the mines. In and out of the warehouses. But for every quay and inlet we watch, how many more are active? We can't monitor everything, and our complaints fall on deaf ears.

'Do you know what these men report, Lisbet?' His voice lowered. Matthew was never one to scream. He didn't need to; the soft vicious tone was far more effective. 'The warehouses aren't sealed. The double locks Salazar promises don't materialise or are left open. Some are guarded, some aren't. Lorries frequent the warehouses, with men hiding their cargo under sheepskin and blankets.'

He had described the activity I'd witnessed on the way back from Sagres perfectly. Another piece of the puzzle was beginning to emerge.

Matthew began to pace, anger and frustration emanating off his lean body. His words tumbled over themselves.

'We are given empty promises. There are no instructions given to the local authorities to prevent the Germans from taking what they want. One man . . .' He took a deep breath, and slowed down. 'One of our men reported confronting a guard. The guard told him that once the wolfram had left the garage, his responsibility ended. The fool wasn't supposed to let it leave the garage in the first place!'

I understood his anger, and his words gave me a better perspective about what was being smuggled from that quay near Sagres.

'You mentioned the Americans. What are they doing about this?'

'Duplicating every blasted thing we're doing!' He banged his hand against the desk. 'Their colonels would rather work independently than build on what we've already learnt. Don't get me wrong – they are helping, but we'd get there a bit faster if we could pool knowledge. Resources.'

Thousands of lives was a high price to pay for a lack of trust.

'What do you think should be done?'

'There's nothing we can do while Salazar sleeps with the Germans.'

'But . . . ?' I prompted.

His head tilted from side to side as he considered the problem.

'The only way to stop the smuggling is to prohibit it. Seal up the warehouses, the quays. Instruct the guards to only allow movement of the ore with the correct authorisation. Hell, put guards in, in the first place,' he growled. 'Then make sure they comply. Supervision. Random inspections. I don't think it would stop it, but at least it would slow it down. And give us a chance.'

'So we're restricted but they're not. How many processing plants there are in Germany?'

'Three that we know of.'

'Presumably processing to capacity. I assume the RAF is doing its best to neutralise them? Although until they do, the unlimited supply fuels the German war machine, and keeps this blasted conflict going.'

'So far so good, old girl. Glad you were listening.' Matthew's voice was flat.

'But what I don't understand is why you're not doing something about it.'

'So you weren't listening, after all.'

'Oh, I was. You said that your lads complain more than Lady Anne. That's all well and good, but when all you do is complain and don't back it up with any action, it's not that effective, is it?'

Matthew stared, as if seeing me for the first time. The mantel clock ticked several times before he responded:

'What are you suggesting?'

'I don't know yet. Let me think about this.'

192

I picked up my handbag and hat. Paused halfway to the door in time to see Matthew sink back into his chair, the picture of frustrated despair.

I was shaking by the time I dismounted from the bicycle in Oeiras. Passed a pair of chattering women as I entered the lavatory of a busy waterside restaurant. For one moment it sounded as if they spoke Italian, and the next Spanish. Then I realised that it wasn't any one language they conversed in, but both. The languages were similar enough to understand one another, and if following the conversation was frustrating, at least hearing their speculation about the romantic prospects of one of the women with some new officer was distracting.

When was the last time I'd been able to laugh that freely? Not since dropping into France, where my life depended on never making a wrong move. Maybe even before then, at the first training school SOE sent me to, where a small group of strangers with different backgrounds and different skills became the best friends I had. The commanding officer was clear about our odds: in all likelihood, only one in two of us would return. I would never have put Robert into the group that wouldn't.

I slipped past a woman preening in front of the looking glass and locked the door to the stall. Intent on applying her lipstick, Laura, the Spanish countess, didn't appear to notice me. Or rather, she didn't notice the blonde Englishwoman. She wouldn't have forgotten the Frenchwoman who'd given her the dressing-down at the casino. I'd have to take my time changing from one into the other.

The cotton shift I'd left home in was wrinkled after being crushed in my bag, but would have to suffice. I hung it on the doorknob and wrapped the wig in my discarded clothes. A knot rose in my throat and I closed my eyes against the tears, bit my fist to stop the howl. Waited until I heard Laura leave the room, before I sat heavily on the commode and wept, my sobs muffled by the damp dress folded neatly in my hands.

That night I dreamt I was standing in the courtyard of the manor house where I trained. The thatched barn is behind me, and crouching on the periphery is the ridge I knew as the Hog's Back, alive with the eyes of a thousand *bufos*. SS thugs watch from the guardhouse, their assault rifles gleaming in the moonlight. My friends stand with me: Dom and Jérôme, Big André and Philippe and Robert. But Dom isn't Dom. She's the dead Frenchwoman, Mireille, and as Robert breaks cover, she throws Alex's sgian dubh. He crumples.

'We don't tolerate traitors,' she explains. I blink and they're gone – vanished into the thistle.

I know I need to break something out, but I don't remember what and there's no one to ask. I reach for my gun, but it isn't in the waistband of my skirt or in my bag. I must have forgotten it at home and instead of the dark clothes I thought I'd worn, I'm wearing a green twinset and a tweed skirt. How could I have done that? I don't *own* a green twinset.

My curse carries on the evening breeze and the guards come to investigate.

'Traitors,' one says. Sees the knife in Robert's body. 'Bloody English knife.'

'Scottish,' I correct automatically.

'Spy!'

The other raises his gun. I know better than to argue. Know better than to run, and I will not beg. I close my eyes and wait for my end.

In the darkness, there's a giggle and a *bang*.

I woke in the darkness of my bedroom, sitting up straight, covered in sweat. Heart pounding, I rested my head against the window frame behind me, allowing the night air to cool my body.

A car growled as it climbed the hill, its occupants laughing and urging it on as it backfired again. Not a gun, just an old jalopy. Padding to the parlour, I poured a large brandy and, saluting the ghost of my fallen friend, drained it in a single gulp.

Even after a second glass, sleep was elusive. I waited for the sky to lighten before dressing in a red linen sheath and a pair of espadrilles. Strapped Alex's knife to my thigh and grabbed my bicycle.

With no destination in mind, I headed to the beach, and the soothing sound of the waves. I turned left at the base of the hill and cycled along the embankment toward Carcavelos until I reached the chunky fort of São Julião da Barra.

As the sky changed from cerulean to lavender, a man appeared on the beach below the fort, running in the surf with an Alsatian dog. He threw a ball into the water, barely breaking his pace. I watched his laughter when the dog returned it, drenching him when it shook the water from its fur. Spellbound, I watched them cavort in the waves until they passed out of sight, their *joie de vivre* restoring some small part of my psyche. I herded my ghosts into their box and shut the lid. There were more important things to consider.

I rose, dusted the dirt from my bottom, and cycled home.

Chapter Twenty-one

So far, I had several pieces to the puzzle but no clue as to what they meant. Mentally I organised what I knew:

One: The Germans were smuggling wolfram from various small inlets along the coast.

Two: The Germans were operating some sort of intelligence ring that allowed the Luftwaffe to target Allied convoys. Major Haydn Schüller was involved, and I guessed, Hans Bendixen. Was Christophe Deschamps?

Three: Matthew was running whores near the port. Were the Germans as well? And if so, how reliable was the information being fed to either side?

Four: Adam's Apple was employed by the British Embassy but kept turning up in a variety of places, and with people whose interests weren't likely to be aligned.

Five: The PVDE – or at least Adriano de Rios Vilar – made it their job to watch the internationals. How much of what was happening were they aware of? And who were they, consciously or otherwise, assisting?

In the City of Spies, no one is who they claim to be . . .

Even their own political police.

In lieu of a pencil, I tapped my teaspoon against the table. The first two items were the big problems. The latter three fitted into them somewhere. Regardless, it was far too large for one person to focus on. I needed help.

I stuffed the blonde wig in my bag and freed my bicycle from the shed. As I opened the tall gate, I jumped back, startled. Claudine stood in the gateway, one hand raised to knock. She was dressed in a bright frock with large cabbage roses. The dress added colour to her dull cheeks, and she looked brittle. And very possibly hung-over.

'Sorry to surprise you. Are you going out?'

'Nothing that can't wait.' I propped the bike against the fence. 'Would you like a cup of coffee?'

She didn't move. 'Christophe didn't come home last night.'

Unsure how to act, I answered carefully.

'Perhaps he came and went. Maybe he didn't want to disturb you and slept in a spare room.'

'None of the other beds were disturbed, and no matter how late, he always comes home.' She swayed and reached out to brace herself against the door. 'And before you suggest it, I don't think it's another woman.'

'I wasn't about to.'

'Good.' Her gaze returned to her feet. 'Maybe we don't have the perfect marriage, but I don't think it's someone else.'

Maybe not *someone* else, but perhaps *something* else? I wanted to pry but in this state, I figured she would tell me what she knew without much prodding.

'Come inside – I'll make you a cup of coffee.'

She didn't move, even with my hand at her elbow.

'He's afraid, you know.'

Trying not to seem to eager, I demurred.

'Of what? What should he be frightened of?'

'I wish I knew. He bought a gun the other week, just after we heard of Martin Billiot's death. Hid it in the car.' Little white lines radiated from her pinched lips, and she suddenly looked old. 'He's afraid, but won't tell me why.'

With the way their marriage appeared, I would have been surprised if he told her the time of day, but looks could be deceiving.

'I know you think I'm foolish,' she carried on in a dead monotone. 'I laugh and I flirt, and then I worry that my husband might be doing the same. But you know nothing of the situation, Solange. *Nothing!*'

My back straightened, surprised at her attack.

'I didn't profess to.'

She burst into tears.

I wasn't good with other people's emotions. Hell, I wasn't even good with my own. What was the protocol for dealing with something like this? At a loss for words, I awkwardly patted her shoulder and gave her my handkerchief.

'Come on, Claudine, let's go for a walk. He might be home, waiting, by the time we're back.'

She followed me on to the street. Waited as I locked the gate. There was something fatalistic about her, about the situation. As if Claudine Deschamps knew her husband wouldn't be coming back.

We bought ice creams from the Italian man near the Tamariz while Claudine spoke of everything except Christophe. I tried to feign interest, I really did, but despite barely interacting with Christophe, I struggled to find empathy for him. I looked away, watched a little girl build a sandcastle. In a world filled with death, with spies and smuggling and Focke-Wulfs bombing convoys, she reminded me that there was something worth fighting for. The doll beside her proved better company than the teenager sitting nearby, with her nose buried in a fashion magazine. The child looked up suddenly and her Cupid's bow mouth opened into a circle before the dark eyes blinked. She scrambled to her feet, her face a picture of beauty.

'Mama!' she cried, running towards us. 'Mama!'

Claudine turned, jumping to her feet. Eyes wide, she stared at the little girl as if she were a vision of Heaven. Or Hell.

'Mama!' The girl's arms lifted, reaching for her mother.

Claudine swayed. I hadn't though it possible for her to lose more colour but she did.

The girl ran past, a blur of chestnut curls and pink pinafore. She fell into the waiting arms of a woman who looked like an older version of the teenager. Not unlike Claudine.

My neighbour crumpled to the ground, scattering chairs and sending the seagulls fluttering. I lunged, trying to help her back to her feet.

'Leave me alone.' She turned her face away.

A small crowd formed around us, patting and consoling her in half a dozen different languages. She struggled to sit, resting her forehead against her knees.

'Leave her alone,' I snapped at the crowd. 'She'll be fine.'

A young man shouldered his way through. Muttering something unintelligible, he picked her up and carried her to a chair underneath an umbrella.

'Thank you,' I said.

He flashed an embarrassed smile and retreated along the esplanade. The waitress returned with a small measure of brandy for Claudine and a glass of wine for me.

'Thank you,' I murmured.

For a moment, she looked as if she wanted to stay and help tend to Claudine, but it was summer, and there were customers to serve. She patted Claudine's arm and gave me a weak smile before fixing a smile on her face and taking an order from the next table.

I sipped my wine and watched the colour return to Claudine's cheeks.

'I owe you an apology, Solange.'

'Not at all.'

'I do.' Her shaking hand stilled my protest. 'And perhaps an explanation.'

'Claudine, you don't.'

She continued in a toneless voice, twisting her wedding ring around her finger.

'My first husband was older than me, and worldly. He was kind at first, but as the years passed, no child came and his eyes began to wander. He left when I was twenty-five. For a little dancer. Seventeen years old and already carrying his child. I was devastated.

'I met Christophe at a Christmas party in '37. He was everything I wanted. Young, handsome, and so dashing in his officer's uniform.' Nervous fingers moved from the ring to the brandy glass, turning it in circles. 'We married within months. Despite the scandal of my divorce, even my parents came. They loved him, but how could they not?'

'In the days before the Phoney War, he travelled a lot. He had to, I understand that. But I was lonely, so lonely. There was another man, a childhood sweetheart. One night, only one night. I didn't love him, Solange. You must believe that. But Christophe was always gone, and Gustave was so attentive. One stinking night.

'Christophe found out. Of course he did. I don't know how. And then the child began to show. It wasn't Gustave's – mathematically could not have been – but Christophe, he didn't believe me. Couldn't forgive me. Isn't that funny, Solange?' Her laugh was bitter. 'My first husband left me because I couldn't conceive his child, and my second husband left when I did.'

She pushed the brandy glass away, and for a few moments we watched the families stroll along the esplanade. A seagull shrieked and dived for some morsel. Just another day in Paradise.

Claudine wiped away a tear, smudging mascara almost to her hairline.

'He was gone then,' she whispered. 'The lovely laughing man – my husband, my friend, my lover. He was gone and I was married to a stranger who hated me. It was almost a blessing when he left to defend the Maginot Line. He wasn't there when my daughter, our daughter, came. And she came fast. My little Adèle wanted to be born, wanted to live. But there were problems, as if God knew I was an unfit mother.' One hand reached out to me, palm up. It was a supplicating gesture, and I didn't know what else to do but to grasp it in my own. I squeezed her fingers, as if I could share my strength with her.

'She was born on the tenth day of May 1940. The same day Germany invaded Belgium. What a day to remember, isn't it? But how lovely she was. She looked just like him. The same eyes, the same nose, the same smile. She even had hair, Solange. A full head of hair.'

My eyes prickled with tears.

'She was with me exactly thirty-one hours. My Adèle. My beautiful Adèle.' Her shoulders hunched as sobs tore through her. A couple, strolling by arm in arm, moved farther away, embarrassed by Claudine's display. 'I've lost her, and now I've lost Christophe. Again!'

There was nothing I could do, but be there for her. The other problems, the wolfram and the smuggling, they'd be there tomorrow. I held Claudine's hand as she wept, wondering how much of her story to believe.

Chapter Twenty-two

I took Claudine home when it began to rain and flicked through her address book until I found Julian's number. If anyone knew how to deal with her, he did. Neither noticed when I made my way home.

I slept badly again, rising before dawn. Paced until I couldn't stand the sight of my villa and stuffed the blonde wig back into my bag. The roads were still wet from the overnight showers, although the sun was bright. I took the coast road, cycling towards São Julião da Barra near Carcavelos. It hadn't taken long to discover that the old maritime fort was now a political prison. I wasn't sure what I expected to see there – perhaps Christophe's face at a window?

A camouflaged lorry turned off the main road and stopped at the gate. The canvas sides hid the cargo; it could have just as easily been provisions as another prisoner.

I left the bicycle on the side of the road and climbed down to the beach. Removed my espadrilles, dug my feet into the cool, damp sand and watched a fleet of fishing boats head out to sea.

The dark man appeared farther along the beach, his dog trotting beside him, carrying a dead branch. My heart skipped a beat.

'For heaven's sake,' I muttered to myself. 'You've seen the man once. Haven't even spoken to him. And for all you know he is . . .'

This time they passed close enough for me to recognise him. I exhaled, feeling weak.

Verboten. This man was forbidden. In every sense of the word.

His dog steamed ahead, then doubled back, dropping the branch and running through the man's legs, tripping him.

'Knut! Come here, you idiot!' he laughed, making the German words seem less harsh.

The dog barked once and complied. Accepted the gentle ruffling of his fur and nudged his master until the man picked up the branch and flung it down the beach. This time the dog dropped the branch at my feet. He barked once, tail wagging, and sat down. Heart racing, I held out my hand, allowing him to take my scent.

'Nice doggy.'

He was having none of it, batting my hand towards the branch.

'Knut, the world is not your playground,' the man panted as he came around a boulder. He stood up straight when he saw me. '*Guten morgen.* I'm sorry to intrude.'

'Good morning.' I choked, strangely tongue-tied.

Even standing on a rock, I had to look up to meet his eyes.

He studied me curiously. 'I know you,' he said in a pleasingly low tenor. 'You're the woman who defended Herr Neumann.'

'Herr Neumann?'

'My lieutenant.' A faint emotion crossed his face as he clarified, 'The one with the scars.'

My own anger burned that I would have to defend that poor soldier to *this* man.

'We all have scars. Just not all of them show.'

I turned to leave, disappointed.

'Thank you. For what you did that night,' he said, surprising me. 'It was very kind.'

'Kind?'

I looked at him over my shoulder. He hadn't moved, watching me with deep-set eyes. At his feet, the dog's tail wagged less exuberantly. He whined, looking between the man and me. And then I noticed the man's bare legs below his shorts, long and muscular, but scars were still visible above the tops of his socks. He'd also been burnt. My tongue stuck to the roof of my mouth as I understood that his revulsion wasn't for the lieutenant's scars – it was for the people who couldn't see past them.

Fascination curled around me and I hated myself for it. Not only did he belong to another woman – the Canary, no less – but he was German. And an officer. I could see past his scars, but how could I see past his nationality? His allegiance?

Solange Verin was a Nazi sympathiser; she would feel comfortable in his company. But what about Elisabeth de Mornay?

The man closed the distance between us and held out his hand.

'My name is Graf. Eduard Graf.' The dog rose to his feet, barked and danced about in a tight circle. He was a beautiful beast, with long lanky legs and a dark pelt. Graf's eyes crinkled at the corners as he stroked the dog's head. 'And this show-off is Knut.'

I stammered my name, blinded as the sun broke through the clouds. The dog slobbered a wet kiss on my arm.

'It would seem he likes you. Well then, Madame Verin, I wish you a good day.'

He was halfway to the beach when he stopped.

'Solange? That means Sun Angel, doesn't it?' He put his hands on slim hips and grinned. 'Somehow, that suits you.'

The butterflies in my belly lasted long after he disappeared from sight.

'Sun Angel, indeed.' I stood in an empty public lavatory and glared at my reflection in the looking glass. 'How he thinks I look like a sun angel when my hair is dyed the colour of a dead mouse, is beyond me.'

I mashed the sun hat on top of the blonde wig, straightened the dark sunglasses and made my way to the gardens near Matthew's safe house.

Matthew had always been a strong proponent of an after-lunch stroll to clear his head. I chose a bench with a good view of the entrance on the chance that he'd retained that habit. A copy of Blake's poems lay open on my lap as I watched the crowd filing out of the doors, with their lunchboxes and paperback novels.

Two women frowned as they drew near. I recognised the bulldog immediately, although it took her a few moments of chewing her lower lip before she made the connection.

'I remember you. You're the new girl who was bringing the file to Sir Matthew.'

I remained seated, hoping my rudeness would send her on her way.

'You have an excellent memory.'

'That's what I'm paid for.' She shimmied past the other woman to sit beside me. 'I'm Mrs Nicola Langston. And this is Betty Jury.'

The other woman was younger than Mrs Langston, her long face framed with mousey-brown hair and jowls. Her eyes were a pretty blue, albeit set too close together. Surprised, she perched beside her friend, twisting around Mrs Langston to maintain the semblance of a circle.

'How do you do?' I didn't offer my own name.

'Wonderful hat. I almost didn't recognise you under it.'

'The curse of fair skin, I'm afraid.'

Would the woman not take the hint and *leave*?

'Have you been here long, Miss ... ?' Mrs Langston leant forward, blocking Betty's view. And mine.

'A few weeks.'

'Ah, Veronica, old girl. Fancy seeing you here.'

A newspaper was folded under one of Matthew's arms while his walking stick tapped the outside of his leg impatiently. He had a collection of them, but I'd never seen him actually use one.

'Hadn't expected to see you today, my dear. Not that it's anything less than a pleasure, of course.'

'And you, Sir Matthew. Have you hurt yourself?'

My barb found an unexpected target; Mrs Langston's eyes widened and she jumped to her feet, waving Matthew into her seat.

'Thank you, Nicks.'

He rested one hand on the silver knob and the other on the back of the seat as he stretched out his perfectly normal-looking right foot. He could have been a gout-ridden eighteenth-century lord. Minus the gout. He shook his ankle, wincing a little.

'Twisted the damned thing. Little more than an inconvenience, and,' he added, winking at Betty, 'marvellous for eliciting a bit of sympathy from the pretty girls.'

She giggled and batted her eyelashes.

'Seems more likely it's hiding a sword, like a swashbuckler from the films.'

Across the park, I spotted Adam's Apple leaning against a tree, watching us.

'Now, Veronica,' Matthew smiled beatifically. 'Don't give my game away. Too early in the day.'

Betty cleared her throat. 'So that's your name, then? You didn't say.'

'Jolly good, I'll do the introductions,'

Matthew flashed a shark-like grin. If he said Pond, or some other variation of Lake as my surname, I'd thump him.

'Do forgive me for not standing.' He shook the ankle again, ever the showman. 'Ladies, let me present Mrs Veronica . . . Ah, old girl, remind me what your married name is.'

It was almost anticlimactic.

'I must remember to make a stronger impression next time,' I stalled, casting about for a suitable surname. My hand brushed Alex's sgian dubh, and smiled. 'It's Sinclair.'

Alex would laugh at the irony; I wouldn't give him my real name, but was happy enough to use his.

'Ah yes. Sinclair,' he repeated. 'Mrs Sinclair is a secretary at Marconi. I'm sure you'll excuse us while I question her mercilessly as to her boss's doings.'

'So you don't work for us?' Mrs Langston asked. 'I'd thought . . .'

Matthew cleared his throat, reminding the women he'd just dismissed them.

'Ah yes. Sorry to intrude, Sir Matthew.' She linked her arm with her friend's, jerking hard on the younger woman's arm to prevent Betty's protest. 'Lovely to meet you, Mrs Sinclair. I'm sure we'll meet again,' she called over her shoulder.

'I'm sure we will.'

Mrs Langston trudged forward, while Betty made little effort to hide her interest.

'I'll have a spare set of papers made up for Mrs Sinclair. Just in case.' Matthew lit two cigarettes, handing me one. 'Dare I ask what brings you here, Lisbet?'

With the Spider, I could have employed any number of clever build-ups. He would enjoy them, proportionate to how outrageous they were, but ultimately he would see through them and I didn't have the time to indulge his humour. Exhaling a cloud of smoke, I opted for the direct approach.

'There are two things I require. Let's start with the easy question.'

Matthew looked mildly interested. He folded his arms and leant back, turning his face into the sun.

'Proceed.'

'What do you know of Christophe Deschamps?'

One eyebrow rose. 'Your neighbour.'

'Yes. He –'

'Disappeared the other night. Yes, old girl. I am aware of this.'

'And?'

'And? Don't look at me like that, Lisbet. First of all, it's unattractive. Second, I had nothing to do with the captain's situation.'

'Situation?'

So there was something going on.

Matthew's eyes remained closed as he soaked in the bright sunlight.

'Please don't hit me. Do remember, I'm already injured.' One eye cracked open to assess my mood. I kept my face blank and waited for him to continue. 'Your Frog has been playing both sides of the lily pad.'

'Can you translate that into English?'

'Certainly.' He sat up and, resting his elbows on his knees, looked straight at me. 'Christophe Deschamps was commissioned into the French army. When France fell, he jumped into Adolf's arms.'

'I know he's close with the Germans. But both sides?'

His mouth twisted. 'He passes on information to the highest bidder, presumably to fuel his gambling habit. And his expensive wife. We know he's untrustworthy, old girl. And season whatever he dishes up with a rather large pinch of salt. Not sure the Krauts, or whoever else he's working with, are as savvy or –' he raised a single finger – 'as forgiving.'

'You're saying they've got him?'

'Nothing of the kind. Only that we haven't. There are a lot of other players out there, not the least of which is the PVDE.'

As Martin Billiot's death could confirm.

'Is he still alive?'

'No idea, old girl. No idea. Hope so. He's likeable in his own way. Utterly rubbish at poker, but likeable. Your second question?'

'Damn,' I muttered, more to myself than to him. 'What do I tell his wife?'

'Why must you tell her anything? A very poor choice for your second question. Simply be there for her, my dear. Be a friend. Or as close to a friend as one in your position can be.'

'My position. Is that all you can say?'

'You're likely to learn more from her about this than me.' He sighed. 'Very well. Usually missing persons are reported to the police. Not sure what they can do right now – but it's as good a place as any to start. Now, my dear, your other question?'

He hadn't confirmed Christophe's death, but hadn't given much hope for his survival. He was right: the only thing that could be done was to log his disappearance with the police and wait. And the waiting was the worst part.

Across the garden, Adam's Apple watched us from behind dark sunglasses.

'I don't trust him.'

'My dear?'

'Your colleague.' I made a vague gesture in his direction.

'Nonsense. I've known Rupert since he was a lad. Worked with his father back when I worked with yours.'

It was a gentle reminder that we both hailed from diplomatic families, and that our loyalty to King and Country was implicit. Only it wasn't. Bloodline didn't destine a person for greatness. Or loyalty. It just made it easier for them to hide.

'Shall I assume your second query deals with young Mr Allen-Smythe?'

Rupert's surname was unfamiliar, but it had been five years since my choice of husband evicted me from my family. And before that, I'd been sent to whichever boarding school was the farthest from Lady Anne, so it was unsurprising that the name was unfamiliar.

'I don't care if he's the old king's love child. He's your problem to deal with, not mine. Just keep him away from me and my cover stories.'

'What's your concern with young Rupert?'

How the devil was I supposed to answer that question? Share my suspicions about a man who shows up in all the wrong places with a man infamous for engineering deceptions? A man whom, by his own admission, he had a soft spot for because he used to work with Allen-Smythe's father?

Across the park, Allen-Smythe's attention didn't waver, making me wonder if Christophe wasn't alone in 'playing both sides of the lily pad'.

'I'm not *concerned* about him. I don't trust him.' I held up a hand for his silence while I explained. 'The more people who know about me, and the work I do for you, the greater the danger I'm in. So while I'd be grateful for the Veronica Sinclair papers, I'd rather keep this, as much as possible, only between the two of us.'

'Fair enough. And the second thing you wanted?'

'Your friend, Bertie.'

'I beg your pardon?' He looked mildly scandalised.

'What have you done with him?'

Matthew sat up straight. 'Why must you always accuse me of all things nefarious?'

'Because you're usually either in the middle of such things, or directing them from the sidelines.'

'What did you think I would do? Hand him over to your lot, or worse – Bendixen?'

There was a plethora of options in between, but little point in listing them out.

'Well, if he's as good as he says, even bandaged, he'd give the Germans a right drubbing.'

'Indeed,' he chuckled. 'What do you want with our little scrapper?'

'Have you sent him back to England yet?'

'Not yet.'

He fiddled with the cane. It was a heavy thing, the silver head moulded into the shape of a leaping dog. Put him in a green velvet waistcoat and breeches, a greyhound rubbing against his white silk stockings, and he'd be perfectly at home in the eighteenth century.

'Why not?'

'You might have noticed he was not in the best of shapes. Thought I'd do the honourable thing and let him heal a bit first. Why the sudden interest? You looked like you couldn't get out of there fast enough the other day.'

He stretched his legs out, feet flexed. Twisted ankle, indeed.

'The room was over one hundred degrees. What did you expect?'

'A better excuse. Would have understood, old girl, if you'd said you were upset at your friend's death. Disreputable as it was.'

'I thought we were speaking of Bertie.'

'Yes, my dear, I understood that, but I'm not sure why. I'll assume . . .' He exhaled and flicked the ash from his cigarette at a nearby bush. 'I'll assume it isn't for his body.'

I choked on my laugh. 'Right you are.'

'So?'

'So?'

'You're getting tedious, old girl. Tell me what you want and then I'll see what can be done about it.'

A young couple wandered our way, swinging their lunch-boxes and leaning into one another. Only when they passed by did I notice that he wore a ring and she didn't. Maybe they had fewer ideals than I gave them credit for.

I lowered my voice. 'I've been pondering your little wolfram situation. And the situation about the sinking convoys. There are a few avenues I'd like to pursue, but as you've requested I operate outside official channels, I need help. Your little East Ender might just serve me well.'

He choked. 'Would you care to rephrase that, old girl?'

'Have your hearing checked, old man. I said "serve", not "service". My honour is not at stake at the moment.'

'That's a first.'

'*My* honour has never been in question. And it's *your* problem I'm trying to solve. Either you give me the resources to solve it, or you can wait for your usual lads to come up with a solution. Remind me – how effective has *that* been so far?'

'What have you found?'

'Nothing yet. I'm only one woman.'

'But you have a plan. Tell me.'

As I explained my theory, my godfather leant back in his seat, a smirk settling upon his handsome face. With a handful of words, I was back in his good graces. And with an East End thug assigned to watch my back.

Hubert Jones was convalescing in a flat just west of the Baixa, close enough to hear the bells from the cathedral. It was relatively anonymous, with a clean-looking café down below. The sort of place the various secret services favoured, making me wonder whether Matthew really had planned to send Bertie back to England after all.

A breeze ruffled the blonde hair of my wig, but didn't alleviate the heat of the afternoon. There weren't many people on the street, but I could feel eyes following me, some appreciative, others deprecating. How many would be selling information about a blonde woman visiting the area, unescorted?

A man walked towards me, holding a parcel. Dark eyes took an inventory before he sniffed loudly, muttering something I didn't quite catch. It was the second time I'd been sniffed at; while I was reasonably certain it had nothing to do with body odour, I had yet to find out what it meant.

I knocked on the door until a hatchet-faced woman opened it, glaring.

'*Sim?*'

She looked even less Portuguese than I did, and spoke with an English accent. An apron was neatly tied around her waist, starched within an inch of its life.

'I'm here to see Mr Aldridge.'

216

She pulled herself up to her full height, no doubt trying to intimidate me.

'What d'ye want wi' *'im*, a toff like you?'

I climbed the last step, forcing her backwards. On an equal level, she was now obliged to look up to meet my eyes.

'A toff like me.'

I moved around her into the little foyer. It was neat and clean, the smell of ammonia and fresh flowers not quite masking the lingering scent of fried fish. A glass door was propped open, allowing a breeze to pass through the rest of the flat. Lace curtains fluttered in the parlour, framing the man sitting on a love seat, a cup of tea in his mittened paws and a wide grin on his battered face. Mr Jones clearly was enjoying the interchange.

'Afternoon, miss.' Jones sketched a mocking bow. 'Welcome to my humble abode.'

'Good afternoon, Mr Aldridge.'

Without waiting for the offer, I sat in the chair opposite him. The dressing around his head had been removed, baring the scars. They were red and angry-looking, but had stopped seeping. The cut over his brow added another scar to his collection.

'You're looking well. Or at least, better.'

'Coulda been worse – at least I have me looks.'

'Indeed.' I reached into my handbag for my cigarette case and lighter. His eyes followed each movement with the hunger of a long-starved wolf. After several months of being banned from smoking in France, I understood that hunger. 'Would you like one?'

'Very kind of you.'

His eyes never left the cigarette in my hand, as if he thought it was some sort of ploy. I lit the cigarette and reached across to put it in his mouth.

'Don't ignite the bandages.'

He inhaled through clenched teeth and expelled the smoke from the side of his mouth.

'What's one more scar?' His voice was harsh, but his face had lost a shade of wariness.

'If you're going to do that, at least stay by the open window,' the woman snapped from the doorway. Her attention was directed at me and the second cigarette in my hand, rather than the thug on the seat before me.

'I don't suppose you could bring me another pot of tea, Mrs Willoughby?'

He put on a woebegone look and, for a moment, I thought she would castigate him. Instead her expression softened and she hastened away. The little thug had the dragon wrapped around his linen-swathed finger.

Mrs Willoughby left the door open to facilitate earwigging, and as much affection as she might have for Jones, she wouldn't think twice about reporting me to whomever would listen. When she reappeared it was with a tea tray and three settings. Rude as it was, Mrs Willoughby was taking no chances that something was about to happen to her charge without her involvement. It was as unsubtle as it was easily averted.

'Ah, Mrs Willoughby, would you mind popping over to the chemist?' Jones said. 'I'm runnin' low on me meds.'

His eyes were wide, but there was a certain flatness to them that belied the pleasant words.

Willoughby's jaw jutted forward and she turned on her heel. Made it halfway to the door before reaching over and snatching the cigarette from Bert's mouth. She stubbed it out and threw the butt out of the window. Her gaze locked on the second one in my hand.

'Try it,' I suggested.

She didn't – her anger echoing on the dark tiles before the front door slammed.

'Charming.'

'Oh, she 'as her moments.'

Hubert Jones's harsh face was ugly and criss-crossed with scars, but he had a puckish charm that made his company entertaining. And he certainly knew how to play Mrs Willoughby. There was potential in the man, and despite myself, I began to warm to him.

I rose to wind the gramophone, peering out of the window to see Mrs Willoughby storm down the street, a blue hat clinging to her wiry hair. Vera Lynn's voice filled the room as she turned the corner.

'Been a while since I been able to listen to English music.' Bertie peered into my handbag, rustling through it until he extricated a silver flask. He opened the cap with his teeth and poured a splash of single malt into the teacups. 'Wasn't allowed in France. Caught bits and pieces from the BBC when I could. Can't get enough of it now.' He held the flask out to me. 'Much obliged, miss.'

'Keep it,' I said. His eyes widened, calculating. 'Call it a get well gift.'

'Ta. So why the visit, princess?' he asked. 'And bearin' presents?'

'How do you find Portugal?'

'Weather's better than Blighty.' He slurped at the teacup. 'Not as that's sayin' much, mind.'

'And?'

'An' I'm not bombed every night. A plus in my books. Mrs Willoughby's accommodating, but I reckon that's not what you want to know.'

What a revolting idea.

'I commend you on the speed of your conquest.' *If not the quality.* 'But no. It isn't.'

He nodded his head. This meeting was the first test, and unless he disappointed me, there would be many. He'd make me work for whatever loyalty he chose to bestow, but for now, all I needed was for him to *want* to work with me. I sat back in the chair and waited.

'They say Portugal's neutral. But there's a lot happening. Under the surface, like. Even up here. I can't go out much, but I sit by the window. I watch an' I listen. That café downstairs is a gold mine.'

'What do you hear?'

'The tides are turning, miss. And about to wash up on Eye-tie shores. The Krauts reckon we'll invade through Sardinia. Could be. That or Sicily. Who knows?' One burly shoulder rose in a careful shrug. 'The local bobbies are – how would you say it? – *disenchanted* with Salazar.' He enunciated the

220

word in a reasonable facsimile of my accent. 'Been brewing for a while, that. Let's see if they have the ball – bottle to do somefin' about it. You haven't answered my question, princess.' He leant forward, his face serious. 'Why are you here?'

Like Matthew, I felt there was little point in prolonging the game.

'I was wondering, Ulysse, if you'd be interested in delaying your journey home. Just a bit longer.'

His expression didn't change, which in itself spoke of his interest. Or that he'd expected something like this.

'What do you have in mind?'

'You've noted that the war's beginning to go our way. I was wondering if you'd be interested in keeping that trend going.'

'What sorta help?' His chin jutted forward in the opening moves of our negotiation.

'Let's keep it simple for now. I need help assessing a current situation, and would rather not go through the official channels. Can you handle that?'

With one mittened hand he batted away the question.

'Assessing? Christ almighty, girl. At least *try* to challenge me!'

'Oh, I will, Mr Jones, once I'm certain you can do what's required. Play your cards right, and you might just have the opportunity to show off those tricks you learnt at Beaulieu.'

Chapter Twenty-three

Instead of returning to the beach at Carcavelos the next morning, I drove Claudine to the police station. Filing a missing person report for Christophe wasn't something she should do alone, and as Matthew gracefully put it, I was trying to be a friend. Or as much of a friend as Solange could be. After twenty minutes of silence, I parked the car in front of the station and pulled the handbrake.

'Are you ready for this?'

'No.' She slammed the car door, took two steps and halted, staring at the building. 'This is real, isn't it, Solange? This is really happening?'

'I'm sorry, Claudine.'

She suppressed a sob and squared her shoulders. A cadaverous officer led her through a set of double doors to take her statement while I remained in the reception area. It was grim: grey walls, grey linoleum floors. Even the air felt grey – grey and grim, heavy with expectancy and despair.

A day-old newspaper was folded on a seat and I thumbed through it. My command of Portuguese was still poor, but I could understand enough. In the last few days, I'd missed quite a bit including news of the food shortages and anti-government riots in the Guimarães district. How had that happened?

Because I lived in an expat community. Because my house-keeper was given enough money to buy whatever was needed on the black market. Because even as a spy, here I was shielded, if not from the Germans, at least from the Portuguese. Barring, of course, Adriano de Rios Pilar's men.

My mood quickly became as grey and grim as the room.

The door burst open, startling me. A man, his hands cuffed behind his back, was pushed through, followed by two more men, a woman, and a pair of PVDE officers. One of them called to the man behind the desk and I understood that these prisoners were overflow from another station.

They looked rough, clad in sturdy burlap clothes, and bruised. One man held his arm gingerly to his chest; the second had a swollen nose and a black eye, and blood trickled from a split lip on the third. The woman looked worse. Petite to the point of being frail, her dark hair straggled around her face, emphasising a haunted, dead look in her eyes. Her ripped blouse barely covered her breasts, and she moved deliberately – every movement designed to mimic normalcy, and yet failing miserably.

Once, in France, I'd seen a woman move like that. The daughter of one of our couriers had been captured by the Gestapo. Not for questioning, but for an afternoon's 'dalliance', and I understood what had been done to this woman. Hated the PVDE officers as much as I hated the Gestapo goons.

A PVDE man, barrel-like and with a greasy moustache, shoved her along. With her hands tied behind her back, she fell and although I wanted to help her, I knew anything I tried would land me on the floor beside her.

For once, I held my tongue. One of the bound men muttered something and crouched next to her. He was either very brave or very foolish. Like Alex.

And like that day, I remained mute. And ashamed. Unable to watch, I fled outside. The air felt dirty, and so did I. What sort of person was I to run away from that?

My hand shook as I lit a cigarette. And another. And another. Until Claudine emerged an hour later, looking as despairing as the Portuguese woman. She dropped on the bench next to me.

'They say they don't know where he is. Told me to check with the embassy or . . . Or his mistress.'

I stared at my fingers laced together in my lap. 'Claudine . . .'

'I know what you're going to say. You're going to ask me if it is possible, but I told you – it is not. Christophe didn't have a mistress – he had no time for one.' She rested her head on the back of the bench and closed her eyes. Under her tan, her skin was grey; the situation had taken its toll. 'I'll go to the embassy to see if they know anything. I should have gone there first. Yesterday. Then I am going to telephone Christophe's friends, the ones I know. Again. Perhaps they can tell me something new.'

'Can I help?'

'Would you know who to call?'

'No.'

'Then you can't help, can you?'

She didn't mean to be cruel, but my shoulders hunched nonetheless.

'No, I suppose not.'

'And after I am done asking questions they cannot or will not answer, I'm going to get myself – how do the British say it? – stinking drunk. You are not obliged to join me. I won't be good company.' She held up a hand to stop my protest. 'It's true. Don't take this the wrong way, my dear, but please, can you make your own way home?'

'Of course. Will you be all right?'

I understood her need for solitude and had no words to salve her pain.

'Always.'

She held herself upright as she passed an American couple, arguing over whether a camera had been lost or stolen.

I didn't believe her.

With no taxis in sight, I took the train. Fighting the undertow of exhaustion, I leant my head against the seat, closed my eyes, and missed my stop. I disembarked at Cascais; it was only a twenty-minute walk and I couldn't bear the press of sweating bodies.

There had been no ransom note, a likely sign that Christophe was already dead or had chosen to go missing. My projects didn't have a much better prognosis: how could one person – two if I included Bertie – crack an espionage ring *and* halt a smuggling operation where Britain's best had already failed?

A youth brushed against me and my handbag began to pull away. Realising that the little sod was robbing me ignited righteous anger. It had been a ghastly morning – a ghastly week – and I'd be *damned* if I allowed the urchin to steal my bag, my papers, my keys, and my bloody PPK.

Leaning back, I counterbalanced him and, anchored by his grip on my bag, he propelled himself around and into my right fist. Blood poured down his face into a mouth open with shock and pain. He let go but I wasn't finished.

In that moment, he had become everyone I hated: the neighbour that betrayed me in Paris; the Nazis; the PVDE goons. It would have been easy enough to kill him. The targets were visible: the bridge of the nose, the base of his throat. Or either side of the throat up to his temples. Maybe another two or three other places. But, angry as I was, I knew that would only brand me as a spy. I stifled the killing rage and made do with a knee to his groin. He doubled over, wheezing and cursing as he shuffled back, disappearing into the crowd.

Applause blossomed around me – tourists and businessmen, mothers and their children. Blushing, I tried to slink away.

'Nice hook you have there, Angel.'

Eduard Graf leant against a rock wall with his arms crossed over his chest, looking as amused as he was handsome.

'He picked the wrong tourist,' I mumbled, feeling my blush notch up another level. Feeling the need to explain, I gave him the only acceptable answer I could. 'I have three brothers. They taught me how to defend myself.'

He stood up and closed the gap between us.

'They taught you well. You saw him off before I could.'

'The bad end to a bad day, I'm afraid, Herr Graf.' The wall of braid across his chest made me realise he was in uniform. It didn't take long to decrypt the insignia, or to realise with a sinking feeling that he was part of the Abwehr, the military intelligence agency known for shagging their secretaries. Or in his case, Spanish countesses. 'Or should I say, *Herr Major*?'

'You may call me Eduard. Why has it been a bad day? You saved your purse, and maybe taught the boy a lesson.'

'I took Claudine Deschamps to the police station to file a report on her missing husband.'

'Ah.'

My hands were still trembling. I clasped them behind my back and hoped Graf didn't notice. Despite the Abwehr's reputation, at least in Portugal, for being inept, instinct told me not to underestimate this man.

'I'm told this is not uncommon. Disappearances.'

'Too many.' Graf fell into step beside me. 'I am sorry for your friend, sorry for her husband's situation.'

'Why? You had nothing with it.' I slanted a look up at him, surprised at how tall he was. I was five foot ten, but he had several inches on me. 'Or did you?' I asked, trying to sound normal. *Why was he here?*

'Me? No. So there would be no point in trying to beat a confession out of me.'

The corners of his eyes crinkled. And as if I wasn't humiliated enough, a deep rumble emanated from my belly.

Please, God, let a tidal wave come and sweep me away!

But the sea remained calm, confirming the fact that God and the universe hated me.

Graf looked away, but I could still see his smile. He spoke after a few steps.

'Please allow me to take you to lunch. Perhaps it will go a small way to improving your day.' My heart picked up its pace, almost to halt at his next words: 'And I missed seeing you on my run this morning.'

'So much so, that you came looking for me?' The words escaped before I could stop them, but what if he had?

'Not at all. Should I be?'

His eyes crinkled at the corners again; he was amused, damn him, although it confirmed that I wasn't – yet – enough of a target to pique his professional interest. His personal interest, however, he was making clear.

A Spanish countess clung to him, and while he wore a wristwatch, there were no rings on his fingers. He was probably sought after by half the women in Lisbon, for one reason or another. While I wasn't keen to add to their ranks, I'd be a fool to turn him away completely. He'd provide Solange Verin with a better, and far more interesting, reason for circulating with the German contingent than Schüller, and if I learnt something from him, maybe about the bombed convoys, so much the better.

'Come, Angel. I offer no more than lunch and if I misbehave, you may punch my nose.'

Angel? If that was how he saw me, I wasn't about to correct him.

'I'm not sure I could reach it.'

My blush returning, I followed him to a little silver BMW. He opened the door and stood back, expectantly. I couldn't help staring at him.

'If your friend needs to file a report on you tomorrow, there are witnesses who see you getting in to my car. If you disappear today, I shall end up in new accommodation, courtesy of Dr Salazar.'

I dropped into the seat. 'From what I understand, your friends are close with Salazar. You might get a medal.'

'Why? Who else have you punched?'

Punched? I wanted to laugh. Shot and stabbed, as well, not to mention being a member of Special Operations. If he captured me, he would indeed get a medal. How depressing.

Graf drove through Cascais to a small fishing village on the far side. Large houses clustered together, crouching behind high walls and hedges. Over Graf's shoulder, the Atlantic threw her waves against the black rocks with such force that the sea spray splashed the road. He stopped the car in front of a small restaurant.

'Welcome to the Boca do Inferno,' he said.

The mouth of Hell. It seemed rather appropriate for the day I was having. And yet, despite the name, it was an oddly idyllic location. The lunch crowd had already departed, leaving the restaurant empty save for the staff cleaning the front room. The maître d' greeted Graf, bowing reverently.

'Senhor. Your usual table?'

'Yes, thank you.'

A boy hastily cleared a table in the corner, next to a wall of open windows, letting in the afternoon sun, the smell of jasmine, and the roar of the Atlantic, a pleasant bass to the folk music playing on the gramophone. A ceiling fan stirred the air around us.

'Beautiful,' I murmured, as Graf held out my seat out.

He laid his napkin on his lap. 'I hope this is acceptable?'

'Perfectly.'

'Good.' He accepted a menu from the waiter, placed it to the side. 'Two bianchi e'mari to start.'

The waiter nodded and retreated.

'White and bitter?' I asked, translating the Italian.

'White wine and campari. An Italian friend introduced me to it. It's quite refreshing.'

'I can order my own drink.'

'I'm sure you can,' he said. 'Please. Order what you like.'

'It's fine,' I told the waiter, wondering why Graf didn't sound as arrogant as Schüller, and despite myself, feeling as if I was playing with fire.

'You speak Italian as well?' he asked.

I nodded, opting for the truth. 'I studied music and found it useful to know what I was singing.'

'How many languages do you speak?'

'French and German, of course. Italian and some Spanish, albeit with an Italian accent.'

He chuckled. 'English?'

Tricky question – and one I couldn't deny if I learnt languages to help with music, so I answered honestly enough:

'Enough to get myself into trouble.' Once his laughter subsided, I continued. 'Their operas aren't brilliant – I didn't spend a lot of time learning them.'

'And Portuguese?'

'People lie when they claim that if you know Spanish, you can understand Portuguese. What about you, Herr Major?'

'Eduard,' he corrected. 'I am not very good at languages, I'm afraid.'

Evidenced by his mistranslation of my name. Not that I was about to correct him.

The waiter returned with our drinks and Graf clinked his glass against mine.

'To one less thief on the streets.'

'And to Galahad, who arrived too late to save the damsel in distress.'

'Ouch.' He smiled. He might not have the movie-star looks of Schüller or Robert, but he was the sort that became more attractive as you got to know them. 'Although the damsel did quite well on her own. The sardines here are quite good.'

'No thank you!'

'Are you not a fan of fish?'

'Herr Major—'

'Eduard.'

For a German, he was remarkably informal.

'Eduard, then.' The white wine was going to my head and I began to feel giddy. 'A human body has 206 bones. Those things have twice the amount, every one honed to razor sharpness. Thank you, but no sardines for me. Not unless they're de-skinned, decapitated, and most importantly, de-boned.'

'Doesn't that take the fun out of it?'

'Life is dangerous enough.'

'Yes,' he murmured. He waved the waiter over and ordered, again without asking for my input. 'Look over there, Angel.' He pointed out of the window towards the ocean.

I could hear the thunder of the surf against the Boca's cliffs, but beyond it the ocean was tranquil enough.

'Yes?'

'She's quiet today. Like Lisbon.'

'I don't understand.'

'Look at it. Blue. Serene. Underneath there is a maelstrom – an undertow that could bring you down before you noticed you were in trouble. Lisbon is not a safe city. Never forget that, Angel.'

'Why are you saying this to me?'

He straightened the silverware in front of him.

'I do not know.'

'So you don't warn off everyone?'

'No.' A half-smile. 'I never felt the need to.'

'I can take care of myself,' I reminded him. Changed the subject before it led to more dangerous ground. 'How long have you been here, Eduard?'

'Just over one year.'

'And before that?'

'Wherever I was sent.' This time his smile was flat and he turned the conversation again. 'As an expert, Angel, what do you think of the Portuguese music?'

At least he'd found a safe topic.

'*Fado*? I love it.'

'You've been to the Café Luso?'

'No.'

The waiter arrived with a bottle of wine. Presented it to Graf. Uncorking it, he poured a measure. As he waited for Graf to taste it, he smiled at me.

'Café Luso? You must go, senhora. Most renowned *fado* in Portugal, not just Lisboa.'

Graf smiled and the ghost of a dimple appeared in each cheek.

'Would you like to go?'

'With such a testimonial, how could I say no?'

If the waiter had said it was a gutter dive populated by thugs, whores and murderers, I'd still have gone.

'Amália sings tomorrow, senhor,' the waiter said, placing the bottle into a silver wine cooler. 'If you wish, I can arrange?'

'If the lady is available?'

What had happened to make me want to go with this man, this *German*? It was more than just wanting an informant within the Abwehr. More than the danger, the thrill of dancing with the Enemy. It was this man. For whatever reason, he intrigued me, drew me to him. Before I knew who and what he was, and even now, after the penny dropped. It was dangerous, it was foolish. And still, feeling as if I was standing at the edge of a cliff, with the full knowledge that more than just my heart was at risk, I murmured: 'I'd be delighted.'

He nodded and the waiter retreated, stopping first at the gramophone in the corner to change the record. The sound of a *fado* guitar, and then a woman's voice soared, intense, compelling.

'Amália?'

Graf laughed. 'I think he's trying to convince you.'

'Shouldn't *you* be working harder to convince me?'

'Why would I? You already said you would go. I assume you understand that it will be in my company, not Pedro's? Of course, if you tell me you'd prefer his company . . .'

'Then I'd suggest you take your countess and we could make an evening of it.'

The waiter turned at Graf's bark of laughter.

'And risk you providing more entertainment than Amália? No, Angel. I think it safest to keep the party small.'

I sipped the crisp white wine, hoping that I didn't live to regret this moment.

Chapter Twenty-four

The high I'd felt in Graf's company dissipated as the little silver BMW disappeared down the hill. What the hell did I think I was doing? This wasn't just playing a role, or doing my job. Playing with Graf would be like playing with a grenade. There were other men who could be just as useful, if not as interesting, to have on my arm. Fully aware that if I had any sense at all, I'd have turned down the date, but hadn't been able to force the words out.

Self-flagellation was never my thing, and rather than examine my actions too closely, I made my way across the street. While I didn't trust her, Claudine had become the closest thing I had to a friend in Lisbon, and she was going through hell.

She stood in the foyer, her back resting against the wall and the telephone's receiver pressed against her ear.

She waved me into a seat and finished her call with a resigned, 'Yes. Yes, I understand. Thank you for your help.'

She replaced the receiver in its cradle and made a rude gesture.

'As if you gave me any help at all, you miserable son of a misbegotten whore.' She spoke with no rancour; it must have burned itself out several hours ago.

'No luck?' I asked.

'Only of the bad variety. No one has seen Christophe. No one knows why he disappeared, or where he might be. Frankly,

Solange, no one cares.' She sank to a settee and dropped her head in her hands.

'I care.'

Perhaps more for Claudine's sake than Christophe's. I didn't trust her, but I did like her.

'I know.' She squeezed my hand and brushed away a tear. 'I'm sorry to have left you to fend for yourself this afternoon. It must have taken you forever to get back.'

Guilt stabbed at me; I'd been enjoying myself while she . . .

'It's of no matter. I just wanted to check in on you.'

'That's kind of you. I'm afraid I'm not very good company. Why don't you take the car? Do a bit of exploring while the sun's still out.'

It was the sort of offer that I'd hoped for, an opportunity to drive down the coast and look for a quay, similar to the one I found on the trip to Sagres, that might be used for smuggling. It was a long shot, a vague hope that if smuggling was as prevalent as Matthew led me to believe, there would be evidence of it nearby. But under the circumstances how could I accept?

'You'll come with me?'

'Too many calls to make. Go ahead, Solange. The keys are on the sideboard.' She gave me a gentle shove towards the door. 'Go.'

As long as no one recognised the Deschamps' Peugeot, I was safe enough. Claudine had provided me with an excuse, should the PVDE or anyone else stop me. I drove without any idea of where to start looking and only a vague assumption that it was possible that with such a coastline, the smugglers would have an outpost in the resort towns between Lisbon and Estoril.

Driving slowly, I chose random paths to investigate. The first ended in front of a small cottage where a child played with a dog. The second ended at a beach, where a courting couple appeared to be doing more than courting. Convinced that sooner or later I would find something interesting, I continued on. No car passed me twice, although the number of people honking their horns and advising me – in several different languages – to learn to drive became tedious.

The sun was sinking to the horizon when I got lucky.

Three hundred yards after turning from the main road, I came to a barrier – the sort that guards a level crossing. The sort that guarded the quay at Cabo de São Vicente.

A young sergeant emerged from a small hut beside the barrier. He tossed the magazine he'd been holding through the open door and strode towards me. He looked at the car's plates, noting the diplomatic tags.

'This area's restricted,' he said in the halting French that came from a list of phrases. With the shoulders of a bull and the face of a labourer, he didn't look local. 'Not allowed to pass.'

Behind him, the warehouse door opened and another man emerged. He stretched in the sun and stared at us. Moved towards us, pulling a pistol from its holster. The last thing I needed was a pair of handcuffs and a PVDE escort. I smiled, hoping it looked engaging.

Hidden behind the dark glasses, I noticed a solitary speedboat moored to the jetty. The sun still shone – albeit barely – and the quay, little as it was, should have been busy. Surely if it were a genuine dock there would be the loading and unloading of cargo, with workmen bustling about?

'Oh, I don't want to pass,' I told the man, my voice blasé. 'What I want are directions. Can you tell me the way to Sintra?'

He relaxed. 'Go back to the big road. Turn left. Stay on road for . . . I do not know. Half hour? Less. You will find it, no problem.'

'*Obrigada*.'

This was what I'd been searching for. I noted the landmarks and turned the car around. By the time I crawled into bed, a plan had begun to form that started with another visit to Bertie Jones.

I closed my eyes and dreamt of scorpions driving speedboats.

The wine was sweeter than the vinho verde I'd developed a taste for. Sweet and warm, but the glass was clean and the café had a clear view of Bertie's safe house. To avoid standing out in the not-very-fashionable neighbourhood, I had donned too much make-up, a black wig and low-cut dress, and placed pads in my cheeks that gave them a fuller look. A foreign look, to be sure, but with my height and colouring, that was unavoidable. And would exempt me from the three hundred escudo penalty a Portuguese woman would be fined for dressing inappropriately.

The tourist book open on my lap was Spanish, pinched off a careless couple an hour before, just before Bertie escorted Mrs Willoughby out of the door. He blew the battleaxe a kiss as she departed, suitcase in hand and a thunderous expression marring her face.

Grateful for a rare dose of good timing, I knew that Mrs Willoughby had been given her walking papers for a reason: Bertie was about to disappear. It was sensible; too many people knew where he was. And with those injuries, he would be easy to find.

Nonetheless, Bertie was well-trained; he'd have a safe house somewhere.

Within minutes, Bertie emerged from the flat, his head hidden under a battered fedora, a small case held in his hand. He walked gingerly, but looks could be deceptive. When he turned the corner, I threw a handful of coins on the table and followed.

For twenty minutes, he led me a merry dance, up steps, down hills, through more alleyways than I'd seen in my life. Bertie was good, and he knew how to shake a tail. Only this tail wasn't about to be lost.

Not until I allowed myself to be distracted by a woman arguing with a shopkeeper, then Bertie was gone.

'Damn,' I muttered, standing in front of a major intersection.

Motor cars of every sort flew past, but there was no sign of the little thug. I backtracked again, this time finding a passageway too small to be an alleyway, heading off from a flight of steps. It was dank and dark, blocked by a rubbish bin and smelling strongly of urine. It was the sort of place I would have used if I was being tailed. I slid my fingers around the reassuring weight of the PPK and stepped into the alley.

Within heartbeats, an iron grip encircled my wrist, slamming it against the wall until the gun dropped. Instinct took over and I raised my knee, aiming for his groin. Bertie slid to the side, kicking at the leg that still supported me.

'Bastard,' I growled. 'It's me.'

I rapped his shoulder twice, then punched his chin as he stepped back.

'What was that for?' he bleated. 'I stopped at your signal.'

239

'Smacking my wrist? Scaring the living daylights out of me? You choose.'

'Why're you followin' me?'

'Why were you trying to lose me?'

'Didn't know it was you at first. Not until you got into the alley. Then smelled you.'

'Over this stench?' I said, offended. 'You stopped when I let you know –'

He had the audacity to laugh. 'I stopped when I smelled you, princess. The double-tap just confirmed it. Not many tarts can afford Chanel No. 5. You might want to think about that next time you masquerade as a dock dolly.'

'Damn,' I muttered, rubbing my wrist. It had better not leave a bruise for Graf to see.

'What're you doing, following me?'

'What are you doing, running?'

'Time to move. You're running me, princess. An' I don't have a problem wi' that. Just don't like some of the friends you have.'

'Who? Harrington?'

'Anyone.' He straightened the fedora, drew me deeper into the passage. 'Figure you're like me. You don't trust no one. They havta prove themselves first. It's why we're still alive.'

'And you don't trust me yet.'

He kept his voice low and leant in to murmur, 'Enough to let you know I got me a job, down at the docks.'

'You can handle the work? Your wounds—?'

'Supervisor. Cause o' me experience.' He flashed a puckish grin. 'What? What'd y' think I did back home? Accountin'?'

'No.'

'Dock supervisor. Before Jerry bombed the East End to the ground. My time to get even.'

'I have no problems with that.'

'Good, then I'll send word when there's news. And sorry.'

I held up one finger before he could say – or do – what was clearly written across his face.

'Touch me and I'll make sure you don't walk for a week.'

'Until next time, then, princess.' He winked and sauntered out of the passageway.

Cheeky little bastard.

Chapter Twenty-five

The gold silk dress was a miracle of design. Its bias cut clung in the right places, covered the scar on my shoulder, and gave my skin a warm glow. To balance the effect, my hair was arranged in loose waves, captured into a low chignon. A thick filigreed bracelet glimmered from my wrist, hiding the bruise Bertie had left.

I sprayed one last puff of perfume, reached for my shawl, and made my way to the silver BMW. Graf leant against the bonnet, smoking a cigarette and staring down the hill at the Atlantic. Claudine would have told me that Haydn Schüller was better looking, but she was wrong.

My instincts told me that this was a dangerous game, one that wasn't likely to end well. I ignored them, burying them under my determination to get the job done. I had the skills. I knew what I was doing. Sort of.

Sensing my presence, Graf looked up, smiling.

'Hello.' I hadn't felt this awkward since leaving the school-room. Tried to hide it behind a cool veneer. 'I didn't know you smoked.'

'I don't.' Graf threw the cigarette butt into the shrubs and kissed my hand. 'You look stunning.'

'Thank you. So do you.' I looked at the dark suit and raised an eyebrow. 'No uniform tonight?'

'Too ostentatious for this evening.'

While not as bad a driver as Claudine, Graf took the winding roads at a perilous speed.

'Practising for Monte Carlo?' I yelled over the air rushing through the windows.

He slowed down immediately.

'Don't,' I laughed.

There was something about the ride, or maybe it was his company, that was intoxicating.

'I thought we'd go for a drink first, if that's all right with you?'

'That sounds lovely.'

'Have you been to the castle yet?'

'No.'

'The monastery? The tower down at Belém?' He pointed to his right – towards the ocean as we sped by. 'No? What have you done with yourself this past month?'

I'd witnessed an attack on a convoy, spied on smugglers, and seen my godfather emerge from a whorehouse. I'd had coffee with the PVDE, socialised with Germans and alcoholics and seen far, far too much of the casino. For fun, I'd ogled Eduard on his morning run. It wasn't quite the standard tourist agenda.

'I took the time to settle in.'

'Lisbon is a beautiful city. There is a lot to see here.'

'There certainly is. And as my guide for the evening, what shall we start with?'

'The Avenida. I must meet a man there. It is only for a few moments. It won't take long.'

It wasn't the answer I'd expected. Was his date with me a cover for some other activity? As Graf parked the car in a side street, my curiosity had shifted from Graf to this contact. Did he know he was using a British agent as his cover? Or was he walking me into a trap?

My long strides matched Graf's as we passed the crowded Rossio and the Estação Central, with its two main arches flanked with three smaller, less ornate ones. A clock at the top proclaimed the time to be 8.25, and we had to move to avoid the wave of people flooding from the station.

Beside it, a porter guarded the entrance to the Avenida Palace Hotel. Two uniformed men smoked not far away. They snapped off the Nazi salute to Graf and I looked away, noticing how the windows aligned on the fourth floor between the railway station and the hotel. Only the fourth floor had all the curtains drawn. Could this be the secret passage that Matthew had mentioned? Funny, I'd expected it to be below ground.

Was this the reason why Graf had chosen this hotel to meet his contact? A rendezvous with someone who wasn't supposed to be in Lisbon? Who could it be? And why now, when it must have been easier to meet this person without me?

We passed under the sparkling lights of an enormous chandelier. Graf ordered two glasses of dry port from a waiter and seated me in an overstuffed chair. He took the seat opposite, facing the entrance. The room was lined by columns, a pale contrast to the patterned red wallpaper.

An awkward silence rose between us. I didn't feel comfortable with my back to the door, although the ornate looking glass behind Graf's head provided a small perspective, and in it appeared the scarred face of Lieutenant Neumann.

'I'm sorry, Angel. Would you please excuse me?' He stood up with an apologetic smile. 'I won't be long.'

'That's fine, Herr Major. Your lieutenant can keep me company while you run your errand.'

I had to stop myself from slipping into the seat he vacated.

Graf snorted, and clapped the lieutenant on the shoulder.

'Good luck, Herr Leutnant.'

'You too, sir.' He shifted from one side to the other, wincing slightly.

'Sit down, Lieutenant, I don't bite.'

I gestured to the waiter to bring a third glass and watched Graf in the looking glass until he turned down a corridor.

'What an intriguing man,' I murmured to myself.

'Yes, ma'am. He is.'

Neumann eased himself onto the chair, one leg stiffer than the other. There must have been hordes of women that had chased him, before the burns. What a waste.

'Have you known him long?'

'Four years, ma'am. Since the start of the war.' A half-smile rose from the beautiful side of his face. 'I drove his tank.'

The question tumbled out before I could stop it. 'How do you get from a tank regiment to a diplomatic role?'

'You get wounded, ma'am.' He looked directly at me, challenging me to look away.

'I'm sorry. Do you miss it? The tanks?'

'I miss my regiment. The 7th Panzers. But as you can see, I can no longer fight.'

'The 7th Panzers? I think I've read about them in the papers. Rommel's Ghost Division?'

245

He inclined his head. 'So fast even the High Command had problems keeping up with us.'

'You were at the Battle of France?'

'Yes.'

'That's where that –' I made a vague gesture – 'happened?'

He spoke without self-pity or anger.

'One moment, we are attacking, fighting just outside Cherbourg. The next, a shell hits.' He ignored my gasp, continuing in that same toneless voice. 'The major pulled me from the tank.'

'And then?'

I was fascinated by Neumann's story – not quite able to imagine this side of Graf.

'The Herr Major commandeered another tank. Delivered me to the medics and returned to battle. He was awarded an Iron Cross for it.' His pride in Graf bordered on hero worship. 'The field marshal himself pinned it on him.'

'And you?'

'Battlefield commission.'

It wasn't something that was normally given for just being wounded. What else had they done?

'And the Herr Major?'

'The second tank was shot out. He joined me in the ward for a while.'

'And now?'

Andreas shrugged. 'Military attaché. As you know.'

Which translated to Military Intelligence. It was an intriguing story, but still didn't explain Graf's almost unheard-of move from a Panzer division to Admiral Canaris's Abwehr. Nor did it answer the question of who he was meeting tonight.

Neumann shook himself out of his reverie.

'I am sorry to bore you, Frau Verin.'

'You're not boring me, Lieutenant.'

On the contrary, Lieutenant Neumann provided a unique insight into Graf. As I waved him to continue, something in the looking glass caught my eye. Two men, plain-clothed, but with a military bearing, walked through the foyer. Graf's tall figure was instantly recognisable, even before Neumann got to his feet and snapped off a crisp salute.

It was the other man who stole my breath. Older, average in height, a face cold and mocking. I recognised him instantly: he was the grey-haired man I'd last seen in the French fishing village. The man who had killed Alex Sinclair.

What the devil was he doing here? And with Graf? Graf was Abwehr. I'd assumed the grey-haired man was Gestapo, or one of the other SS divisions. I didn't realise they operated outside Germany and the occupied territories.

Unless they'd followed someone here? Someone who'd perhaps killed several of their number? Someone like me? Did they know who I was? Did Graf?

No, I decided. If they were after me, I'd already be surrounded. The man's reflection gave as little away as Graf's did as they completed their conversation. He remained still, watching Graf move towards us.

I forced my hand away from the PPK in my bag. There was a chance that the grey-haired man wouldn't equate the urchin in France to the elegant socialite in front of him, and I didn't want to have to use the gun. Not here, where I had no hope of surviving a shootout.

I pretended to admire my manicure as Graf sank into the chair the lieutenant vacated, waving his adjutant away.

'Many apologies for my absence, Angel. The meeting was unavoidable. Its length, unconscionable.'

I surreptitiously wiped my damp palm on the brocade upholstery.

'Think nothing of it.'

A stray thought occurred to me: if I was reluctant to cause a scene in the hotel foyer of a neutral country, what if the grey-haired man was too? Was he waiting for me outside? Would Graf defend me or hand me over?

One thing was clear: if I survived the day, I would have to ignore Rios Vilar's warning. It was time to go hunting, and at least this time I knew the face of my prey, even if I lacked his name.

I took a sip of the port, noticing that its taste had soured.

'Was it successful?' I asked. 'Your meeting?'

For an instant he allowed a weariness to creep across his face.

'Only time will tell. Finish your drink, Angel. We're late for our reservation.'

My eyes scanned the room as I rose, but the grey-haired threat was not in sight. Feeling the reassuring weight of the PPK concealed in my clutch bag, and the sgian dubh strapped low on my calf to accommodate my gown, I allowed Graf to steer me from the hotel.

Every nerve was alive. To the threat of the grey-haired man, as much as to Graf.

Café Luso was once a wine cellar of one of the Bairro palaces, and by ten o'clock the room was crowded and already thick with smoke. The tables radiated from an area cordoned off by thick red ropes, where a slight man sang in front of a mural of another *fadisto*, singing to a crowd on the streets. The painted man cavorted but the live one's eyes were closed, his delicate hands extended as his voice soared.

Graf seemed more at ease here than he did on the streets in his uniform. And I took comfort in the crowded room. If there was a kidnapping on the cards tonight, it would be damned difficult to do it here.

'Don't let his innocent look fool you,' Graf murmured, and it took a moment to realise he spoke of the *fadisto*. 'This song is very political.'

'I thought you didn't speak Portuguese?'

'I don't, but I have learnt words – phrases. Enough to get by.'

He's been here before. With other women? The Canary?

'Oh.'

I suppressed the stab of jealousy and the knock-on horror: he was an Abwehr officer, and my decoy as much as I was his.

'The song is loosely based on history,' Graf continued. 'Just enough to keep him out of trouble. But he does not welcome us here.'

We were surrounded by Portuguese couples, the women with their hair cut in the 'refugee' hairstyle, their dresses based on French designs.

'Us?'

'The Germans, the Italians. Europeans. Not so much the people, I think, as much as the strife we bring.'

'He favours the Allies?'

249

'Most Portuguese do.' Graf paused to order a bottle of wine from a passing waiter. 'You didn't know?'

'No.'

Graf seemed unconcerned by the Portuguese's sentiment. What *were* his politics? Could a Nazi be sitting with a Frenchwoman, drinking vinho verde in a *casa do fado*? Could he blithely accept a singer who disagreed with his leader's policies – when Salazar, however covertly, was rumoured to support Hitler?

Who *was* Eduard Graf?

'Why are you here, Solange?'

His question so closely mirrored mine that all I could do was blink and take his question at face value.

'Because you suggested a night of *fado*.'

'That's not what I meant. You don't court the aristocrats, although I suspect they would accept you. But nor do you seem overtly political. Why did you leave France?'

Keep the lies close to the truth . . .

'I made a mistake.'

He put down his glass. 'A mistake? One that landed you in Portugal?'

'One that could have landed me in Fresnes.' I shrugged. 'I turned down a date with a neighbour. In retaliation, he accused me – to a gendarme – of being a Resistance fighter.'

It was the same story I'd told Adriano de Rios Vilar. It was always easier to be consistent when it was the truth.

He looked politely amused. 'And are you? Is that where you learnt to fight?'

'I told you – I have three brothers. And if I was a Resistance fighter, do you really think I would have left France? That I would be here with you?'

250

'Perhaps not,' he answered. 'There was no one who would speak on your behalf?'

'This neighbour was well placed. I did what I had to do.'

His face became serious and he put his hand over mine.

'Remind me to thank that neighbour of yours,' he murmured.

He wouldn't thank the neighbour, or me, if the grey-haired man figured out who I was.

The *fadisto* finished his set, bowed, and left the stage. His guitarists sipped water and tuned their instruments. The noise levels rose when a beautiful woman made her way through the crowd. She paused at the red ropes before taking her place behind the microphone, dark hair shining under the gaslights.

'Amália,' Graf said, unnecessarily.

Unlike the young man, Amália was quietly confident. She straightened her black shawl at the opening notes of the first song. The *fadista*'s black gaze was piercing and when she opened her mouth, the most extraordinary voice emerged. I understood why Graf and the waiter had insisted that I hear her.

Amália's skill humbled me. Enjoying my response, Graf refilled my glass, his fingers brushing against mine, evoking all the wrong emotions. He was Abwehr – my enemy – and my instincts should be telling me to bolt. Instead, for the first time since landing in France, they urged me to relax and enjoy the temporary illusion of safety.

Because it wouldn't last.

Part 3

Late July to August 1943

Chapter Twenty-six

Rupert Allen-Smythe stood near the Tower of Belém, a thin silhouette against pale, delicate stonework. He spoke to a man who, not unlike the tower, was short and squat. A snap-brim hat hid his face, but I recognised him, by face if not by name. Like Allen-Smythe, he kept cropping up, often in the same company. German company. While someone like me, with no official links to the British embassy, could get away with it, I struggled to find a reason, above board, for his actions. Curious, I had begun to follow him, often wearing the blonde wig or a short auburn one to keep the PVDE's attention away from Solange Verin.

Allen-Smythe favoured tourist attractions for his meets and maintained a rough pattern that allowed me to find him in the morning and, even if he managed to lose me, to pick him up again by mid-afternoon. Patterns were as dangerous as they were foolish. And while Allen-Smythe's stupidity was clear, there was little evidence of any wrongdoing. Yet. But I trusted my hunches.

A peal of bells reminded me of my own meeting. According to the tourist books, the Mosteiro dos Jerónimos was commissioned in 1502 by King Manuel I and designed by a chap called Boytac. It had stonework that 'wonders and delights', statues of Prince Henry the Navigator and Our Lady of Belém. The architecture was Manueline, which as far as I could tell was a flamboyant mix of Gothic and Moorish. An equally impressive building stood next to it with the ubiquitous tourist bus parked in front. That was one thing about meeting in tourist areas: it was easy to hide in plain sight.

There was no sign of Bertie, and with Allen-Smythe lurking less than a ten-minute walk away, I hid my unease behind a bland veneer, blending in with the clergy and tourists to admire the architecture, the statues, the fountains. There was still no sign of my thug when I circled back to the archway fifteen minutes later. Had he been compromised already? Or was I being set up?

With heightened senses, I'd almost expected the shot that rang out. Just not its proximity. Dropping to the ground, I held my hands protectively over my head. While terrified screams swelled and plaster rained down on my shoulders, a few things were clear: one, there was no familiar punch as the bullet tore through my flesh; two, the gun sounded like a revolver, and based on its pitch, German; three, the shooter was an idiot – revolvers were unreliable at distances. Unless this was a crime of opportunity, and if that was the case, was I the target?

Tourists moved slowly, stunned by the ugly reality of war in this holy place in neutral Portugal. Most had never heard a gun before. After a quick scan to confirm that no one had been hit, I rose, searching for a glimpse of the shooter.

A second shot rang out and something drove me on to the ground. The force was accompanied by the smell of unwashed man and I reacted, trying to flip him off me.

'Stay the hell down. You can strangle me later, princess,' Bertie growled, his weight on mine ensuring my compliance.

Over his shoulder I saw a jagged hole in the masonry marking the spot where my head had been only moments before. Bile rose in my throat along with the realisation that I was the target, and that without Bertie's intervention, I'd have been dead. My muscles released and I closed my eyes. I would *not* be ill. Not here. Not now. And not in front of Bertie Jones.

'Stay here.' He shifted to his knees, and I hoped that in his frayed and stained clothing, he made less of a target than I did. 'I don't see him. Bastard'll be long gone by now.'

He helped me up and threw his dusty jacket over my shoulders. Hidden in the crowd of tourists, he half carried me into the chapel.

'Christ almighty, princess,' he murmured. 'Someone's out to get you.'

The grey-haired man? No. He wouldn't have used stealth, even here, where his jurisdiction was limited. And he wouldn't have missed. Allen-Smythe? Possibly, although as far as I knew, he had no reason to kill me.

Whoever it was, was someone new. Shaken as he was, at least I could rule out Bertie. I didn't trust him any more than I needed to, but it was reassuring that it wasn't him. As with the grey-haired man, Bertie wouldn't have missed.

Which made this assassin as much a coward as they were incompetent. It wasn't a comforting thought; even incompetents got lucky sometimes.

Hiding behind bravado, I joked, 'Good thing their aim is rubbish.'

He snorted a reply, but his arm was firm against my back, leading me past a bewigged statue and a few tombs. When my legs would no longer carry me, I sank on to a wooden pew.

'Did you spot him?'

'No.'

'Did anyone else notice that I was the target?'

He shrugged. 'Don't reckon so.'

It could have been anyone: Allen-Smythe, the man he was talking to – anyone. But it was too soon after my potential sighting of the grey-haired man to discount that possibility. What was worrying was that I was dressed as Veronica. Was she the target or had someone connected her to Solange?

'Whoever it was, disappeared right quick. Bloody daft though. Could have taken down a battalion, much less you, princess, with a rifle from one of them turrets.'

Struggling to get my pounding heart under control, I didn't bother to correct his terminology.

'You said you had news?'

He leant back in the pew, wincing as it creaked. Slid a few inches away and bowed his head in a reasonable facsimile of religious devotion.

'Turn away from the wall,' he murmured. 'Someone might be watchin'. You don't want them readin' your lips.'

A few feet to my left, seven wooden doors were framed by elaborately carved masonry. The closed doors could have hidden anything from trysting lovers to assassins. He was right to be cautious.

'Your news?'

Bertie pulled a rosary from an inner pocket, crossed himself and fidgeted with the malachite beads. Head down, I struggled to hear his words.

'You were right – something's up. Portuguese man named Pires approaches me. Wants to know if I'm interested in makin' a bit extra, on the side, like. I tell him that I lost everythin' fleein' France. I'm interested. He says it's easy money. Keep an eye on what ships go in an' out of the harbour. Let him know what flag they fly an' the state they're in. Bit more if I know the cargo.'

It wasn't a bad result after only a week in the new job.

'You said yes, of course.'

'Too bloody right. I'm tryin' to find out who he really is, who he's workin' for.'

'Good.' I made a mental note to buy myself a rosary; they seemed just the thing to hide trembling hands. 'Until then, make sure he thinks you're his man. See who else he leads you to.'

'Aye.' Bertie nodded. 'You know the Pastelaria Suíça?'

'I can find it.'

'Next Thursday. Two o'clock. If there's news, I'll leave a message in the drop. Get outta here, princess. And be careful, will you?'

Most of the tourists had fled when the shots were fired, but a small group of French-speakers remained, the overweight tour guide determined to persevere. I waited at the back of the group as she stopped her flock. She glanced outside, her struggle to maintain a calm veneer clear, her voice breaking when she spoke.

'Before we leave the nave, I must tell you: when King Philip II of Spain visited the Chapel of Saint Jerónimos, he was so taken by the saint's terracotta likeness that he exclaimed *"No me hablas, Hieronimo?"* Won't you speak to me, Jerome? And so, follow me and I will show you this wonder.'

Unless Jerónimos was about to give up the name of my would-be assassin, I wasn't interested. The tour moved to the next room, and I melted away.

There was work to do.

I had been in Portugal for less than two months, and to my knowledge at least, I hadn't blown my cover, irked, or threatened anyone enough to eliminate me. Sure, there were people who didn't *like* me – the nasty Spanish countess Laura, Bertie's old housekeeper Mrs Willoughby – but there was a fair distance between not liking someone and wanting them dead.

What about that old battleaxe who worked in Matthew's office? What was her name? Nicola something-or-other. Langston. Had she confirmed that there was no Mrs Sinclair at Marconi and deduced that I was a spy? And what was to say my assassin disliked me? Maybe they didn't know me. Or maybe they pretended to be my friend. Claudine? Gabrielle?

There was no need to limit the list to women.

There was the grey-haired man, of course, but I was certain he was Gestapo. Killing from a distance wasn't their style. And with a handgun? In a monastery crowded with tourists? No. Whoever it was was an amateur. Someone like Rupert Allen-Smythe? Or someone I had won money from on one of my trips to the casino?

My head was pounding when I spotted Julian's car parked outside Claudine's house. It wasn't alone; several other cars were parked along the road and the gate was open. It was too early for a party, but this was one curiosity that was easy enough to figure out.

Instead of the maidservant, Julian stood by the door.

'Oh,' he said. 'It's you.'

'Who were you expecting? The Pope?'

He stood back to let me in, his face unusually dour.

'Why not? Everyone else is here. And dare I say, you seem to be in a foul mood, Madame Verin.'

From his expression, I guessed I wasn't the only one.

'What happened?'

'The police came this morning. They've found Christophe.'

'Ah.' My temper melted away, leaving me with displaced remorse and little to say. 'Where?'

'In the mortuary.'

'Oh hell.' My shoulders dropped and I rubbed my eyes. My hunt would have to wait, at least for a few days. 'What happened?'

'His body was spat up by the Boca do Inferno.'

The same place Graf had taken me for lunch, that first time. I remembered the angry roar of the waves attacking the black rocks below. It was a beautiful and frightening place. There wouldn't have been much left of him to identify. I wasn't fond of the man, but not even Claudine's husband deserved so ignoble a death.

'I'm so sorry. How's Claudine taking the news?'

'As you'd expect. The well-meaning souls in there are helping her drink herself into a stupor.'

261

'So glad she's surrounded by friends,' I murmured, staving off a fresh panic at how close I'd come to joining Deschamps in the mortuary.

With a quick hand at the small of my back, Julian prevented my escape.

'Come in, Solange. Join the circus.'

'Were they able to confirm . . . ?' What? How he died? Who killed him? How I was going to prevent myself from saying anything untoward? I fluttered my hand in vague clarification. 'Were they able to confirm what happened?'

'The coroner is doing the post-mortem tomorrow, but with two bullet holes in the back of his head, even the locals should be able to figure that one out.'

An execution, and professionally done. Christophe had clearly been involved in something way over his head, but what? And with whom?

'They're certain it's Christophe?'

'Claudine identified the body.'

I cringed. 'Ah, Julian. She shouldn't have had to see that.'

'She identified him by his wedding ring. That and a scar on his leg. The face? Unrecognisable.' His blunt words only underlined his sorrow, and not for Christophe, I was certain. 'Come inside, she'll be glad to see you.'

He escorted me into the parlour with the piano. Its cover was down and a group of men sipped cognac around it, while Gabrielle and two other women fussed over Claudine. She shook them off as she saw me.

'Solange.' She held her hands out to me.

I stepped through them and hugged her.

'I am so sorry.'

'Let me get you a drink,' she insisted.

I wanted to tell her to sit down, but remembered how I was after the news of Philip's death reached me – the manic urge to keep moving, to focus on other people so that you didn't have time to think of your own loss. I nodded.

An older man in uniform waylaid her en route to the sideboard, whispering something in her ear. Maybe he knew the right thing to do, or say, because I didn't. All I could offer was my presence, and hope it would be enough.

Julian pressed a glass into my hand. A sickly-sweet cherry-flavoured swill oozed down my throat, and I struggled not to spit it out.

'Are you trying to kill me, you mad Irishman? What the blazes is this?'

'Ginjinha.' He maintained a straight face. Barely.

'And people enjoy this?'

'Not all, apparently. Your man is in the library, by the by, if you're looking for him.'

'My man?'

If he was referring to Schüller, I'd thump him.

'The Herr Major is in the library with the other Herr Major.'

Julian enunciated each word, as if talking to a stupid child. His nostrils flared a bit, highlighting the distaste in his voice – perhaps for Eduard, Schüller, or the two of them hiding away during a condolence call. Most likely the latter.

'Really?' I cleared my throat, grateful for an excuse to leave the parlour. 'What's he doing in there?'

'Why ask me?' He shrugged, smirking as my empty stomach protested a second introduction of cherry moonshine. 'Go and find him if you're that curious.'

He flicked his fingers at the door and sauntered away.

The library door was closed and cigar smoke wafted from within. I raised my hand to knock but paused, hearing the low hum of their voices.

'Rome, of all places,' Schüller was saying. 'You were right about the Allies landing in Sicily – fucking Martin – but bombing *Rome*?'

The clinking of ice on crystal filled the silence, and then a second, unfamiliar voice.

'It is the Italian capital, Herr Major. And thus a target. I expect there's worse to come.'

'What will they bomb next? The Vatican?'

'Not unless His Holiness declares war on the Allies.' Graf sounded amused. 'I don't see that happening, Herr Schüller, do you?'

'You must admit it was a clever gambit,' the second voice drawled. 'No one, excluding yourself, Herr Graf, questioned the gold mine of intelligence handcuffed to a waterlogged corpse.'

'Fucking spooks. No honour in it.' Schüller said.

'My dear Major,' the second voice continued. 'If that's your opinion, you're in the wrong line of work.'

'Don't be daft. I find a convoy, and sink the bastards. All by the book. Do let your friend Köhler know that, will you, Graf?'

So Schüller *was* behind the air attacks – fed by information from men like Bertie's Pires – but who was Köhler, and why the enmity from Schüller? I stored the name for future use and leant closer to the door.

'The only difference, Haydn,' Eduard explained, 'is that they drew us away from their trap, whereas you drew them into ours.'

'What is more astonishing is that we fell for it.'

The smug, sardonic voice was unfamiliar, but the other pieces of the puzzle came together. The mysterious Major Martin wasn't a German agent; the poor fellow was a decoy used to lure the troops to Sardinia, leaving Sicily open to the Allied attack ten days ago. Mission accomplished, and may he rest in peace.

There was a snort and the glugging sound of glasses being refilled.

'Not that it matters any more. The only hope is to recover from this. And we will, gentlemen.'

'Hear, hear!' Schüller's voice slurred.

It was as good a time as any. I knocked and peered around the corner.

'Am I interrupting?'

Three men sat around a small table, each exhibiting exhaustion in different ways. Eduard was pale under his tan, but his calm demeanour gave little of his thoughts away. Schüller sprawled out in an armchair, his booted feet resting on an ottoman. Dark circles ringed his normally bright cat's eyes, a fat cigar clamped between his teeth.

The third man looked as if he expected me.

'Frau Verin.' He came to his feet and closed the distance between us, moving gracefully for an older, overweight man. 'It is delightful to finally meet you.'

265

If he was trying to catch me off guard, he had another think coming. I extended my hand.

'A pleasure. I'm afraid you have me at a disadvantage, Herr . . . ?'

Eduard's face remained impassive as the man raised my hand to his lips.

'Frau Verin, may I present Herr Kapitän Bendixen?'

Hans Bendixen. Finally, a face to match the name. He wasn't attractive, wasn't even memorable, except for those eyes. Dark, clever eyes.

'Monsieur Reilly said you were hiding away in here. I didn't mean to interrupt.'

'My fault, my dear Frau Verin,' Bendixen interjected. 'I needed to pick the Herr Major's brain for a few moments. But on a happier note, I'm hosting a small soirée tomorrow night. Do tell me you'll come.'

'On a Sunday?' I raised an eyebrow, and Bendixen laughed as if it were a joke.

'Why not? It's just a few friends.' He leant over my hand in a half bow. 'I shall expect to see you gracing Major Graf's arm.'

And with a wolfish smile, the captain left the room.

Chapter Twenty-seven

The talk was banal, and stilted. Eduard and Schüller might be colleagues, and professionals, but they weren't friends. Andreas Neumann's knock on the open door was almost a relief.

Schüller rolled his eyes as the lieutenant limped into the room. The good side of his face held a tinge of sadness beneath its usual professionalism.

'You asked for an update, sir.'

He waited for Eduard's nod before handing him a folded piece of paper. He opened the flimsy note, frowning. A crease appeared, and then deepened between his brows.

'What is it?' Schüller asked.

For a moment Eduard looked like he wanted to ignore the question, then handed him the note. Schüller read aloud.

'"RAF bombing of Hamburg commenced 00.57. Rubble blocked passage for firefighters. Fires raging."' Schüller frowned at Graf. 'I thought you were from Munich?'

'I am.' He flicked his hand in the *keep reading* sign.

Schüller grunted and complied. '"Second attack at 16.40. USAF targets U-boat pens and shipyards." Fucking Yanks.' He crumpled the note into a ball and threw it in the corner. 'I'm going down to the harbour.'

He brushed past Neumann, slamming the door behind him. For a few moments there was an uncomfortable silence until Neumann cleared his throat.

'I apologise for the Herr Major's rudeness, Frau Verin.'

'Never apologise, Lieutenant, for things that aren't your fault.'

I looked down for a moment, not sure how to feel, but knowing that the flames wouldn't be limited to the docks. I'd been in London during the air attacks of '40 and '41. The Blitz. Knew what it felt to survive systematic attacks, day and night. Knowing that you weren't safe wherever you went. Going to bed with shoes pointing towards the door; skirt and cardigan and handbag nearby. To carry all the important things with you, because your home might not be there when you returned.

Did I wish that on the Germans? No. I wouldn't wish that on *anyone*.

'Any news of them?'

Eduard's voice was calm, but his face was taut. There was something wrong, something that went beyond the sadness for the people of Hamburg, or the strategic loss this would entail. Something . . . *personal*.

'No, sir. Too early for that.'

Eduard nodded, his eyes on the wall above the lieutenant's shoulder.

'Dismissed,' he murmured.

Neumann didn't linger. I was torn between allaying my curiosity and asking, and allowing him the time alone, in Claudine's library, with his own thoughts. Sensing his reluctance to talk, I reached for my bag, surprised when his soft voice stopped me.

'Have you eaten today?'

*

268

It was still early, but the Baixa was busy – local workmen rubbing shoulders with sailors and prostitutes.

'What sort of place are you taking me to?' I murmured, but Eduard kept moving, and even I had to work to keep up with his long stride.

There was no sign advertising the restaurant, just a simple door, left open.

'Are you certain this is right?'

As soon as the words left my mouth, I heard the sound of guitars. Followed Eduard through an unmarked door and down a decrepit flight of stairs to a basement that looked like it was a cave. Rough rock walls, and tables that would give my naked elbows splinters. Two men, brothers maybe, strummed guitars and crooned *fado* from the corner, while a table of three Portuguese men sat nearby. There wasn't another German in sight. We followed the maître d' to a table near the back wall, and Eduard ordered drinks before even looking at the menu. A brandy for himself, a glass of vinho verde for me.

'Hamburg?' I broached the subject as soon as the man left.

His shrug was unselfconscious. 'I have friends, family there.'

'But you're from Munich?'

With a slight tilt of his head, his dark eyes met mine.

'And you are French. From Paris. Do you have no relatives elsewhere?'

Once again, a Gallic shrug and a truth that was easier than a lie.

'My grandmother was from Alsace. I was named for her.' Sensing more than he would say, I put my hand over his. 'I am sorry. For whatever people you have there.' It was still the truth.

The man returned with our drinks, and Eduard removed his hand from mine. He opened his mouth to say something, and then closed it, over a rare muttered oath. Still holding my glass of wine, I followed his gaze.

One of the Portuguese men sitting near the singers turned. Large intelligent eyes catalogued every detail, before Adriano de Rios Vilar inclined his head towards me in silent greeting. An equally silent reminder of his determination to preserve Portugal's neutrality. I had only spoken to him the once, but had sensed his attention on and off since then.

Was it a coincidence that he was in the same restaurant we were, scant hours after learning of Christophe's death? No, he had already been here when we arrived. Did Eduard know him? Was this planned?

I didn't believe in coincidence, although I wasn't sure which part of the puzzle he fitted into. As far as I knew, he could still think I was nothing more complicated than a Frenchwoman stepping out with a German. Unless he knew about Veronica. Or my hunt for the grey-haired man. Or the matter of the work I was doing for Matthew, any of which would upset his delicate balance.

Focused on Rios Vilar, I almost missed the man walking down the rough stone steps. Reacquainted myself with the small details. The way he moved, like a shark through water. Cold, dead eyes. A faint scar on his cheek that gave his mouth a sardonic, cast. The pale hair, slicked back from a high forehead. As if cast from my own thoughts, the grey-haired man strode through the restaurant towards us. Dressed in a suit, rather than uniform, as he was in France, but no one could confuse this man with anything other than what he was. Two men trailed behind him; their suits were inexpensive, ill-fitting, and didn't hide the bulge of a sidearm.

At a gesture, the two men remained at the bottom of the steps. How had they found us in this remote restaurant? Were they following us?

I fell back on my training. Not the skills learnt from Special Operations – the ones learnt from Lady Anne. I could almost feel her icy poise flow though my veins.

'A friend of yours?' I asked Graf.

Eduard's face settled into a polite-but-neutral expression.

'Not quite.'

The introductions were brief; just shy of curt.

'Frau Verin, may I introduce you to Herr Köhler?'

I extended a cool hand to the man who had shot dead Alex Sinclair, allowing only a faint irritation that this man would interrupt our dinner to show on my face. People saw what they wanted to see, maybe even this man.

'Good evening, Herr Köhler,' I murmured, keeping my breathing deep and even. Extracting my hand from his, I noticed a red smudge, barely perceptible, across his right cuff.

Pale eyes clawed over me, but Köhler's expression remained unchanged.

Eduard's voice held a faint irritation. 'Is there something I can do for you at this hour, Herr Köhler?'

'My apologies, however, I need a word with the Herr Major.' The faint mocking smile as he spoke to me.

'Can't it wait?'

A languid gesture took in the dinner table and restaurant.

271

'I am afraid not.'

Eduard exhaled. Folded the linen napkin and placed it on the table.

'Of course,' he said, gesturing for Köhler to lead the way.

The two henchmen followed them up the steps as the singers' voices swirled around each other in a crescendo.

Would both henchmen leave if they thought I was a risk? If Köhler was telling Graf who I really was? I didn't think so, although they could be waiting outside.

What information would pass hands? Did it involve me or some other unfortunate soul?

I raised the glass only to put it down. The sgian dubh was strapped to my thigh, but how far would it get me against three armed Gestapo bastards and an Abwehr agent who, despite his loyalties, I rather liked?

At the table near the singers, the Portuguese men had stiffened, their attention on the dark velvet curtain at the top of the steps, separating the restaurant from the outside.

Why? Why be concerned when one German came to speak with another? *Why were they here?*

Under the tablecloth, I eased my skirt high enough to grip the hilt of the dagger. Who was Köhler and what was his agenda? The Gestapo's reach didn't usually extend this far, certainly not into a neutral country. Even if the Abwehr didn't have the best reputation here, they reported to Admiral Canaris; they weren't part of Himmler's SS.

My left forefinger tapped out the time on the base of my wineglass as five minutes extended into ten, into twenty, my attention ping-ponging between the stairwell and Rios Vilar.

Finally, Eduard's tall frame re-emerged. While he looked, if possible, even more exhausted, he moved with his usual grace through the small room, stopping briefly to speak with a waiter, but ignoring the Portuguese men at the other table.

'Apologies, Angel. Unfortunately, that was unavoidable.'

He squeezed my shoulder as he slid past me, and then paused.

'Problem?' I couldn't stop myself from asking, fingers tightening around the sgian dubh.

He hummed a non-response, his eyes still at my shoulder. The scar, as usual, was covered, but had Köhler asked him about it? Well, if so let him. Even if Graf ever saw it, the timeline was off; this scar couldn't be confused with a wound taken in June.

'Eduard? Is everything OK?'

He met my eyes and offered an apologetic smile.

'Certainly.'

Despite sensing Rios Vilar's attention, I took a small sip of wine and raised an eyebrow, willing him to fill the silence with an explanation.

His half-smile acknowledged my tactics and allowed me a small victory.

'There was a risk that Herr Köhler wished to discuss with me.'

Another sip, this one larger. 'And?'

A small shrug. 'I do not think it is important – he did.' He held up a hand to stop further questioning. 'That is all I can tell you.'

All he could tell me, or all that he was willing to tell me with Rios Vilar and his men sitting a few feet away? He smiled, but the tension didn't abate.

My hand brushed the hilt of the sgian dubh as glanced across the room, meeting the Portuguese man's eyes. Between him, the grey-haired man, and the blasted soirée at Bendixen's villa, it wasn't likely to abate any time soon.

Chapter Twenty-eight

Three risks that I knew of, and that didn't include the attempt on my life at the monastery; of the three, Köhler was the easiest one to mitigate. I could eliminate him. I could find out where he lived and make *him* disappear. However, while that would get rid of the man, it would shine a light on the problem. I had no choice but to watch the situation, and take action only when I was in direct danger.

My reflection didn't reveal any hints of anxiety. The Balenciaga dress brought out the green of my eyes and was complimented by an emerald and diamond necklace won from Laura's husband in a game of baccarat. I looked calm and confident. Ready.

I breathed in the night air. Roses and jasmine, undercut by the ozone that preceded a good storm. I closed the balcony's French door and turned on the wireless in time to hear the BBC newsreader commenting on the combined initiative between the RAF and the USAF in bombing Hamburg.

It was a storm of a different sort, and while I couldn't help but pity the people of Hamburg, I hoped that this show of force, this co-ordination with our allies, might bring about a quick end to this blasted war.

Maintaining a polite chatter on the drive to Bendixen's villa, I kept my opinions to myself. Eduard downshifted the BMW and passed through a high wooden gate, nodding to the sentry who waved us through. There were two villas ensconced behind the barricade. The lights blazed in the first, but her twin shimmered from behind closed shutters.

'Welcome to Villa Girasol,' Eduard murmured.

'Who lives in the other villa? I can't imagine your safety-conscious friend happily living so close to someone else.'

'Certainly not. He has tenancy over Villa Bem-me-Quer as well.'

One man, with two large villas. I'd bet the second villa was where he based his operations. He wouldn't trust the leaks in an office any more than Matthew did. I would have to find an opportunity to investigate.

'Stop looking so grim, Angel. It's a party,' he said, helping me from the car as the valet looked on. 'At least try to pretend you don't dislike our host.'

'I don't dislike Herr Bendixen. I've only met him once.'

He hummed a non-reply and led me through the grand foyer, past heavy chandeliers and oil paintings, into a ballroom lit by countless candles. Familiar and unfamiliar faces, flushed with too much drink, nodded to us. With the exception of the Spanish countess, who glared at me.

Standing beside Schüller, she was splendidly dressed. Her gown, the colour of a good burgundy, brought out faint red highlights in her dark hair. A filigreed torque encrusted with rubies, pearls and garnets clung to her slender throat, reminding me of a cuirass I'd seen in a museum.

'Good evening, Countess. Herr Major,' Eduard said, polite as ever.

'Frau Verin, how lovely you look.' Schüller bowed to kiss my hand.

Laura's smile reminded me of a shark's. 'I was sorry to hear about Hamburg being bombed, Eduard. I do hope your wife's family is safe.'

Wife? I'd never seen a ring on his finger; the only jewellery he wore was a Cartier wristwatch. Married. Christ almighty, did he have children as well? Clearly they were the *they* he'd asked Neumann about.

Why should I be upset? He wasn't my lover, just a man that, as Solange Verin, I stepped out with. A convenience. A useful addition to my cover story, and someone to escort me into the right circles to perform my mission for Matthew. I shouldn't be jealous. Wasn't jealous. Was only curious. That was natural, wasn't it?

His wife. What was she was like? Tall and blonde? Elegantly heartbroken that he was here? Did she know that he stepped out with other women? Maintained a dalliance while he was stationed abroad? Not only with me; that dalliance had gone a damn sight further with Laura.

What did it matter? I knew what the Abwehr's reputation was. Shouldn't have – no, *didn't* – expect anything else. And to be fair, he had never acted inappropriately with me, had never promised anything.

Who was I kidding? I'd been attracted to him from the first moment I saw him, and despite myself, that attraction had only grown as I'd begun to know the man. How had that happened? When had he changed from being something convenient to being something . . . more?

And how had I got it so wrong? Not only to fall for a German officer, but also a philanderer. I didn't know whether to kick myself or scream, and in this company I could do neither.

Eduard's face was impassive. 'Thank you, Laura, for your concern.'

It wasn't concern, it was bloody malice. I raised my head a little higher so that I towered over Laura and murmured, 'And my thanks, Countess, for the necklace. I trust you'll excuse us.'

Under the false gaiety lay something even darker and more desperate than my mood. Even the more moderate drank heavily, trying to convince each other, and maybe themselves, that the events in Italy, in Russia, were temporary setbacks. That Mr Hitler would find a way to lead them to victory.

Fools. If they thought the surrender of '18 was bad, this would be far worse.

A woman teetered past on high heels, while on the far side of the dance floor a young adjutant craned his neck. With a sinking feeling, I knew who he searched for. It seemed that Bendixen believed in social graces, but only when they were useful. This soirée was an elaborate ruse to ensure his men were in one place without attracting undue Allied interest. I anticipated the words before they were spoken:

'Herr Major?' The adjutant was young, perhaps seventeen or eighteen years old, and fresh-faced. That didn't make me detest him, or his message, any less. 'The Herr Kapitän has requested your presence. Immediately, sir.'

Eduard glanced at me. 'Has he?'

'He's waiting for you in the library. My apologies, Fräulein.'

I sighed. 'Go ahead, Eduard. I'm certain Haydn wouldn't mind keeping me company.'

The young adjutant's face brightened. 'Have you seen Major Schüller, ma'am? The Herr Kapitän requests his presence as well.'

Yes, of course he did.

I tapped one fingernail on the crystal champagne flute as Eduard pointed the lieutenant in the direction we'd last seen Schüller and took his leave. Over the next few minutes, one by one, senior officials exited, leaving their women milling around in pairs and trios. And despite stepping out with an officer, I was still an outsider; each time I neared a group of women, they changed the subject.

Bored, I sipped another glass of champagne and watched the only other outsider edge towards a door. I had no intention of confronting her, but my legs thought otherwise and I found myself following the countess. Laura kept to the shadows, pausing and looking over her shoulder, one hand on a door knob. She slipped through and allowed the door to softly close behind her.

I covered the distance in a handful of steps, paused outside with my back to the door. Smiled and fanned myself as a couple sauntered by. I heard Laura unlock and open another door.

Then silence.

Grateful for any distraction, I followed. It could be a trap, and save for the knife on my thigh, I was unarmed. I placed my hand on the doorknob and took a deep breath. Felt it turn and the door ease open. The room was dark, the pale moonlight revealing a desk with two visitors' chairs. Framed watercolours of the monastery and the ruined castle hung on the walls, flanking a pair of French doors.

Laura was outside, sliding along the shadows between the villas, pausing under a magnolia tree. She turned around and I froze, hoping the night and my dark gown hid me. Her gaze passed over me, and her shoulders relaxed a fraction as she leant against the tree, intent on the second villa. I took advantage of her distraction to slip outside.

Just in time to see a man step through the door. He was almost upon her when she called out.

I edged closer, intrigued, hiding behind a low hedge.

The man turned, one hand reaching for his service pistol, his posture aggressive. A slow smirk spread as he recognised her, and Schüller swaggered towards the countess. Wasn't he supposed to be with Eduard? Had the meeting already finished? I turned to go, but my gown caught on a bramble. I tried to free it as Laura's slim arms wound around Schüller's neck. His hands bunched the burgundy silk of her dress, drawing it to her waist as he pushed her against the tree.

Oh hell. At least I now knew who his lover was, should I need to find him. Not voyeuristically inclined, I looked away towards the blazing villa, to the one from whence Schüller emerged and up at the ivy wall above them, cursing my bad luck.

A dark shape caught my eye. Actually, there were three. Three black objects, carefully hidden in the leaves.

Another piece of the puzzle fell into place. My skirt freed from the shrubbery, I retreated to the ballroom and was standing by a modern representation of an old master's oil painting when Laura strode past, face taut and angry as she called for her cloak.

I acquired a fresh glass of champagne, silently congratulating whoever had irritated her, until my mind wandered back to the three baubles. Harmless, if you didn't know what they were. I sipped the champagne and sat in a corner, considering how to get word of this new twist to Matthew.

Eduard found me there, two glasses and perhaps forty minutes later. He looked as grim as I felt.

'What happened?' I asked, forcing myself not to shake off his hand.

It was now clear that his attention to me was as contrived as mine had once been for him. More than my ego hurt.

Normally astute, his attention was focused on the news. He took a deep breath and shared it with me.

'Nothing that will not be common knowledge tomorrow. The Italian Grand Council has been convened.'

Suddenly my bruised ego seemed a small thing.

'Convened? Why?'

'Why do you think?' That he was snapping indicated his level of irritation. His response was immediate. 'I apologise, Angel. There is no excuse for being short with you.'

The Italian Grand Council? That could only mean . . .

'They're deposing Mussolini?' I whispered, a maelstrom whirling in my mind.

How had Bendixen heard the news so soon, and what did it mean for the war?

*

We drove in silence, each of us wrapped up in our own thoughts. Three baubles hidden outside a window, a deposed dictator, and a wife I knew nothing about. Matthew would hear the news of Mussolini before I could get word to him, but the baubles? I'd draped one just like it out of the window whenever I transmitted on my wireless, holding my breath in case someone would see it, or the radio detection vans would find me.

Three baubles meant at least three wireless operators operated out of the Villa Bem-me-Quer. This was where Bendixen and Schüller transmitted fleet locations to whichever Luftwaffe base was close enough to attack convoys heading around the Cabo de São Vicente.

They had to be stopped. Permanently.

'You're quiet this evening.'

I opened my mouth to claim exhaustion, and was horrified when a different set of words spilled out:

'You didn't tell me you were married.'

'Angel.' His shoulders dropped; he didn't want to have this conversation any more than I did. 'You had a husband before. I do not like the idea, but I accept it.'

'Good. That's good of you,' I muttered. 'To accept the existence of my dead husband.'

I braced myself for some story of a man far away from home. Graf ran his hand through his hair. Instead of abating, my words stoked his anger.

'Angel, do you truly think I would be here with you if I were still married? What kind of man do you think I am?'

An Abwehr officer. Who's possibly hunting me.

'You're not?'

282

'Franziska died five years ago. Her car skidded on black ice and went into the River Elbe.'

'Oh, Eduard, I am sorry!'

For her death and for his bereavement. For my appalling behaviour, and the tears I didn't know I was holding back.

'Thank you.'

We were at an impasse. Eduard drove on in silence, maybe expecting a different reaction.

Until a loud crack split the night.

Chapter Twenty-nine

The car swerved, and I screamed. Eduard thrust me forward, banging my head against my knees. I stayed hunched over, groping for the dashboard as he accelerated.

'Stay down.'

Pulling his pistol from its holster, fury turned his pleasant features into something unfamiliar and frightening. The hand gripping his pistol held me in place. The car screamed to a halt outside my gate and, in a tone I'd never heard from him, Eduard ordered me to remain in the car.

He disappeared down the hill, Luger in hand, while I lay curled on the floor of the car aware of the possibility that he wasn't the target. A clever assassin would approach the car now, with Eduard out of sight. I was hampered, although not harmless. Did he know that? Did the assassin know what I was capable of?

If he didn't yet, he soon would.

Who was he? And, for all that Rios Vilar and his men watched me, were they a part of this or just observing to ensure I wasn't disrupting the balance? If they weren't trying to kill me, would they prevent someone else's attempt?

Apparently not.

Eduard tapped on my window, shielded me with his body as he helped me from the car and ushered me through the gate.

I went straight to the sideboard in the parlour and poured two large brandies. Handed Eduard one and slumped into a chair.

'Someone shot at us. Someone had the unmitigated affront to *shoot* at us!'

Eduard knelt in front of me, holding my hand in his.

'I can only apologise, Angel. I would never willingly endanger you.'

He thought they were shooting at him. Maybe he was right; just because I had been shot at twice now, that didn't mean he wasn't the real target. I hadn't considered that, but even if it weren't true, I wasn't about to correct him.

'Why? Why were they shooting at you? At us?'

'I'm a soldier. People have been shooting at me for years.'

'Stop making light of it,' I snapped. 'Portugal is supposed to be a neutral country, and that blasted road isn't a battlefield. Who is trying to kill you? Why?'

He let go of my hand and began to pace.

'I work in military intelligence, Angel. Or rather, counter-intelligence. You know that.' He turned and faced me.

'So, it's someone you're after who's trying to kill you? Was this the risk that Köhler told you about?'

He shook his head. 'I do not know who shot at us, Angel. Not yet.'

'Köhler . . . ?'

'Spoke of a different risk.'

'Christ.'

Anger made me shiver and Eduard held me close. Another feeling rose, strong enough to subdue even my anger. A need to move closer, be closer. Not to feel less alone, like the night in the farmhouse with Alex. This was something more though, something I was reluctant to give a name to. My hand went to the back of his head, pulling his lips to mine. He tasted of brandy, warm and sweet. He pulled away far too quickly.

'I am sorry Angel,' he said, retreating again to the open window.

With the high fence surrounding the property, it was unlikely anyone would see him, or be able to take a shot, but it was also unlikely he saw anything more than the trees. If that.

Was he rejecting me? Could that really happen after a kiss like that? Or was it something else: the ghost of a dead wife?

Indecision dissipated and I followed him, sliding my arms around his waist and resting my head on his back. For a few minutes we stood like that until he turned, breathing my name into my hair.

'Angel, you know I care for you.'

'And?'

He remained quiet, and then I understood.

'Oh. You want to be seen with me, but not to be with me.' I straightened my back and tried to hide behind an aloof veneer. 'I see.'

'No, Angel. I do not think you do. Things are . . . uncertain here. My work. The people I must associate with. I cannot allow that to endanger you. I will not.'

'Do you want to break it off with me?'

'No!' His reaction was visceral. Calming himself down, he looked at the ceiling, the floor, at the storm breaking outside, and finally at me. 'No, although I should.'

Any association with Eduard Graf was dangerous. I didn't want to look too hard at my reasons for wanting it to continue, only knew that I did.

'Then the risk is mine to accept or not.'

His head was shaking before I'd finished my sentence. 'No, Angel. I cannot allow that.'

'Yes. You can. Stay with me.'

'You don't know what you are saying. We were shot at. You are frightened.'

His hand was at my nape, strangely gentle.

'I'm not frightened. I'm angry. Stay with me,' I pressed, even though I could see he was resolute.

I wanted to kick something. Take his gun and run out and find the assassin. Kill the bastard now to prove that without the threat, I would still want him. Me, not just Solange Verin. I might hate myself for wanting this man, this *decorated* Abwehr Officer, who hunted people like me. But I did want him. Despite all reason.

And I knew he wanted me as well. Or at least, he wanted Solange, and that was good enough.

'Give me the time to figure out who is trying to kill me and why. If this, you and me, is meant to be, there will be another time. And I will look forward to it.'

He raised my hand to his lips and stood back.

'You don't strike me as the fatalistic sort, Eduard.'

'No,' he said, his voice holding a different sort of resolve. 'I am not.'

'Very well.' I tried to force a rational tone. 'But it's not safe for you to leave. The sniper may still be outside. If you won't sleep with me, then stay in a spare room. I won't have you leave only to have to pick up your body outside my door tomorrow.'

Chapter Thirty

Eduard's car was still parked outside my villa, although Andreas Neumann had picked him up shortly after dawn. Eduard had apologised, not qualifying whether it was for the shots of the night before, the rejection of my bed, or the shredding of my reputation, but mitigated the statement with a kiss that left me – and his adjutant – in little doubt of his intentions.

The storm had passed overnight, and the morning sun was bright and hot. With Claudine in isolation, Gabrielle Ribaud visiting friends in Sintra, and Julian doing whatever it was that Julian did, I spent the morning listening to the wireless and trying to sort through my own emotions. The latter was shoved aside when the formal announcement was made at midday: the Italian Grand Council confirmed that Benito Mussolini, Il Duce, had been replaced by Pietro Badoglio.

Unable to remain alone with my thoughts, I went for a walk, half hoping to draw out whoever had tried to shoot at me. The afternoon passed without incident and the sun was sinking as I walked up the hill. As I passed the arched buildings at the base of the casino, a pale car slid past me, the driver hunched low in the seat, unrecognisable under a dark fedora. It idled at the side of the street for a few moments before the ignition was cut.

The best agents took pains not to stand out, but this man acted like a spy in a bad film.

I dipped my head, hiding my face under the sun hat's brim and watched as one leg slowly emerged from the car. The rest of his body followed, pausing to look up and down the street – checking to see who else was watching. Almost unconsciously, my hand grazed my thigh, reassured by the familiar feel of the sgian dubh.

The man pulled a black briefcase from the passenger seat and adjusted his hat. He glanced right – uphill – first, and then downhill before crossing the street. He was evidently used to cars driving on the left-hand side of the street.

British? Or someone who had spent a fair amount of time there?

He adjusted his grip on the briefcase and straightened. Rupert Allen-Smythe was appearing in far too many places for a low-level diplomat.

Instinct propelled me down the incline and into the hotel. Past the first foyer and into a rose-coloured armchair near the bar as he approached the concierge. Through the glass doors, people were beginning to congregate on the patio with their pre-dinner gin and tonics. I leafed through a copy of *Time* magazine and watched the concierge pass a key to Allen-Smythe. There might have been a perfectly legitimate excuse for the subterfuge, but something felt wrong. The Palácio was too public – too much a British hotspot.

A small man in a crisp suit stood at my elbow. His hair was slicked back and his small moustache was shiny with wax.

'May I help you, madame?'

His supercilious voice was inordinately loud, but he blocked me from view as Allen-Smythe crossed barely five feet in front of me into the bar.

If Allen-Smythe saw me, he didn't show any concern. Unsurprising, as he had only seen me as blonde Veronica, not Solange, with dark hair dishevelled from a day at the beach.

'A cup of tea, please.'

I opened the pages of my book, dismissing the waiter. When he passed from sight, I slid into the next chair over, changing my view from the arched hallway to the dark panelled walls of the bar. Allen-Smythe sat at the bar, fiddling with his cuffs. At his feet was the black briefcase.

Next to him another man sat in a low chair, a half-drunk aperitif in front of him, and to the other side, a trio of men laughed, their noses red from sun and liquor.

The exchange happened so fast I almost missed it. As Allen-Smythe adjusted his tie, the gentleman seated by himself crossed his leg, his foot sliding his own briefcase forward.

Allen-Smythe twirled the ice in his drink, and glanced again in the looking glass. He wasn't preening – he was watching. He made a show of checking the time before draining his glass and reaching into an inner pocket to retrieve his wallet. He dropped a note on the bar, and exited with the other man's briefcase.

Everyone knew the Palácio was Allied territory, which made it probable that his contact was British, although Allen-Smythe's overacting would have had him laughed out of a variety show.

The Spider should have known better than to keep a bloody idiot on his books.

Allen-Smythe was waylaid at the entrance by an older couple. I scooted around him and charged up the hill, cursing myself for not letting the air out of Allen-Smythe's tyres when I had the chance.

Hoping I hadn't lost too much time, I threw my bag onto the passenger seat of Eduard's BMW and fumbled for the wires, striking them together until the BMW woke with an angry roar and catapulted down the road. I was about to make the sharp right turn leading towards the Palacio when Allen-Smythe's silver Peugeot slid past. It turned on to the Estrada Marginal, heading towards Lisbon.

Half-hidden behind his dark fedora, Allen-Smythe's face was expressionless.

The BMW responded to the change of direction with beautiful precision. The last rays of sun glinted off the Atlantic to my right. I allowed a second and then a third car to drive between us, trying to mask my pursuit.

I had learnt my lesson at Sagres; my PPK was hidden in the bottom of my bag. It would be difficult to get to while driving. There was a chance that Eduard kept a spare in the glove compartment. Keeping one eye on the Peugeot, I rummaged in the glove compartment at the first stop sign. Papers that I would review later. A crushed pack of cigarettes – strange, I'd only seen him smoke that once – and a French letter. What the blazes was he doing with that? The bloody fool had a French letter in his glove compartment and turned me down? Half the Abwehr were shagging their secretaries and he turned *me* down. What was wrong with him?

I muttered a curse, and stepped on the accelerator.

If he was shagging his secretary, I'd kill him.

If he was shagging *anyone*, I'd kill him.

Allen-Smythe turned off near Oeiras, but instead of heading towards the beach and Schüller's rooms, he weaved through small streets, sometimes speeding, sometimes creeping – doing a bloody poor job of trying to shake a would-be tail. It was a miracle he had survived so long.

Another red light allowed me to extricate the PPK from my bag.

Allen-Smythe picked up the Estrada Marginal again, passing a monument and continuing along the south front of the Praça do Comércio. He turned up the Rua da Prata into the Baixa. A right turn led us past the little church of St Maria Madalena and the larger cathedral.

It was difficult to keep cars between us now. This was territory I hadn't been trained for. On foot, I could pick up a tail or lose one as easy as breathing.

Allen-Smythe wasn't subtle. He might be taking detours but was heading inexorably towards the Alfama district. He turned off and cut his engine. I drove past his parked car, certain that his destination was the ruined Castelo de São Jorge. Convinced there was no above-board reason he would want to visit at this hour, I ditched Graf's BMW near Santa Luzia and continued on foot.

My espadrilles allowed me to scale the steep, cobbled streets with barely a sound. The Bairro Alto would be kicking off soon, but this side of town was quiet enough for sounds to carry. Garlic and fish battled with the stench of sweat and urine. Short dark men, stocky and sullen watched from a restaurant lit by lanterns as I paused for breath at the base of the castle ruins, only looking away when a young woman arrived with a tray of drinks.

What could these men recount? A European brunette following an Englishman around the castle? They didn't know me; didn't travel in the same circles I did. What was the worst they could say? That I was a jealous woman, following my lover? And bad taste in men was neither a crime, nor overly noteworthy.

I waited just beyond the entrance to the ruins, the PPK a reassuring weight in my hand. Seconds ticked into minutes with no sign of Allen-Smythe. And the minutes ticked into an aeon. The shadows lengthened, but it was still too early for the searchlights to scrape the sky. Finally, muffled footsteps approached. I moved closer to the wall and held my breath. Still carrying the briefcase, he slipped past with a furtive grace.

What a bloody stupid place for a meeting, although given Allen-Smythe's gross incompetence, it shouldn't have surprised me. The more interesting question was who he was meeting. The man he was with at the Torre de Belém? Whoever he'd commissioned to kill me?

He skirted the perimeter of the ruins, passing under archway after archway, only occasionally pausing to look over his shoulder. At the base of the fortress, he veered right.

I gave him enough time to clear the alley and cross the arched bridge into the fortress. Crouching low to avoid being exposed, I scurried after him. Picked him up when a falling rock gave away his position on the ramparts. I clambered up the steps on my left and stopped just short of the top. When Eduard had brought me here, we'd followed the rampart around to a dead end. Allen-Smythe must have known about it. I eased back, evading that trap.

Allen-Smythe doubled back – crossed an empty courtyard to a flight of steps at the far right side in a game of bloody snakes and ladders. I took the long way, skulking in the shadows. Climbed rough, steep steps and crouched behind the crenellations. Allen-Smythe's frame was silhouetted against the twilight as he ducked into the watchtower. I counted the seconds until he exited. I followed him, flicking the safety off the PPK with a too-loud snick although Allen-Smythe showed no sign he'd heard it.

I edged towards the watchtower, leading with the muzzle of the gun. Expected to walk into an attack but the room was empty.

Footsteps echoed to my left and a sliver of pale skin glowed in the moonlight as Allen-Smythe crossed another courtyard. The bastard moved fast. Legs burning from the crouch I'd been forced to maintain, I followed him down the steps.

I heard the second set of steps too late. Should have been listening for them; Allen-Smythe had come here to meet someone, not just lose a tail. I'd allowed him to distract me while his partner's firm hands on my back shoved me forward.

'Lisbet, no!'

Matthew's voice carried across the dreamscape, as my nails raked against the raw stone, scraping for purchase. I tried to catch myself against the archway and missed. My knee smashed against a step. Then my wrist, my hip, my shoulder. Fire exploded in my head and I heard a howl of protest, not recognising it as my own as I landed.

Two shots reverberated and someone patted my cheek. I couldn't see anything as velvety darkness took the pain away.

Chapter Thirty-one

I woke in a strange bed, in a room that smelled of ammonia and fresh flowers. My left hand was immobile, but with enough determination, the right one rose until every muscle cried out in anguish. Ignoring the pain, I fumbled for the pistol I usually kept under my pillow, but came up empty. The gun was gone.

Where was it? Where was I? Panicking, I tried to move, but my body refused to obey. My head pounded and tears of frustration threatened. Bright light stabbed at my eyes and I extended my other senses until my eyes could adjust to the light. Cars hummed on the streets below. The low din of nearby conversation competed with the dolorous sound of a *fado* guitar. I wasn't familiar with the song or the singer; the recording wasn't mine.

Footsteps clicked by, two voices murmuring about an accident. *What the hell had happened?*

Slowly, in flashes, my memory began to return. Following Allen-Smythe to the castle. Hands pushing hard at my back. Falling. Hearing my real name ringing off the stones. There was another man, the one who'd pushed me. Who was it? The same one who'd been trying to kill me, or someone else? Where was he? Something scratched at the back of my mind – a bit of information – but when I tried to pull it forward, it eluded me.

Stomach clenched, I took an inventory. My ribs felt like some-one had taken a cricket bat to them, but felt bruised rather than broken. My toes finally moved; at least I wasn't paralysed. Only my left arm refused to comply.

I counted to ten and cracked open my eyes again. The room was whitewashed, with pale curtains fluttering in the breeze. A watercolour of the seafront hung above a table holding a vase of flowers. My arm looked rather less pastoral, splinted and cushioned upon my chest.

Rupert Allen-Smythe. Next time I saw that misbegotten bas-tard, I'd shoot him. And if Matthew had anything to say on the matter, I'd shoot him too.

What I'd mistaken for a pillow was a thick band of cotton wrapped around my bruised chest. My head ached, but there were no bandages, save for a damp plaster near my hairline. I hoped it was only sweat, but my fingertips came back tipped with pink.

'So. You are alive?'

The voice was deceptively calm, as the man rose from a chair near the door. His body was tense, the shoulders stiff and his dark eyes snapping with anger.

'So it would seem,' I croaked. I cleared my throat and tried again. 'Where am I?'

'*Who* are you?'

The voice was familiar; the tone wasn't. I tried to raise myself to see his face, but the effort was too great and I sank back into the pillows.

He moved to the foot of the bed, staring at me for a few long seconds. Poured a glass of water and, cradling me in one arm, held me as I drank.

'Thank you.' I reached for his hand, but he pulled back.

'Who are you?' Eduard Graf repeated.

'I thought I was the one concussed.'

From his expression, my joke fell short of the mark.

'You are not.'

It was bad – I knew that. My medical situation, far less critical than the situation with Eduard. How many lies and half-truths would it take to recover from this? What if he'd already told the Germans about me?

'Eduard?'

'Who are you, Solange?'

'The same woman I was yesterday.'

Only I wasn't, and I didn't need to hear him call me Solange rather than Angel to confirm that. My cover was blown and, as much as Portugal pretended to be a neutral country, Eduard could arrange for me to 'disappear' if he wanted to. So could Matthew. Would it be a race between the Germans trying to kill me and my godfather shipping me off on the next plane to London?

Eduard broke the silence. 'You have one cracked rib and a broken arm. You were pushed down a flight of steps in a ruin you should not have been to. In a city you rarely visit.' My eyes struggled to focus as he paced in front of the window counting out my infractions on his fingers. 'Having hot-wired *my* car.'

I winced; I'd forgotten that detail.

'Ah . . . I can explain that . . .'

He continued as if I hadn't spoken. 'You held a pistol in one hand and a knife in the other. And I could not get there in time to stop you from falling.' He clenched his fist, every inch the Panzer commander. This man would take no prisoners. 'It was you, wasn't it? The man who shot at us was after you, not me.'

My mouth went dry. I tried to fashion a plausible excuse, but came up blank.

His voice lowered. 'Do you know why I left the car in front of your house? Do you?' He didn't wait for an answer. 'I thought they were after me. I did not know if they'd cut a line to the brakes. If I would not be able to stop and would continue down the hill and into the Atlantic.'

Cold sweat prickled my skin. I hadn't considered that his car might have been sabotaged – hadn't thought of any risks. I just knew I had to follow Allen-Smythe.

'Did you even think of that?'

'Eduard . . .'

'Of course not. You do not think before you act. You simply assume everything will be fine. But that has not always been the case, has it?'

I had no idea he'd read me so well.

'I don't know what you're talking about.'

'So you hot-wired my possibly sabotaged car and drove to São Jorge for the fun of it?'

'Something like that.'

'Stop lying!'

He took one step towards me. Swivelled, and drove his fist into the wall. I stared at him. This quiet man, this *gentle* man, was incandescent. At me. And didn't care who heard it.

'Please keep your voice down.' I glanced meaningfully at the door.

Furious, he stormed to the door and locked it, but when he spoke, his voice was again low and measured.

'I am a fool. I should know no one is who they say in this damned city.' He looked to the ceiling and took a deep breath before staring into my eyes. 'You were there to meet Harrington, and I would like to know why.'

It felt stupid to do so, but I still asked who he was referring to. His look was answer enough.

'I know you were there,' he grated. 'What I want to know is *why* you were meeting him.'

'Eduard, I swear, I wasn't meeting anyone. Not your Harrington, not Salazar, not anyone.'

He stared at me for a few moments. Then leant forward, one arm on either side of my bound ribs, his face a breath from mine.

'Then why did he scream "Lisbet" as you fell?'

Chapter Thirty-two

Matthew's carelessness had all but confirmed that I was an English spy. How could I rationalise the irrational? Especially when Eduard was fully justified in feeling betrayed.

He waited for my answer, but all I could think of saying was: 'Why on earth would he do that?'

'That's what I'd like to know.'

Keep as close to the truth as you can . . .

'Fine. You've accused me of acting on impulse, and you're right. I was walking up from the beach, and stopped for a cup of coffee. I saw one man leave with another man's briefcase.' I shrugged. 'I called out, telling him of his error, and when he didn't respond, I went after him.'

'You knew something wasn't right, and yet you followed.'

'Ah. Yes. Sounds rather silly, doesn't it?'

'Without wondering who he was meeting or whether he'd be armed. Who he was working for or where he was going. How insane are you?'

'Insane enough to be certified. Clearly.' Which of course would be better than jailed or dead. 'Why were you there?'

'I finished a meeting, saw my car – *my car* – screaming by, and you expect me to do nothing?'

'Oh hell.'

His eyes narrowed at my curse, but otherwise he ignored it.

'I commandeered a car and followed.'

'Christ,' I muttered.

Had I been so intent on tailing Allen-Smythe that I'd missed Eduard tailing me? Who else could have been tailing me?

'Then I see you pushed and Harrington shooting over your head. He hit one man. The other shot at me, and ran off.' He rubbed his face, grey from exhaustion. At least some of the anger had dissipated. 'I do not understand, Solange, why an English diplomat was standing over you, protecting you.'

'Nor do I,' I said, thinking quickly. 'Unless he thought I was someone else?'

Eduard frowned. 'So you don't know him?'

Evasion was easier than outright lies. 'Why would I?'

'I hoped you would tell me.'

'I can't tell you what I don't know.'

I tried to keep my eyes steady as they met his. Warring emotions played across his face: the anger that hadn't fully subsided; exhaustion that could only partially be blamed on his work; and a desperate desire to believe me.

My eyes began to burn with tears. I tried to wipe them away, but couldn't raise my arm high enough. It was bad enough having to cry, but weeping in front of Eduard was mortifying. I tried to muster the shreds of my bravado.

'But while I'm delighted that you care enough to yell at me, can it please wait? I'm not feeling very well at the moment.'

The words were barely out of my mouth when my stomach revolted. I lunged for the bowl on the bedside table. Felt Eduard's hand steady my back as I vomited.

'Oh God, how humiliating.' I fumbled for a glass of water.

'The painkillers,' he explained. 'Sometimes they have that effect.'

His weight sagged against the bed and his linen handkerchief brushed against my cheeks. For whatever reason, he was allowing me to get away with my story.

He's a good man, Lt Neumann had said. *Honourable.*

But he was a German officer. Tasked with rooting out enemy spies. Like me.

The painkillers were making me sleepy as well as maudlin. I closed my eyes to escape his censure, hoping I would survive the hospital, and the repercussions of the last few days.

The man sitting beside my bed was slightly shorter than Eduard and swarthy. Avian black eyes watched me and, given the certainty that Eduard was having my room watched, I was grateful for my godfather's Mediterranean disguise.

'You gave us quite a scare, old girl,' he said.

'You shouldn't be here.'

'And you shouldn't have been at the castle.'

'What happened?'

Matthew wound a gramophone in the corner – the sounds of a Verdi duet masking our conversation.

'It would appear you stumbled into something rather larger than anticipated.'

'Yes, well. I'd rather guessed that when I felt a pair of hands at my back.'

He studied a painting on the wall before speaking.

'You were right about Allen-Smythe. He was passing on secrets to the Germans.'

'What sort of secrets?'

'Mostly who we were interested in, and the steps we were taking to . . . ah . . . keep watch over them.'

Probably not what he really meant, but I didn't have the energy to argue.

'And where is he now?'

'The city mortuary. The gentleman who pushed you panicked when he saw me. Got off one shot at me, and one at Rupert. Young Allen-Smythe presented a better target.'

'You mean, he killed his own contact? Why would he do that?'

'Jolly good question. For which I can only guess that he was afraid Rupert would betray him.'

'Do you have him? Or the man who gave Allen-Smythe the briefcase?'

'Not yet.'

'Did you at least see him?'

The door to my room opened and a doctor walked in, trailed by a pair of nurses. Matthew retreated to the window. The doctor removed the stethoscope from around his neck and checked my breathing, or what he could do through the yards of linen bandages. Grunted and said something to the nurses, and something else to Matthew, who nodded, as if he understood the doctor's orders.

Waited for the door to close firmly behind the trio before he spoke.

'My dear?'

'Where's the man who tried to kill me?'

'I don't know. Whoever he is, he's wounded.'

'You shot him?'

'No, your German friend did. Went a little mad, that boy. Jolly good shot, by the by.'

'Speaking of which, do you have my gun?'

'Sorry, old girl?'

'Never mind,' I mumbled, feeling sleepier by the second.

If Matthew didn't have it, then maybe Eduard did. Or it was lost. I felt more of a pang for the sgian dubh than the PPK. Something else worried me – something else I needed to tell him. And then I remembered.

'I found it.'

'Found what, my dear? The fountain of youth? Love? Your gun? Damned silly thing to lose. Especially for a yahoo like you.'

'Love?' I blinked. 'Why would you say that?'

'Last time you acted so foolishly, you ran off with de Mornay. Just be careful, Lisbet. Falling for that boy is not a good idea. The Abwehr have a reputation here in Lisbon. Most are indeed more concerned with their pleasure than their jobs. But not that boy. Eduard Graf is a damned sight more dangerous than your husband was.'

'No joke.'

'No, indeed.'

'Are you going to send me back?'

'To France?'

'To London, you dolt.'

'Why would I do that?'

'He knows that I'm a bit more complicated than he thought.'

Matthew snorted. 'You're a bit more complicated than the German naval codes, Lisbet. But no, until the risk is real, I'd rather you stayed.'

'It isn't real?'

Hard to believe, when I was lying in bed with ... what was it? A broken arm and a cracked rib after being pushed down the steps of a bloody ruined castle.

'Graf hasn't yet alerted his masters to his suspicions. I'm not sure he will.'

Well, that was interesting. But it was time to confess.

'Someone is trying to kill me. Not Graf.'

'Yes, old girl. I had noticed that.'

'It wasn't the first time. That someone has tried to kill me, that is.'

He pursed his lips. 'Do you know who? Why? Where they are?'

'If I did, they'd already be dead. Do you?'

'I do not. And I suggest you take care of that problem. Do let me know if I can help.'

I believed him, but by his own admission, his organisation had too many holes. Sleep again threatened me, and I fought it, determined to let him know what I'd learnt. In case Eduard changed his mind. In case the Gestapo came for me in my sleep. He was halfway to the door when my whisper stopped him.

'I found them, Matthew,' I repeated.

'Them? There's more than one?'

I shook my head and he retraced his steps, the genial Spanish façade receding as the avian predator took over. I was no longer his recalcitrant godchild, but the agent, the informant.

'Who have you found?'

'The pianists, Matthew,' I mumbled.

He patted my shoulder with an awkward affection.

'Time for bed, old girl. You're beginning to speak nonsense.'

I was losing the battle to stay awake, but this was important. I couldn't let them sink another ship.

'Germans,' I mumbled. 'There are three of them.'

He held himself very still. His black eyes sharpened as he moved closer.

It took all my reserves, but I forced the words out.

'Wireless transmitters. Run by Hans Bendixen at the Villa Bem-me-Quer.'

And then I closed my eyes. It was bad enough that Eduard had heard enough to suspect I was rather more than I claimed. The problem was that someone else suspected me as well. And had already tried to kill me. Again.

The nurse had just finished changing my bandages when the door opened with an unceremonious bang. She turned, a string of rapid Portuguese on her tongue, stopping midstream when she saw the offender.

'I'm sorry, sir.'

She picked up the dirty bandages and sidled out, leaving room for Rios Vilar.

The PVDE man strode past her as if she didn't exist, taking up a position at the foot of my cot, arms crossed over his chest and brow lowered.

'I am glad to see you alive, Senhora Verin.'

He didn't look it. He looked like he'd happily put a bullet between my eyes.

'An unfortunate accident?' he asked, his voice incongruously pleasant.

'Unlike Monsieur Billiot,' I said, 'I try to survive any accidents.'

'Most people try to survive accidents, senhora. I am glad you were more successful than Senhor Billiot.' He pulled a chair close, but instead of sitting down, braced his hands on its back. 'Would you care to tell me what happened?'

'Don't you know?'

He blinked. If he was feigning emotion, he was doing a bloody good job of it.

'Why don't you tell me.'

It would have been easy to lie: a story of a horseback riding accident, a slip on the rocks, anything. But this man had me watched for months; there was no point. Taking a deep breath, I repeated the story of seeing a briefcase stolen, and on a foolish whim, following the offender.

'Silly thing to do,' I concluded. 'Clearly.'

'Clearly,' he echoed. 'Senhora, I do not think I need to repeat myself and tell you that these are dangerous times. The war progresses, both sides are jumpy. Desperate. Both sides will do whatever they must to succeed. If you get in the way, you are in danger. If you are a part of it, you are in danger, and due no protection from the state. Do I make myself clear?'

'Yes.'

I wondered what protection he had offered to date? How many times had I been attacked with no one to guard my back?

'Good.'

He let his hands drop to his sides and turned to the door.

'Senhor Rios Vilar?'

309

The painkillers had loosened my tongue and the urge to ask the question in the back of my mind bubbled to the surface. He paused, turning back to me with his head tilted in silent inquiry.

'Yes?'

'If things are as you say, and the war progresses, which side will you choose?'

'You know the answer to this.' His laugh was mirthless. 'Portugal, Senhora Verin. For me, it is always Portugal. Nothing else matters.'

It was still about the fine line of neutrality. One that he might now think I'd crossed. And if he did, then my life might well go the same way as Martin Billiot's.

Chapter Thirty-three

After three days, neither the PVDE, the Gestapo, nor Eduard came calling.

Matthew did, briefly. Long enough to interrogate me on the wireless devices. I told him of meeting Köhler, first in France and again in Lisbon. He confessed to knowing little of the man. Agreed to keep an eye on the situation but felt it unlikely the man would be here because of me.

I agreed. Didn't think he'd be a bad enough shot to miss twice, maybe three times.

With regards to the PVDE, Matthew could shed no light.

'Some PVDE officers favour the Nazis, as you know. But Rios Vilar?' His shrug was no answer.

Three days. Seventy-two hours. On my own, staring out of the window, wondering what would happen upon my release. Or whether someone would tire of waiting and have me killed in here.

I was bored. I was cranky. And I was *damned* if I'd allow myself to be an easy target. I could brood about Eduard as well from home as I could in the hospital, and could protect myself better there as well. On a walk around the ward, I acquired a skirt one size too large, a jumper one size too small and left the hospital.

The taxicab dropped me off at a hotel in the Bairro Alto. I went in the front door, and out of a service exit in the back. Took the train to Cascais. Doubled back. It was exhausting and I didn't have a lot of energy to spare, but if Rios Vilar still had his men following me, chances were good that they were as exhausted as I was. I unlocked my front door, turned on the wireless and poured myself a drink.

The BBC and its Spanish equivalent recounted the Allied successes in Italy, the continued bombing of Hamburg, the Russian victories on the steppes. The local English station spoke of food shortages and the resulting strikes in the Bairro, where the workers had stopped work on Tuesday and were now locked out. It had escalated into demonstrations, shots fired, and the city filled with troops. The German channels claimed these 'disturbances' were fostered by the British.

I lit a cigarette and took my brandy to the piano, picking out a tune with my right hand. Perhaps I could check in with Bertie. Make sure he hadn't left something out of his last report. Wasn't there something he'd said . . . ? Something that my memory was aware of and that I just couldn't pull forward. What the devil was it?

A loud knock sounded on the gate.

I ignored it. An assassin wouldn't announce his presence, and whoever else it was, could go hang.

The knocking became insistent. I walked upstairs and eased out on to the balcony. The angle was wrong, but could just barely see the top of Claudine's head when she stepped away from the door. The last thing I needed was to be more fodder for the Estoril gossip machine.

'Go away!' I bellowed, not caring who heard.

'For pity's sake, open the door, Solange!' Claudine shouted. 'I'm not leaving until you do!'

'Bloody Frenchwoman,' I grumbled, but padded down to meet her. Yanked the door open with my good hand, ignoring my ribs' protest. 'What do you want?'

The black dress accentuated her pale skin and haggard appearance.

'I heard you were in hospital! I wanted to see how you were.'

A wave of guilt overwhelmed me. I'd forgotten about her own situation, and had been unnecessarily harsh. I stood back to let her in.

'Broken arm. I'll be fine. The funeral?'

'Yesterday.'

'I'm sorry I wasn't there.'

'I didn't expect you to be. I was just worried about you.'

I shook my head. 'Nothing more than a silly accident. Forgive me, Claudine. I'm just feeling sorry for myself.'

'I can understand that.' She ducked under my good arm and entered my house. 'Self-pity isn't good for you. Did you fall off that bicycle? I told you that you should give it away and buy a car.'

'I like that bicycle,' I said, feeling strangely protective of it. Scratched my nose and waited for her to leave.

'It *was* the bicycle! I knew it!'

'She tripped in the old castle ruins and had a nasty fall, Claudine,' Eduard said from the doorway.

I was shocked by his sudden presence. Had he deliberately used Claudine as a Trojan horse? He stood back, his hands in

313

his pockets. He was casually dressed, without a tie, and a light breeze ruffled his hair.

'Oh, you must be careful. Some of those rocks . . .' Claudine's voice trailed off, and she fluttered her hand at my arm, hanging from a sling fashioned from a floral scarf. 'Obviously.'

'Frightfully clumsy.'

I was surprised that Eduard would give me an alibi instead of exposing my lies. I forced a weak smile, hoping Claudine didn't see through it.

'Coffee?' I offered, although I wasn't sure if I wanted either of them in my home.

Claudine winced. 'I'll make it.'

She pottered around my kitchen while I retreated to my parlour. Eduard sat in the armchair, watching while I paced around the room. I didn't know how to react. His absence had been a palpable force and I wasn't certain how things stood between us.

I halted in front of him, standing with my good hand on my hip.

'Why are you here?'

'The door was open.'

'That's not what I asked. Why are you here, Eduard?'

I jerked my head to the kitchen, asking why he'd given me the alibi. He shrugged and gave my half-empty glass a flat look. Damned if I'd let him judge me, I drained the blasted thing. And refilled it. Let him comment on that. Sensibly, he refrained.

'You should have sent word – I would have picked you up at the hospital.'

'After our last conversation?'

He raised an eyebrow, as if that was an answer. It wasn't. We sat in awkward silence until Claudine bustled into the parlour and set the tray on the table. The rich smell of coffee wafted through the room and I breathed deep enough to cause a stab of pain to shoot through my ribs.

'Careful,' Eduard murmured.

'So what news, Herr Major?' Claudine asked. 'I heard there was quite a bit of excitement at the embassy the other day.'

I closed my eyes, allowing their words to wash over me. Sipped the coffee and expected to hear news of Italy.

Instead Eduard said, 'Yes, Bendixen was quite inconvenienced by it.'

'By what?' I asked, suddenly interested.

'Oh, that's right. You were in the hospital,' Claudine said. Eduard remained silent as she explained. 'The PVDE raided his home, and the villa next door. It would seem they found evidence that he had people watching the ports and relaying information to the Luftwaffe.'

People like Bertie's contact Pires. Was this before or after Rios Vilar issued his last warning? That raid would have upped the stakes between the Germans and the Allies, perhaps causing the increased tensions he noted? I made a note to contact Bertie and see what he knew of this.

'Ah,' I said, my voice calm, although my mind raced. 'Didn't someone mention that at a party not too long ago?'

'Well, of course,' Claudine said, 'we all knew about it, but for the Portuguese to have evidence? Now that Mussolini has been deposed? It not something Dr Salazar can ignore.'

Eduard's face was still closed, but the way he watched me made me wonder if he thought I'd had a role in the raid. For that matter, so did I. Had Matthew taken my news seriously enough to act on it so quickly?

'What sort of evidence could they have found?' I asked.

'Copies of what appeared to be transmissions,' Eduard finally said.

Ah. Well then, God bless German efficiency. Duplicates and triplicates of everything.

Another thought, less welcome, came to mind.

'Eduard, what will this mean for you?'

'The raid on Bendixen's villa?' He shrugged. 'Nothing, as far as I know. I am with the Abwehr, not Naval Operations.'

'What do you think will happen?'

'I would guess that a case will be made at the Portuguese High Court. If the evidence is solid and if the case goes against us, those whose involvement can be proved will be evicted.'

Would Bertie's name be on any list or was he too small fry?

Claudine flapped her hand. 'It's happened before – a slap on the wrist. Nothing more.'

'As you just commented, the political climate is changing,' he reminded her. 'No assumptions can be made.'

'Pah. You'll see – Salazar will have it all thrown away.'

I shared a glance with Eduard, sensing that he lacked Claudine's certainty.

'Well,' she said, standing up, 'I'll leave you then. You most likely have some catching up to do.'

And she had gossip to spread. Eduard saw her out of the door and locked it after her. I waited in the parlour. He hadn't told

Claudine the truth, but he *was* part of the Abwehr. Had he told anyone there about me?

I started with the easier question: 'Why did you lie to Claudine?'

He didn't answer at first. Took my brandy glass, sweating near the piano, and emptied it out of the window.

Not a good sign.

'What lie? Did you not fall down the steps in the old castle?' His voice was too cool, and I half-expected the next question. 'What did you see at Bendixen's villa, Solange?'

I made a face. 'Haydn Schüller. Having your countess in the bushes.' My eyes snapped open. 'Haydn? He was coming from the other villa when he met Laura. Is he involved in this, then?'

Éduard shrugged. 'Why were you following her?'

'Following her?' Sometimes a half-truth was useful. 'Why on earth would I do that? It was warm inside. I went outside for a breath of fresh air. Only it wasn't so fresh, and I came back inside rather than interrupt them.' My moue of distaste was genuine enough. 'Did I miss something interesting?'

'More interesting than that? I should think not.'

I cleared my throat. 'Then why did you ask? Do you think someone shot at us because they thought I saw something? Neither Laura nor Haydn have made any attempt to keep their affair a secret. What? You can't possibly think someone was shooting at *me*?'

'In truth, I did not.' He leant against the wall, crossing his arms over his chest. 'But after your "accident" in the ruins, I do not know.'

317

'Laura was outside as well. If someone shot at us because of something I may have seen, do you think they went after her too?'

Not for a moment did I believe that. Not when someone had shot at me at the monastery *before* Bendixen's soirée. But Eduard seemed to consider it.

'I saw her a few days ago. She did not appear to be suffering from any attack, thwarted or otherwise.'

'I don't know what to say. I can't imagine why anyone would want to shoot me, but if they are, then I'd really like my gun and knife back. If there's a chance . . . Well . . . I want to be able to defend myself.'

He nodded slowly. 'You may have them back on three conditions.'

'Which are?'

'One – you tell me how you got hold of them.'

I played lightly with the truth. 'The gun? I acquired it in France.' I remembered Scar and Pig-eyes, the two Gestapo agents I'd killed at Franc Laronde's house. 'To protect myself.'

'A PPK isn't something easily acquired.'

'For a price, anything can be bought.'

He frowned, clearly wondering what price I'd had to pay.

'I'm not like Laura,' I snapped. 'I don't barter my body for *anything*.'

'I know.' He cleared his throat and continued. 'And the knife?'

'A gift.' I stared back, refusing to be ashamed. 'From a friend who's now dead.'

'A German gun, popular with the Gestapo, and a Celtic blade.'

'The Scots were in France before the war, Eduard. Keep the gun if you must, but I'd like the knife back.'

He didn't look happy. 'Was he your husband?'

'Who?'

'The man who gave you the knife. The one who's dead?'

'What? No. My husband died in the early days of the war, the Scot somewhat later.'

'He was your lover?'

There was a French letter in his car; he hadn't been a monk since his wife died, but he wouldn't apply the same latitude to me. Nevertheless, I wanted there to be truth – as much as I could afford – between us. At least about this.

'Briefly,' I admitted. 'And the only one other than my husband, before you ask.'

For whatever reason, it was important he know that.

'Was he involved with the Resistance?'

'Alex?' I laughed, sadly. 'No. Not at all. Just a man who was in the wrong place at the wrong time.' Before he had a chance to draw any parallels, I added: 'Your second condition?'

'That you allow your curiosity to go unsated. This is Lisbon, it is not safe to be too curious. You will not follow anyone. You will not get yourself in any other mischief.'

I nodded, finding it easier to lie to him non-verbally.

'Your third condition?'

He looked like he wanted to ask something else, but instead threw the challenge out.

'That you prove to me you can use them. You're a danger to yourself without them, but if someone is out to kill you, I'd rather you be ready for them.' He picked up my handbag. 'Get in the car.'

It looked like Eduard Graf had made up his mind.

At least for now.

Eduard was serious about the shooting lessons. We drove out towards the sparsely populated area near the Boca do Inferno. He pulled a satchel from the boot of his car, ignoring the telltale clink of wine bottles.

'If you're going to seduce me, Eduard, that's fine. But with all the painkillers I'm taking, I don't think you need more than one bottle.'

He gave me a flat look. Stalked to a fallen log and lined up three empty bottles.

'Damn,' I muttered, giving the cast on my left arm a dark look.

He paced back about twenty yards and checked the pistol. With a complete lack of concern, he raised it, squeezed the trigger, and the rightmost bottle shattered. It was a good shot and he should have been smug, but his face was blank as he handed me the gun. Adjusted my posture, damn him, and had me fire off a shot.

I would have loved to show off, to prove that I could do it, if not as well as he could, then certainly not far off. Instead, the pain in my ribs set off my balance, and with only one hand on the pistol, I missed.

He stood behind me, his warm body supporting me, closed his hand over mine and took aim. Dizziness that had little to do with the painkillers had me sway on my feet. Eduard tightened his hold and the report of the gun echoed over the waves as another bottle shattered.

We stood at the makeshift range, Eduard patiently correcting me, until no bottles were left and the nearest tree was filled with lead. My right arm shook from the exertion, and my left arm itched. Special Operations' instructors were good, but Eduard Graf was better. Even exhausted, I was now hitting the knots in trees.

'The sun is going down,' I murmured, not wanting to admit I was too exhausted to continue.

'One more time.'

Eduard refilled the clip and moved behind me to correct my stance. I blew a lock of hair out of my eyes, rubbed my forehead with my sweating arm and took aim. Missed spectacularly as Eduard's lips lingered at the nape of my neck.

'Stop distracting me.'

I lined up another shot, my concentration challenged by his proximity. His chuckle shot a spark down my spine and I closed my eyes.

'I'm distracting you?'

He straightened my right arm as it wavered. Then drew the back of his hand down the sensitive underside before wrapping his hand around mine again and squeezing the trigger twice, hitting the knot both times.

'You're cheating, Eduard.'

His hand dropped to my hip and, despite the risk of another rejection, I leant my head back against his chest.

'Do not stop,' he murmured.

I wasn't sure if he meant my shooting or my advances. I straightened and emptied the clip into the tree, the cartridges catching the fading light as they fell in elegant arcs away from the pistol. Squeezed the trigger until the mechanism clicked on an empty chamber. Tossed the gun a few feet away, and turned in his arms.

He was waiting – pulling me closer. I ignored the pain in my ribs as I pressed against him.

'Goddamn you, Eduard Graf. If you reject me now, I'll shoot you. I swear I will.'

'The clip is empty.'

'I don't care.'

My fingers fumbled with the buttons on his shirt, hating the cotton that separated us, awkward with haste and the encumbrance of the cast. Eduard stepped back and shed both shirt and vest, not giving me time to stare as he closed the distance, his fingers, more nimble than mine, going to the buttons of my shirtwaister, cupping my breast through the thin cotton and groaning.

'I can't get this dress off.'

'Let me.'

He made short work of the buttons and eased the sleeve over my cast.

I should have been embarrassed standing in the half-light in my brassiere and knickers, yards of linen protecting my ribs, but I threw my head back and let him look. Revelled in the expression on his face. Wanted to see him, feel him.

Have him.

'Angel?'

I took a deep breath and closed the space between us, wondering why something that should be wrong should feel so right.

As if everything I'd done for the past year, the past twenty-eight years had led me to this point, lying with this man above the cliffs named after the Mouth of Hell.

He unfastened my bra, his trousers. The discarded clothes made for a comfortable mattress. The sky, a canopy of pinks and blues, until Eduard made me blind to everything but the look on his face, the feel of his lips, his hands, and his body.

Until he made me his.

'A redhead,' he murmured.

'What?'

I followed his eyes lower down my body, and grabbed for his shirt to cover my modesty. What little was left of it.

'Why did you dye your hair?'

'It seemed the thing to do.' I couldn't let him distract me. 'Why now, Eduard?'

'What? This?' He nuzzled my neck. 'You smell good.'

'Thank you.'

There it was again. The scratching of the memory. Smell.

I stopped when I smelled you, princess.

That night at the castle ruins, the person near the steps. I'd thought it was a man, but anyone could wear a disguise, and I'd fallen into the age-old trap: I'd seen what I expected to see. But on some level, I registered more; a perfume with a mix of musk and night flowers, as unique as the woman who wore it. I knew who she was. Pictured her with the gaslights bringing out the red in her chestnut hair. She didn't have a reason to want me dead, but then, this was the city of spies, and no one was who they pretended to be.

Why was she meeting Allen-Smythe? Was it for money? Her husband's losses at the casino were well known. She wasn't German, but spent far more time with them than even I did. Was it ideology? She didn't strike me as either a fascist or a communist. Was it the thrill of the chase?

I leant back in Eduard's arms and sighed. I'd have a devil of a time neutralising her.

His teasing voice became serious. 'Angel, at least twice in the past week I came close to losing you. Maybe more. I cannot lose you, and if the only way I can keep you safe, is to keep you by my side, then I will do that.'

I smiled, unwilling to correct him. He couldn't keep me safe from an assassin. Only I could do that, and only if I was able to stop her first.

Chapter Thirty-four

It would have been easier if it was Köhler. One assassin, one threat. This complicated things. While easier to find on any given day (half of Estoril knew where she lived), I couldn't just knock on her front door, point the PPK at her forehead and pull the trigger.

To make matters worse, they were watching me. It was more intense than the usual *bufos*. I felt it the last few days. Couldn't see them, but could sense their presence; a sort of malevolence that was directed at me. Was it my would-be assassin? Or one of her henchmen?

I stared out towards the sea, the glass of brandy untouched at my elbow. The evening was cool, stars glowing in the sky, and the sea a fair bit calmer than the tempest raging inside my mind. Whoever she really was, she had done a jolly good job of hiding in plain sight. And I had underestimated her – almost paying for that error with my life. Twice.

What could I safely assume?

She had both a revolver and a rifle, although displayed rather poor skill with both.

She was aiming at me on the night of Bendixen's soirée. And having shot at me clad as both Veronica and Solange, she knew I was more than I seemed, although she might not realise which side I worked for.

She may or may not have told her masters about me, depending on the level of threat she felt I posed. Although her attempt to kill me gave a fair steer on that. Anger more than fear made my hand shake as I lifted the glass to my lips.

She was most likely working for the Germans. The communists had their hands full on the Eastern Front and were, at least nominally, our allies.

She would have a safe house where she could leave her disguises and any equipment without worry that her husband would find it. Equipment. Perhaps she was a wireless operator; there were the three baubles outside Bendixen's villa, but that didn't seem right either. Bendixen would have staff to do that; there was no reason to be covert, especially with the Portuguese government turning a blind eye.

With Eduard asleep in the bedroom, I couldn't begin the surveillance until the next day. She had hunted me for the better part of a month. Tomorrow would be soon enough for me to return that favour.

With both aliases potentially compromised, I opted for a simple knitted cap, a bulky shirt, and trousers. If no one looked too closely, I could pass as a man, with the added bonus of not further constricting my still sore ribs and hiding the brace on my arm.

Her social schedule was busy enough and, as I soon learnt, predictable. Luncheon with friends, shopping, dining out and often finishing the evening at the casino. She met one lover in his apartments in Carcavelos and another in Lisbon. And although both could be ruses to gather or pass on information, based on the sounds from within, I was relatively certain they lacked any platonic nature. It didn't surprise me, given what I knew of her, and what I knew of espionage, but that didn't stop distaste from blossoming.

It was more than a week before she veered away from Lisbon's shopping district up a short passageway and into a building, not far from the one Bertie had stayed in while he convalesced. It wasn't the elegant town house I would have expected. On the lower side of bourgeois, it was clean enough and nondescript. Exactly the sort of safe house I had in a different part of the city. Intrigued, I slipped through the door behind her, taking note of the flat she entered and continuing up the stairs to the next landing.

Five minutes. Then ten, and still no sound from the flat below. I couldn't wait her out much longer, but in truth there was no need. I knew where her safe house was, and would be better served returning when there was no risk of getting caught – either by her, or by a curious neighbour. I eased myself from my perch and made my way outside into the sunshine.

With plans to return later in the evening, I made my way to the embassy's annexe, with the hope of encountering my godfather.

I bought a fresh pack of cigarettes and waited for him to leave.

From the way he was dressed, I guessed he was heading to the port, in search of whatever intelligence the dock dollies, as Bertie called them, could offer up. Within two blocks, he turned and closed the gap between us.

'You're losing your touch, old girl.'

Digging my good hand into my pocket, I shrugged.

'If I didn't want you to see me, you wouldn't have.'

'You're looking better than you were the last time I saw you. Nice outfit,' he commented, avian gaze raking me up and down. 'Although I preferred the blonde wig. And the female couture.'

Another shrug. 'This is better for shadowing. Walk with me.'

He fell into step. 'Who might you be shadowing, or should I refrain from asking?'

'I'm trying to figure out why someone is trying to kill me. Someone with links to your friend Allen-Smythe. What do you know of his activities?'

He tilted his head to the side. 'Still frightfully little, although that's changing by the day. We're still trying to find the man who passed him the briefcase, as well as the contact he passed information on to. Doubt we'll ever find out why. I don't suppose you've figured that one out too, my girl?'

'For money?'

'What a bloody stupid question,' he admonished. 'I really do expect better of you. Of course for money. Although it would seem admiration also factored in. Sad, really. His father –'

'I'm not concerned about his lineage. What sort of intelligence was he passing on?'

'As far as I know, your name never came up, if that's what you're asking. You're not listed in any of our files.'

'And yet, he saw us together. Could have easily found out there's no Veronica Sinclair at Marconi. Could have seen me in the casino or anywhere else in Estoril. Heaven knows, I saw him about.'

He inclined his head, acknowledging the point.

'So, his area of focus?'

Matthew sighed. 'He was one of my men working to foil the wolfram smuggling. It would seem he passed on any updates as to how we were dealing with the situation. Any new complaints, anything. To be fair, what he passed on was relatively low-level.'

'And my work with Bertie?'

'He knew nothing about that.'

'Can you be certain of that?'

Matthew pursed his lips and drew me into an empty bar, ordering two beers.

'In our line of work, my dear, there is rarely certainty. We have to make do with probability. With calculated risks. So, while I don't *think* he knew who you are, I cannot guarantee that. What do you want? I'd rather not extricate you with everything else going on, but I'd also rather not have you dead. Become rather fond of you in the past few decades, I'm afraid.'

'Jolly good.' He ignored my sarcasm and I continued. 'And I'd rather not leave yet either. As far as I know, she is acting on her own.'

'She?'

'She. Sometimes women make good spies.' I stated the obvious. 'And assassins. Who would have thought it?'

A ghost of a smile passed over his face.

'Who indeed. You know who this woman is?'

'I do.'

'And you won't tell me?'

'With the leaks in your organisation? No chance.' I pushed the beer around in a small circle, relenting. 'But if I can't handle her, you'll be the first to know. And I'll need to get out fast.'

'And your Abwehr friend?'

'Knows I am more than I admit. And that someone wants me dead. Ironically, the latter bothers him more than the former.'

'Does he know who it is?'

Interesting that he was less curious about my would-be assassin than he was about Eduard Graf.

'No. Not yet.'

'Why not?'

'Why? Because I haven't told him. The damned woman is working for the Germans. She's on his side. And while he might suspect I'm more than I seem, I'd rather not confess to being a British operative. He's bloody Abwehr, Matthew. Part of their job – *his* job – is to root out people like me.'

'Would it make any difference if I asked you – again – to be careful?'

I nodded and made to move away when he grabbed my arm. 'I will do.'

He released me and stood back. 'If there's a risk—'

'I know.'

'I know you know.' He cocked his head to the side, eyes narrowed as he studied me. 'There's something else, isn't there? Something you're not telling me.'

'There's always something I'm not telling you. It's rather a *quid pro quo*.'

Matthew was already shaking his head. 'It doesn't work like that, old girl. Not when your life's on the line.'

I shrugged. 'There isn't much you could do, even if I had proof.'

'Proof of what?'

'Someone is watching my home.'

'This is Lisbon, my girl. Someone is watching *everyone*. I told you that the first day.'

'It feels different. More intense. I haven't been able to find them. Yet. Whoever they are, they're good, but I can feel eyes on me every time I come in or go out. Bloody inconvenient.' My blasé tone fell on deaf ears.

'More than the usual *bufos*?'

'I think so, yes.'

'I don't like this, Lisbet. Do remember to be careful.'

'Always.'

She wasn't difficult to find. Her chestnut hair glowed in the sun as she sipped cocktails with two German women at a bar near the beach. Sensing that she'd be occupied for some time, I made my way into Lisbon and her safe house.

Her front door wasn't designed to deter a trained burglar, and gaining entry was easy enough. She wasn't stupid, though, and had set up tricks to determine if anyone had been in. A tripwire near the door led to nothing more serious than a small array of potted plants, which would acknowledge an unauthorised intruder. There were also a few threads hanging from doorknobs and a book at an awkward angle where everything else was aligned. I'd used similar tricks when living in France.

I started with the usual places, peering into drawers and closets, shoeboxes and hatboxes. Found an appalling array of clothing, but little else.

Moved to the bookshelves. Romantic novels in Spanish, and a few on horticulture. These offered gardening tips and a handful of French letters. The other books, in German, provided a bit more insight. The countess hadn't struck me as being interested in military history, but the language made me wonder just how far her links to Germany went.

Frustrated, a glance at the clock on the desk confirmed that while quite a lot of time had passed, I had no proof, much less any inkling, as to why the countess had targeted me.

The floorboards sounded solid, as did the walls, and the only thing living under the bed was a dust ball the size of a small cat. And then it was too late. A key in the lock gave barely enough time to turn off the light and crawl beneath the bed.

Heart pounding and fighting the urge to sneeze, I watched slim ankles in Italian shoes cross the floor, followed by heavier boots. She turned in a 360 degree arc, as if cataloguing anything that might be out of place. Her skirt fell a few inches from my face, and she moved closer to the man.

Not only was she not alone – she was about to entertain. On the bed above me.

The skirt was quickly joined by a blouse and a lace camisole. And then a heavy *clunk* as the man's belt buckle hit the floorboards. His trousers weren't the fine material of an officer's uniform, but the heavy denim of a workman.

Wouldn't it be funny if it was Bertie?

On second thoughts, it wouldn't be funny at all.

From the sound of it, there was no love involved, just an animalistic coupling that made me ashamed to witness it, yet unable to escape.

With one hand on my PPK, I closed my eyes against a growing dread about what I was about to experience, and an even bigger dread of what *she* might have seen if she had been watching me as closely as I now watched her.

The bandage at the top of her arm could have hid a bullet wound, and was all the confirmation I needed. She moved to the bathroom after he finished, while he sprawled, naked, on a chair in the parlour. He was fair-haired, taller than Bertie although not as tall as Schüller or Graf, with the thick body of a labourer, and as his splayed legs demonstrated, an impressive suite of assets.

She emerged, clad in a blue silk kaftan. Her voice no longer held the husky tones of pre-sex, but the tone was low and the German consonants lacked any hint of what I had believed to be her native accent.

She handed the man a folder from her handbag, waiting as he leafed through it. He grunted some sort of approval and tossed the dossier onto a sideboard. Perhaps it wasn't so interesting after all.

And then he pulled her forward. She accommodated him by raising the hem of the kaftan and straddled his hips. Locked her lips on his and guided him inside.

What was in that folder to warrant such a reaction? And despite the plethora of French letters in the horticulture books, none were used. Did she *want* to get pregnant?

A harsh rip and the blue silk fluttered to the floor; his mouth was on her breasts as she rode him.

This time, it didn't last as long, and the man exited while she ran a bath. I crawled out from under the bed and locked the door to the flat. The folder was gone, but she was alone. It wasn't going to get much better than this. I sat on an armchair facing the bathroom door, PPK in hand, and waited.

She took her time cleaning herself up. I didn't blame her; I felt as if I needed a hot shower myself.

The door opened and she stood for a moment, silhouetted by the gaslights, towelling dry her long chestnut hair. Her eyes widened when she saw me, but she quickly hid her surprise behind a calm demeanour. Her chin lifted a notch, defiant.

Feeling oddly calm, I smiled.

'*Guten abend.*'

Chapter Thirty-five

She seemed equally calm; only a slight narrowing of her eyes warned that she was about to move. She threw the towel at my face and I batted it away as she bolted backwards into the bathroom. My bruised ribs made me slower than usual, as I jumped over the low table and braced my good arm against the door. I slid my foot into the breach to prevent her from locking me out. Heard a drawer roll open and pushed hard, taking the chance that with her attention diverted, I could get inside.

The door gave way, and instead of seeing a pistol pointing at my head, the countess stood in the middle of the bathroom, her hands at her sides. Smirking.

She hadn't had enough time to booby-trap the room, and there was no window to escape from, so at first I wasn't sure what she was smiling about. Then her jaw tensed, making a crunching sound. I wasn't fast enough to get to her before the capsule between her teeth released the arsenic, or whatever other fatal cocktail the Germans stuffed into their L-pills, into her body.

Special Operations had given me a similar pill, but I had thrown it away at the first opportunity. Why die when you could fight back? Laura held my gaze as the poison took effect. Soon she struggled to stand and sank to one knee, one pale hand on the countertop.

'You stupid, stupid woman,' I whispered as she fell to the ground.

Kneeling beside her head, I asked the only question needed: 'Why?'

She closed her eyes, her slight smile spiting me until the end. If she felt any pain, she kept it to herself, along with all the other secrets she held.

'Stupid, stupid woman' I repeated.

My heart was still pounding, although less from exertion than it had been minutes before. Throughout the whole event, there had been no crashes, no screams. No logical reason for anyone to come and investigate, but logic had little to do with my life and I didn't want to be found here, with the body of a dead Spanish countess, whoever or whatever else she happened to be.

I wiped down the surfaces I had touched. Any other secrets the flat held would have to be found by the police. Pulling my cap low over my eyes, I exited quickly from the flat. As far as I knew, unseen, although I wasn't about to take the chance of the police, or worse, the PVDE arriving.

I had gone to Laura's safe house with the intention of getting answers, not seeking her death, and despite her repeated attempts to murder me, there was neither joy nor satisfaction in it. The evening left me with sadness, anger over the unanswered questions I had, and a growing sense of foreboding. What if she'd kept incriminating information on me? Who was the German man she gave the file to and what was in it?

And what, if anything, did he know about me?

*

336

I was spoiling for a fight by the time I returned to Estoril. Tired of being on the run, of being attacked and stalked, I had had enough. Dressed again as Solange, albeit in dark clothes, I circled the streets around my home, looking for anything out of place. Couldn't see anyone, but felt a presence. Was it one of Köhler's men? One of Eduard's? Or the PVDE?

The Deschamps' home was dark. Not good if I had to scream for help, but at least Claudine wouldn't be a witness to whatever happened after I managed to draw my watcher away.

I passed through the gate. Paused. Turned around to leave, sensing him following me. I moved up the hill, past the other houses and villas, until dwellings were sparse enough to have truly dark patches between them. I was tired. Past tired. My arm hurt and my ribs hurt. But at least I was alive, and wasn't inclined to give that up.

Blending into the shadows, I allowed him to get in front of me. A large man, far taller than the gardener-*bufo*, and unfamiliar, but what was in his hands told me all I needed to know. First, like me, he knew that the report of a gun would bring unwanted attention. The garrotte, on the other hand, was quiet enough. And with the cast on my arm, he would think he had the advantage.

He was wrong, but I had to move fast. He must have heard me, deflected my blow and tried to get the garrotte around my neck. Raising my left arm, I stepped back, catching the wire on my cast. White pain reverberated up my arm, and I used that pain to fuel my anger. I grabbed the handles from him and lashed out with a leg.

'*Fotze*,' he grunted, stumbling, and falling to the ground.

The lights went on in a nearby house. Someone called out, their words unintelligible.

Time was running out. Garrotte in hand, I slipped behind him, sliding the wire over his hand and tightening it around his neck.

'Who are you? Who do you work for,' I whispered in his ear. First in German and then in English, because it didn't matter any more if he knew who I really was. There was just enough slack in the wire that he should have been able to answer. He chose to resist instead.

With no choice left, I tightened the wire.

When he stopped moving, I patted down his body down, looking for clues. Pocketed his papers, and left him where he lay, the wire still around his neck.

Chapter Thirty-six

According to his papers, Alois Bergmann was born in Hannover and was in Lisbon for business, working for a German shoe company. Utter rubbish, of course. Shoe salesmen don't skulk around, stalking women with garrottes and guns. Gestapo agents, however, do.

Had Laura arranged this before she died, or was this the work of Köhler? No, the grey-haired man would be here, supervising my demise, if that was the case. But the questions remained about Laura . . . until they didn't. Sometimes the obvious answer was the right one. She might have been irked that Eduard threw her over for me, but found solace fast enough with Schüller. No, it wasn't jealousy. The connection had to be through Allen-Smythe. If I'd seen him cropping up in all the wrong places, he might have seen me. Might have even connected Solange to Veronica.

And if that was the case – if whatever they thought I knew was enough of a threat to kill me – then who else had they shared the threat with? Who else would be coming after me to retaliate for their deaths?

With the body just up the hill, the knock on my front gate was not unexpected, but I tightened the sash on my dressing gown and stepped out on to the balcony. Two uniformed officers stood on the street outside with Claudine Deschamps. I stubbed out a cigarette on the ashes of Bergmann's burnt papers and took my time going downstairs to greet them.

'Senhora Verin?'

'Yes?'

They showed me their ID. They were regular police, not the PVDE – a good sign.

'May we come in?' The shorter of the two spoke. He was built like a barrel, but his eyes were sharp.

'Of course. The coffee is still hot. May I offer you a cup?'

Ignoring Claudine's look of distaste, all three followed me into the kitchen. I poured three cups and put the sugar bowl on the table.

'I'll fix a fresh pot,' Claudine said.

My neighbour poured her coffee down the drain and measured fresh grinds into the bowl.

'What can I do for you?'

Barrel cleared his throat. 'Did you hear anything . . . ahh . . . untoward last night, senhora?'

'Me?' I exchanged a wide-eyed glance with Claudine. *Nothing to see here, officer. No answers to give . . .* 'Nothing at all. What's happened?'

'Someone was killed. Farther up the hill,' Claudine piped up.

'A man was found dead,' Barrel clarified. 'We are treating it as a suspicious incident.'

Keeping my eyes wide, I gasped.

'No! So very many suspicious incidents these days. You know about Martin Billiot and, of course, Madame Deschamps' husband? Ghastly.' I reached for her hand and gave it a little squeeze. Felt a slight pang of guilt when she turned away to wipe away a tear. 'Do you know who it was? Who did it?' I kept a straight face as I added, 'Do I have anything to worry about?'

'No, no, senhora. I am certain you don't. You heard nothing? Saw nothing? I am sorry, but we must ask.'

'No.'

'Did you know a man called Bergmann?'

That was fast; I hadn't expected them to discover his name so soon. My frown was genuine enough.

'I'm afraid not. Did you, Claudine?'

She shook her head. 'The name sounds German, but he wasn't an officer. I didn't know him.'

The younger policeman looked at the cast on my arm.

'An accident, senhora?'

The cast was filthy, but the area where plaster was missing was hidden by the sleeve of my dressing gown.

'I had a nasty fall at the castle.'

They looked between us for a few moments before Barrel nodded.

'Very well, then, we won't waste your time.'

'Thank you, sir.'

'Thank you, senhora.'

I saw them out and locked the door after them.

'How awful.'

Claudine's hands shook as she poured the hot coffee into a cup.

'Do you think it was related to Christophe? You said –'

'Claudine, I have no idea.'

I met her eyes directly, trying to assess whether she was lying as well.

'Do you think . . . ? Would Eduard know?'

'The man has only just died, Claudine. Besides, you know that if Eduard knew who killed Christophe, he would have already brought the man to justice.'

Her eyes filled with tears and she squeezed my hand.

'I know he's busy with Herr Köhler, but could you ask him to look into it?'

'I think you think I have more sway over Eduard Graf than I do, but I'm happy to ask. What do you know of Herr Köhler?' I kept my voice light, hoping she'd read the question as little more than idle curiosity.

'I haven't met him yet,' she said. 'But Haydn doesn't like him. Says he's Gestapo, sent here because Herr Hitler doesn't trust the Abwehr, and thinks they're plotting against him. Haydn says he's causing problems for *everyone* here. Not just the Abwehr.'

'Problems? Do you think he was involved with this Herr Bergmann?'

'I don't know. I don't think so.' She shrugged. 'I'm surprised Eduard hasn't said anything to you.'

'Why would he?'

'Haydn says he knew Köhler in Germany. That Eduard Graf seems to be the only person Köhler *isn't* looking at. Why do you think that is?'

I sipped my coffee and shrugged. 'I couldn't tell you. Eduard doesn't speak of his work to me, but I *can* tell you this – if Köhler isn't interested in Eduard, it's because he knows Eduard is loyal. And if you want me to ask Eduard about Christophe, I will. But I doubt he'll have any answers.'

Claudine nodded, seeming to believe my words.

I only wished I did. If Eduard Graf knew Köhler back in Germany, and if Köhler knew who I was, how long would it be until Eduard handed me over to him?

In the middle of a hot Portuguese summer, it hadn't taken long for Laura's body to be found, and the count was brought down to the mortuary to identify her remains.

'He doesn't believe it was suicide,' a woman at the next table whispered to her friend. 'After all, why would the countess be in *that* part of town?'

'Was there any sign of . . . well, you know?'

'Murder?'

'As well.'

'The word they're not saying is "rape",' Gabrielle said, sipping a glass of Pernod and staring out across the beach where a sea of tourists sunbathed. 'There will be a post-mortem of course. And then an inquest. Count Javier will see to that. And given that Laura had the morals of a street cat, they'll find something, although I'm not so sure it'll be rape.'

Under the circumstances, it was safe enough to ask.

'What do you think happened?'

'Heaven knows, Solange. There were enough people who probably wanted to kill her, including her husband.' She raised her shoulders in a quintessentially Gallic shrug, and tucked a strand of incongruously blonde hair behind her ear. 'Maybe it was suicide, but why kill herself?' She lowered her voice. 'Unless she had a secret she didn't want let out?'

'Maybe she was expecting?' Claudine suggested, staring into her own glass.

'Well, if she was, she'd have palmed it off on her husband.' Gabrielle flipped her hand, the sunlight dancing off her rings. 'No, I think it was murder.'

Claudine nodded, and I followed her lead, but one thought kept scratching at the back of my mind: Laura wasn't working alone. The inquest would find the poison, and whoever was running her would be alerted. L-pills were given out to prevent spies from surrendering their secrets; that she had one might raise eyebrows, might draw her handler into the open.

Unless of course, what drew him into the open was me. And the prospect of retribution.

Part 4

October 1943

Chapter Thirty-seven

Retribution, if it was coming, was taking its time, and as I hunted my hunter, the Portuguese Attorney General, prodded by the British mission in Lisbon, put together the espionage case against Bendixen and his operation based on the information they'd found in the PVDE's raid on Bendixen's villas.

The case was tried in the military courthouse near the Baixa. It was a nondescript building in an innocuous square, but on this day it was far from average, and the courtyard pulsed with people from just about every nationality. They weren't here to watch a trial; most wouldn't be allowed inside. They were here to watch a spectacle: history being made, the first time since Salazar changed the law that a case was brought to trial of a foreign power committing espionage on Portuguese land, where the nation they were spying against wasn't Portugal. No one knew what would happen. Would Salazar order the court to take the easy way out, claim insufficient evidence of espionage and dismiss the case. Or would the men be convicted; expelled or incarcerated? Either way, Bendixen and his men were now out in the open.

The prosecutors went after the big names, including Bendixen and Schüller. People like Bertie, and even Pires, were considered too small fry to worry about, and while Pires was no doubt wondering where his next bribe would come from, Bertie had discreetly passed on information detailing how the dockside part of the network operated.

The October sun blazed down on the Rua do Arsenal. Gabrielle stretched out, trying to catch the best of the sun, while I hid under my floppy hat and dark sunglasses.

'I heard the most extraordinary thing the other day,' she said.

Julian and Claudine exchanged an eye-roll, but Gabrielle waited until I responded.

'Dare I ask?'

'Well, I overheard it from a pair of diplomats. English, you know, so I can't vouch for it.'

Even Knut, panting at my feet, looked bored.

'And?'

I reached under the table to ruffle his fur, wondering how Eduard was faring inside the courthouse.

'It would seem that Mr Churchill went to Parliament, and revealed that Salazar gave him approval to construct an airbase.' She raised her sunglasses and watched us closely to gauge our responses. 'On the Azores!'

I straightened up slowly. This was big, and potentially spelled the end of the war. I hadn't heard anyone speak of it before, although wouldn't be surprised if both sides hadn't made a case for access to the islands. A base on the Azores would allow us to fight Hitler's U-boats from the air, without having to rely on the carriers, without having to worry about refuelling. It meant we could better protect our convoys. And with fewer subs threating our shipping, and a better supply chain, it would be a strategic coup.

Between that, and the possibility of Bendixen's intelligence network being blown apart in the courthouse a few streets away, this was shaping up to be a jolly good day for the Allies.

'If it's true –' I kept my voice slow, measured – 'it'll give the Allies quite an advantage, won't it?'

'Hitler's been pressuring Salazar for years over those islands,' Julian noted, dryly adding: 'Who'd have thought a bunch of rocks in the middle of the Atlantic would be so important.'

'Who indeed?' Gabrielle asked, leaning back with a look that almost seemed self-satisfied. More than was warranted for a bit of gossip, salacious as it was.

Before I could think about what it meant, a shout came in the direction of the courthouse.

'It's about to start. Let's go.'

Julian paid the bill, and we weaved through the crowds.

'What do you think will happen? I mean, with Gabrielle's news?' Claudine asked, falling into step beside me.

'I don't know. As you once said, Claudine, if this had happened before Mussolini fell, it wouldn't even be in question. But when even Franco is cutting his losses, and now the Azores?' I shrugged. 'Heaven only knows what Salazar will do.'

It was down to Rios Vilar's delicate line of neutrality, assuming that it still applied. I couldn't see how Salazar could really maintain neutrality if he let the Allies build that base.

'Has Eduard mentioned anything about it?'

'No.'

If my voice sounded grim, it was all too genuine. If he knew about it, he hadn't shared that news with me. Neither had Matthew, although to be fair, both were focused on the court case, tasked with relaying updates back to their respective embassies.

'What Salazar wants, the judges will deliver. Everyone knows that,' she sighed.

And with Bendixen gone, would the smuggling ring be broken? With less naval intelligence, less tungsten steel, and with the added threat of an airbase in the Azores, how much longer could the war last?

And what then?

Gabrielle and Julian weaved through the crowd like dancers, while our path was cleared by an 80 pound Alsatian, but that thought jostled me worse than the crowd. What will happen when the war ends? These people had become friends. And Eduard . . .

As I took a steadying breath, forcing my sudden panic into a box labelled 'cross that bridge when I come to it', a man emerged from a side door, back straight, body vibrating with anger. Sunlight glinted off the medals on his chest as he shoved a PVDE officer out of his way and slipped into a dark Peugeot.

'Oh, heavens, Solange. It's Haydn. What's happening?' Claudine pushed forward but the Peugeot was already out of sight. She turned to me, eyes more bereft than curious. 'That can't be good news.'

'I don't know. If he was found guilty, surely they wouldn't let him go.'

There wasn't enough time to consider it; a short man in a smart suit appeared at the top of the steps. When the crowd quieted down, he relayed the verdict. His voice was lost in the crowd's echo:

'Guilty.'

Men filed from the building – journalists and witnesses, prosecutors and defendants. Anyone lucky enough to have a ticket to the circus. Knut barked when Eduard appeared, deep in conversation with Andreas Neumann, and dragged me through the crowd to his master.

'It's done?' I asked, reaching for his hand.

He looked drained, forcing a weary smile for my benefit and ruffled the dog's fur.

'Every scrap of paper that was seized ended up in that damned courtroom.' Eduard's voice was heavy. 'Proof undeniable, they decided, of our guilt in the matter.'

'And the verdict?'

'Incarceration and expulsion for anyone associated with "this unfortunate affair", depending, of course, on the severity of their actions.'

'Not much worse than it was before the laws changed.'

'Never before have the English presented proof like this. Names and dates. Copies of the transmissions. *And we handed it to them on a silver platter!*'

'Bendixen?'

'Diplomatic immunity, although I imagine he'll be recalled to Berlin.' His words rang out like a death sentence.

'You wouldn't be recalled as well, would you?' I asked, grabbing at his arm.

'Me? I had no part in that operation.'

He sent Andreas ahead to secure a table away from the square and stood with his hand on my waist, as we were buffeted by the next wave of people emerging from the courthouse. A swarthy man spat at Eduard's feet, signalling the mood.

The level of noise rose as Matthew appeared in the doorway, sporting a pale suit and a wide grin. Swarmed by reporters and their cameramen, he waved away the kudos, giving credit to the 'fair and just' Portuguese courts.

'Was there any hint about how the Brits knew where to look?' Claudine asked.

'Anonymous tip.'

'Anonymous, faugh! *Someone* must know something.'

Matthew swaggered forward, a wide grin on his face, and the walking stick swinging jauntily with each step. Claudine added, 'Pretentious bastard.'

Eduard shrugged and tilted his face into the sun. He wouldn't meet my eyes – a fair indication that he still wondered if I was the one who had betrayed them. There must have been no evidence presented to confirm that possibility and my sigh of relief was genuine enough.

Another black motor wound its way past the police lines and idled in front of the steps. It would seem that Matthew had finally begun to think of his own security. He paused on the bottom step, looked around as if about to relay a forgotten titbit, as the car door opened. Instead of a uniformed driver, a man in a dark shirt and trousers jumped out. Despite the heat, a black knitted cap was pulled low over his face. Two others, similarly clad, rushed Matthew. He moved with the grace of a younger man, sidestepping the first assailant. Dropped a shoulder and swung the swagger stick like a cricket bat, catching the other man behind the knees. The man staggered back, tripped over a step and sank to the ground. Matthew was already facing the second attacker. The crowds, contained by the PVDE, erupted in screams.

Restrained by Eduard's hand and the press of the crowd, I remained an observer. Kidnappings were common, but this was my godfather, and no one moved to help. He stood alone, wielding the stick like a cricketer, fighting off an attack by three men. One kicked out and Matthew stumbled to one knee. The second assailant manhandled him into the back seat and tossed the stick in after him. The crowd surged again and all I could see was the car speeding past the police barrier. Unmolested.

'One less problem,' a German voice muttered somewhere to my left.

'Shocking.'

The woman beside me fanned herself with a lawn handkerchief and shook her head. Eduard herded us from the square, with Julian scribbling furiously, a cigarette dangling from his lips.

What would happen to Matthew? Beaten, tortured? His body ending up like Christophe's, mangled and bloated, spat up from the Boca do Inferno?

Not if I had anything to do about it.

Eduard followed me into the parlour. He wound the gramophone and a *fadista*'s soulful voice filled the room. I was seething, but managed to maintain a cool voice.

'Interesting conclusion to the case. Did you know about it?'

'It was a foregone conclusion. The evidence the Portuguese – in reality, the English – presented was overwhelming.' He poured two brandies and handed me one.

'Yes, you've said that all along. That wasn't what I asked.'

'Did I know that the Englishman, the one who called you "Lisbet", would be attacked? Kidnapped? I did not.'

I scanned his face, his eyes. If he lied, he was better at it than I realised.

He raised a finger, stopping my protest.

'I have accepted your arguments that you do not know him.'

'But you don't believe them.'

'No, Angel. I do not.' He looked tired and sad. But oddly, not angry.

'What are you telling me, Eduard? That you don't trust me, or you don't care?'

His laugh grated at the back of his throat. 'That was never the question, Angel. You know I care. Far more than I should.'

'But you think I'm an English spy.'

It was a foolish challenge, breaking the rules of our détente. Maybe it was time.

His dark eyes captured mine; he was as willing to walk into the minefield as I was.

'A spy, perhaps. Maybe English. You are not what you seem, but I have known that for months.'

'And it's never bothered you?'

'Oh, it bothers me.'

'But not enough to make me disappear?'

'Jesus God, Solange, what do you think I am?'

'Loyal to your Reich.'

'Loyal to my *country*.' He held up one finger to make his point. 'I am German. I fight for Germany. Do not fault me for that. I have never faulted you for fighting for what you believe in.'

'So you do think I was the leak?'

'No, you did not have access to Bem-me-Quer and were never inside. Do I think sometimes you pass on gossip to your Englishman? Yes, Solange, I do. However, these things are common knowledge within days. You fight with the tools you have, and while I do not like it, I accept it.'

'Isn't it your job to root out spies?'

'My job has many aspects.'

Was one of those to arrest Matthew? Me?

The PPK was in my handbag, the sgian dubh at my thigh. Close enough if I needed to defend myself, but could I really stab Eduard?

The answer bubbled up on a wave of despair. *No. Not even to defend myself.*

Leaning against the sideboard, he watched my face, gauging my response as only a lover can.

'I am a soldier, Solange. I accept that if I die in the service of my country, I die with honour. There is no honour in kidnappings. In making people "disappear". But I am not everyone and I am frightened of the game you play.'

'I've never played with you, Eduard.'

'Yes. I know.' His smile, tired yet genuine, didn't last long. 'But I know the way your mind works. I do not know what it is, but Harrington has a hold on you. I do not like it, but I am not foolish enough to think I can sever it.'

'I don't know what you're talking about.'

'No? As you wish. All I ask is that you are careful. Whoever you really are, *here* you are a Frenchwoman, involved with a German officer. If you start asking about Harrington, trying to find him, the question must be asked – why is she interested? People will look at you closer. At me. I cannot allow this.'

He was right. I would happily take risks on my own behalf, but with Köhler lurking about, I couldn't risk drawing his attention to Eduard. Even if he was, by Claudine's reckoning, the one man Köhler wasn't looking at, I'd seen the Gestapo play the long game too many times to trust anything about them. To save one man I loved, would I be forced to betray the other? I sat down hard and looked down.

Eduard's hand covered mine.

'I cannot allow you to jeopardise yourself. I would not be able to protect you.'

'I don't need your protection,' I muttered.

Eduard's hand on mine was warm and secure. A knot rose in my throat, but I tried to brazen my way through this.

'What makes you think I want to do anything anyway?'

He snorted. 'Angel, I would expect nothing less. Listen to me – this kidnapping wasn't sanctioned. It confirms our guilt, makes us seem like animals. It is dishonourable. Do this for me – allow me to find out what happened.'

I gasped, unable to believe what I was hearing.

Eduard Graf took a deep breath.

'Allow *me* to find your Englishman.'

Eduard left early the next day, the *Ritterkreuz* around his neck, a tangible reminder of his bravery. He rarely wore his uniform, much less the "iron necktie", and I felt an odd foreboding when he kissed me goodbye.

He'd asked me trust him, but how could I, when the only rationale he would give me was that he wanted to keep me safe? Why would an Abwehr officer do that?

He couldn't really expect me to sit around and do nothing. And he wouldn't, of course. The only problem was that I had no plan. No starting point and no resources to find, much less free, my godfather. Certainly not without putting Eduard into Köhler' cross hairs.

I prowled through the house, making and discarding cups of coffee. Opening windows, only to close them moments later.

Why would this German officer risk his life for a woman whom he didn't entirely trust and a man who worked for his enemy?

I had never asked him about that first evening, when he'd met Köhler at the Avenida Palace. Never asked about Köhler at all. Or his absence in the days between his accusing me of working with Matthew after the incident in the old castle, and his showing up at my house. Never pressed him as to why he pinned the Iron Cross to his uniform, but not the Nazi party badge. Was it as he had said, that his loyalty was to his *country*?

He was a good German, but maybe not a good Nazi?

If that were the case, then what the devil was he up to?

Chapter Thirty-eight

The Pastelaria Suíça, located beside to the Rossio and some of the best shopping in Lisbon, did a good late-afternoon business. The locals referred to it as Bomparnasse, a nod to the Parisian district Montparnasse, combined with the Portuguese phrase for 'good legs'. An obvious reference to the risqué refugee community that congregated there for coffee and pastries.

A group of men sat beneath the awning, speculating on what had happened to the English diplomat when security was at the point where a seagull needed to show papers at the border. It was the question on everyone's lips.

Bertie and I communicated via dead letter boxes and newspaper advertisements, only when he had information to relay, and I hadn't physically seen him in months. There was no time to make the appropriate arrangements to meet, but he'd mentioned this place before and it was better than waiting down at the docks. If I was lucky, he'd head here after his shift. And hopefully it was an early shift.

A storm was brewing, and more than just on the political front. Dark, heavy skies threatened rain, and despite this, there were no tables available outside. I sat inside, in the corner, near a rotating fan that pushed tepid air around, listening to émigrés' stories: the Portuguese minister, now forced into retirement, who'd helped French Jews escape before they could be sent east to the work camps; the horrible acts of the Gendarmerie, bastards in Occupied as well as Free France. Speculation on how one Otto Skorzeny had rescued Mussolini from where he was imprisoned in the Apennine Mountains. And what Hitler would now do with his shamed poodle.

Three hours and a few cups of coffee later, Bertie swaggered in with two other men. He ordered a beer and sat down with his chums. Quaffed half of it before he ran his hands over the stubble on his head. To a chorus of catcalls, he pulled out the empty chair next to me and sat down.

'This seat free?'

He spoke in French, keeping in line with his alias, and flashed a rakish smile. Charm oozed from his battered face, and even with half-healed burns, he had a confidence that Lieutenant Neumann had yet to find.

'And if it wasn't?'

'It isn't now.' Bertie chuckled, then lowered his voice. 'You look good as a brunette, but if you wanted to see me, princess, you coulda left a calling card.'

I snorted. 'It's a hothouse in here. Let's go for a walk.'

'Ah.'

He grinned and helped me to my feet, winking at the two men, who were now calling out advice.

'Well, that was discreetly done,' I said.

'Had to maintain my reputation, princess. What can I do for you?'

We stopped across the square at a tobacconist edged with a carved wood frame and blue tiles that featured a frog and a crane. I bought two packets of cigarettes and handed him one. Meandered a little farther before I spoke.

'I need your help.'

'An' here I thought you wanted me for my good looks an' charming personality.'

'Of course.' My voice was dry.

'My rapier wit?'

'That too,' I replied, deadpan.

'My body?' he asked, throwing his arms wide.

'Don't push your luck.'

Dark clouds hovered over the Tagus, but the air remained still. I pulled a lace fan from my handbag and created the small breeze that Nature had withheld.

'You have Nazi scum you want me to question? No? So if it's not that, I'm guessing it's the English diplomat you're after. The one what was kidnapped yesterday.'

'Why do you say that?'

'He was the one what brought you in to question me. Reckoned you'd be around, sooner or later. Figured you'd want to find him.'

'Do you know where he is?'

'No.'

'Can you find him?'

He shrugged.

'I think you can.'

'What makes you think that?'

'Because,' I said, pausing to light a cigarette, 'I think he's been taken to one of the quays.'

He hummed a response – looked interested.

'One of the quays from where they smuggle wolfram,' I amended.

'Why?'

'They're remote. The security infrastructure is already in place. Do I really need to continue?'

'Right. So assumin' he was taken to a quay, d'you have any idea how many o' those there are?'

'Tens, hundreds. I don't know. A lot. But they won't want dock workers around while they question him. Find me a quay – another quay – that isn't used often.' Thought a bit, then clarified. 'Or even better – find me one that closed recently. One that started to turn the workers away in the last day or two. It can't be far.'

His face was carefully blank. He raised his index finger.

'One condition.'

'Yes?'

'When I find out where your toff is stashed,' he said, crossing his arms over his chest, 'I want in on getting him out.'

'Why?'

He shrugged. 'Boredom.'

'You're willing to blow your cover for *boredom*?'

'Listen, lady, I've been trained, same as you, to do more'n pass on gossip. You want to go in after him? Fine. But you're not having all the fun. I'm going in with you. You got that, princess?'

I looked up at the grey clouds amassing on the horizon and wondered if it was a symbol. None of the men I knew trusted me to do this on my own, but I wasn't stupid. Knew I couldn't pull this off without help. Matthew Harrington had been missing for more than twenty-four hours, and each moment that slipped by took him farther away. I'd take help from whatever quarter I could find it, whether it was an Abwehr officer, a half-English thug, or anything in between.

Chapter Thirty-nine

The next day, the storm finally broke. Big fat drops bounced off the ground and slid off my umbrella.

'Would you like to move inside, madame?' The waiter's once-crisp jacket stuck to his shoulders.

'No, thank you, but another Pernod would be nice.'

Moored boats bobbed in the harbour, like toys on the steel-grey Atlantic. The atmosphere on shore wasn't much friendlier.

Eduard had come to see me at midday. He had no news and I suspected his call was to make sure I was at home, rather than planning anything untoward. Inactivity wasn't in my nature and after he left, I wandered through the shops and cafés, bars and restaurants, relying on the gossip mill to provide a clue as to Matthew's whereabouts.

'I heard he played cricket for Oxford,' a woman sitting nearby said. 'With that swing I believe it.'

Utter rubbish. Matthew, like my father, graduated from St Andrews.

'I heard he was part of the Geneva Convention after the Great War,' another said.

Hogwash, although he probably would have loved to play a part in it.

'You're both wrong,' a third corrected. 'He was in London, apprehending an East End gangster family.'

He was a diplomat, you old bat! Not a bobby.

Speculation was rife, and not limited to his career. A mistress in the Baixa. Another in the Algarve. Young, old, female, male. If a story could be conceived, it was attributed to my godfather. None had any substance. Whoever had taken him had paid the right people to be quiet.

The waiter set my drink in front of me as lightning split the sky. Ozone fizzled, almost tangible.

'I love what you've done with your hair,' Julian drawled, interrupting my thoughts.

The storm's electricity had sent my hair mad. It was now secured in a twist, fastened by a well-placed pencil.

'Go away.'

'It suits you. Brings out an unexpected bohemian look.'

'I'm armed.'

I picked up a butter knife from the table and waggled it at him.

'Of course you are.' He slid his drink to safety under the umbrella, and sat across from me. 'Everyone is. Especially now. Wouldn't be surprised if you had a pea-shooter in your bag.' He reached across. 'Can I see?'

I slapped his wrist.

'Finally, a break from the sun,' he sighed. 'Weather's turned, but then, a lot of things are turning. The Allies are crawling up the Boot, the Krauts are on the run, the Danes have lost their government and the poor bastards out there –' he swept his arm out towards the city – 'they're still starving. Yet all we can talk about is the English diplomat. This whole thing's depressed her, you know.'

'Who?'

'Claudine, of course. She's single-handedly trying to drain her wine cellar. Drowning her sorrows – wallowing in misery. Call it what you will. Wouldn't be surprised if her little befuddled mind has juxtaposed the Englishman for that waste of space she married.' He paused and then crossed himself. 'God bless his miserable soul.'

Julian leant in to take a sip of his whiskey, ignoring a large drop that fell from his nose onto the back of his hand.

'What's your excuse?'

'Pardon?'

'You look as rubbish as she does. Pondering great truths or are you, too, mourning the dashing Englishman?'

'Mourning?' I schooled my features to give nothing away. 'He's dead then?'

'Who knows?' He rubbed his nose. 'Might be, if the right people have got hold of him, but I think that if they wanted him dead, they'd have killed him on the steps. No, they'll keep him alive, until he tells them whatever they're after. Assuming, of course, that he knows anything. What happened to send you on a mad crawl through half the bars in Estoril?'

'Consider me a restless version of Claudine.'

He didn't laugh; he *brayed*. 'Only you're a lick more sensible, not as drunk, and your man might be overworked, but he's not dead.'

'You've seen him?'

'A few hours ago, through the window of a car. Blasted thing almost hit me.'

'How did he look?'

'Exhausted. Aren't you concerned for my safety?'

'No. Did you dent the BMW?'

'No sympathy from my dearest friends.' He pulled a long face at my snort. 'All right, then – a dear friend of one of my dearest friends. And, to be fair, you look like you might need sympathy more than I do. When was the last time you saw your dashing hero?'

'An hour around lunchtime.'

'Conjugal visit? Oh, you're not married, are you?' In the rain, his face softened. 'From what I understand, between this, and Gabi's news about the Azores, the German embassy has been set on its arse. No one claims to have the Englishman. Although whether to believe them is a different matter.' He ran his fingers through his slicked-back hair. 'I do wonder if they're related.'

That was interesting. 'How so?'

'Just a guess, but he was in the courthouse. Was he involved in orchestrating the raid? How did he know where to raid?' Julian took another sip of whiskey, and breathed a happy, fumy sigh. 'Although rather a bit late, if you ask me. The proverbial horse has already bolted.'

Unless, as Julian said, they were after whoever had passed on that information to Matthew. Me. I picked up my empty glass, wondering whether I should order another one. How long before Matthew broke? How long before it wasn't a few random thugs who hunted me, but the whole bloody German mission?

'At least in France we didn't have this sort of behaviour. Kid-nappings on the streets, in broad daylight. And no one raises a finger? Julian, this war is making savages of us all.' I was proud that my voice didn't wobble.

365

'War does that, my love.' He stared over the rocks. 'At least they leave the everyday man alone.'

'And who's that, here? The starving hordes on the street? The refugees from across Europe? Was Christophe an everyday man? Are you? A novelist who enjoys needling one side or the other, depending on the day?'

'Depending on my mood,' he corrected, taking a sip from the delicate crystal.

'So both sides alternate between loving you and hating you. What's to say you won't be next?'

He leant back in the chair, the rain slick on his face. The corners of his mouth twitched and he swished his glass around. Stopped when he realised it was being diluted, and placed his hand over the top.

'Ah, my dear. That's easy. A. I'm not important enough, and B. It won't happen to me simply because I don't care if it does. It's the moment that you begin to care, dear woman, when you have something that makes you want to live, that things go wrong.'

Was that it? Had I survived this long because I'd never really cared? But now there were people I cared for: my Machiavellian godfather; the broken Frenchwoman getting drunk in the dark up the hill; even the barmy Irishman across from me. And Eduard.

God help me.

'Ghastly night to be out.' Julian pushed my glass towards me. 'Right then. Finish your drink and I'll drive you home.'

My front door had been jemmied, but the lock hadn't been fully reset. If they were still inside, they'd have heard the roar of

Julian's car, or watched from a window as I staggered through the gate.

Feeling more sober than I had in hours, I pulled the PPK from my bag and checked the clip. Eased the door open with my shoulder, and led with the gun's muzzle, jumping when a flash of lightning blinded me. Thunder could hide a multitude of other sounds, but not footsteps. I eased out of my shoes.

I smelled fresh flowers and then . . . the nasty tang of Gitanes. Followed the stench down the hallway. As on my first night in Estoril, this intruder didn't care if the smoke alerted me to his presence.

Friend or foe?

There was no light shining from under the door. I slowly turned the doorknob, easing the door back enough to make room for the gun's nose. I crouched low. If the intruder fired first, they'd go for a chest or head shot.

The glowing cigarette gave away his whereabouts, although there could have been more than one. Holding my breath for the count of three, I took one step in and slid to the left. Then my pistol was at his head.

'Careful, princess, gunshots are messy.'

'Jesus Christ, Bertie, I could have killed you.'

I slid the safety on and slapped the back of his head.

'Better men have tried. Oh, wait. You're not a man, are you?'

He grinned as I flicked the light switch, bathing the room in a warm glow. The East Ender looked rougher than usual – his clothing was filthy and his face streaked with dirt. His gaze followed mine to the brown stain high on his arm.

'Nothin' important,' he said, dismissing the wound.

I narrowed my eyes, wondering what he wasn't telling me.

'Bad news?'

'Not really.'

'You found him?'

The little man smirked. 'Did you ever doubt it?'

'Well, it bloody took you long enough!'

'Two days, princess, an' I'm counting from the time the toff disappeared. Weren't you taught patience in that posh school of yours?'

'What? Between learning how to shoot and to kill people with my hands?'

Chuckling, he sauntered to my sideboard; admired the view before filling two glasses with Carlos Primero.

'Am I going to need that much?'

My stomach rebelled against the thought of more bad news.

'You might. Sit down.'

I shouldn't have underestimated him; he'd found Matthew, of course he could find me. I hadn't overtly kept him in the dark, but hadn't offered any information on myself, my alias, and certainly not where I lived. But there were more important things to consider.

'What have you learnt?'

'About your life as Solange Verin? Your aspirations to becoming the next Frau Graf? Tsk, tsk. What would they say back in Blighty?'

'I imagine they'd give me a medal, but I was asking what you found out about Harrington, not about me.'

'Dangerous game you're playing, just as you know. Graf doesn't have a reputation for being a fool.' He smacked his lips. 'Excellent brandy. Right, right, don't give me that look. Sir Matthew. You were spot on when you thought he was at one of the quays.'

'You've found him?'

'I found the quay. Halfway between here and Sintra. Not far from the one you showed me in June. Small, an' up until now, active enough, pulling in half a dozen labourers to work on the docks a few times a week. Been there before, y'know. Wolfram goes in. It's decanted into barrels – marked as lead, mind. So as if anyone's poking around, it looks above board. Then it's onto a speedboat an' out to fuck-knows-where. Pardon the language.'

'Of course.'

'So the night before the kidnapping, they turn away the crew. No explanation, just a get-thee-hence. Repeated the next night. Now the quay's shut for business. Boarded up, but wiv' an armed guard at the gate, an' men patrolling around the warehouse.'

'Who has him?'

'Germans.' He held up a hand to stop the next question. 'Not sure which group, although if I had to guess, it's the Navy Intel arseholes, out for a bit of revenge after what happened at the courthouse. 'Sides, they know which quays the smugglers use.'

That made sense. 'Is he alive?'

'If he's dead, why keep it closed?'

I hummed a response, then asked: 'How do you propose we get him out?'

He reached into his pocket and pulled out a folded document. Smoothed it out on the table and used our two glasses and an ashtray to hold down the edges. It was a map of central Portugal – towns and cities shown in strong black print. Bertie had pencilled in markers along the coastline.

'Drew this when you had me look into the smugglin'. I've worked out of a good number of the quays, but the one you want is here.' He pointed to an inlet about five hundred yards from the coast road. 'Lorries usually come down here at night, an' leave before sunrise. Not any more.'

'You confirmed this?'

'Thought this was the one yesterday. Spent the night stakin' it out. Saw men moving about but not the same – not like there was a shipment coming in, or goin' out.' He paused, the glass halfway to his lips. 'You hear that?'

'I didn't hear anything.' I reached for my pistol.

Bertie held up a finger for silence and grasped his gun as the front door opened. I held myself flush against the wall as Bertie turned off the lights and moved to the other side of the door.

Approaching footsteps became louder. A single set, and whoever it was made no attempt to hide their presence. I closed my eyes and said a little prayer as the parlour door swung back with an almighty crash. We moved quickly, our guns aimed at the man backlit by the hallway lights. The muzzle of his Luger alternated between us.

'Who are you?' Bertie demanded in French.

'Who the hell are you?' Eduard responded. My breath escaped with a soft *whoosh*.

'Thank God,' I whispered, sliding the safety into place. The men still had their pistols trained on each other. 'Put your guns away, both of you.' I turned on the lights. 'What are you doing here, Eduard?'

'Ah, the estimable Major Graf,' Bertie murmured. His gun didn't move. Neither did Eduard's.

'Who's he?' Eduard's expression was one of grim resignation. 'What have you done now?'

I opened my mouth but words refused to emerge.

'Just once, Angel. Just once can you not stay away from trouble? I asked you to leave this to me. Not only did you ignore me, you rushed headlong into it with this riff-raff!'

Bertie put the gun on the table, but kept it within easy reach, palming the map and reclining in the armchair. He wore a look of sublime amusement.

'Riff-raff?'

'For heaven's sake, Eduard. Do you really think I'm the sort to sit on my hands and wait for someone else to solve my problems?' I raged.

'Sometimes I wish you were.'

The words hung in the air. His shoulders were stiff and he looked as if he wanted to hit something. If he took one step closer to me though, at that moment, I might just have hit *him*.

'Then you're with the wrong woman.'

Eduard took another step towards me when Bertie interrupted, gun back in his hand.

'Touch her, mate, an' I'll put a hole in you.'

Eduard might not have spoken French fluently, but he understood enough to flush an angry red.

'Who are you to give me orders?'

'I'm the one what's holding the gun.'

'Leave off, Ulysse.' I used his codename to remind him that this was my operation, and despite Eduard's untimely appearance, I was in control. 'He's angry, but he won't hurt me.'

'Not your skin I'm worried about, princess. Me, I don't like the idea of being in the same room as the Gestapo.'

'Abwehr,' Eduard corrected. 'I am not Gestapo.'

'Maybe you're not.' His voice was conversational. 'But the princess here, she seems fond of you. So if you're stayin', I'll take me leave.'

'Stay.'

I stared at Eduard, hoping instead *he'd* leave.

He didn't. He stared at me with an unreadable expression, his eyes moving from Bertie to me and back.

'If you have something to say, Eduard, then bloody say it. I don't have time to play games.'

He raised one eyebrow. When I remained silent, he relented. 'I know where he is.'

'I'll bet you do,' Bertie drawled. His gun was still centred on Eduard's chest.

'Put the gun down, Ulysse,' I snapped, my voice as short as my patience. He gave me a level look, but obeyed.

Eduard's anger hadn't quite subsided but it appeared that he was beginning to realise what he was dealing with.

'You're serious about seeing this through?'

'I am.'

He stared at me for a few seconds before he sighed and turned to Bertie.

'Put that map back down. I'll tell you how we're going to get Harrington out.'

'And you'd do this why, Herr Major?'

I could see indecision warring against the anger. He lifted my glass from the table and drained it before putting it down with a loud thud.

'I could say it's because I don't want her to go alone.'

'She won't be alone, mate. Why are you really doin' this?'

Eduard stared at Bertie, assessing him. Whatever he saw must have reassured him because when he spoke, each word came as a blow.

'I need Harrington alive.'

'And why's that?'

'Because he is facilitating a meeting that is very important to me.' He took a deep breath and closed his eyes, before revealing the truth, in front of a witness, that undid me. 'And to the people I represent.'

Chapter Forty

'Represent? *Who* do you represent, other than the Third *bloody* Reich?' I snarled, to hide my shock. 'And how the hell did you know to come here? Do you have someone watching me?'

'In a manner of speaking.' His mouth twisted wryly. 'Claudine telephoned. She said she saw a burglar breaking into your home.' He looked Bertie up and down. 'It would seem I found him.'

Bertie raised his glass in a mocking salute.

'Weren't lost.'

Eduard pretended not to notice. 'I ran out of a meeting thinking you were in trouble. Foolish me.'

'Sit down, mate. Give the lass a break. She and the diplomat go way back.'

Bertie switched from French to English as he offered up more than one truth to Eduard. I dropped my head into my hands. In mere minutes, Bertie had confirmed more to Eduard than I had in all the months we had shared a bed.

'And you know this how?' Eduard answered in the same language, surprising me. His accent was almost perfect. Where had he learnt it? And, more importantly, why? What was happening? He'd said he was bad with languages.

'She saved me from being deported. She and the toff what got kidnapped the other day. Could say I owe them.'

'Deported, why?'

'I seem to have upset your lot back in France.'

Eduard closed his eyes. 'I asked you not to get involved with anything stupid, Solange. I *begged* you.'

My patience was at an end and I snapped at him.

'You don't need to be involved in this, Eduard. I'm sure the *party you represent* will be just as happy if we free Matthew without your assistance.'

'What do you think you can accomplish? You and that thug?'

'Sticks and stones . . .' Bertie murmured.

'Don't underestimate us, Eduard. Your help would be brilliant, but quite unnecessary.'

'What are you saying?'

'That thug there . . .' I pointed to Bertie. 'That *thug* was trained to do things you could never imagine.'

'Speak for yerself,' Bertie murmured.

The penny dropped. 'The Department of Dirty Tricks,' Eduard groaned. 'God in Heaven.'

I was angry enough to continue: 'And so was I.'

'You? Special Operations?' He rubbed his face. 'I really am a fool.'

'I wasn't the one who used you as a cover story!'

'When did I do that?'

'Our first date. Your meeting in the Avenida.'

His face flushed, red and angry. 'I didn't use you, Angel. I wanted to take you out, but I had to meet someone that night. Someone who would leave the next morning.'

He acted as if Bertie wasn't there. Maybe he trusted his words to go no further. Maybe he didn't care. But I knew one thing:

Köhler hadn't left the next morning. Or at any point after that. I couldn't let it go.

'Someone who needed to be kept incognito? I saw Köhler, you know.'

He returned to the window, staring out into the inky blackness as he collected his thoughts.

'He was not the man I intended to meet, but do you know who he is?'

'Gestapo.' The storm outside had passed. Inside, it had only begun. 'What are you involved in, Eduard?'

'I can't tell you.'

'Can't or won't?'

'Can't.' His eyes met mine and I could see the regret in them. 'I will tell you, when I can. But not yet, Angel. I am sorry.'

'Let me see if I understand this – you can't tell me why you're involved with the Gestapo?'

Bertie was more of a barometer for trouble than I was, but he was also a good judge of character. Now he was looking at Eduard as if considering options. And those options seemed to exclude, at least for now, murder.

'Maybe, princess,' he said slowly, his eyes now locked with Eduard's. 'Maybe you should tell Fritz here just why you want the toff back.'

Eduard's jaw clenched, but turned his gaze to me. 'Angel?'

'What the devil are you playing at? I already admitted to being in Special Operations.'

'That's not what I said, princess. Tell him about the toff.'

How the hell had Bertie found out about that?

Both men watched me expectantly, the silence as palpable as it was uncomfortable.

'Do you really want to know, Eduard, why Matthew screamed "Lisbet" when I fell?' The anger dissipated; I was tired, although strangely not frightened. If Eduard was going to move against me, he already had enough ammunition. And secrets of his own.

'Your code name?'

'No.' I stood in front of Eduard, my eyes locked on his. 'Because Matthew Harrington remembers a child too young to pronounce her own name. Matthew Harrington isn't just my handler – he's my damn godfather.'

The words hung in the air like a heavy smog. Eduard fought to hide his shock well while Bertie grinned.

'S'ppose that gives you the right to be angry, princess,' he said.

Eduard lit a cigarette, flinching when I snatched it out of his mouth.

'You don't smoke.'

I took a deep drag, smashed it on the windowsill and threw the butt into the garden.

Bertie sniggered. Eduard glared. I finished my brandy.

Seconds ticked on the grandfather clock in the hallway. I refilled my glass. Neither man commented.

'So, Fritz, you have a plan?' Bertie asked.

Eduard relented. 'Show me that map.'

Bertie waved his hand, inviting Eduard to look.

'Let's see how clever you are, then.'

Eduard traced one long finger down the coastline from Estoril to Sintra. Stopped and tapped against a small inlet.

'Here,' he said. 'It's not the biggest quay, but it is remote enough to hide someone.'

It was the same quay Bertie had found, but he gave nothing away.

'How do you propose to get him out? Boat?'

'No. One man on the jetty with a machine gun would cut us down in a heartbeat.'

'Even disguised as joyriders?'

'It could work for Solange, perhaps, but not for you, *mate*.' Eduard drawled the last word, echoing Bertie's accent.

'An' what would you suggest, yer lordship? Waltzing in an' asking for his nibs and a by your leave?'

Eduard studied the map in silence while Bertie rolled his eyes. Finally Eduard straightened and turned to Bertie.

'You come in by speedboat, that part will work, but not into the inlet. You land here, and move across by foot.' His fingers traced the map – long, elegant pointers.

'And me?'

Eduard glared. 'You stay safe.'

'Like hell I will. Either I go with you or I go by myself.' I folded my arms across my chest. 'Your choice.'

Bertie shrugged, barely able to hide his mirth. Eduard was rather less amused.

'Just what are you proposing, Angel?'

'I can shoot better than most. But you knew that. A lot of others don't. What if I become your camouflage?'

He didn't look convinced. 'How?'

'Most men, military men, don't see women as a threat. Get me a uniform, the sort your people wear. I'll drive your staff car.

We gain access from the coast road, pass the checkpoint Ulysse marked here, and regroup at this point here.'

'And, lovely as you are, you think you can sail through unmolested?'

'Yes, Eduard. I do.' My smile was humourless. 'Because I'll be driving a German officer.'

A dark silence slithered into the room and wound itself around my throat as we worked out the details of the operation. If we went in as he'd suggested, shots would be fired. Would Eduard – a good German, loyal to his country – willingly shoot his country-men to save a man who was going to simply *facilitate* a meeting for him? What sort of meeting was worth this?

'You can't get him out by diplomatic means?'

He rubbed his eyes. 'Not without the trail leading back to me.'

He didn't need to say aloud what would happen to him if that occurred. The Germans weren't squeamish when it came to executing traitors. Which meant that if the kidnapping wasn't sanctioned, neither was the rescue.

'You don't need to do this, Eduard.'

'Actually, Angel, I do.'

'Not for me, you don't.'

'That's my cue to take me leave.' Bertie paused at the door, yanking his non-existent forelock. 'Princess, Fritz. Try not to kill each other before we rescue the toff, will you?'

Eduard waited until he heard the outside gate open and close.

'I told you, I need your diplomat alive. If not, everything I've worked for dies with him.'

He was working with Matthew? Why on earth would he be doing that?

'I cannot let that happen,' Eduard continued. 'I would prefer you to stay here.' He held up one hand, stilling my protests. 'But I know that would be useless. Unless I tie you to the bed, you'll find a way to be there anyway.'

'What choice do I have? How long will he be questioned before he gives away my name? My *real* name.'

'Which is?'

'I rather like the way you call me "Angel",' I admitted. 'But my parents named me Elisabeth. Why didn't you tell me you spoke English?'

'You never asked.'

'I'm asking now. You can't speak French. Your Portuguese is abysmal. But you're fluent in English?'

'My father liked the English. He thought it was a useful language.' His laughter was mirthless. 'I don't think he understood just how useful.' He stood up, signalling the end to the conversation. 'I have things I need to arrange. I'll pick you up at nine o'clock tomorrow.'

I watched him leave – this Abwehr officer who was willing to liberate a captured enemy diplomat. An *English-speaking* Abwehr officer, who shunned the other members of his organisation, instead socialising with the key players in Naval Intelligence. Who represented people requiring ties that Matthew Harrington could provide.

Who really *was* Eduard Graf?

And did Köhler know?

Chapter Forty-one

A crisp breeze blew through the French doors, an innocent promise of autumn that belied the day's agenda. The blonde wig was perched atop the bedpost, having refused to be coaxed into a military style; I would have to rely on pads and cosmetics, to transform my face into a stranger's.

A motor rumbled outside, and I hid the wig inside the closet, slipped the Luger and two spare clips into my handbag and locked the doors behind me.

Eduard, dressed in his uniform, lounged against the bonnet of a black Mercedes staff car. The October sun shone off his hair, and if he was still angry from the night before, he hid it well. So did I. There would be a conversation, with the last remaining truths being aired, but not yet.

Claudine, standing on her balcony, raised a hand in greeting as I climbed into the Mercedes.

'Maybe it was a good thing that I couldn't arrange the wig into a knot,' I said. 'Claudine is a better guard dog than Knut.'

'She thinks we are going for a picnic.'

'Why?'

'Because I told her so.' Eduard started the engine and looked over at me. 'What is wrong with Knut?'

'He licked my hand within seconds of meeting me.'

'He has good taste.' He handed me his cap and put the car into gear. 'We will stop along the way so you can change. There is a uniform in one of the bags.' Eduard's mood was as serious as mine. 'Are you certain you want to do this, Angel?'

It had little to do with 'want'. I had no lust for battle, but even if there wasn't a threat to me, I couldn't leave my godfather to the Nazis. It was that simple.

The trees whipped past, interspersed with the pastel houses that became less frequent the farther we drove from Lisbon.

'Angel?'

'It was my idea,' I reminded him. 'And there's no other choice.'

The car slowed down. 'You could stay home and let me take care of this.'

'And wait to hear how you and that East End idiot botched it?'

Eduard reached for my hand. 'I cannot speak for your thug, but please, Angel. Have faith in me.'

'I do.'

Despite everything, I did have faith in him. It was trust that I struggled with – still struggling to separate Eduard the man from Major Graf, Abwehr officer. And rely on a feeble hope that he wouldn't betray me.

So, maybe I did trust him.

He turned the car on to a dirt track and cut the ignition. Handed me a bag with a reasonably unwrinkled drab green tunic, skirt, and cap.

'You want me to change *here*?'

'We haven't passed another car for ten minutes and it isn't safe to use a hotel, even if we could find one. Go ahead, Angel. I'll keep watch.'

He reached into a second bag, stored in the well behind the driver's seat. It looked heavy.

Wild horses thundered about, trampling my poor brain. My mouth was dry and my tongue tingled with the remnants of something bitter. Good Lord, we'd had a few drinks; it was our last night together, but not enough to rate a hangover of this magnitude.

My body refused to move. Protested everything about the situation, down to the lumpy bed. That realisation brought on waves of nausea and fear. My own bed wasn't lumpy. I forced my eyes open, bracing myself against a stabbing bright light.

The blurry outline of a man's hand was silhouetted in front of me, and cool dry fingers fluttered at my neck. Something smelled familiar, but I couldn't place it. All I knew was that it wasn't Eduard, and I wasn't home. And a strange man's hands were at my throat.

Red-hot anger burned through my fear.

To hell with you! I silently screamed, balled my hand and let it fly. My fist found its target and the man recoiled with a loud *oof*.

'I see you're awake then,' he said in English, rubbing his jaw.

The accent was public school, sharp as cut glass. I waited for the retaliatory blow to fall, but instead he faded from sight. Water gurgled as the fuzziness began to fade. I accepted the glass from my captor and flung it into his face.

'Insult *and* injury, Lisbet?' Matthew pulled a handkerchief from a pocket and dabbed his face. 'Was that really necessary, old girl?'

I snarled. 'What do you want?' I looked about the spartan room – the white walls, the battered institutional desk and green filing cabinet. An office, obviously, but it could be anywhere. 'Where the bloody hell have you taken me?'

'Extra ammunition?' I asked.

'And a few charges,' he acknowledged. 'Your man says he can set them.'

He took out four spare clips, slipping two into his pockets. Reached into my handbag and pulled out my Luger to check it, grunted, then checked his own. He leant back against the car, facing away. As awkward as I felt, he looked worse.

'Eduard, if you're guarding my modesty, you're a little late.'

He snorted, but sat down again in the driver's seat, keeping his eyes straight ahead. It wouldn't be the first time he'd seen my breasts and despite the gravitas of the day, I wanted to tease him.

'Eduard.'

I moved closer and ran a finger down his arm.

Eduard cast a quick glance my way. His eyes widened as we heard the hum of an engine.

'Angel!'

I didn't think – I reacted. Clad in skirt and camisole, I launched myself at him, my knee hitting the steering wheel as my leg straddled his. With a pang, I remembered another country, and another man's kiss to hide behind. Alex Sinclair had fought for something he believed in. He was too young to die, and so was I.

An old wagon bumped into sight, two men in the front and another two in the back. They called out to us, and Eduard, one hand buried in my hair, waved them off, his lips not leaving mine.

'Did they recognise us?' I asked once the sounds of their vehicle had faded.

He shrugged. 'I doubt they saw anything other than your breasts.' His hands caressed me for a moment more before lifting me off his lap. 'Get dressed. We have work to do.'

The old soldier stood in front of a hut, a clipboard in his hand. He was of average height, stocky, with a face scarred from weather and combat. His MP 40 *Maschinenpistole* was slung low across his body. I'd expected another pimply faced youth to guard the quay, not a veteran of the front lines with a paratrooper's sub-machine gun. I met his gaze as he glared, first at me, then at Eduard, reclining behind me in the big Mercedes.

'What's an *alter Hase* like you doing on guard duty?' Eduard asked.

The guard ignored the question. 'Turn about, this area is restricted.'

'I'm well aware of that. Please raise the gate, sergeant.'

'Against orders, sir. None to pass.' He raised the machine gun menacingly.

'Herr Kapitän sent me.'

Did Eduard know which captain was in charge, or was he bluffing? From his impassive face it was difficult to tell, and I resolved never to play poker with the man.

'I have my orders, sir.'

Dogmatic, intense. Not easy to brazen through, but for one thing . . .

The voice of a commanding officer.

'Raise the gate, sergeant!' Eduard barked.

His body leant forward, his voice battlefield precise. Instead of my lover, in the rear-view mirror, I saw the Panzer commander, leading his division as it trampled through France. Felt a stifling fear.

'I'm sorry, sir. My orders are clear.'

A dark shape moved behind him, but I couldn't look away from the weapon aimed at me.

'As are mine.' Eduard ordered. 'Drive on. Run the fool over if he doesn't move.'

Crouched low, I revved the ignition and crashed through the barrier. The guard jumped back. I expected to hear gunfire, feel metal rounds riddle my body.

In the rear-view mirror, the guard aimed his weapon. The scarred finger squeezed the trigger and I braced myself for the impact.

There was a flash of sunlight on silver and the old veteran slumped into Bertie's arms. My breath came out in a soft whoosh as I slowed the car. I hadn't realised I was holding it.

'Did you know that was going to happen?'

'No.' A fine sheen of sweat shone on Eduard's brow, and I realised that he had never actually believed that his bluff would work. It became more difficult to breathe, and I clawed at the top button of my tunic. Eduard's hand stilled mine, his soft voice slowing my pounding heart. 'You did well, Angel. Stop the car and give your goon a moment to catch up.'

I forced my heart back into rhythm. It was bad enough that Eduard had seen my weakness. I couldn't allow Bertie to witness it as well.

Bertie dragged the guard's body into the hut and emerged moments later, wearing his uniform and holding his machine gun. He sprinted to catch up to the car.

'A fucking sergeant? What d'you think I am?' he muttered, jumping into the back seat.

'The same size. The colour suits you,' Eduard said.

'Sod off, Fritz.' Bertie's voice had lost his usual banter. 'You wasn't followed?'

'No,' I said. 'I've been watching for that.'

'Good. An even dozen of 'em in there, princess. Three questioning your toff.'

'He's still alive?'

'He was, an hour ago. Maybe not so comfortable, but still breathin'.'

'Where are the other nine?'

'Around the warehouse. Place is stacked with barrels.'

I blinked, bit my lip. 'Wolfram?'

'Disguised as lead. See if we can get it on to the speedboat before we leave. You have my charges, Fritz?'

'In the bag.' Eduard passed one of the canvas satchels to Bertie. 'Careful with them. How are they armed?'

'Mostly sidearms. Lugers. A few have K98ks. Nothing like this.'

He stroked the lean metal of the MP 40. There was little doubt that he'd keep it after all this. A souvenir or a tool for other times, although he'd have the Devil's own time getting that back to Shoreditch.

'Slow the car, princess,' he said as the first outbuilding came into sight. 'I get off here.'

'Don't forget to wait for my signal.'

Bertie nodded, slid from the seat and into the trees.

I closed my eyes and prayed to a god that had long since stopped listening.

Chapter Forty-two

Two armed guards came out of the warehouse. They wore plain clothes but their bearing was military. The first one blocked our path, left arm raised, warning us to stop. When we didn't, he pointed his Schmeisser at me, reinforcing the message. The other stood back, weapon ready.

Worry exploded into panic and I struggled to maintain control, stamping down on the insidious fear as well as the brake. Gravel crunched under the wheels as the Mercedes halted.

Under the soldiers' watchful eyes, I opened the door for Eduard. His uniform was the entry key and the soldiers responded. Tall and aloof, he stalked towards the warehouse. I followed, hands clasped behind my back to hide their trembling. And the Luger tucked into my skirt.

'Bet he's shagging the driver,' one of the soldiers muttered. 'Fucking Abwehr.'

Any reply was silenced by Eduard's icy stare.

The soldier at the door was a broad man of about thirty with the big hands of a farmer, and the demeanour of one who takes rather than gives orders. He allowed us to pass and closed the door behind us.

'You can wait for the major in the office,' he said, dismissing me. 'There's coffee.'

Once my eyes adjusted to the darkness, I scanned the warehouse. Barrels were stacked along one wall, almost to the ceiling. A catwalk ran along the back wall, perhaps ten feet deep, that ended in an enclosed room with another man standing just outside, smoking a cigarette. His rifle was propped against the wall.

In the far corner of the ground floor, under a naked bulb hanging from the ceiling, Matthew Harrington slumped in a chair with his hands tied behind him. His eyes might have been vague, but his croak was recognisable: 'If she was blonde, she'd be a dead ringer for Veronica Lake.'

Arsehole.

The men nearest to him shrugged, and one cuffed the back of his head. So far I'd counted seven.

'The office?' I asked.

'*Ja*. Stairs are over there.'

The guard flicked the end of the cigarette over the railing as I approached. His eyes burned with barely concealed lust as I climbed the stairs. I played it for all it was worth, slowing my pace, and adding an exaggerated wiggle. Behind him, another man sat at a desk, riffling through papers.

Eight and nine.

The soldier wolf-whistled as I sashayed past. I tilted my head and gave him a reasonable facsimile of the sultry look Veronica Lake was famous for. His eyes were glued on the expanse of my legs, although the man at the desk barely looked up. I ran my hand up my leg, raising the hem of my skirt, inch by inch.

The soldier closed the door about the time my hand reached the tip of the sgian dubh. My hand closed around the dagger and when the soldier pulled me close for a kiss, I drew his head down and plunged the knife through his tunic, under his breast-bone and yanked it upwards. A rush of blood cascaded over my hands but I was already moving towards the desk.

The other man fumbled for his sidearm, and in an instant I recognised him: he was the man from Laura's apartment. The lover she'd given the folder to.

I dropped to one knee, as I'd seen Alex Sinclair do so long ago in that field in France, and flicked the little knife.

'Crazy whore!' His words were cut off with a gasp. He stared at the blade sticking out of his chest, his pistol clattering to the floor. I closed the distance, pulled the knife out and sliced his throat.

'Fucking Nazi.'

I returned the compliment, kicking his corpse for good measure. Grabbed the papers and stuffed them under my tunic for safekeeping. Laura had been dead for months. These wouldn't be the same papers, but they might be of interest to someone at the embassy.

A quick glance at the wall clock confirmed that it had been less than five minutes since we entered the building. If Bertie's numbers were right there were only ten of them left. And we still had the element of surprise. I slipped my knife back into its sheath, took the rifle and stepped on to the catwalk.

This crazy plan might actually work.

Bertie was perched high on the barrels across the way. He held up his hand, thumbs up, maybe congratulating me, maybe asking if I was OK. I held up two fingers, letting him know there were two fewer men to deal with.

He held up three with a smug grin. Not counting the guard, that brought the count down to eight, and the action – the *real* action – had yet to start.

Down below, Eduard stood above Matthew. One of my godfather's eyes was swollen closed and there was a gash at his temple. But he was breathing.

'Get up!' Eduard barked.

Matthew didn't move, and I looked away. A pack of cigarettes was perched on the balustrade and I would have given anything in that moment for the chance of lighting up. Instead, I loaded the dead man's rifle, and moved into the shadows, before anyone could notice me.

'What did you do to him?' Eduard asked one of the men. 'Drugs?'

'Not yet. Orders were to hold off until an interrogator arrived.'

'Yes, I can see how well you followed them.'

Sarcasm was lost on the man, who spat at Matthew's feet.

'Open your eyes, you English bastard!' Eduard barked, removing his sidearm and sliding the safety off. I picked up the rifle and lined up my shot, and waited for Eduard to make his move.

The strange thing about a Luger: when it fires, the knee joint mechanism jerks up, so fast it's a blur. Clever thing. It jumped twice and the two men to the left of Matthew fell. With a loud report from my rifle, the third sank to the ground. Eduard kicked Matthew's chair, toppling it to the ground. He knelt, worked on the ropes.

Pandemonium.

I aimed just ahead of the soldier running at Eduard. The bullet clipped his arm. He roared but didn't stop. With one fluid movement, Eduard picked up his gun and shot the soldier through the heart.

A tremendous explosion rocked the warehouse and I fell to my knees. Watched helplessly as the rifle dropped over the balustrade. Reached for my pistol, bracing myself for the second charge.

Eduard had thrown his body over Matthew's to protect him. Now he knelt with his Luger clutched in both hands while Matthew acquired a sidearm from one of the bodies.

Two; three; another three . . . no – four. Assuming no one was killed in the blast, perhaps another three men were left. Other than the greedy flames, there was no movement below. No stutter of gunfire; no soldiers racing at us. I edged down the stairs, my back skimming the wall.

At the base was a small stack of barrels. Over the hissing of the fire, I heard breathing, and tightened my grip on my pistol. The man's weapon was in front of me seconds before I could locate the rest of him through the smoke. The flames glinted off his fair hair, and the pistol in his hand.

For a moment, I thought it was Köhler, but the eyes, the cheeks were wrong. I straightened my back and squared my shoulders, watching as recognition dawned.

'You,' he said. 'You're that woman. The one that was following the English spy.'

Was that it? Laura was worried because of what she'd thought Allen-Smythe revealed. She was targeting me to protect *her* asset. And then, presumably herself when I connected them. The flames were coming closer; the smell of burning wood, oddly comforting. They moved up the walls and now licked at the ceiling, coming closer and closer.

'The countess mentioned a tall woman. One that just wouldn't die. Me, I can fix that.'

'Sorry to disappoint you.'

The roof groaned as I squeezed the trigger. Instead of the bark I'd expected, the gun made a small click. The clip was empty.

The man smiled. His forefinger began to contract and I lunged to the side, damned if I'd allow him to kill me. Not now, when we were so close.

I was on one knee when the bullet whistled by my ear.

I lunged forward, my hand on his wrist, forcing it away from me. He was stronger than I was, and I struggled to maintain control. I did the next best thing, forcing his finger on the trigger, firing shot after shot until his clip was also empty. A well-placed knee evened the odds, and his fingers released the empty gun. Throwing it to the side, I tightened my hand and lunged forward again, as I had learnt on Special Operations' practice field. Holding the grip until his body crumbled, his breath gone. Slit his throat to make sure he was dead.

'Angel!'

Eduard's voice bellowed over the rumbling flames and the creaking of the burning building. I ran for the door. For Eduard. For safety.

A section of the warehouse caved in, sending flames and sparks scattering. I fell to my knees outside, gasping in the clean air, the pistol resting against my thigh.

Eduard dropped to the ground beside me. Pulled me hard into his arms.

'Don't you ever, *ever* do that again!'

I couldn't find my voice to respond. Coughed, trying to clear the smoke from my lungs.

'Matthew? Bertie?'

Eduard pointed at the boat pulling away from the pier. Bertie's stocky figure stood at the controls as the boat skimmed the whitecaps. Matthew leant against the neat rows of barrels stacked behind them.

'Your thug will drop Harrington off at the boat he came in on and do God-knows-what with the barrels. ' He held up a finger. 'Don't tell me. I don't want to know.'

'And us?'

'You change into something less disreputable. There's a canteen of water somewhere in the car.' Debris had fallen on it, but so far the vehicle was still intact. A muscle in his jaw jumped as he took in the bloodstains on my tunic. His eyes widened at a thought: 'You're not hurt, are you?'

'Me? No. Are you?'

'No.'

'Thank God.' I cleaned my blade as best I could and paused. 'Are we safe?'

'Should be.'

'Good.' I replaced the blade in its sheath on my thigh. Took a few moments to collect my thoughts. 'Survivors?'

'Four.'

I turned almost hard enough to pull a muscle.

'Sit down, Angel, and wash your hands. We're the four.'

Multiple footsteps disagreed. Three men emerged from behind the guard hut, their machine pistols aimed at us. In the centre, the elusive grey-haired man from France.

Köhler.

Chapter Forty-three

'You disappoint me, Major Graf. A decorated hero, such as yourself, working with the British?' Shaking his head, Köhler eased the butt of the rifle on to the ground and leant against it. With us sprawled on the ground, exhausted, and surprised by his silent approach, Köhler had the advantage. 'Still, I'm grateful that you didn't die in there. We have a few things to discuss, you and I.'

I kept my head down, avoiding Köhler's interest. He had played the long game. I'd suspected as much from the moment Claudine told me that he was looking at everyone other than Eduard. He'd waited for Eduard to do something to betray himself. Something like rescuing a captured English diplomat. And he'd waited here to witness it. We'd played right into his hands.

'You, Herr Graf, are a traitor to your country.'

Eduard's posture was as casual as Köhler's, his tone almost amiable.

'On the contrary, I am loyal to my country. Always have been.'

Truth shimmered through his words and not for the first time, I wondered what game Eduard Graf played. And whether it would end here.

At a sign from Köhler, the goons kicked our pistols out of reach.

It's when you care too much, old girl . . .

Exhaustion gave way to anger.

Bollocks, I thought, shifting my legs. *It's when you care that you fight the hardest to survive.*

The wind blew a spray of cooling ash towards us. An ember landed on my jaw and I shouldered it away. Something about that gesture attracted Köhler's attention. His loose posture sharpened and in two steps, he was in front of me. Grabbed my hair, pulling it back until his eyes met mine.

I remember you, they said, as he nodded to himself. *I remember what you did.*

On my knees, I raised my chin, and squared my shoulders. This man would not win. He would not beat me. He couldn't in France, and he wouldn't here.

'Well, well. You survived. How delightful.' His smile was chilling. 'I look forward to our conversations.'

There were three of them, and two of us. The odds wouldn't be so bad if we hadn't been disarmed. Eduard met my gaze, his eyes questioning, horrified. If Köhler had recognised me before, he hadn't said anything to Eduard. Explanations would have to wait. Köhler's goons hauled us to our feet, and led the way, one on either side of Eduard. Köhler and I followed, his fingers firm on my arm.

I gestured to the burning warehouse.

'A rather elaborate ruse, if all you wanted was a conversation.'

His laugh rasped like fingernails down a blackboard.

'That depends on the nature of the conversation, doesn't it?' He had wanted proof. Of Eduard's loyalties, and now of mine. 'I'd be interested to hear how you got here from France.' His fingers tightened on my arm, although his expression remained polite. 'And how you got into France in the first place. From England, wasn't it, Frau Verin? Or should I say . . . oh, what was it?' He pretended to think about it until naming my previous alias. 'Nathalie Lafontaine? Is there perhaps another name you wish to share?'

Köhler had made it his business to learn the name I'd used in France. And if he hadn't made the connection to Special Operations on his own, the little wireless operator might have told him before she died. It was astonishing that he hadn't recognised me until now. Or had he? Had I too played a part in his long game?

The Gestapo had no authority to arrest us in Portugal, but Köhler could still make us disappear. Maybe we'd be sent to Germany, maybe just killed and disposed of. After being questioned to the point where death seemed a better option.

'I don't know what you're talking about.' The lie, ridiculous as it was, came naturally.

He laughed, 'Of course you don't.'

The large saloon car parked near the guard hut hadn't been there when we'd arrived; they must have been waiting nearby. And the moment we got in, our chances of escape dwindled. It had to be now.

If I was going to die, I might as well die fighting. I dropped my head, letting him think me beaten. He grabbed my elbow, pulling me forward. But not before my hand clasped my blade, freeing it from its sheath and plunging it into his belly.

'This is for Alex Sinclair,' I whispered in his ear.

Warm blood spilled from Köhler and I pulled the knife up as far as it would go. My eyes remained locked on his, watching the surprise turn to fear. His left hand tried to staunch the flow of blood. His right raised the machine pistol pointing at Eduard, but he was already moving, reaching for a goon's gun while his attention was fixed on us. There were two shots.

Köhler's strength was fading. I knocked the gun from his hand. Stepped away, letting his body drop to the hard ground.

'I should have killed you in France,' he whispered.

I settled one knee on his wounded abdomen, and watched the light leave his eyes.

'Yes, well. You tried. And failed.'

I should have felt triumphant, but all I felt was an exhaustion that reached to my very core.

Eduard helped me to my feet, scanning me for wounds.

'How badly are you hurt?'

'Not as bad as him,' I said, using Köhler's sleeve to clean his blood from Alex's blade. 'Why was Köhler convinced you are a traitor?'

'He was wrong. I would never betray my country.'

He'd said that before, and now I thought I understood. He wouldn't betray Germany, but he would do whatever he could to prevent it from betraying itself.

'How did he know we were here?'

'I don't know.' Eduard's dark eyes mirrored my own exhaustion. 'Köhler knew there was a leak in the Abwehr, someone was liaising with the British. I didn't think he thought that was me. That I was working with Harrington. Maybe I missed something. Maybe Harrington did. All I can hope is that Köhler's suspicions about me went no further.' His eyes went to the sky, but then sharpened. He frowned his eyes meeting mine. 'How did you know him?'

I held up the sgian dubh, let it lie flat in my hand.

'This blade once belonged to a man named Alex Sinclair. He was my friend, and Köhler killed him.'

'Why?'

'Alex tried to save a girl that Köhler and his Gestapo friends kicked to death.'

I replaced the knife in its sheath, reacquired my PPK from Köhler's corpse, and allowed Eduard to help me to my feet.

We hadn't moved more than five feet before we saw the man leaning against Köhler's black saloon car. He was unarmed, but the men flanking him weren't.

'Bloody hell,' I whispered.

Chapter Forty-four

'Senhora Verin,' Adriano de Rios Vilar said. 'You continue to surprise me, despite all my warnings.'

Exhausted, I let my hands drop to my sides. I was out of ammunition and out of the will to fight. Eduard wasn't. He lunged in front of me, shielding me from the Portuguese PVDE officer and his men. Rios Vilar continued as if Eduard had remained at my side.

'May I ask what happened here?'

Those large, beautiful eyes were as opaque as they were steady. Covered in blood and the soot from the still-burning warehouse, with the body of Köhler and his two goons behind us, there was little point in protesting my innocence.

'If you've been there long enough, then you'll know.'

Eduard bristled and my fingers tightened on the empty gun, still in my hand.

'Stand back, Major Graf,' Rios Vilar said.

Beside him, his men raised their weapons, pointing them at Eduard. Eduard's shoulders tensed, but he stood back. Rios Vilar nodded, his attention still on my face.

'Is he safe?'

'Unless you plan on shooting him. Or me.'

'That is not what I asked. Do not take me for a fool, senhora. Is the *English diplomat* safe?'

If he was going to kill me – kill us – in reprisal, at least it was for a good cause. I raised my chin.

'Yes. Yes he is.' My anger returned, overriding my better judgement. 'No thanks to you and your men. Bloody line of neutrality and you allowed this, the kidnapping of a diplomat, to happen on your watch?'

A faint smile appeared that did not reach his eyes.

'On my watch? What I witnessed was him being rescued by – forgive the presumption, Major Graf, but by people with his interests at heart. Thus saving us the embarrassment of his disappearance.' He sighed and looked at the blaze. 'Although you have left me a bit of a mess to clean up, senhora.'

'A bit of a mess,' I echoed.

'You were not here,' he said.

'I what?'

My knees buckled and Eduard reached out to steady me.

'You were not here, and this ... this *incident*, will not be talked about. Am I clear?'

I wasn't so certain, but nodded nonetheless.

'Good.' Rios Vilar waved at the Mercedes. 'Now go, but understand that I will not clean up after you again.'

Waves of confusion battered my mind. Eduard's hand was warm on mine as he tried to guide me away. I pulled away and turned back to Rios Vilar.

'Why are you doing this?'

His lips pursed, and his head tilted to the side. He studied me for a few moments before the faint smile returned.

'Because of my ... how did you call it? Bloody line of neutrality, of course.'

He gestured to one of his men, who tossed a water bottle to me. My arms refused to work, and I watched its trajectory – watched it land at my feet. Stared at it because at that moment, struggling to comprehend Rios Vilar's actions, I couldn't think of what to do with it.

'Clean yourself up and go, senhora. Before I change my mind.'

He gestured to his men and they moved towards the bodies of the Gestapo thugs.

I bent, and held the bottle in my hand. Eduard pried the PPK from my other hand and led me to the Mercedes.

Before I sat in the passenger seat, I turned to Graf.

'Why? Why is he helping us?'

'He isn't helping us, Angel,' Eduard said. 'He's helping Portugal. Things are changing. The war is changing. Salazar is no fool. He has allowed the Allies to use the Azores as a base, and this court case was another, perhaps more subtle show that he does not want to be seen on the losing side. It is the first time someone, agents of another government, are tried for espionage on Portuguese land. He could have dismissed the case, yet he did not. Harrington's kidnapping would be an embarrassment he would not tolerate.'

'Then why . . . ?' I glanced back to where the PVDE men were dragging the corpses towards the warehouse.

'Why did he not do something?' Eduard's laugh was mirthless. 'Because we did the dirty work for him. But do not think it is over, and do not think that man is on your side. His masters are Portugal, Salazar, and his captain, Agostinho Lourenço. And I am not sure of the order.'

I looked back at the Portuguese men. Rios Vilar had stopped directing his men and stood, arms crossed, watching us. A thin finger of apprehension traced down my spine.

'Come, Angel, before he changes his mind.'

He didn't need to tell me twice.

Chapter Forty-five

The late afternoon sun glowed red as it sank towards the horizon. A red sun at night was supposed to indicate a sailor's delight, but what did it mean for a spy? A midnight flight? The ocean was to my left and we were heading north, maybe north-west. Away from Estoril. Wherever Eduard was taking me – it wasn't home.

What was north and west? There wasn't enough water in the bottle to do more than rinse my hands and face. My body was still covered in blood, the smell, the feel of it choking me. Fear, barely suppressed during the rescue, returned, reminding me how close we had come to ending up dead.

We drove past a signpost for a town I'd never heard of and I looked at Eduard's profile, wondering what he was planning. His hand dropped from the steering wheel on to my knee. He squeezed it and downshifted into a turn. Bile rose in my throat.

'Stop the car!'

'What?'

'Now!'

The Mercedes hadn't quite halted when I catapulted myself from it. Dropping to my knees, I was sick, heaving long after there was nothing to left to expel. Angry tears streamed down my face and tremors racked my body, and still my stomach convulsed.

Eduard kept one hand on my back, steadying me, as the other held my hair away from my face. I was ashamed of my reaction. Maybe even ashamed of my actions.

'You did what you had to do,' he said.

'Does that make it any better?'

I looked down at myself. Dried blood stained the tunic. I rubbed my hand against it, desperate to be free of it – free of the coppery stench. Free of death.

My fingers fumbled with the tunic's buttons, tearing the last two off in my haste to be rid of the garment. Something fluttered free. I was too clumsy to catch it, but batted it away from the vomit and pounced on the papers before the breeze could scatter them.

Holding them under my knee, I pulled my arms free of the tunic, throwing it aside to claw at the shirt underneath. It stuck to my body, still moist with blood. I ripped it from my shoulders, catching at the cuffs. I pulled, but they wouldn't give way.

I couldn't stifle the sob.

Eduard took my trapped hands in his. Murmured nonsense as he undid the buttons, freeing me from the stench. He held me against him as I wept; I didn't regret killing Köhler or his men. Didn't regret the men from the warehouse; they would have killed me, given the chance. But so much blood. So much blood on my hands.

'What's this?' Eduard asked, reaching for the papers.

I looked him blankly, then at the papers. There were rows and columns, letters and numbers – codes that made no sense. I forced my brain to slow down, to concentrate. There were three typewritten sheets. Some rows had ticks next to them, but most didn't. I blinked and the pattern began to emerge. The items with ticks had dates that had passed. Other columns included a time and location, sometimes a handwritten note in the margin. I flipped to the last page, saw a date some months hence and understood what we held.

So did Eduard. 'Sweet Jesus, Angel. Do you know what this is?' His dimples flashed as he began to laugh. 'God in Heaven, you stole the wolfram shipping schedule! Did you know what it was when you took it?'

I shook my head.

'What did you do? Take it just because it was there?' I shrugged and he handed the sheets back to me. 'What do you plan to do with it?'

His voice was neutral, and his face gave nothing away. Was this a test, or something else?

I had neither the resources nor the inclination to act on them myself, but this information could do damage to the smuggling operation enough to put a dent in the German war machine. I tucked the papers into my blouse and buttoned it up.

'I'm sure I can find a use for them.'

'Yes, I am quite sure you can.'

Eduard helped me to my feet and opened the car door for me. He didn't look upset by this new twist.

We continued north-west and I continued to speculate. Why wasn't Eduard upset? Köhler was no longer a threat, but there was no way of knowing whether his suspicions of Eduard had gone any further. Unless Eduard thought the investigation into him would end with Köhler?

There was another possibility. He might not be a traitor, but I now knew, or at least suspected, that he wasn't working for the Führer. And that made me a risk. Would he set me up to be caught with stolen documents down my blouse and blood, literally, on my hands? My hand crept to the knife strapped to my thigh. The handle fitted into my hand, and I braced myself for an answer I didn't want to hear.

'Eduard?'

'Angel?'

'We're not going home, are we?'

'Not yet.'

I cleared my throat and freed the sgian-dubh; keeping it close to my side. Hidden by my skirt, my forefinger tapped the tip of the blade, testing how sharp it still was.

He glanced my way and smiled, a sweet, slightly nervous smile.

Just beyond Sintra, we turned into a long drive and stopped at a gate. Thick hedges abutted it, and some way beyond it loomed the upper floor of a peach-coloured villa. Eduard fumbled in his pocket for the keys and pushed the heavy wrought-iron gate open.

He nosed the car through and returned to lock the gate. The hedges were high enough to detract the casual observer from peering through, but wouldn't stop a determined prisoner from climbing out.

The car bumped over the gravelled road, its protests only slightly louder than that of my heart. Eduard cut the engines outside the villa and looked at me.

'Where are we?'

'Villa Aurora. A friend of mine gave me the keys.' Eduard looked everywhere but at me.

'Why?'

I put my hand on his arm to get his attention.

'Eduard. Why are we here?'

'Holiday?'

He stared at me. Hunger, and fear too, reflected in his gaze. Maybe nerves. He looked at the villa and spoke more to it than to me.

'I thought it best we spend some time away from Lisbon, from Estoril. Unless, my Angel, you want to return home like that?'

Pink streaks ran down my arms. My fingernails and my soul were caked with blood. He was right. With the *bufos* on every corner, it would only be a matter of time before someone linked me to the massacre at the warehouse.

Who I was, what I did, the company I kept, made me a target for both sides. I leant my head against the seat and sighed.

'And the *bufos* won't have seen us here?'

'Did you see another car?'

My hand slashed away that argument.

'You know as well as I do that it's the *bufo* you *don't* see who is the most dangerous.'

He snorted. 'I wouldn't fancy his odds against you, Angel.'

'Angel of Death,' I muttered.

'Who's in need of a bath. Come on.' He stepped out of the car and moved around it to open the door for me. Saw the knife in my hand and sighed. 'There should be no one else here. You won't need that, but hold on to it if it makes you feel better.' He tilted his head and looked down at his own hands.

'I *really* hope you do not need it. I've had enough killing for one day.'

So had I.

I tightened my grip on the knife and stood up, wincing as my muscles protested.

Eduard pulled a dress pack I hadn't noticed before from the Mercedes' boot and led the way into the villa, pointing out the various rooms we passed before stopping outside a closed door.

'The master bedroom.'

The room was magnificent, decorated in whites and creams. The centrepiece was an enormous walnut four-poster bed, with acres of mosquito netting gathered at each corner. Dark heavy wood furniture was dotted around the room: a dressing table, a wardrobe, a chest of drawers, and a pair of night stands. The only colour was the huge bouquet of red roses dominating the dresser. Drawn like a moth, I couldn't help sniffing the blooms as Eduard hung the pack in the wardrobe.

'Beautiful.'

I breathed in their scent, grateful to smell something other than blood and cordite.

'The bathroom is directly across the hall. Take your time – we'll have a late dinner tonight.'

I kept the knife in my hand as I wandered through the villa, not sure what I expected to find.

Each room held a fragile beauty; the mistress of the house had excellent taste. One parlour was decorated in shades of blue, with Wedgwood-like designs edging the walls just below the ceiling. An ormolu clock sat on the mantelpiece above a fireplace, held upright by two bronze Cupids.

Another was more masculine. Heavy furniture uphol-stered in dark green leather guarded the many bookcases that lined the room. The faint aroma of pipe tobacco lingered on the air.

I moved to the next room, finding works of art, of beauty, of a time I'd almost forgotten. When I returned to the master bedroom, I heard the sound of rushing water. Eduard had run a bath for me. Water steamed from the copper tub, carrying with it the aroma of perfumed bath salts.

'Bathe, Angel,' he smiled – that sweet smile that I loved. 'Because, quite frankly, you stink.'

Without a word, I closed the door behind me, locking it. Put the knife on a countertop and delicately sniffed my shoulder. He was right; I did stink.

I cleaned the knife first with soap and water, then eased myself into the bath. I jumped every time I heard a sound, listened for the rumble of engines, the sound of voices, anything that would herald an attack. All I heard was Amália's voice, soaring from a gramophone recording.

Slowly, I allowed myself to let the water heal me. I left my discarded clothes where they lay. I didn't want to put them on, didn't even want to touch them. Wrapped myself in a fluffy white towel and padded across the hall.

A silk dress the colour of double cream lay on the bedspread. Delicate lace, shot through with silver thread, raised the plung-ing silk neckline of the underdress to the base of the throat, leav-ing the arms bare. The lace continued over the sheath to drop a hair's breadth below the hemline. Matching underwear and shoes completed the ensemble.

I looked around for Eduard, wanting to ask where he'd found such a creation. There was no sign of him.

I towel-dried my hair, combed it, and twisted it into a chignon at the back of my head. Slipped into the brassiere and underwear. Strapped the knife high on my thigh and stepped into the dress. I was fastening the shoes when Eduard arrived, wearing his dress uniform and the Knight's Cross.

He handed me a glass of champagne and stood back to admire me.

'You'll do,' he said.

'You think?'

'Yes. I like your hair like that. When it dries, it curls.'

He stood behind me. Placed his hands on my hips, his lips grazing my nape and sending shivers up my spine.

'Keep it up, Graf, and we'll never leave the room.'

He chuckled, and clinked his glass against mine. We drank in an awkward silence. Finally Eduard stood, and placed the empty flutes on the night table.

'Are you ready?'

'For what?'

'I thought we might see a bit of Sintra before dinner. If that's all right with you?'

'That's fine.' I followed him outside to the Mercedes. 'Did I tell you how much I miss your little BMW?'

'Me too.' He smiled but again his humour didn't reach his eyes. 'Andreas will deliver it tomorrow.'

'He knows we're here?'

'Yes. Why?'

I stared at the retreating villa and wondered if this was a ghastly charade to keep me off balance.

'No reason.'

We passed the town, the Mercedes growling on the steep inclines. Eduard was unusually taciturn and I stared out of the window at the scenery: the ruins of a Moorish castle at the top of the mountain; the red brick palace halfway down it. Beautiful villas and churches, bedecked with spires and turrets. Eduard parked the car along a side street and helped me out of the door. There was no restaurant in the immediate vicinity.

'Is it far?'

'No. You'll be fine. Even with your high heels.'

A small tic in his jaw betrayed his nerves. From the day or from what awaited us? Would he dress me up only to kill me?

We didn't pass another car, another soul as we walked up the steep hill. The wind carried rose petals down to us, circling us before tumbling down the street.

A small church was tucked away around a bend. It was less ornate than some of the others, painted yellow with white trim and a large white archway. A square bell tower rose on the right side and the ground outside the double doors was strewn with more rose petals.

'Someone must have got married today,' I noted.

Eduard choked. I looked away, realising he'd read that as a broad hint. We'd been seeing each other for months, but there had been no talk of the future, much less one that was shared. I wouldn't ask, and he hadn't offered. It was something I shouldn't want.

He looked awkward as he asked: 'Would you like to go inside, Angel?'

I shrugged. If he wanted to say a prayer for the people we'd killed, that was fine with me, although I would struggle to muster any remorse for Köhler's death.

Petals swirled around my feet and for a moment, I envied that bride, coming through the doors on the arm of a man she loved, safe, and secure in their future together.

Eduard took my hand and led me up the steps. Inside, the church blazed with the light of dozens of candles. Enormous bouquets stood as sentries just inside the door; smaller wreaths with white ribbons hung from the end of each pew leading the way to the altar, framed by more flowers and an enormous stone arch. The evening light shone on an old priest as he rose from his chair, hands clasped and head bent. He straightened his cassock and beamed at us.

'You are late, my children.'

'I'm sorry, we hadn't realised the church was closed for the evening,' I apologised.

The priest looked surprised, but Eduard froze. Panic flashed over his face.

Panic? Now, but not when a gun was pointed at him?

'Eduard? What's going on?'

He took a deep breath. His mouth opened once or twice.

'Angel ...' he started, then bit his lip. Wiped one of his palms on his trouser leg and tried again. 'Angel, you are a difficult woman. You are arrogant and opinionated. You drink too much, smoke too much and keep very bad company. You gravitate towards trouble with no care for yourself, and act with a ruthlessness that is not ladylike. But you fight for what you believe in and you make me want to fight with you. For you.'

My heart was pounding, the blood rushing in my veins.

'Eduard? What are you saying?'

He looked pained and shook his head.

'This is not coming out right.' He closed his eyes and tried again. 'Angel, you are a danger to yourself. And to me, if anything should happen to you. So I must do what I can to protect you.'

He rubbed his face, muttering to himself. Reached into his pocket. My heart was pounding, unsure what to expect. What did he mean by protecting me?

A black box was open in his hand. Inside it, a small gold ring. The candlelight danced off it as he uttered a single word, barely audible over my beating heart. The world shrunk, its entirety gleaming in that band. I couldn't take my eyes off it, or the man who held it. All humour left his face. His dark eyes were serious and he slowly sank to one knee.

'Angel?'

'Eduard.'

I hadn't realised I was crying until a tear dropped on to our linked hands. There was fear in his eyes – worry that he'd gone too far and would lose me. Was he offering to marry me for just that: to keep me alive? I loved him, desperately, but I wanted more. Needed more.

I dropped to my knees so I could look into his eyes.

'Eduard. Do you love me?'

'Haven't I just said so?'

413

'Perhaps somewhere in the catalogue of my faults.'

He looked at the ceiling, the stone balustrade that guarded a narrow catwalk. Did it remind him of another catwalk only a few hours ago?

'Solange, Lisbet, whatever your name really is. I love you more than my life. Will you marry me?'

I couldn't understand the words, asked him to repeat them. The word he uttered was one I rarely heard him use.

'Please.'

A lump rose in my throat, and the tears, previously a trickle, now poured down my face.

'My name is Elisabeth.' I wiped the tears away with the back of my hand. 'Elisabeth Daria Grace de Mornay. And yes, Eduard Graf. Even though that was the least romantic marriage proposal. Ever. Yes, I will marry you.'

Part 5

Lisbon, January 1944

Chapter Forty-six

Almost every pier was occupied, with ships of every imaginable size, shape and nationality. Bright flags crackled overhead while skiffs ferried goods and men back and forth from the larger ships. The breeze smelt of salt water and winter.

We weren't far from Lourenço Marques – the restricted area where English ships docked and unloaded. Special precautions had been put in place by the Portuguese government to keep the Allied ships safe, including very visible police barricades. Bertie had unloaded the wolfram shipment there last October. He remained coy about how it was managed and how he continued to fox the Germans by 'diverting' shipments. He was making a small fortune from it, but as long as he kept the wolfram away from the Germans, the British government was happy to look the other way.

Under heavy security, an English frigate bobbed on the tide, safe from the Nazis' wireless operators and the planes they commanded. Or as safe as we could make it.

Eduard squeezed my hand as a young sailor approached and saluted smartly.

'Major Graf?'

The man displayed only respect, making me wonder, not for the first time, what exactly Eduard would be doing in Berlin, and why he needed to sail to France first.

'At ease, man. Give me a few moments to say goodbye to my wife. I'll be with you directly.'

The sailor picked up Eduard's case and stepped back to allow us the illusion of privacy. Lieutenant Neumann had already taken Knut aboard, and the only goodbye I had left was the one that was most difficult.

I brushed a lock of my hair out of my eyes, hoping Eduard didn't notice as I struggled to maintain my composure. He tucked the strand behind my ear and pulled me close.

'Maybe next time it'll be red, yes?'

His expression was so hopeful that I had to laugh.

'We'll see.' I leant into his kiss and whispered, 'Remember your promise, Eduard – nothing stupid.'

His smile didn't reassure me.

'It is not me that I worry about. Be careful, Angel. It is not safe here. Not yet.'

'Berlin isn't safe either, Eduard. Not with everything going on. Köhler's investigation –'

He put a gentle finger over my lips to silence me.

'Has gone nowhere.'

I stepped out of his reach and glared.

'If you die on me, I swear to God, I'll dig you up and shoot you myself.'

'I know.' He pulled back and reached into his pocket for a small velvet box. He stared at it for a few seconds before handing it to me. 'Something to remember me by while we're apart.'

'As if I could forget.' I snorted, but took the box. 'What is it?'

'Open it and see.' He smiled.

A white-gold locket rested on a bed of black velvet. Fili-greed flowers styled after Mucha's paintings were etched around the edges. In the centre a young girl knelt in front of a box, her long hair flowing behind her as she held a sapphire set as a star.

'It's beautiful,' I breathed.

'Pandora. She reminds me of you. If someone tells you not to look in a box, you will find a way to peer inside.' Eduard's voice was tinged with amusement. 'Watch.'

His fingers showed mine the hidden catch and the locket sprang open. A tiny copy of the photograph the priest had taken of us on our wedding day was set on one side. Eduard looked formal, perhaps afraid of what he was getting himself into. He was more relaxed in the other one, grinning from the ramparts of the Moorish castle.

'You can change the photographs if you wish.'

'They're perfect,' I whispered, holding up my hair so he could fasten the locket around my neck.

'You're crying.'

'I'm not good at goodbyes.'

'It's not a goodbye, you little fool.' He dropped a kiss on the tip of my nose. 'I will be back before you know it.'

I held my breath and tamped down the tears. My first hus-band had said the same thing to me once. Only he didn't come back. And I wasn't as sure as Eduard was that the threat from the Gestapo was gone. As if he knew what I was thinking, Eduard touched the locket at my neckline.

'I promise.'

Eduard's last kiss was over far too quickly. His tall frame broke away, leaving me feeling bereft. He strode after the sailor, turning once to mouth the words 'I love you'.

A cold breeze blew, ruffling his hair. I stood on the jetty watching him disappear into the hatch of a U-boat. I turned to the sea, with a rising sense of déjà vu.

'You've already taken two men from me,' I said to the sea, shielding my eyes from the sun. 'You cannot have this one, damn you.'

Through the haze of tears and misery, I drove Eduard's BMW back to Estoril. A little white envelope fluttered to my feet as I opened the gate. I brought it into the house, poured a glass of cognac, and lit a cigarette. Placed my hands on the countertop and resisted the urge to cry. Then gave in to it.

I raged at the fate that had made me fall in love with a German officer, only to have him summoned to Berlin. Even if he arrived safely, the Allies were bombing Hitler's capital on a regular basis. And if the bombs didn't find him, there was the Gestapo. When would it end?

The fury dissipated, leaving me exhausted. I flicked the envelope through my fingers. There was no name, no return address, no distinguishing marks. I ripped it open, finding Claudine's childish scrawl:

I know you won't want to be alone just now. Julian, Gabi and I are having cocktails this afternoon at the Tamariz. Come and join us! Any time after four . . .

She signed her name with a ridiculous flourish, and I wanted to weep again, touched by her caring. The clock on the mantle read a few minutes to five.

Why not?

I stubbed out the cigarette, slipped on my coat and locked the door behind me. I walked down the hill and paused at the corner, waiting for a dark saloon car to pass before I could cross the street, staring at it as it slowed. It veered sharply to the kerb, brakes screaming. It was like watching Matthew's abduction again, only this time the men ran straight at me. Two of them. Wearing balaclavas.

They reached for me, and after months of complacency, my timing was off. One man grabbed my right arm, and then my body began to remember. I leant into him, driving my knee into his crotch and yanking the sgian dubh from my thigh. I dropped into a crouch, edging backwards until my back hit a low wall.

A little crowd gathered across the street, returning from the beach with their towels and sand pails. They stood. And watched. And did nothing.

'Help!' I screamed.

The man, still clutching his crotch, hissed, trying to draw my attention from his advancing colleague. I slashed and the little knife grazed his arm. Two against one. I'd had worse odds, until my heel caught on a crack in the pavement, and I lost my balance.

As I flailed, a white cloth brushed my face, stinking of something acrid and unfamiliar. Strong hands gripped my arms, supporting me as my legs ceased to work.

And then, there was only darkness.

*

421

'The airfield. You will be on the scheduled flight back to Blighty. I apologise in advance that your trip might not be the most comfortable, but they still watch every move we make. You'll need to change into this.' He pulled a folded uniform from the cabinet. 'You'll be masquerading as the co-pilot.' A roll of dressing was placed on top of the uniform. 'Who is a man, needless to say.'

What the devil was going on? I tried to sit up too fast and the room spun.

'Why? Why now? After all these months, why me?'

'You know better than ask that, old girl.' Matthew perched on the side of my cot and laid a steadying hand on my arm. 'Your Major Buckmaster sent word. He's recalling you to London. The kidnapping was a fake. Staged, if you will.'

'Let me see if I understand this. I risk my cover story, my life and the lives of two good men to rescue you from your kidnapping, and in return you plan mine?'

'Yes, my dear. That about sums it up.'

'And you couldn't just summon me? Let me know?'

He sighed. 'Don't you think Jerry would notice if you packed up house and waltzed on to the next flight to London the moment your *husband* sails off to Berlin? What do you think would happen to him? Do consider the company he keeps.'

I knew the company he kept: the German company, and the role he had undertaken – at their behest – with the British. The very thought made me feel ill.

'You must tell him, Matthew,' I said when my breathing allowed it. 'He'll come back expecting to find me.'

'And *Solange* will have disappeared.' He stressed the name, watching my reaction. 'We need his reaction to be authentic. Otherwise your cover story, and his allegiance, will be called into question.'

'Let me explain his *authentic* reaction. With no ransom and no word, he'll search for me. And when he realises you're involved, he'll go after you as well.'

Matthew stared at me, his expression inscrutable.

'You really do care for him, don't you?'

'He's a good man, Matthew. He risked his life to save yours. And so did I. Tell him. Let him know I'm safe.'

'*Solange* was his wife, Lisbet. You mustn't confuse the two.' Again that look – that warning. 'Elisabeth, you haven't done anything stupid, have you? You must know that not even your group of yahoos would tolerate an agent genuinely married to an Abwehr officer.'

It was nothing I hadn't already considered, but his words fuelled my anger.

'Matthew, there's no need to threaten me, or be insulting. I suppose I could always write from England.'

'Don't be daft,' he snapped. 'I'll tell him. Anything else, while I'm playing messenger boy?'

I thought about that for a second.

'Why, yes, Matthew. There is.'

He didn't quite roll his eyes. 'And that is?'

'Bertie.'

'What about him?'

'What will happen to him after I leave?'

'Ah, your little East End friend. He's done well, hasn't he? We'll keep him here, of course.' Outside the window an engine roared into life. 'Your chariot awaits. Payne will escort you out. It was supposed to be Fitzgerald, but his arm is being stitched up.' He gave me an arch look. 'By the by, that's a nice little toy you have.' He pointed to the sgian dubh where it sat on the desk next to my handbag. 'However did you acquire it?'

I grunted, and struggled off the cot. Matthew rested a hand on my shoulder.

'Get dressed, and then wait for Payne. We must make it look authentic. This time, try not to grab his testicles, his wife might object.'

'If he knocks me out again, I won't just grab them, I'll rip them off. And next time you play this game with me –' I closed my hand around the sgian dubh – 'I'll go for yours.'

I waited for the door to close behind Matthew, and slowly began to dress, binding my breasts and tucking my hair into the cap. The shirt and tie covered my necklace, and my bracelet and earrings were buttoned into a pocket. I left my wedding ring on. Buck and Vera would already know of 'Solange's' marriage, but what was more worrying was how they would act on it.

The disguise wasn't perfect, but was good enough to convince anyone who didn't look too closely.

I held the little knife in my hand, and waited in furious silence for Payne and the flight home.

To whatever lay in wait for me on the other side.

Chapter Forty-seven

The aeroplane rolled to a halt on the runway in Bristol. The pilot and I remained in the cockpit until the others disembarked. A dusting of snow blew across the tarmac as I followed him into one of the metal huts.

Vera Atkins waited just inside. One gloved hand adjusted the impeccable tilt of her hat, and then she moved forward to greet me.

'Welcome back to England, Cécile. Did you have any problems getting in?'

'A bit of flak as we crossed over France, but nothing significant,' the pilot answered.

'Excellent. Thank you very much,' she said, dismissing him. 'Come, my dear. Dinner's waiting for you in the main hangar, then we'll get you to London. Buck is quite keen to speak to you.' She linked her arm in mine, a civilised escort. 'We'll drive back after dinner, and do feel free to doze on the way, Cécile. It's a long drive, and Maurice is expecting you at Orchard Court at eight o'clock sharp tomorrow morning.'

Eight o'clock sharp. This wasn't going to be good.

Mr Parks was immaculately clad in his usual dark suit and tie.

'Good morning, madam.'

I forced a polite smile. 'Good morning, Mr Parks. Did you miss me?'

'Frightfully dull without you, madam. Please follow me.' He led the way through the lift's gilded gates. 'Pardon me for saying, but you're looking well. It's nice to see a tanned, friendly face.'

The lift stopped on the second floor, and Parks opened the grates.

'This way,' he said, although I knew the way. We walked to the end of the corridor, and Parks knocked on the door. At the muffled response he peered inside. 'Miss Cécile is here to see you, sir.'

Maurice Buckmaster mumbled something and Parks closed the door. I knew the drill. Followed Parks down the short hallway to Special Operations' Orchard Court suite waiting room. Or rather, its bathroom. I flicked on the lights and perched on the toilet's closed lid and leant my head against the cool tiles. If I had to be locked in the loo, I might as well be undignified about it.

The first time I was locked in here was the day of my interview, a year and a half ago. I'd been kept waiting rather too long and by the time they came for me, I'd been on the verge of walking out of the lavatory, the flat, and the interview.

Now, I was back. My body was scarred from German bullets, and my soul from the deaths I had seen, and caused. I wanted to open the locket and look at Eduard's face, but dared not. Not in this place. They knew about him, and might eventually learn of the locket's secrets, but not yet. I wasn't ready.

There was a polite knock on the door. Vera opened it. She had freshened up and was impeccably dressed in a smart tweed suit with a gold cat pinned to her lapel. If the late night drive from Bristol had drained her, it didn't show.

'I apologise for making you wait, Cécile. We're ready for you now.'

Buckmaster stood as I followed Vera into the bedroom that served as his office. He was tall and slim, with an angular face and thinning hair. He vigorously shook my hand, then waited for me to sink into an armchair before perching on a corner of his desk, legs swinging.

'Welcome back, my dear. Excellent showing down in Portugal. Particularly liked your style, stealing the wolfram whilst rescuing Sir Matthew. Excellent use of your assets.'

If he was aware of the rescue, he knew who'd helped me. I hoped my polite smile hid the burning in the pit of my belly.

'Don't forget the shipping schedule.'

'I was more impressed by the way you set up the Germans from a legal perspective,' Vera said. 'Relying on Salazar's instability to help your case. Most would have just blown up the villa, as they were trained to do. I'm glad to see you've learnt to curb your temper.'

If she'd seen the warehouse she might have rethought that assessment. She allowed silence to blossom between us, her blue-grey eyes intent on mine. Eduard did this too – using silence to compel people to incriminate themselves. I wasn't that foolish. I lit a cigarette and waited.

'I am, however, most intrigued about this marriage of yours,' she continued.

Her tone was light, conversational. It gave nothing away, but implicit in it was the threat: betraying your country is treason.

'Of course,' I echoed. *I, Elisabeth Daria Grace de Mornay . . .*

'It takes a strong will to live that sort of deception.'

Maurice didn't take his eyes off my face. I shrugged, desperate to change the subject. Or for Buck to tell me what fate he'd decided for me.

'I never doubted the strength of your will, Cécile. Quite frankly, what does concern me is any emotional entanglements you may have formed with this man. As Solange you spent a lot of time with him, were intimate with him. How much do you know of his business? The reason he was in Portugal?'

'He was a military attaché.'

Buckmaster flipped his hand impatiently.

'Yes, yes, and Harrington is in charge of passports.' I frowned as he leant forward. 'Last summer you accompanied him to the Hotel Avenida.'

How the devil had he heard of that?

'I had drinks with him there several times. Which time are you referring to?'

'Perhaps the first week in July?'

That first date, before hearing Amália sing. When Andreas Neumann kept me company as Eduard disappeared for a meeting. With Köhler.

'What about it?'

'Did he ever speak of it?'

'He apologised. Said it was something he had to do. I remember being quite out of sorts with him for leaving me waiting downstairs with his adjutant. Even less so when I recognised the man he was with as Gestapo.'

Vera smiled. 'Yes, I can't imagine you enjoying that. How did he explain it?'

'He didn't. Said he couldn't.' They exchanged a glance, sharing some secret that I was not privy to. 'Is there something I should know?'

'Well, yes, Cécile. You should know what happened there. Do remember to ask the major next time you see him.'

My heart quickened at the thought of seeing him again. Then, fast on its heels, I realised that they weren't as upset about my liaison with an Abwehr officer as they should have been. That I had been taken straight to Baker Street, instead of that school in Wandsworth where they usually debriefed returning agents. That they were implying that it wasn't Köhler whom Eduard had intended to meet that night. So had Eduard, but if it wasn't Köhler, then who?

'Who? Who was it?'

'Ask the major,' Vera repeated.

They knew. They knew what Eduard was involved in.

'He's working for you, isn't he?' The words came slowly, grating like a car not quite in gear.

'No, no. I would love for it to be true, but no. Your major is a good German.' Buckmaster's voice was wry. 'And loyal to his country.'

Eduard used the same words, with the same emphasis. His *country*. Not to the madman running it. They all but confirmed my suspicion. A coup. He was working on a *coup*. I remembered the lectures when I trained, heard the rumours that circulated in the Resistance. It wouldn't be the first attempt to get rid of Hitler and his band of lunatics. The Bürgerbräukeller in Munich, 1939;

430

Paris, Berlin, Russia. The number of attempts was growing, but the rabid bastard always managed to escape. The conspirators were arrested, deposed, or dead. I couldn't bear the thought of that happening to Eduard.

The fool! The bloody, brave, patriotic *fool*! And he accused *me* of doing stupid things?

I looked out of the window and composed myself. There was no point in letting Vera and Buck know the depth of my feelings; they would only use it – use me – to further Eduard's rebellion.

Was that it? Were they going to send me to Berlin? I kept my voice cool.

'Should I see him again, I shall.'

'Good,' she said with an enigmatic smile. 'Do that, Cécile.'

Buckmaster's chair squealed as he leant back.

'I must say, it wasn't easy getting you back. Your friend in the Foreign Office kept his cards close to his chest. Officially, you were never in Lisbon. As there was never any paperwork seconding you, the bean counters didn't understand why we wanted you back when they didn't think you were there in the first place.'

I studied them both – Maurice's animated face, and Vera's cool one. Drew in a deep breath and exhaled slowly. Leant forward and matched her level gaze.

'Why did you want me back?'

Already suspecting the answer, my heart sang.

Berlin. Send me to Berlin. Send me to Berlin to work with Eduard.

'Because, my dear –' Maurice's face was suddenly serious – 'we have another job for you.'

431

Historical Note

When I tell people my debut novel takes place in Lisbon during the Second World War, they give me a strange look. 'Lisbon,' they ask. 'Why Lisbon? Portugal was neutral.' And it was, sort of. As the only European capital that was both neutral and a port city, Lisbon quickly became a centre for intrigue, with exiled aristocrats, diplomats, businessmen, artists, refugees and, of course, operatives, obsessively watching each other. As I began to learn more, it became the perfect backdrop for *City of Spies*.

This book is fiction, and while I've tried to stay as close to the facts as possible, there are times where I intentionally deviated from history, and other times unintentionally. All mistakes are my own.

Special Operations Executive

Special Operations Executive (SOE) was officially formed on 22 July 1940, at the instigation of Prime Minister Winston Churchill, as a single organisation to conduct espionage, subversion, sabotage, and reconnaissance. He directed Hugh Dalton, the Minister of Economic Warfare and newly appointed with the political responsibility for SOE to 'Go and set Europe ablaze'.

SOE recruited agents from all classes, backgrounds and occupations and provided rigorous training that included map reading, demolitions, weapons, Morse code, fieldcraft, and close combat, and inserted agents into all countries occupied or attacked by the Axis, except where agreement was reached with other Allied countries.

In 1942, realising they were missing a trick, SOE began recruiting women as field agents. These women trained alongside the men, (often being used as an example to spur the men on), and were commissioned either in the Women's Auxiliary Air Force (WAAF) or the First Aid Nursing Yeomanry (FANYs), before being deployed. SOE sent 39 women into France, and all but 13 of these amazing women came back.

The City of Spies

Lisbon was the real-life City of Spies. There would always be elements of this in any neutral capital, however Lisbon was uniquely placed as a port on the Atlantic. It hosted large swathes of exiled nobility and aristocracy from across Europe, desperate refugees fleeing the Nazis, diplomats, merchants, smugglers, and of course spies.

Passenger ships and the Pan Am Clipper connected Lisbon to New York. The British Overseas Airways Corporation (BOAC) operated a scheduled flight to Bristol, and on 1 June 1943, this flight was targeted by the Luftwaffe and shot down by a Junkers fighter over the Bay of Biscay, killing 17 people including the actor Leslie Howard. Quite a lot of conspiracy theories surround this event, including one that the Germans believed Winston Churchill was on the flight. Leslie Howard was a gifted actor, director, and producer, but also worked with anti-German propaganda. There were also theories that he worked for British

Intelligence, which might have made him a target in his own right. I'm not sure we'll ever learn the truth.

Several other real-life spies involved with Operation Fortitude, the military deception aimed at convincing the Germans that the allied invasion would be targeted at Calais, either operated out of Lisbon or visited the city to meet with their handlers. And yes, there really is a 'secret' passageway between Rossio Station and the Hotel Avenida, which enabled diplomats and operatives to conduct clandestine business and to be out of Lisbon before anyone knew they were in it.

In April 1943 the body of 'Major Martin' was found off the coast of Spain. This was part of Operation Mincemeat, another Allied deception. The body (of an already-dead street tramp) was dressed as an officer in the Royal Marines, and carried documents pointing towards an Allied invasion of Sardinia and Greece. The Germans bought it, moving Panzers, troops, fighter aircraft and ships to better defend the area. On 9 July 1943, the Allies invaded Sicily (Operation Husky), which ironically, Hitler was convinced was the feint.

Dr António de Oliveira Salazar, the Portuguese dictator, had risen to power after the *coup d'état* of 28 May 1926. Opposed to democracy as well as communism, his policies were conservative, nationalist, and Catholic. And while he distanced himself from German fascism/Nazism, he did consider Germany the last bastion against communism. Portuguese neutrality was a balancing act, and perhaps necessary for its survival. Siding with the Germans risked breaking the Anglo-Portuguese pact, and most likely losing some, or all, of its colonies. Siding with the Allies, would likely have risked tipping Spain over to the Axis, or even opening themselves up to an attack from Spain. It wasn't until October 1943, when the tides of war were truly turning towards the Allies that Salazar allowed the British access to the Azores to build a base (Operation Alacrity).

Despite Salazar's assertations that Portugal would not take advantage of its neutrality to profit from the war, it did. Previously a relatively poor country, it profited from the refugees who sold their belongings to buy a ticket to Britain or America, bribes, the Nazi gold, and Wolfram. Wolfram, or Tungsten, was sought after by both sides for war munitions and small mining communities suddenly found themselves wealthy. Although Portugal set up quotas for both the Allies and the Axis, British Intelligence had gathered evidence of the Germans smuggling the mineral out by a plethora of routes, some simple, some complex, and believed that there was a large amount of Portuguese involvement in these operations. Salazar firmly denied any official involvement.

Meanwhile, German Naval Intelligence was tracking the routes of the British convoys crossing the Atlantic. In addition to having people monitor the docks, the Abwehr set up brothels in the dock areas of Lisbon to attract the British seamen with the aim of extracting dates and routes, and if a target seemed particularly good, they would radio a Luftwaffe base in the south of France, who would then send out the Focke Wulfs to sink it. The Shetland and Volturno were real, and were only two of several ships to have been sunk this way.

Salazar's surveillance and state defence police, the Polícia de Vigilância e de Defesa do Estado or PVDE was founded and led by Captain Agostinho Lourenço ('the Director'). It was broken down into two sections: Social and Political Defence Section, and the International Section, which not only controlled the flow of immigrants and refugees, but also took care of counter-espionage and/or international espionage. Officially, they maintained a neutral stance towards foreign espionage activity, as long as there was no intervention in Portuguese internal policies, and in June 1943 the Criminal Code was amended to criminalise espionage of foreigners against 3rd parties in Portugal.

In early October 1943, the PVDE raided 3 villas belonging to German agents, including Hans Bendixen's Bem-me-Quer, and while they found wireless equipment, they claimed to have found nothing suspect. In *City of Spies*, I took the liberty of raising a 'What if' that deviated from historical fact.

Acknowledgements

There's a photo on my desk of six people clad in 1940s-style khaki tunics huddled around an Enigma machine. Over quirky cocktails, my Zaffre/Watson, Little 'dream team' and I discussed WW2, espionage, and publishing the *City of Spies*. Katherine Armstrong, Jennie Rothwell, Francesca Russell, Alexandra Allden and James Wills, I am eternally grateful for your patience, insight, and the opportunity you've given me. You, and the rest of the team that weren't with us that night, Nick Stearn, Stephen Dumughn and Steve O'Gorman, have made *City of Spies* a much better book!

Writing a book takes a lot of hard work and perseverance, and I'm very fortunate that I have a wonderful group of family and friends who celebrated the 'ups' with me, and rallied me through the 'downs' of the publishing rollercoaster. First and foremost, my mother who might not have lived to see my book written, but always knew it would happen. My dad (a backseat historian), who used to print out a copy of my manuscript and advise on some of the technical details. My brother Stephen, sister-in-law Emily and their children Matthew and Alexandra who always offered love and pragmatic advice.

Massive thanks as well to Justine Solomons who is the beating heart of the publishing community BytetheBook – and who introduced me to my agent; to Antonella Pearce who introduced me to BytetheBook, and to Sérgio Vieira who suggested I write about Portugal. That led to a few trips to the National Archives in Kew, which is a truly magical place.

Joyce Kotze and Karen Pettersen were incredibly patient, reading several drafts of the novel, treating each version as if it were new, and didn't think I was (too) mad for talking about my characters as if they were real people.

The Quad Writers have sadly now disbanded, but provided great insight and support – thanks especially to Martin Cummings, Kevin Kelly, Barry Walsh, and Rob Ganley. And throughout the process, my friends kept me sane, providing support (and wine) along the way: Michelle Perrett-Atkins, Alison Hughes, Luma Rushdi, Sharon Gayler, and Monique Mandalia.

Last but certainly not least I would like to thank my readers. I hope you've enjoyed reading Elisabeth's story as much as I loved writing it!.

Touring the City of Spies

When a Portuguese friend of mine suggested basing my book in Lisbon, I knew I would have a lot of research to do, but what I didn't know was that this global city, rich in history and culture, would itself become one of the main characters in my debut novel.

While I'm particularly interested in Lisbon's role during WW2, there is enough to do and see to intrigue history buffs, foodies, and anyone looking for a friendly, easy-to-access city for a long weekend.

Looking straight ahead is an easy way to miss some of the most interesting bits of any city, so look up at the architecture, down at the black-and-white mosaic paving stones, and around, where you'll see the iconic blue tiles that Lisbon is famous for. You won't be disappointed. Oh, and pack your trainers or comfy shoes. Lisbon is a walkable city, but your legs will definitely feel the workout at the end of the day!

All aboard Tram 28!

When friends from abroad visit me in London for the first time, my first suggestion is to take a ride on the hop-on/hop-off bus to get a feel for the city and explore some of the key landmarks. The best (and in some ways even better) equivalent in Lisbon is the little yellow Tram 28. The trams themselves are iconic, dating back to the 1930s. From the polished wooden benches you can see: the baroque Basilica da Estrela and the Jardim (garden) across the way; São Bento Palace (the Portuguese Parliament building); The Chiado (the nearby arts quarter); and the Praça Luís de Camões (the main plaza of Bairro Alto, the beating heart of Lisbon's nightlife). You can also access the shopping areas in the Baixa, the Se Cathedral, and the Portas do Sol in the Alfama. This plaza has wonderful views, and is also the closest stop for the castle, but beware: it's a steep walk uphill!

Walking through history at the ruined São Jorge Castle

For a history junkie like me, the castle is one of the most fascinating places in Lisbon. Evidence of people occupying the castle hill dates back to the Phoenicians in the 8th century BC, and fortifications from the 1st century BC. It was also occupied by the Carthaginians, Romans, a few Germanic tribes, and the Moors before the Portuguese reconquered it in 1147. The castle started to decline in importance in the 16th century, and despite reconstruction projects introduced in later centuries, it is now largely in ruins. Catch a concert there if you can, but even if you can't make one, it's a fascinating place and the views over Lisbon and the Tagus are spectacular – particularly at sunset.

Fado in the Alfama District

Alfama is one of the oldest districts in Lisbon, running from the castle right down to the Tagus. It hosts the Lisbon Cathedral, the Convento da Graça, and a plethora of *fado* bars and restaurants.

Fado, if you haven't heard of it, is a haunting style of music where a solo singer is accompanied by a traditional Portuguese guitar. But Alfama isn't the only place to hear *fado*; the last time we were in Lisbon, we followed a fellow diner's recommendation and visited Senhor Vino's – a *casa do fado* that wasn't the easiest to find, but which was certainly worth the trip!

Eating and drinking in the Bairro Alto

The Bairro Alto benefitted from the urban regeneration of the later decades of the 20th century and is now the beating heart of Lisbon's nightlife with trendy bars, clubs and restaurants.

When you eat out in Lisbon, make sure to try the local dishes. Lisbon is a port famous for its fish and shellfish, with a culinary focus on spices that complement the food rather than heavy sauces, which makes sense considering Portugal's former colonies. I can also highly recommend the local wines – and of course the after-dinner port. During our time there, we quickly ended up foregoing menus and relied on the recommendations of our servers and fellow diners, and were never disappointed. Also, make sure to try the delicious Portuguese pastéis de natas (custard tarts) before you leave – my other half was addicted to these.

The Rossio

The Rossio has been one of Lisbon's main squares since the Middle Ages; a site for protests, bullfights and executions. While I'm pretty sure the latter two don't happen there anymore, it is still a popular venue for protesters – and for Lisbonites and tourists, due to its proximity to cafes and restaurants. In the 1940s, the easy walk from the train station made it a gathering spot for refugees fleeing the war.

Looking down at the square you'll see black and white cobble-stones arranged in a wave pattern, and at the centre is a column dedicated to King Pedro IV. There are two beautiful baroque fountains on either side, the Dona Maria II National Theatre to the north.

Oh, and that train station? It had a 'secret' passageway to the Hotel Avenida next door which was only blocked up in the 1970s. Fascinating to imagine what went on there . . .

Be a culture vulture in the Chiado

Based in the historic centre of Lisbon, this picturesque neigh-bourhood hosts a number of art museums, theatres and galleries, including the National Museum of Contemporary Art in the former Covent of St Francis, the Teatro Nacional de São Carlos (the opera house) and the Archaeological Museum in the former Carmo Church.

Heading West

There are many things to see outside the city itself, so make time to explore some of the gems that the coastline has to offer.

Belém

A few stops west on the Metro from the Cais do Sodré is the district of Belém. Here you can visit two UNESCO World Herit-age Sites: the magnificent Jerónimos Monastery; and the nearby Tower of Belém, which served as the ceremonial gateway to Lisbon for Portuguese explorers embarking on or returning from their travels. These voyages are showcased in the Museum of Discoveries (Padrão dos Descobrimentos) which was built in 1960 in honour of the 500ᵗʰ anniversary of the death of Prince Henry the Navigator.

Also found here is the Belém Palace, the current official residence of the Portuguese President. From Belém, you can look across the river to see the Cristo Rei, the statue of Christ, arms raised in blessing.

Estoril, Cascais and the Mouth of Hell

The villages of Estoril and Cascais flourished during the 1940s, where exiled aristocracy rubbed shoulders with diplomats, refugees, and (of course!) spies at the villas, beachfront restaurants and the Casino Estoril, which was the inspiration for Ian Fleming's *Casino Royale*. The promenade between Estoril and Cascais provides tourists with a scenic (and easy) walk along the beachfront, with plenty of places to stop for refreshments.

Continuing further along the coast from Cascais, past striking beaches and cliffs, you'll find the Boca do Inferno (Mouth of Hell). Once a sea cave, it collapsed leaving a cavern and sea arch. The Atlantic's waves give this opening a beating, and during nasty storms the water is known to explode upwards, giving the site its (rather melodramatic) name.

I've tried to do justice to Lisbon in *City of Spies*, but whilst sipping a glass of Douro red in the Rossio, one thing kept coming back to me: I may have finished writing my novel, but I don't think the real city of spies is done with me yet . . .

Q&A with Mara Timon

1. What inspired you to write *City of Spies*?

About a decade ago, I saw a documentary about Special Operations Executives and became intrigued by the 'Baker Street Irregulars'. Instructed by Churchill to 'set Europe ablaze', they seemed to revel in breaking rules, not the least of which included recruiting women to work behind enemy lines. I began to binge-read the biographies and autobiographies of their agents, and at that point something clicked; a need to write stories about (fictional) female SOE agents.

The first story I wrote was about a young woman, newly drafted into the SOE, and her work in Occupied France in 1943. In the story that character met another SOE trainee called Cécile (who we now know as Elisabeth). Before long, I began to feel Cécile standing behind me, poking my shoulder and saying, 'Hurry up – you'll write my story next.'

If you've finished *City of Spies*, you know that she does tend to get what she wants. I'll get back to that first story once Cécile/Elisabeth finishes with me.

2. How much research did you do before you started writing?

The Portuguese friend who suggested I write about Lisbon had given me a high-level picture of the history, but I wanted to get a better feel for it before deciding to base a story there. A good deal of the information was online, and the National Archive files were brilliant. It gave me an idea of which way the story might go, but then I made my own life difficult: I don't plot out my books before writing them. I know where they start and have a rough idea of where they may end up, but the characters themselves direct what happens in between. Which meant that some of my research, while giving me a good perspective, wasn't used, and more research was required as the story developed.

3. Did you make any surprising discoveries during your research?

Well, for starters, I had no idea how much was really going on in Lisbon during the war. Smuggling and espionage, yes. But there were also youth marches that weren't too different from the ones in Germany, and while many members of Salazar's government and his police force were pro-Axis, a number of them used their diplomatic powers to help European refugees, e.g. by providing them with visas and safe houses.

I was more amused than surprised when I discovered that there really was a 'secret' tunnel between Rossio Station and the Hotel Avenida next door. There was no doubt in my mind that it was well used, allowing people to sneak into the city for a dodgy meeting and then get out before anyone knew they had even been in Lisbon. I'd actually hoped to be able to walk through it on my last trip to Lisbon but discovered that – sadly – it had been blocked off in the '70s.

Also, as I read about the real spies that operated in Lisbon during the war, I kept coming across the name Dusko Popov, codename Tricycle, and found that intriguing. Why that name? Officially it was because he was running a trio of double agents, although some claim that it was because he always had a beautiful woman on either side of him. Popov, and his promiscuous lifestyle, became the primary inspiration for Fleming's 007.

4. *City of Spies* includes some fictionalised versions of real-life people, such as Maurice Buckmaster and Vera Atkins. Why did you choose to include them and not create completely fictionalised characters?

Why create fictionalised characters when the real-life people not only existed, but were so well documented – and interesting? If I can't find out who did something in real life, I'll make them up, but using real people makes me feel closer to the history. What I write is fiction, but I do try not to misrepresent them!

5. What drew you to Elisabeth as a character? Why did you decide to tell her story in particular?

I created Elisabeth in a previous story, and as bonkers as it sounds, she wouldn't leave me alone. I love Elisabeth. She's strong, determined, and fights for what she believes in, and in trying to do the right thing, often finds herself in trouble. She also – to quote Eduard Graf – 'drinks too much, smokes too much, and keeps very bad company.' She's a lot of fun to write about because I genuinely have no idea what she's going to do next.

As to why I decided to tell her story? Well, that was her doing. I'd created Elisabeth in an earlier book and noticed that she kept cropping up. By halfway through that story, I could feel her tapping my shoulder, telling me to hurry up. That I was going to write her story next.

6. Are you planning to continue Elisabeth's story?

I don't think she'd have it any other way! In the next book, we'll see Elisabeth joined by two other Special Operations Executive agents as a (fictional) all-female Jedburgh team, paving the way for the Normandy landings.

7. Why set the book in Lisbon and not Berlin or Paris?

I was on the Eurostar, with two colleagues, heading to Paris for a meeting. One of my colleagues, knowing that I was working on a book, asked me how much research I'd be doing while we were there. The other colleague – a Portuguese man – suggested that I base my next book in Lisbon. It was a gentle nudge in the right direction, and my research drew a portrait of a country with split loyalties, precariously neutral, with a capital that, partly based on its geography, became a magnet for spies and espionage.

It was the perfect place for Elisabeth to get into mischief, but don't be surprised if I do set a future story in Paris or Berlin!

8. Do you have a favourite character in the novel?

Isn't that like asking a mum which child is their favourite? Elisabeth is my favourite, of course, but I suspect the question is really 'who is my favourite *after Elisabeth*', and the answer to that is Hubert Jones. Bertie started off with a big personality that just kept growing, and I loved writing his banter with Elisabeth, and the way he verbally fenced with Eduard. I'm not going to rule out having him show up in another story!

9. If the SOE still existed, it would have just celebrated its 80th anniversary. Why do you think there is still such interest in the work that the SOE did during the war?

I think people have always been interested in the exploits of spies – it's wonderful escapism – and the SOE were the bad boys and girls of the spy world. They didn't play by any established rules, and their agents were more than just spies – their remit was sabotage and subversion. They blew up trains, bridges and factories, while fostering revolt (often working with local resistance groups). They were Churchill's Department of Dirty Tricks. He told them to 'set Europe ablaze!' and they did. Their real-life exploits still read better than a lot of commercial thrillers.

Fun fact: Anne-Marie Walters's autobiography *Moondrop to Gascony* won the John Llewellyn Rhys Prize in 1947.

10. Do you feel that more should be done to celebrate and promote the work that female agents did during World War II? What, do you think, would be a fitting tribute that hasn't already been done?

Yes, of course. People don't seem that surprised when I tell them I write about fictional female spies during WW2, but they are usually shocked when I mention that there really were 39 female SOE agents who operated in France, and that 13 didn't make it back.

That being said, there's a lot of work going on now to promote the female agents. There are several new biographies out now, and I believe a movie is in the works about Nancy Wake ('the white mouse'). The advocacy group Hope Not Hate has produced Heroes of the Resistance podcasts, some of which relate to female SOE agents, and this year two female SOE agents have had blue plaques raised at their former residences: Christine Granville (born Krystyna Skarbek, and the longest serving female agent of WW2) and Noor Inyat Khan (who was killed in '44 and was posthumously awarded the George Cross).

Is it enough? No, but it's several steps in the right direction.

11. Do you think you would have made a good spy?

I'd love to say 'Yes!' but the truth is closer to 'probably not'. I'm far too what-you-see-is-what-you-get!

12. What was your favourite part of the writing process? And what did you find most challenging?

Favourite: When the story is in full swing and my characters are 'speaking' to me. I'm racing with them into action, and I can barely write fast enough to keep up.

Most challenging? When my invisible friends aren't talking to me. It usually means that I've made a mistake somewhere and have to go back and figure out what it is, and fix it. Sometimes it's not an obvious error, and sometimes it's an error that has already rippled through a fair part of the story. Re-work isn't so much fun, but the end result is always better.

13. What does an average writing day look like for you?

In the 'new normal' of working from home, I've repurposed the time I used to spend on the morning commute for writing. I normally get up around 6:30 and brew a large pot of flavoured coffee (chocolate raspberry, pecan praline, or whatever I can find) and trundle into my writing room. Don't get excited – it's only the spare bedroom, and these days doubles (or is it triples?) as my home office. I'll work until about 8, before I switch hats for the day job.

Lunchtime provides an opportunity to retreat outside and do a bit of plotting while I walk or run along the canals and, once I finish work, I go back to working on the story for another couple of hours.

When I'm editing, I print the story out and edit on paper as well as on screen. I'm sure there's a scientific reason behind it, but often I'll pick up mistakes on paper that I won't when I'm reading it digitally.

14. Do you listen to music while you write?
Sometimes, but not always. The music will often depend on who I'm writing about and what they're doing. I've got wide-ranging (and eclectic) taste in music and probably confuse my neighbours.

15. Which books or authors are you inspired by?
Where do I begin? I'm inspired by the real women of SOE: Violette Szabo, Krystyna Skarbek (Christine Granville), Virginia Hall, Nancy Wake, Anne-Marie Walters, Noor Inyat Khan, the Nearne sisters, Odette Sansom, to name a few. I started binge-reading their biographies and autobiographies, fascinated by the way their stories read like thrillers. There are a lot of great books to choose from, but new readers might want to start with: Clare Mulley's *The Spy Who Loved* (about Krystyna Skarbek), Sonia Purnell's *A Woman of No Importance* (about Virginia Hall), and Imogen Kealey's *Liberation* (about Nancy Wake).

I love Ben MacIntyre's books, in particular *Double Cross*, which told of the spies involved in tricking the Germans into believing that the Allies would attack Calais and Norway, instead of Normandy.

I'm also a big fan of Jack Higgins, especially the early books. He's a master at making the reader feel sympathetic to his bad-dies, who aren't really bad at all, just fighting on 'the wrong side' of the war, which makes for a much more interesting read.

16. Do you have any advice for new writers working on novels set in the past?

Do your research. It's a pet peeve of mine when I pick up a book and read about characters that don't act believably within the confines of the period, where the story doesn't align with the history. There will probably be points where you consciously veer from fact, but that shouldn't detract from the storyline.

17. What's next on your to-be-read list?

JOSEPHINE: Singer, Dancer, Soldier, Spy by Eilidh McGinness.

It's a biography of Josephine Baker, a black American-born entertainer, who was recruited by France's Deuxième Bureau (military intelligence), to collect information on German troop locations from high-ranking officials. She used her work as an entertainer to carry information for transmission to England (written in invisible ink on her sheet music or hidden in her knickers). After the war, she was awarded the Croix de Guerre, the Rosette de la Résistance, and was made a Chevalier of the Légion d'honneur by General Charles de Gaulle.

While still in France in the '50s, she became a civil rights activist, using her ever-growing platform to speak out against racism. In '63, she spoke at the March on Washington – the only official female speaker – at the side of Rev. Martin Luther King Jr, and after his assassination was offered unofficial leadership of the movement by his widow. She declined.

Josephine Baker was a real-life action hero, and I'm really looking forward to learning more about her.

18. What's the best piece of writing advice that you have been given?

The first piece of advice I ever got was 'write about things you know'. That probably works for a lot of people, but I like to use my writing to tell a story while also learning about a place or a period in history.

The best advice I received, or rather the advice that worked best for me, was to 'write the book you'd like to read'. The corollary to that is 'listen to your agent and editor', because they'll definitely take your story to the next level!

19. Has there been any part of the publishing process that you found surprising?

I was initially surprised when I realised how long the publishing process takes. I'd signed with Bonnier Zaffre in August 2018, with *City of Spies* being published in September 2020, although when you break down all the steps along the way, it does make sense. And while patience is not really a Timon trait, the team are great to work with and the time has gone by very quickly!

20. Describe your next book in 15 words, or less!

Three female SOE agents work to destabilise German operations ahead of the Normandy landings.